Wrong'un

By Keith A Pearson

For more information about the author and to receive updates on his new releases, visit…

www.keithapearson.co.uk

Copyright © 2018 by Keith A Pearson. All rights reserved. This book or any portion thereof may not be reproduced or used in any manner whatsoever without the express written permission of the author except for the use of brief quotations in a book review.

Author's Note

Whilst *Wrong'un* is a standalone novel, you'll appreciate, and hopefully enjoy the story to a greater degree if you've read the first book in the series, *Who Sent Clement?*

If you've already read it, welcome to Clement's next adventure...

HAMPSHIRE — 1999

1.

The balance had shifted. Moments of lucidity were infrequent and his mind was dissolving into a murky soup of confused thoughts.

Sir Charles Huxley knew he couldn't put it off any longer. Time, he thought, waits for no man. His time was short and he knew it.

As he shuffled into the study on unsteady legs, he concentrated intently on keeping the task from slipping into the soup, from where he feared it would never return.

He eventually reached his chair and slowly lowered himself onto the leather seat.

Safely ensconced behind his desk, he allowed himself a moment to gaze wistfully around the room. The study had all the ambiance of a gentleman's club; panelled walls entombing the finest antique furniture, hand-crafted in oak, mahogany, and leather. The lingering scent of vintage port and cigar smoke triggered memories of the countless after dinner drinks he'd enjoyed with the great and the good in that very room. Those were good times, when the house was a home.

His attention turned to a picture on the desk, cased in a silver frame. Two faces stared back at him, smiling — his wife and only child. A moment of happiness captured when William was still full of childhood wonderment, and Victoria was unburdened by poor health. His addled brain tried to calculate how many years had passed since that moment. Sixteen, maybe seventeen — he couldn't be sure.

He came to the conclusion the specific number didn't matter. They were both gone now. His son had spent three years at university, rarely returning home before moving overseas to work for a charity in some god-forsaken corner of Africa. He hadn't seen William in almost three years. As for Victoria, her health deteriorated and almost a decade had passed since she'd been stolen from him.

He was alone, rattling around in the old house with just his memories for company. They too would soon be gone.

He let out a deep sigh, opened a drawer in the desk, and withdrew a ream of vellum writing paper; his full title and address embossed at the top in gold leaf. He lamented the fact he would never get to use the full stock of expensive paper.

As well as the writing paper, he also withdrew an envelope containing a grainy, black and white photograph and a copy of a certificate, together with a pewter trinket box, roughly the size of a paperback book. The trinket box had been given to him by an elderly constituent — a poor man of few means — and it was Sir Charles's intention to bequeath it to William. Although it held no monetary value, he was sure William would appreciate the Latin inscription on the lid, right up until the moment he opened it.

For the thousandth time he considered the ramifications of what he was about to do, and for the thousandth time he concluded he had no choice.

He reached for a fountain pen and began to write.

The words flowed as the nib scratched across the paper; his handwriting erratic, but legible. Although the physical act of putting words on paper was simple enough, dredging his broken mind for the right words was no easy feat. If that were his only challenge, he'd have been grateful, but guilt, regret, and shame tormented him with every completed line.

Of everything Sir Charles had accomplished in his seventy-two years, all would be forever tainted by one unfortunate incident thirteen years prior. However, it wasn't the incident itself he was ashamed of, although he deeply regretted it. No, it was the years that followed where he had ample chance to make amends but he passed it up for fear it would destroy everything he had worked so hard to build. Unlike the vintage port he used to sup, his secret had not improved with age.

It mattered not. His letter would ensure the sins of the father would soon be passed to the son, in the hope he might be a better man and right his wrongs.

He floundered for a moment; searching for a specific word to end a sentence. Scouring his mind, frustration mounted and he gripped the pen hard in one hand while the other balled into a fist. Three heavy taps to his temple failed to dislodge the word. Whatever it was, the word was gone. He returned the nib to the end of the sentence and completed it with the best alternative his mind could summon.

He ended with what he hoped was a sincere apology, and signed his name. The letter was complete, but he felt no better for it. He never really thought he would.

He then tucked the letter into the pewter trinket box along with the photograph and the tattered certificate — three pieces of a jigsaw, conveniently sorted for his son to piece together.

Closing the lid, Sir Charles sat back in his chair while keeping his gaze fixed on the pewter box. Seconds passed and he could already feel his mind drifting away from the contents, and the possible implications once his son read the letter. Perhaps no bad thing.

A sudden knock on the study door startled him. His head snapped up as the door creaked open, and a middle-aged woman stepped into the study. She looked as haggard as she probably felt.

"Everything okay, Sir Charles?"

Originally employed as a housekeeper, Lizzie had somehow become Sir Charles's full-time carer. Having previously worked as a nurse, she was more than qualified for the role but it wasn't exactly a career move of choice.

Lizzie's decision was born of necessity.

Almost four years had passed since her husband died unexpectedly; bequeathing Lizzie a mountain of debt. Despite her best efforts, the bailiffs eventually came calling and the marital home was duly repossessed. The only reason she'd taken the job at Hansworth Hall was the accompanying offer of staff accommodation. At the time, the offer was a blessing, but she soon realised her subsidised home was a curse. Too much of her modest pay went on servicing debts, so while she continued to diligently save every precious pound, Lizzie remained trapped.

"Pour me a brandy," Sir Charles ordered.

Lizzie paced over to the desk and took a seat on an oak chair, opposite her employer. She paused for a moment as she studied the old man's wizened features. His face was almost skeletal now, on account he frequently forgot to eat the meals she'd prepared for him. Her attempts to remind him had been met with hostility — the once erudite and witty charmer now a confused and temperamental curmudgeon. Lizzie knew Sir Charles wasn't long for this earth but she needed him to hang on for at least a few more paydays. By then, she hoped her savings would be sufficiently bolstered to allow an escape.

"Now, now," she replied, her tone almost maternal. "You know you can't take alcohol with your medication. Can I get you a cup of cocoa instead?"

"No. Take a letter for me."

Lizzie closed her eyes and counted to five. Sir Charles didn't appear to notice or care, and began his dictation.

"Dear Margaret. Firstly, I understand Dennis has been unwell recently. Please pass on my wishes for a speedy recovery."

Lizzie opened her eyes and leant across the desk. This wasn't the first time Sir Charles had regressed to his days as a government minister. Two years had passed since he was diagnosed with Alzheimer's, bringing the curtain down on Sir Charles's forty year career as a politician, and in a cruel twist of fate, within a month of his party losing power in the 1997 election.

"I'm not your personal secretary, Sir Charles," she sighed, choosing not to inflame his mood by pointing out that almost a decade had passed since Margaret Thatcher had been ousted from 10 Downing Street.

"Just get on with it, woman," he bellowed.

Arguing with him was pointless. She knew the only way to steer his confused thoughts in a different direction was to change the subject.

"That box is pretty. Is it silver? It looks expensive," she remarked, pointing to the trinket box on the desk.

Sir Charles stared at Lizzie and then at the box. A bony hand suddenly snatched it away and returned it to his desk drawer.

"It's priceless, woman," he spat.

Lizzie nodded as he slammed the drawer shut. With that gesture, his anger appeared to dissipate and he fell silent.

"It's late, Sir Charles. Would you like any help getting ready for bed?"

"Yes," he replied, his voice barely a whisper.

Lizzie moved around the desk and helped him from the chair, only to be met with a string of mumbled expletives. Undeterred, she took his arm and they shuffled out of the study.

Unbeknown to Lizzie, it would be their final walk together as death would come calling in the night and finally put an end to the old politician's misery.

PRESENT DAY

2.

The air is heavy with a cocktail of scents: aftershave, perfume, and the combined morning breath of a hundred commuters, crammed into the carriage. Despite the best efforts of my fellow passengers on the Jubilee Line, the liberal application of designer fragrances struggles to mask the communal halitosis.

The tube train rattles onwards and the melancholy faces continue to stare at anything but one another.

It's with some relief I'm finally able to prise myself from the packed carriage and step onto the platform at Westminster tube station. The morning commute from rural Hampshire is a tedious journey, taking over two hours, and I'm grateful I only have to complete it once a week.

I wait a few seconds for the crowd to thin before making my way towards the exit. A dozen yards ahead, two unkempt youths in baseball caps are leant against the wall — one plump, one rake thin, both clearly angry with life. They glare in my direction as I approach.

"Look at that Tory wanker," the plump one mutters to the other, loud enough for me to hear. I'm not sure if that was his intention but it matters not — I've heard that particular insult before and I'm sure I'll hear it many times again.

As it happens, the obese youth is correct. I am a member of the Conservative Party, although at heart I'm politically agnostic, and by virtue of the fact I'm a somewhat uncomely, middle-aged bachelor, I'm no stranger to an occasional bout of self-gratification.

Nevertheless, such assumptions from people who don't know me, rile. I stop dead in my tracks and approach the youths.

"Sorry, gents," I say politely. "I didn't catch what you said."

"Didn't say nothin'," the plump one retorts.

"Oh, in which case, please accept my apologies. I could have sworn you called me a Tory wanker."

They swap awkward glances but remain silent.

"Well, for future reference, I personally prefer the term Tory tosser — it has a softer ring to it, don't you think?"

Puzzled faces replace awkward glances. Unsurprisingly, they have little to say now.

"Have a good day, gents."

I give them a parting nod and continue my way along the platform.

Progress is slow as I continually sidestep commuters heading in the opposite direction; many of whom are young and pretty. A number of them are also female; a species I seem to repel for some reason. Perhaps repel is too strong a word, but I certainly lack the physical characteristics to attract women. Indeed, a girl at university once described my appearance as extraordinarily ordinary, like white bread or magnolia paint. Not ugly, but not handsome. Not short, but not tall. Not fat, but not thin. She further theorised that sleeping with me would be akin to eating boiled rice when hungry — functional, but incredibly dull.

I avoid eye contact with the pretty young things and head towards the exit.

A minute later, the escalator delivers me onto the featureless concrete concourse where the majority of my fellow commuters either make for the exit on to Westminster Bridge or head right towards Whitehall. I do neither, and dart down a commuter-free walkway with a revolving door at the end; a police guard stood the other side. Apart from those who work here, very few people know of this entrance to the home of British parliament.

I swap nods with the policeman and head towards my office.

I'm not sure it's any cause for celebration, but this year marks my tenth anniversary as Member of Parliament for Marshburton; one of the smallest constituencies in England with only sixty thousand residents. I cannot say I had any great appetite for a career in politics but my late father, Sir Charles Huxley, was a well-respected minister and assumptions were incorrectly made that I might like to follow the same career path.

I vividly recall the day I received a visit from the chairman of the local Conservative Party. A blusterous former Naval officer, he literally press ganged me into standing as the local candidate after my predecessor unexpectedly stood down; the result of an unfortunate misunderstanding with his expenses, so I was told.

Despite the last-minute campaigning, and my numerous threats to quit, I was duly elected. One minute I'm plain old Will Huxley, the next I'm The Right Honourable William Huxley MP. In hindsight, I can see how and why I was elected. After a scandal, what better way to placate the constituents than to offer them a candidate with a back story. My father had served the good people of Marshburton for more than four decades and my surname alone offered a return to the good old days. It was a smart move by the chairman. Not so smart on my part.

Nevertheless, I had a job to do, and I naively thought I could make a difference. In my first six months of office I was stringently mentored in the hope my star would rise. Those hopes were quickly dashed when it became clear I was more interested in people than politics. And so, I became just another invisible backbencher — a mere pawn in somebody else's game; to be whipped, bullied and occasionally flattered into doing what I'm told.

Still, someone's got to do it, and as my only previous work experience was an eight year stint volunteering for an overseas charity, I wasn't exactly blessed with alternative career options.

"Good morning, William," Rosa chimes as I step into the office.

"Morning," I reply while pulling out my chair.

Before my backside even touches the seat, Rosa floats across the carpet and stands in front of the desk, her ever-present notepad in hand.

"I'll get your tea in a moment, but we've got a full diary today so I wanted to check you're on top of everything."

Vexed, I stare up at her and try to hide my annoyance behind a feeble smile. "Yes, yes. I'm totally on top of everything."

She tilts her head and tucks a strand of chocolate-blonde hair behind her ear.

"Are you absolutely sure, William?" she asks; the merest hint of incredulity breaching her usually soft tone.

"Well, most of it," I reply sheepishly.

"What are we going to do with you?" she chuckles. "Get your diary ready. I'll be back in two minutes with that tea."

She drops her notebook on my desk and turns away. I watch her as she effortlessly moves across the office and out of the door.

Rosa is now in her third month of employment as my personal assistant, having previously spent much of her career with a corporate law firm. My previous PA, Joyce, who'd been with me since the day I started, unexpectedly quit ten weeks ago. She cited personal reasons for terminating her position without notice, but she did have the decency to recommend Rosa, and I'm very pleased she did.

I'm not by nature, a particularly organised man, and coupled with my goldfish-like memory, I fear I wouldn't be able to function without an efficient assistant. And while Joyce was as prickly as she was professional, Rosa is charming, witty, and, it must be said, quite beautiful. Factor-in she's twenty-five years younger than Joyce and exceedingly good at her job, it makes Rosa a most agreeable upgrade.

However, there is one problem — I face a daily battle not to fall in love with the woman.

Truth is, it's a battle I'm losing, but the chance of my affections being reciprocated are close to zero. Politicians aren't the most lovable of creatures, and I'm already behind most men in the lovable stakes. So, I do what any stiff upper lipped Englishman would do, and keep my counsel. In my defence, I fear even hinting at my true feelings might scare her away, and I can't afford to lose another personal assistant.

Rosa returns with two china cups on accompanying saucers, and places them carefully down on my desk. I open my briefcase and retrieve a battered diary. Rosa stares at it with mock disdain.

"Ah, that reminds me," she remarks before scooting back to her desk.

After rifling through her handbag, she skips back with a mobile phone in hand.

"For you. A present."

"That's very kind of you, Rosa, but I already have a mobile phone."

"Ah, but this is a smart phone. You can use an app to synchronise our diaries."

I tentatively take the mobile phone. I'm perfectly happy with my old Nokia handset because I have no desire to be enslaved to a digital overlord. Call me old fashioned, but I like to open my diary without fear it will delete itself.

"This looks expensive, and to be honest, I wouldn't have the first clue how to use it."

"It's my old phone and it was in a drawer doing nothing. And don't worry, I'll set it up and show you how it works."

A kind gesture, and despite my reservations, it would be remiss of me to decline.

"Thank you, Rosa."

"My pleasure, and I promise it'll make your life easier. Leave your old phone with me before you go to your meeting and I'll transfer everything over."

It feels like saying goodbye to an old friend as I hand over my antiquated relic of a phone.

"Now that's sorted, we'd better crack on."

Rosa then plucks her own phone from a jacket pocket and jabs the screen with an elegant finger. She then lists the various meetings and obligations I have scheduled throughout the day; varying from tedious to mind-numbingly dull. I politely nod and check each appointment against my own diary, silently praying I haven't missed anything and inadvertently supplied the kindling for Rosa's diary burning threat.

Once the diary is checked and I've been furnished with a pile of manila folders, we move on to the next order of the day — sorting through the never-ending correspondence. My mind begins to wander as Rosa churns through a raft of letters and memos, requesting a response to each one. We now have this task down to a fine art and Rosa, efficient as always, takes responsibility for the lion's share. There are a few, however, which require my input.

"Dinner invitation from Martin Faversham."

"Tell him I'm busy until Christmas."

Rosa scribbles something on the letter and moves to the next item.

"A request for you to attend the opening of a new media suite at Marshburton High School next month."

"What on earth is a media suite?"

"I'll tell them you'll be there," Rosa replies without seeking my consent. "You might learn something."

"Fine," I groan. "Next."

Rosa churns through another dozen demands on my precious time. I reluctantly agree to seven of them and notes are scribbled to make excuses for the rest.

"And one final item: a request for a meeting from Dominic Hassard."

"Who?"

"Your estate agent in Hampshire."

"Oh, him. What does he want?"

"The lease on Hansworth Hall expires next month. I believe the tenants want to renew."

"Just tell him to renew it on the same terms."

Hansworth Hall has been the home of the Huxley family since 1808. A grand regency house sited within ten acres of formal gardens, it was purchased by my fourth great-grandfather, Thomas Huxley. He made his fortune during the industrial revolution and cemented his place amongst the landed gentry. On Thomas's death, the house passed to his son, Augustus, before it tumbled down the family tree to my father, and eventually, me. I am now the seventh generation of Huxley to own Hansworth Hall, although I haven't stepped foot in the place for over twenty years.

It would be fair to say I have a love-hate relationship with our family home. I love the architecture, the history, and the beautiful grounds, but I detest so much else about the place. I was an only child, and with no nearby neighbours, I would wander around the grounds with just my own thoughts for company. Then my mother passed away when I was fourteen, and my father decided it would be better for me to board at school. I hoped to escape the loneliness but it followed me for my remaining years of school, and beyond to university.

After university, and much to my father's disgust, I chose to volunteer at a mission in Uganda. I still recall the ferocious argument which ensued after I told him of my career plans — an argument which culminated in three years of estrangement. Our relationship had deteriorated to such a degree, he didn't even tell me he'd been diagnosed with Alzheimer's. I was twenty-four when I received a call from his doctor — told by a stranger that my father had died.

I spent three weeks back in Marshburton, with little desire to return and take up permanent residence at Hansworth Hall. I was as alone as I'd ever been, and to make matters worse, I faced a significant inheritance tax demand. I had no option other than to auction most of the contents and rent the place out.

I returned to Uganda and tried to put Hansworth Hall out of my mind. The loneliness came with me and even today, it has never really gone away.

"I hope you don't mind, William, but I took the liberty of looking at the current lease."

"I neither mind, nor care."

"You do realise the tenants are paying significantly less than the full market value?"

I let a lazy gaze drift over her head while sipping tea, in the hope she gets the message. She doesn't.

"I have a few contacts in the property business, from my time at Stephens & Marland. Surely it's worth your while exploring other avenues before you commit?"

Rosa looks at me, expectantly. I know she's only trying to help but I really couldn't care less about finding a new tenant, irrespective of any potential rent increase. I don't need the money, and the current tenants have never caused me any bother.

But, those big cinnamon-brown eyes.

"Okay," I sigh. "I'll leave it with you."

A wide smile breaks across her face. "I appreciate your faith in me, William. I won't let you down."

With that, she scoops up the pile of papers and heads back to her desk. I breathe in her sweet perfume and without thinking, sneak a glance as she shimmies away.

Delusional fool.

I gather my things and head off to the first appointment of the day.

3.

You can spot a new member of the house within seconds. They are like the new intake at school; full of innocent wonder, and fear. Even after ten years, I can still appreciate the former, although I have little patience for the latter. The Palace of Westminster, or Houses of Parliament as commonly labelled, possesses an architectural gravitas few buildings in the world can match. It is more than just the structure though; it is the weight of responsibility placed upon those sent to conduct the business of democracy. It is said that a man tired of walking these corridors is a man tired of service. It may, in these times of gender equality, be an obsolete quote, but the point remains valid.

"Excuse me," a portly man, clearly flustered, says as he steps into my path.

"Yes?"

"I, um, seem to have lost my bearings," he replies awkwardly while stealing a glance at his watch. "I'm looking for the conference hall."

I look him up and down. His crumpled, off-the-peg suit and polyester tie do him no credit.

"You're new here?" I ask.

"Second week."

"And you'd like me to give you directions?"

"Well, yes… please."

"And what's in it for me?"

21

"I beg your pardon?"

I offer a wry smile. "*Quid pro quo.*"

His confusion appears to mount as his mouth falls open. No words follow.

"Your Latin a little rusty?"

"I never studied Latin."

"A favour or advantage granted in return for something. It's how this place functions; a fact you should be mindful of."

"Um, okay…"

I have no time to tease him any further and point him in the right direction. He might well be a few seconds late for his meeting, but I hope the lesson proves adequate compensation.

I watch him waddle off and shake my head when he immediately takes a wrong turn. I conclude he won't last — this is no place for those of an indecisive disposition, or cheap suits for that matter. Maybe I'll keep an eye out for him; try to steer the poor fellow in the right direction.

I continue on my way.

My first meeting of the day is with the Chief Whip, Nigel Naylor. A career politician, Nigel is several years my senior, and thinks himself something of a charmer, particularly with the ladies. I don't care much for the man — he is a bully and a blaggard, although one might argue both are necessary characteristics for a man in his position.

The job of Chief Whip is to ensure we, the elected members, toe the party line when votes are cast in the house. If a bill is put forward, the cabinet will decide upon a position, and we are encouraged to vote in accordance with that position. Nigel Naylor is the one to administer that encouragement, by fair means or foul.

I reach his office and knock at the oak door.

"Enter," a voice booms.

I open the door to an office far grander than mine. Not that it bothers me, but there is a pecking order to the allocation of offices here at Westminster. New arrivals, like the chap seeking directions, are housed in glorified broom cupboards, while the so-called 'Big Beasts' — long-serving members whose authority and reputation proceeds them — enjoy suites with views of the Thames. The Chief Whip is one of the biggest, and most fearsome of beasts to prowl the corridors of power, and afforded an office to match such status.

"Ah, William. Thanks for popping by."

As if I had a choice.

Nigel offers me a seat on a wooden chair — one I suspect he deliberately chose because it offers little in the way of comfort.

"What can I do for you, Nigel?"

There is no point in any pretence. Nobody is ever summoned to Nigel's office unless he wants something.

"The greenfield bill," he replies, leaning back in his leather chair.

"What about it?"

"It goes to the house next week and I wanted to check we're all on the same page."

"And what page is that?"

"The one that begins with a yes vote," he replies with a thin smile.

The bill in question contains legislation which would allow the building of new homes on certain greenfield sites. Essentially, it's a charter to turn parts of our countryside into sprawling housing estates, and I am vehemently against it.

"No."

"No?"

"I'm not on the same page, Nigel. I don't think I'm even reading the same book."

"Oh, I see. Perhaps I can encourage you to be a little more forward thinking?"

With vast swathes of my constituency situated within the greenbelt, I was always going to be steadfastly opposed to the bill. With that, it is no surprise I've been singled out for Nigel's attention.

"If I vote for this bill, Nigel, I'll be lynched the next time I step foot in Marshburton."

He sits forward and rests his elbows on the desk. "I might be able to help you with that."

And so it begins.

Before he utters another word, I know Nigel will now offer me something to take back to my constituents — a small token to sugar the pill, if you will. This is how the political system works. Every time somebody gets what they want, others will pay a price to some degree. Failing that, a muddy middle ground is established where nobody loses and nobody wins, and very little is achieved. A colleague once suggested it's much like walking into a shop and asking for a pullover in either blue or red, and leaving with a purple hat that doesn't quite fit. No decision made here is ever universally popular so we spend an inordinate amount of time analysing the least unpopular option and hope enough of the electorate agrees with it. There will always be casualties, and today, the good people of Marshburton are in Nigel's sights.

"I'm listening."

"Affordable homes."

"What about them?"

"We're looking to launch a pilot scheme to help first time buyers, and I'm sure I can convince the housing minister to trial it in your constituency."

"Which would suggest you first need to build some houses?"

"Correct."

"So let me get this straight. You want me to convince my constituents that allowing a housing estate to be built in the middle of open countryside is a price worth paying so first time buyers can get on the property ladder a little easier?"

"Yes, although I'd hope you'll frame it a little more positively, William."

"They won't buy it."

"Why not?"

"Because no matter how much a handful of first time buyers might like the idea of subsidised housing, the majority don't want a scaled down version of Basingstoke built on their doorstep."

"What's wrong with Basingstoke?"

"Ever been there?"

"No."

"I rest my case."

He sits back in his chair, presumably pondering his next move. It's quick to come.

"So, you won't even float the idea to them?"

"I can't. No."

"That's a shame, William. The PM had high hopes this might be an opportunity for you to show you're a team player. She's had her eye on you; thinks you have potential."

There are three stages in any negotiation with Nigel. Stage one is where you're offered something as a subtle bribe, although it's usually nowhere near adequate recompense for what you're being asked to give up. Stage two is where you're offered a career carrot, attached to a stick of indeterminable length. And stage three is just blatant threats.

We've now entered stage two.

"I am a team player, Nigel, but my constituents are as much part of my team as the party are."

He frowns, and the mask of civility slips.

"Your father wouldn't have thought twice. He'd have seen the bigger picture, been the bigger man."

A low blow, but one I've faced countless times. No matter what I do, it seems I'm destined to remain in my father's shadow.

"I hate to break it to you, Nigel, but my father is dead. What he may or may not have done in this situation is therefore academic."

A slight twitch of his upper lip signifies we're about to enter stage three.

"There's nothing I can do, or offer, to make you vote in favour?"

"Nothing. Sorry."

The problem Nigel has with stage three, at least in my case, is there are no threats he can levy. There are some in this house who are motivated by their thirst for power or career advancement. Threaten to take away that power, or pull a few rungs from the career ladder, and most will yield to Nigel's wishes. My motivations lie beyond his grasp.

"Your loss," he spits. "Shut the door on your way out."

His expression is that of a schoolyard bully, offered a tuna paste sandwich in lieu of lunch money — there is no threat where there is no fear of loss.

I do as instructed.

As I wander back to my office, a familiar feeling resurfaces — guilt. Not for the way I dealt with Nigel, but the issue itself. Our country *is* in desperate need of more housing and countless governments of every hue have struggled to address the problem. I wish I had an answer but I don't, and that is my frustration. I can argue that we shouldn't build homes in the countryside, but where do you build them?

But housing is not the only national issue to permanently remain on every government's agenda. There's the evergreen problem of funding the Health Service, social care, defence, transport, policing, and education. Then there's the environment, trade, immigration, security, taxation, and the vast complexities of extracting ourselves from the European Union. A raft of monolithic issues; each one so cumbersome that a change of direction, even by the odd degree, requires almost generational patience. No government has a generation to make a difference so all we can do is set the direction of travel and hope to make some headway; until the next government is appointed and another path is set. It's no wonder we seem to go around in circles.

And that is why, more often than not, I feel completely useless. I do miss my voluntary work. The times I could make a tangible and immediate difference to the lives of others. You help dig a well and see clean water flow from a tap. You toil to construct a prefabricated classroom and hear children learn to read. You assist with administering simple medicines and watch the sick get better. Perhaps self-indulgent, but you get the chance to see your efforts rewarded. I can't say I get that same gratification when voting for the renewal of our nuclear arsenal.

But here I am. Still.

A question asked by many, and of myself, is why I don't just pack it all in and return to my voluntary work. The only answer I can offer is duty. Not to my constituents, not to my colleagues, or even my party — I have a duty to my father. After our argument, I returned to Africa without closure. Our mutual stubbornness ensured we never got the chance to heal our rift. My primary reason for being here is to try, in some way, to make amends by pursuing the career he hoped I'd pursue.

It is a shame so many of my colleagues don't understand my motivation, and wrongly assume I have the same political aspirations as my father. So, it remains a stick for the likes of Nigel Naylor to beat me with, albeit a hollow one. And in some way, it nicely sums up where twenty-first century politics is heading — a Punch & Judy show performed by caricatures. Pick a side and heckle, "That's the way to do it!" or "Oh no it isn't!" Repeat ad infinitum until nobody knows what to believe.

It's not difficult to understand why the British public, on the whole, are now so disillusioned with politics.

I, more than anyone, share that disillusion.

4.

"That was quick," Rosa remarks as I stroll back into the office.

"Brief, and strained."

Her eyebrows arch. "Have you upset the Chief Whip again, William?"

"Possibly. He'll get over it."

She moves across the office and stands in front of my desk as I take a seat.

"Here," she says, handing me a piece of notepaper. "You can fill the time before your next meeting by catching up on your calls."

I take the notepaper and inwardly groan at the long list of names, numbers, and Rosa's accompanying notes.

"I said you'd call Mrs Henderson first."

"Mrs Henderson?"

"Nora Henderson, from Marshburton."

"Of course, yes. What does she want?"

"Her husband passed away last week."

I'm genuinely shocked. "Oh dear. That's terrible news."

Nora and Arthur Henderson are, or *was* in poor Arthur's case, community stalwarts in Marshburton. Decent people with no pretensions.

"Did she mention where the funeral is going to be held?"

"St Mark's Church."

"Right."

I hate funerals as much as the next man, but I particularly hate church funerals — they are no place for an atheist. Despite attending a Christian school, I have long since come to the conclusion there is no God. My opinion was forged during my teenage years, at my mother's bedside, watching her waste away. Where was God then? My prayers went unanswered as I watched her die. Consequently, I'm often lost for words when it comes to offering the bereaved comfort. My platitudes about better places and eternal peace carry the stench of insincerity.

"William?"

"Sorry, Rosa," I splutter, returning to reality. "I was just thinking about Arthur."

"Were you close?"

"Not especially, but I knew him well enough."

Rosa steps around the desk and places a hand on my shoulder. It's not in her job description, but I appreciate the attempt to offer comfort, even though her touch only heightens the feelings I'm already struggling to quell.

"Would you like me to call Mrs Henderson?" she asks in a soft voice.

"No, thank you. I'll call her now."

Rosa's fingers linger on my shoulder before she turns away and heads back to her desk. With such a solemn task to perform, it would be inappropriate to watch her shimmy away. I stare at the phone and dial Nora Henderson's number.

Seventeen long, painful minutes ensue. I do my best to keep her spirits buoyed and offer a few amusing anecdotes about

Arthur. She cries, a lot. I'm not sure my anecdotes help and I end the call with the poor woman in a much worse state than she was seventeen minutes earlier.

"Not your forte, William?" Rosa remarks from the other side of the office.

"What isn't?"

"Tea and sympathy."

"You noticed?"

"I could hear Mrs Henderson sobbing from over here."

"I tried my best, but what can you say?"

Rosa shakes her head. "It's not about saying anything, William. It's about listening."

"You think my anecdotes were inappropriate?"

"Maybe a little."

I suppose she has a point, and I consider calling Nora back. However, one thing I've learnt in my time serving as a politician is that deeds are greater than words.

"Can you send her some flowers please, Rosa, and a card."

"Would you like me to write the message?"

"I think that might be sensible."

She nods and scribbles a note to herself. I return to my list of calls.

I manage to strike four calls from the list before I'm due at my next meeting. Rosa furnishes me with the necessary paperwork and I leave the office again, destined for another meeting I'd rather not attend.

The only consolation is my route passes through the cathedral-like central lobby; an octagonal hall constructed in stone, with an intricately tiled floor, mosaic-covered walls, and grand arched windows. No matter how many times I've passed through it over the years, I'm still taken with the same sense of wonderment I experienced on the first occasion.

Beyond the breathtaking architecture and decoration, there is an almost palpable aura of historical reverence. Many times, when the lobby is closed to the public and the palace is near silent, I have taken a seat on one of the leather benches positioned around the perimeter. I have enjoyed moments of quiet reflection and visualised the great men and women whose footsteps once echoed through the hallowed lobby: kings and queens, popes and presidents, and figures who had carved their place in history. Perhaps a ridiculous notion considering my atheism, but I occasionally sensed the presence of their spirits, and in particular, one spirit who cast the longest shadow — Sir Charles Augustus Huxley.

Today, alas, there is no time to reflect on architectural majesty, or figments of an overactive imagination.

My meeting proves to be every bit as tedious as I had feared. Two hours of discussion on a subject I have little interest in, with colleagues who can't see beyond their own agendas. Such a waste of time. Just for once I wish the wheels of bureaucracy could be lubricated with a little common sense. My wish is futile though, and the wheels continue to grind and jar like I suppose they always have and always will.

Fortunately, lunchtime brings some respite. I head back to my office to find Rosa putting her coat on.

"I'm just going to grab a sandwich. Can I get you anything?" she asks.

"No, thank you. I might pop out for some fresh air shortly. I'll pick something up while I'm out."

She smiles at me as she buttons up her coat. "Fancy some company?"

Don't embrace false hope, William.

"That's very kind but I have a speech to prepare for later. I don't think I'd be good company."

"Oh, okay. If you're sure," she replies. She then turns her collar up and heads for the door.

Perhaps I imagined it, but I'm sure I detected the slightest trace of disappointment in her voice. It could just as easily have been relief, though, and I instantly dismiss it. I possess too little experience to understand the nuances of the female vernacular.

I sit down at my desk and run through my commitments for the afternoon: two back-to-back meetings, a debate in the house which will almost certainly attract no more than a dozen or so members, and finally, I've pulled the short straw to give a speech at a business event north of the river.

Much like my life, the outlook for the rest of the day appears dull and uninspiring.

I clear a couple of the more urgent calls from Rosa's list and leave the office in search of lunch. I could choose to eat at the subsidised member's canteen but socialising with colleagues does quash my appetite somewhat.

Once I've navigated security, and the throngs of tourists in Parliament Square, I take a stroll through the quieter back streets towards St James's Park. I pop in to a sandwich shop and order the same thing I order every single day: chicken salad on whole wheat bread, with the merest lick of Dijon mustard. I no longer have to ask for my order, such is my predictability. I like predictability. I like routine.

Sandwich acquired, I head for St James's Park and locate an empty bench. The early October sun provides just enough warmth to be comfortable and the park is relatively busy with tourists and office workers taking advantage of the mild autumn weather. As I sit and eat, people pass without a glance in my direction.

I am fortunate, unlike a number of my colleagues, to enjoy anonymity. No journalists or paparazzi are interested in anything I do, or say for that matter, and that suits me just fine. I have no desire for media attention, nor do I wish to become one of those celebrity politicians who leaves the commons for a stint on Celebrity Big Brother or some other god-awful reality show. No shame, some people.

And of course, there are those who unwittingly attract the media spotlight due to an indiscretion or lack of good judgement. Extra marital affairs, drugs, prostitution, gambling, alcoholism — the men and women who serve in parliament are no more virtuous or immune from life's temptations than the rest of the population. The only difference is the media love a good scandal involving a politician and we make for easy prey. I've seen good colleagues have their lives torn apart for some minor indiscretion that would go unnoticed in any workplace but ours. It doesn't seem fair, but public scrutiny comes with the job and requires us to live saintly lives. That's not so difficult for me, but some of my colleagues do find it a chore.

I finish my sandwich and sit for a few minutes; simply to enjoy the tepid sunlight and distinctive scent of London in autumn.

All too soon I feel compelled to check my watch — forty minutes until my next meeting. With a puff of my cheeks, I reluctantly climb to my feet and take a slow walk back to the office.

I return to find Rosa on her mobile phone, listening intently to whoever is on the other end of the line. I wonder if it's a boyfriend, or potential suitor. I know she's not married as there's no ring on her finger. She's never mentioned a partner but I can't imagine such a fine woman wouldn't be without her pick of admirers. I've never brought the subject up because I'm fairly sure I don't want to hear the answer.

"I've got to go," she says hurriedly before disconnecting the call without a goodbye.

I glance across at her, half expecting a throwaway comment about who she was talking to; like people apologetically do when taking a personal call in the workplace. No such comment is forthcoming. Perhaps she's embarrassed, or conscious her three-month probation period is still in force. I'm a little disappointed she thinks I'm petty enough to chastise her for making the odd personal call.

"Nice lunch?" she asks while slipping her phone into her handbag.

"Most pleasant, thank you. I hope I didn't interrupt an important call."

"No. Nobody important."

She smiles but doesn't expand on her answer. Part of me is relieved she didn't confirm she was chatting to a partner. I let it go.

"Oh, I've sorted your phone," she calls across the office, changing the subject.

With much enthusiasm, she scuttles over and sits down at my desk. I'm then given a concise tutorial on using the device. I had no idea a small block of glass and plastic could do so much, and by the time we're through, I have to begrudgingly admit the new phone is indeed much smarter than my dumb Nokia.

Phone sorted, I grab the folders I require for my meetings and ask Rosa to ring a few people on the list to see if she can deal with their queries. In many cases, people think I have some magic wand I can wave at their problems. Granted, a sternly worded letter on parliament stationery does often help, but there are simply too many people with too many problems for one man to deal with.

"I'll probably go from my meetings straight to the house, so I won't be back until late afternoon."

Rosa nods and I head off to my first meeting.

I can't recall his name, but a famous American economist once quipped that meetings are a great way to appear busy while achieving nothing — both my meetings offer credence to that statement.

Two hours later I enter the house, or the House of Commons to give it it's full name; the heart of parliament where the elected members debate and vote on bills. Once a bill is approved, it's then sent to the House of Lords for scrutiny and ratification. Dozens of bills are put to the house every week and attendance of members is usually determined by how important or contentious the bill is. The debate in the house this afternoon relates to a bill on vehicle noise limits; a subject clearly of little interest to the majority of members judging by the woeful turnout. There are over six hundred members of parliament and just sixteen are present.

I do my best to engage in the debate but it's so intolerably mind-numbing, my attention drifts for long periods. When one of my colleagues launches into a lengthy diatribe about the evils of noise pollution, the small audience collectively groans. By the time it's over, I'm so utterly bored of the subject, I simply abstain from voting on the basis I have no idea if the bill is worthwhile or just another piece of needless legislation.

I finally escape, and with less than an hour before I'm due to give my speech, I hurry back to my office.

Another list awaits me.

"I've tried to deal with as many as I could but this lot insist on talking to you," Rosa says apologetically, handing me the list.

"They'll have to wait until tomorrow. I'm running late."

I print off a copy of my speech and tuck it into my jacket pocket. I then check my appearance in a small mirror, affixed to the inside of the door. I'm not a vain man, but I'd rather not deliver my speech with a crooked tie or stray tuft of hair.

"How's my diary looking tomorrow morning?" I ask Rosa while adjusting my tie.

"You're in luck. Your ten o'clock meeting has been postponed so there's nothing until the afternoon."

"That's a relief."

"And you look fine," she adds.

I feel my cheeks flush at Rosa's compliment, if indeed it was even intended as a compliment. People say *fine* all the time and it now lacks any real meaning: *How are you? I'm fine. How was the meal? It was fine.* Something that is neither good nor bad is just *fine*. Perhaps that makes it the perfect word to describe my physical appearance. Or perhaps I'm just over analysing a throwaway remark.

"Thank you," I reply, still facing the mirror so Rosa can't see my pink cheeks.

I bid her a good evening and hurry out of the office, hoping I've left sufficient time for my journey, and that my speech is slightly better than *fine*.

5.

The tube carriage is packed with commuters and I'm grateful the journey from Westminster to Temple is only a few minutes. I escape the crush, scoot up to the station concourse, and make my way towards The Strand; one of London's most famous roads where the likes of Charles Dickens and Virginia Woolf once lived. My destination is The Montgomery; an imposing Art Deco hotel where two hundred guests are awaiting my speech at six o'clock sharp.

This is one of many events I'm asked to attend throughout the year and they usually fall into one of three categories: events in my constituency which benefit the community or local business, charity events which are always good for the party's public relations, and then there are events which return a favour for a party benefactor, or a lobby group whose interests align with ours.

In this instance, the event has been arranged by an organisation that represent independent retailers, and want to highlight the plight of town centres, particularly in some of our key marginal constituencies. I'm guessing they would have ideally liked the Minister for Business to attend, but he was unavailable, and so was their second, third, and fourth choice of speaker. So, they're stuck with me, and the only reason I've been sent is because I once sat on the backbench business committee. Essentially, the organisers asked for a box office name and have been sent an extra.

With fifteen minutes to spare, I make my way through the lavishly decorated foyer and head towards the conference hall at the rear of the building. I've attended events at this particular venue many times and spoken on two prior occasions, so I know what to expect — a crowd of suits who are completely indifferent to a politician's views and will therefore spend the entirety of my speech eyeing the free bar. I am merely the bread before a liquid banquet.

I approach the entrance where a makeshift reception desk has been set up. Two middle-aged men in grey suits are stood behind the desk, checking-in the delegates and handing out name badges on bright red lanyards. I approach the nearest man.

"William Huxley, here for the first speech."

"Ah, yes, Mr Huxley. We were expecting you at five thirty."

"I beg your pardon," I reply with a frown. "I wasn't told that."

"I'm pretty sure we would have informed your office what time to arrive."

"I doubt it. My personal assistant is extremely efficient."

"Nevertheless, I'm afraid we've already moved your slot."

"To where?"

"Third slot from the end."

"So how long before I'm on?"

"Oh, not too long," he replies dismissively. "Maybe an hour or so."

Just as I'm about to protest, a voice booms from the public-address system to advise the first speech is imminent, and the free bar is closed.

"Sorry, Mr Huxley, I'm required elsewhere," the man squawks. "Jeremy here will sort you out," he adds, before leaving his befuddled companion to placate me.

Jeremy tells me there is free water available by the now-closed bar and they've reserved a seat for me at the back of the room.

"Somebody will come and collect you five minutes before your slot."

He hands me a name badge, and before I can raise a complaint, he scuttles away.

This day just gets better and better.

I turn and survey the sea of heads facing the stage. The chairs have been arranged into two blocks, each ten seats across and ten deep, with an aisle running down the middle. I slope over to my allocated seat and tear away the sheet of paper taped to the back; my name scrawled across it in marker pen.

The woman in the adjoining seat turns, looks up at me, and smiles. I'm immediately dumbstruck. She's maybe thirty years of age with dark, shoulder-length hair, and dressed in a perfectly tailored business suit.

With my irritation immediately quashed, I return an embarrassed smile and take my seat.

I keep my gaze fixed on the stage and try to ignore the prickly sensation that comes from being in such close proximity to an attractive woman. Her perfume engulfs me; a floral scent, heavy on the patchouli. I take a quick glance towards the floor and stare at her high-heeled shoes, probably designer, and her naked ankles. Perhaps it's my imagination, but I'm sure I can feel the warmth of her body, radiating towards me.

The only way to ease the awkwardness is to concentrate on my speech. Just as I'm about to pluck it from my pocket, I feel a light tap on my shoulder. My head snaps to the left to find the woman smiling at me again.

"Excuse me. May I ask a favour?" she asks.

"Um…yes, of course."

"I just want to grab a glass of water before they start. Would you mind watching my seat?"

I nod and she touches me on the shoulder again. "Thank you."

The woman then gets up and glides towards a table by the bar, laden with bottled water and glasses.

I try to pull myself together as I watch her go. This is ridiculous. For ten years I've stood and debated in the House of Commons; the most vociferous, intimidating forum in the land, yet upon meeting an attractive woman, I become a blubbering wreck.

What is wrong with me?

It's a purely rhetorical question because I know full well what's wrong with me. I spent fourteen of my formative years at an all-boys school, and with no siblings I had little opportunity to develop relationships with any females, besides my mother. By the time I started university, the problem was already so deeply entrenched I avoided girls wherever possible. I chose to bury myself in my studies rather than confront my shyness. That, in hindsight, was a mistake, and one I'm still paying for today.

The woman returns and takes her seat.

"Thank you," she says, before placing her glass on the floor.

I return an awkward smile, willing her not to engage in any further discourse.

She sits forward and turns to me, her hand outstretched. "I'm Gabby, by the way," she says.

Please, leave me alone.

I tentatively take her hand. "William."

I would usually avoid prolonged eye contact with an attractive woman but her lustrous green eyes have an almost familiar quality. I continue to stare into them, hoping a connection to that familiarity will spark, but nothing comes. In the end, I maintain my gaze just a little too long and she turns her head towards the stage. Her hand slips away from mine a second later.

I would usually retreat back into my shell at this point but the familiarity is still niggling enough for me to pose a question.

I steel myself. "Erm, I'm sorry, but have we met before?"

She turns to me. "I don't think so. I hear that a lot, though. I must have one of those faces."

"Right, yes. Sorry."

"And besides," she replies, her smile now a grin. "I would hope you'd remember me if we had met before."

"Yes, yes, of course," I bluster, conscious my cheeks are reddening. "It's…it's just that I meet a lot of people in my line of work and I'm not blessed with a particularly good memory."

"And what is your line of work, William?"

Telling somebody you're a politician, specifically a Conservative politician, does tend to pour cold water on a conversation. But seeing as I'll be introduced on the stage in an hour's time, there seems precious little point in evading her question.

"I'm just a humble politician."

Her pupils widen a fraction as her sculpted eyebrows arch. "Oh, really? How fascinating."

Is she being sarcastic?

"It's not as fascinating as it sounds."

Without warning, she suddenly places her hand on my knee. "Well, Mr Huxley, I hate to break it to you, but shouldn't you be up on that stage about now?"

I stare back at her, confused. "How did you know my surname?"

Her gaze slowly falls towards my groin. I instinctively drop my head in the same direction, fearing my fly is undone.

"Ohh, right," I say with some relief. "My name badge."

"Yes. Your name badge," she coos. "And my memory, thankfully, is pretty good — your name is on the list of speakers."

"I've been rescheduled. Some mix up with my office, apparently."

Before she can reply, thumping music bursts from the speakers behind us, and the lights dim. A cloud of dry ice drifts across the stage and coloured light beams burst through the fog, dancing in time to the beat.

"Bit over the top, don't you think?" Gabby shouts in my ear.

I nod, and we join the rousing applause for the compere; a plump and overly energetic man with delusions of his own importance. Why anyone thinks this an appropriate entrance for an event of this nature, is beyond me?

Just when I think his behaviour can't get any more ridiculous, he starts clapping his hands together over his head. A few idiots in the front rows copy his actions and that only serves to encourage him.

"Don't indulge the fool," I mutter to myself, perhaps a little louder than I anticipated.

Gabby chuckles again before leaning over and whispering in my ear. "That's an unusually candid statement for a politician."

I don't know what to say in response, so I say nothing.

Mercifully, the music ends and the plump compere gets down to business, going through an admittedly slick introduction before he announces the first speaker.

"Ladies and gentlemen, please give a warm round of applause for Gavin Grant."

The crowd oblige and Mr Grant, whoever he is, enters the stage. It takes barely two minutes for me to determine Mr Grant is insufferably dull, as are the next four speakers. Perhaps I'm being unfair as it's not so much the speakers who are dull — it's the subject matter. Talk of footfall trends and retail indicators is of little interest to me. The crowd seem to be lapping it up, though, and I become increasingly concerned my own speech might dampen their enthusiasm.

Before I have a chance to reconsider the content of my speech, Jeremy reappears and beckons me through a door at the side of the auditorium. I nod at Gabby before I depart and she mouths the words, 'Good luck'.

I follow Jeremy along a corridor and enter a small anteroom adjacent to the stage. The plump compere is seated in the corner reading a newspaper and nods at me over the top. I return his nod as Jeremy offers me a glass of water.

"I'm good, thank you."

He places the glass back on the table and checks his watch. "Three minutes, Mr Huxley."

I take those minutes to check my speech again. Too late now to make any significant changes and I'm not one for ad-libbing.

Suddenly the door leading up to the stage bursts open and a sweaty man with a rotund face appears; the sound of applause following him into the room.

The compere folds his paper and gets to his feet.

"Ready?" he asks me.

"I guess so."

Without another word, he heads towards the stage as the applause peters out. Butterflies begin to dance as the compere begins my introduction.

"Break a leg," Jeremy quips while waving his arm towards the door.

The compere bellows my name. This is it. I draw a deep breath before making my way through the door and up five steps to the stage. The compere steps towards me and offers his hand.

A quick handshake, a slap on the back, and he directs me towards the lectern. I shuffle over and welcome the barrier it creates. I turn to my right, looking for assurance from the compere but he's already heading back down the steps.

The applause dies out and a sea of faces stare expectantly in my direction.

I extract the two sheets of folded paper from my jacket pocket and lay them on the lectern. After clearing my throat, I prepare to deliver what I hope will be a rousing opening line.

"Ladies and gentlemen. This government is, and always will be, the friend of business."

I pause for effect and deliver the next line with conviction.

"Before changes in legislation under this government, businesses had been strangled by *ted rape*."

Oh, Christ! Red tape, man. Red tape!

I hoped my spoonerism would go unnoticed. Apparently not and stifled laughter fills the auditorium.

"Taxi for Ted Rape," a voice from the audience suddenly heckles.

The dam bursts and laughter roars across the room.

There is no coming back.

It takes almost a minute for the laugher to die down, by which point my credibility is in tatters. I make no effort to deliver the rest of the speech with any conviction and tear through it in half the time I anticipated.

The final line is met with a half-hearted ripple of applause before more laughter ensues. I turn and take the walk of shame towards stage right.

The compere passes me en-route, shaking his head and frowning. The greeting in the anteroom is equally frosty and the next speaker barges past me, mumbling something under his breath.

"Probably not your finest speech," Jeremy helpfully points out.

"It was just a slip of the tongue."

"A quite unfortunate slip of the tongue."

"Yes, well, I didn't expect them to be so childish about it."

We reach an impasse and I decide it's probably best to leave. No matter how much I might need a drink, particularly a free one, I have no desire to endure more ridicule.

"I think I'm going to head off now."

"Right. I'll walk you out," he replies, possibly relieved I'm not going to ruin their event any further. "I've got to notify the next speaker, anyway."

I follow Jeremy out of the anteroom and along the corridor. We enter back into the rear of the auditorium where the crowd are thankfully engrossed by the speaker who barged past me. Jeremy shakes my hand and disappears.

As I make my way past the back row of chairs, I notice the two empty seats at the end. It seems Gabby couldn't tolerate any more speeches and has already left. Can't say I blame her. I reach the reception desk where a young woman is sifting through a pile of papers. As I pass, she calls after me.

"Mr Huxley?"

I turn and face her. "Yes."

She hands me a folded piece of paper. "This was left for you."

I take the paper and open it up, half-expecting it to be a summons for slandering Ted Rape.

It is not a summons but a scribbled note…

I bet you could do with a drink!

I'm at the bar across the road and I don't much care for drinking alone. Please don't leave this damsel in distress —
Gabby xx

I read it twice to ensure I haven't misread her intent.

A quick check of my watch — not quite seven thirty. There's nothing in my diary tomorrow morning and she is certainly correct regarding my need for a stiff drink.

I give the matter a few seconds thought and conclude it would be ungentlemanly to decline Gabby's invitation. And besides, where's the harm in having a few drinks?

6.

I dart back through the hotel foyer and out onto The Strand. There is only one bar opposite, and I dash through the traffic to the other side of the road, and enter.

The interior has all the hallmarks of an identity crisis; as if the owners couldn't decide if they wanted to open a nightclub, a traditional pub, or a soup kitchen. The walls are painted in burnt orange and teal while the furnishings look like they've been liberated from a skip. Perhaps the schizophrenic styling is all part of the latest hipster trend which seems to be plaguing our capital city.

I scan the tables, most of which are empty, and spot Gabby at the far side of the room. As I'm about to make my way over, she stands and waves, then slithers past the tables towards me. Once she navigates the assault course of furniture, her stride becomes more confident, more purposeful.

Her approach ends with us stood barely a few feet apart; well within my personal space.

"You obviously did need that drink," she remarks.

I return an awkward smile. "Um…yes. What can I get you?" I splutter.

"Gin and tonic, please."

I shuffle towards the bar and Gabby joins me; stood so close her arm is pressed against mine. I resist the urge to step to my right, and hail the barman.

"Two gin and tonics, please. Make them large."

As the barman pours our drinks, Gabby leans closer towards me. "I didn't take you for a gin man, William?"

"At this precise moment, I'm an any kind of drink man."

The stupidly-bearded barman returns with our drinks and I pay.

"Shall we grab a seat?" Gabby asks.

I nod, and follow her across the room to her table at the far side of the bar.

We sit, and she raises her glass. "Cheers."

I reciprocate and we chink our glasses together before I take a large gulp of gin and tonic. Silence descends and I choose to dispense with the usual small talk.

"Excuse me for asking, Gabby, but why did you ask me to join you?"

She puts her glass down and puckers her lips. Perhaps my question was a little blunt.

"That's a very direct question," she replies.

Not a great start.

"Sorry, I didn't mean to offend. Subtlety is not my forte, I'm afraid."

"Clearly. But to answer your question, I thought your speech was fascinating and I couldn't pass up the opportunity for a little one-to-one time."

"You thought it was fascinating?"

"Don't sound so surprised, William. You're clearly an intelligent, erudite man."

She takes a slow sip of her drink, keeping her eyes fixed on me. The glass is returned to the table and she continues. "And those are qualities I really admire in a man."

Such is my lack of experience with the opposite sex, I have no idea if she's being friendly or flirtatious. Best play safe.

"I appreciate your positive feedback, Gabby."

She starts laughing. I don't get the joke.

"What's so funny?" I ask.

"You, William. I can honestly say I've never met a man quite like you. You're so very formal, aren't you?"

Besides her obvious beauty, she's also highly perceptive. Whilst most men seem able to effortlessly drift from one persona to another, depending on their social situation. I have one persona and evidence suggests it is not best suited to wooing a lady.

"I don't know what to say, Gabby. I am who I am, I'm afraid."

"Don't apologise. I think it's quite endearing."

"Do you?" I reply with some surprise.

"Oh, absolutely."

She seems comfortable to maintain eye contact whilst I struggle to hold her gaze for more than a few seconds.

"Can I ask you a question, William?"

"Of course."

"What do you do when you're not practising politics?"

I'm not one to lie but I'd rather not tell her the truth. While I'm in London, I spend nearly all my time at work. And when

I'm not there, I'm usually to be found drinking alone at a bar near my flat in Blackfriars. It should be said that the frequency of my visits to Fitzgerald's bar has little to do with my appetite for alcohol, and a lot to do with the fact I'd rather sit amongst strangers than sit alone in my flat.

"It's a very time consuming job. I have precious little time for much else."

"How does your wife feel about that?" she asks.

"I'm not married."

My answer hangs in the air as Gabby mindlessly taps her fingers against the side of her glass. For the first time I notice an absence of any rings. I have no intention of asking her relationship status, and fill the silence with a fairly inane question.

"You never said, Gabby. What is it you do?"

"I'm a marketing consultant. I specialise in the retail sector, hence my attendance at the event."

"And are you based in London?"

"I'm based here, there, and everywhere. It's a fairly nomadic existence," she replies, perhaps wistfully.

"Do you enjoy it?"

"I love my job but I don't like the life that comes with it."

"What do you mean?"

"I mean, I hate the loneliness, William."

Without waiting for my response, she empties her glass and stands up. "Same again?"

I nod and she heads back to the bar. I watch her go while pondering her remark about loneliness. It does seem extraordinary that such an attractive woman should be lonely. I'd have assumed men would be queueing up for her attention.

She returns with two glasses of gin and tonic and places one in front of me.

"This city," she says as she takes her seat. "So many people yet it's one of the loneliest places on earth."

"If you don't mind me saying, I wouldn't have considered you to be somebody who struggles to find company."

"Why? Because I'm a woman?"

"Well, no, because you're very…erm, attractive."

"And attractive people don't get lonely?"

"I wouldn't know."

She snorts and shakes her head. "Now *that's* not a particularly attractive trait."

"What isn't?"

"Self-pity."

"I didn't mean to suggest I had any pity for myself. I was simply stating a fact."

"A fact or an opinion?"

"An opinion based upon factual evidence."

She leans across the table and her eyes lock onto mine again. "Well, we'll have to agree to disagree on that one."

Her gaze lingers for a second before she sits back in her chair.

"Does it scare you, William?"

"What?"

"Being alone?"

It doesn't scare me. It terrifies me.

"Sometimes."

"It scares me," she says. "That I might end up a lonely old spinster living with a few dozen cats and a sack full of regrets."

It could be her soul bearing, or the gin swilling through my system, but I suddenly feel a connection with Gabby. Despite the vast differences in our physical appeal, perhaps we have more in common than I first imagined.

"Loneliness," I reply in a hushed voice. "The worst kind of poverty."

"That's a very profound quote. Who said it?"

"I did."

"Born from experience?"

I have no idea why I should be talking so candidly to a virtual stranger. Perhaps it's out of necessity — so rare is the opportunity to discuss affairs of the heart that I can't let the opportunity slip by.

"I have no close family, and few real friends," I reply.

"I know that feeling."

"Your family…"

"Both my parents are gone," she interjects. "I lost my mother when I was eleven, and my father while I was at university."

"I'm sorry."

She bows her head a fraction and bites her lip. I wish I could lean across and offer some physical comfort but not even two double gins are enough to bolster my reserved nature. Then I recall Rosa's sage advice after my conversation with Nora Henderson. It's better in these situations to listen rather than talk.

"Tell me about them."

"Who?"

"Your parents."

I'm relieved to see her face brighten, and silently offer thanks to Rosa. Strangely, I feel a pang of guilt for sharing a drink with another woman. I dismiss it as illogical.

For ten minutes, I sit and listen as Gabby pours her heart out. Clearly she had a very close relationship with her parents, particularly her father, and hearing her talk so fondly of him triggers another pang of guilt, and regret.

She ends with an apology. "I can't believe I just bored you witless, talking about my parents. I'm so sorry. What must you think of me?"

"I think you needed to talk."

She reaches across the table and places her hand on mine. "I did, and thank you for listening, William. It's been a long while since I've been able to really talk about my parents with anyone."

Her hand is warm, and she gently brushes her thumb across my wrist. It is as disconcerting as it is wonderful, to feel a woman's touch.

"You don't have any siblings?" I ask.

"No. I've got a few cousins who I see now and again, but we're not close."

I'm not sure what else to say on the subject of families, and I'd rather we moved on to something less depressing. I offer to acquire more drinks and slink back to the bar.

The only member of staff is dealing with another customer so I take a position towards the end of the bar and wait. It proves an opportunity to contemplate the fortuitous hand fate has played me after that car crash of a speech.

A hand of an altogether different variety suddenly touches my left arm. Dragged from my thoughts, I turn to find Gabby stood beside me.

"Have you ordered my drink yet?" she asks.

"No."

"Good. I was going to head back to the hotel and grab a bite to eat in my room."

Normal service, it seems, has been resumed. It looks like another evening sat alone in Fitzgerald's.

"Oh, right. Well, it's been lovely chatting with you, Gabby."

I offer my hand and her brow furrows slightly. "I was kind of hoping you might like to join me."

"Oh."

"But honestly, William, if you're uncomfortable with that then I totally understand. I just don't like eating in restaurants."

I realise my hand is still outstretched, and my mouth is possibly agape. I pull myself together.

"I wouldn't wish to condone inviting strangers to your hotel room."

"I guessed you probably wouldn't, which is why I feel comfortable inviting you. I'm a good judge of character, William, and I have no reason to think you're anything other than a total gentleman."

I've been labelled a gentleman many times before and in my view, it translates as safe, dependable, and predictable — not exactly traits to set the heart racing. Perhaps it would be nice, just for once, to be thought of as roughish, a charmer, or even a bit of a bastard.

"Thank you. I'd be honoured," I reply, gentlemanly as ever.

Gabby takes my arm and we head back on to The Strand, and the chilly night air.

"Where are you staying?" I ask.

"Just there," Gabby replies with a nod towards the Montgomery Hotel opposite; the venue we left an hour ago. I hope we can avoid bumping into any of the delegates who will no doubt still be enjoying the free bar.

We approach a pedestrian crossing and wait for the lights to change. I sneak a glance to my left, at my beautiful companion, and I immediately feel ten feet tall. I may have skulked out of the Montgomery Hotel with my tail between my legs but I will be returning with my head held high.

Could this be the start of a long overdue new chapter in my life?

Dare I even hope?

7.

The foyer in the Montgomery is quiet as we cross the polished floor to the lifts. Gabby then presses the button and we watch the lights on the adjacent panel change as the lift descends.

"Are you hungry?" she asks as we wait.

"Peckish," I confirm, although a mix of apprehension and excitement have somewhat stifled my appetite.

The lift chimes and the doors open, revealing a plush carpeted floor and mirrored walls. We step inside and Gabby presses the button for the ninth floor. The doors close and we turn to face the mirrored wall, and the odd couple staring back at us. We look every bit the parody of a middle-aged politician and a disproportionately young and pretty mistress, despite the fact I'm unmarried.

I choose to look at the floor as the lift ascends.

Another chime and the doors open. I let Gabby lead and she turns left into the corridor while extracting a key card from her jacket pocket.

She stops outside room 904. "This is me."

I follow her into a room which isn't quite a suite, but nonetheless grand with two huge arched windows dominating the rear wall. The decor is a palette of browns and creams, although I suspect the overpaid interior designer sold them as *latte* and *cinnamon*.

"I've never been in any of the rooms here. Very impressive."

"I spend most of my time in grotty motorway hotels," Gabby replies, placing her handbag on the dresser. "So I like to treat myself when I'm in London."

"You never said. How long are you in London for?"

She bends down and opens the mini bar. "I'm not sure yet. Drink?"

"Please."

Caps are popped from tiny bottles and gin and tonics poured before she places the glasses on a table between two wingback chairs.

"Come and sit down," she orders.

I do as instructed, immediately reaching for one of the glasses. Gabby slips off her jacket to reveal a sleeveless white blouse beneath. Her shoes are then kicked away before she takes a seat.

"God, that's better," she sighs. "A long day on my feet wearing new shoes. Not such a good idea."

She takes a sip of her drink and sits back in the chair, crossing her legs.

"Are you comfortable there, William? You can take your jacket off, you know."

Perhaps a sensible suggestion as I do feel a little warm all of a sudden, not least because of Gabby's blouse, which is virtually transparent; her lacy bra and ample chest clearly visible beneath.

"Yes," I concede. "Good idea."

I sit forward and slip my jacket off. As I look for somewhere suitable to hang it, Gabby gets up and takes it from me. "I'll hang it up in the wardrobe."

I watch as she pads across the carpeted floor towards the wardrobe. I remind myself that I'm only here for a bite to eat and some company. I am a gentleman, and as such, I must banish the lecherous thoughts which are creeping ever closer.

She closes the wardrobe door but doesn't return to her chair.

"Actually, I feel a bit grotty," she calls across the room. "Do you mind if I grab a quick shower and change before we eat?"

I shake my head.

"I'll be five minutes. Promise."

She disappears into the bathroom, leaving the door slightly ajar. Moments later, I hear the shower pump whine and the splashing of water on tiles.

It takes only a few seconds for a devilish voice in my head to suggest Gabby left the door ajar for a reason.

Don't be stupid, man.

The devilish voice then sets a scene for me; one where I approach the bathroom door and open it. I stand for a moment, drinking in the picture of a naked Gabby, lathering her body beyond the glass shower screen. I quickly strip off and take a step towards the cubicle, just as Gabby turns; the full beauty of her body on display. She smiles, and beckons me to join her.

A stirring in my underpants drags me back to reality, just as the whine of the shower pump ceases. I breathe a sigh of relief my fantasy was nothing more than that. Even the thought of making such a comprehensive fool of myself delivers a cold shudder.

The bathroom door swings open and I expect to see Gabby exit, dressed in casual attire. I suppose attire doesn't get much more casual than the white towel just about covering her modesty.

"Silly me," she grins. "Forgot my clothes."

The stirring in my underpants returns as Gabby swings the wardrobe door open. I take a large gulp of gin and tonic, and try my damnedest not to watch her scouring the contents of the wardrobe.

I fail, and watch on before she suddenly stops her search, and turns back in my direction. "Would you be a sweetheart and pass me that bag please, William," she asks, pointing to a leather holdall at the foot of the bed, a few feet from my chair.

This is not good. This is not good, at all.

I am suddenly thirteen again, stood in line at the school tuck shop — the moment I first experienced an involuntary and extremely inconvenient erection. My erection on this occasion may not have been aroused by maize-based snacks, but the awkwardness is the same.

"That bag?" I gulp, pointing to the only bag in view.

"Please."

I rue the decision to remove my jacket as long seconds pass. With no plausible excuse not to, I tentatively stand and scuttle towards the holdall in a stooped, crablike manner.

"You okay there?" Gabby asks.

"Erm, yes. Just a slight twinge in my back. It'll pass."

I grab the holdall and continue to shuffle forward, enacting a passable impression of Quasimodo.

"Here you go," I grunt, handing it over.

"Are you sure you're okay?" she asks again, more than a hint of concern in her voice.

"Honestly, it's fine."

I shuffle backwards which, in hindsight, was a mistake considering how unfamiliar I am with the layout of the room. As I smile at Gabby to indicate just how fine I am, my right foot catches the leg of a stool next to the dresser. My arms flail, and as I stumble backwards I trip over my own feet and crash to the floor, flat on my back, winding myself in the process.

"Oh my God, William," Gabby shrieks. "Are you okay?"

I raise my head to look up at her, and then let my eyes fall south. I wish they hadn't. In my supine position, the erection appears untroubled, standing proud like a pole in a wool twill tent.

I look back at Gabby but her eyes must have followed mine, and she is now staring at the bulge in my trousers.

I work with some of the most adept liars in the country, but even they would struggle to concoct a plausible explanation for my predicament. There is little I can say.

I lift myself up onto my elbows and attempt to catch my breath. I'm expecting Gabby to scream at my deviancy any second, and I'm already plotting my escape once I find some breath.

Much to my surprise, there is no verbal onslaught. Instead, Gabby steps across the carpeted floor and stands by my outstretched legs. I look up at her, apologetically. In turn she smiles, and does the one thing I would have least expected — she slowly peels the towel away and drops it to the floor, revealing her naked body in all its glory.

My look of apology morphs into confusion as she takes two steps forward and kneels down next to me.

"What caused that then?" she purrs, nodding towards my groin. "Were you thinking of me in the shower?"

I look up at her, trying my utmost to focus on her face, rather than her naked breasts.

"Possibly," I wheeze.

"So what do you think? Is it as nice as you imagined?"

"Better. Definitely better."

"Maybe you should get up and take a proper look, just to be sure."

She stands and takes a few deliberate steps backwards before placing her hands on her hips. I require no second invitation and use the dresser as support to clamber up. Seconds later, we are stood five feet apart, facing one another; Gabby seemingly at ease with her nudity, and my trouser pole fully extended.

The situation is beyond surreal and I have no idea what to do, other than gawk at the naked woman in front of me.

"Well? Better?" Gabby asks.

"Immeasurably."

She suddenly moves towards me, not stopping until there are barely inches between us.

"Still hungry?" she whispers as I feel my belt being unbuckled.

"No," I whimper.

Our eyes remain locked as she skilfully removes my belt and undoes the single button holding my trousers in place. As her eyes narrow a fraction, I feel a hand unzip my fly while the other slips beyond the waistband of my underpants.

I almost pass out when that same hand grasps my phallus and tugs it free.

"Jeeesssus Chriiiist," I groan, temporarily forgetting the fact I don't hold religious beliefs.

I close my eyes for a second or two, and open them to a view of Gabby's head as she ducks down. Despite being fairly sure what is about to happen, I am ill prepared when the actual event occurs.

My first reaction is to make a sound I am unlikely ever to repeat, and it takes every ounce of strength to prevent my knees from buckling. The sensation is exquisite; unlike anything I have ever experienced. And while I have little to judge her technique by, I cannot imagine how it could possibly be improved.

My only concern is the potential brevity.

Fortunately, she stops just before I reach the point of no return. She stands up but keeps one hand tightly gripped around me.

"Three minutes," she says.

"Sorry?"

"I'll give you three minutes to get undressed and shower."

"Then what?"

She nods towards the bed. "Then we'll see if that bed is as comfortable as it looks."

Gabby releases her grip and slowly moves towards the bed, maintaining eye contact.

"Okay," I blurt and make a dash for the bathroom.

I hurriedly strip and hop into the shower cubicle. Twenty frustrating seconds are wasted as I try to work out how to turn the damn thing on. Eventually, a stream of water cascades from the shower head and I lather my body with the hotel shower gel, all the while counting seconds in my head.

It is only when I step from the cubicle I take a moment to consider the situation I find myself in.

Never, as I walked into the hotel foyer a few hours ago, could I have envisaged being in such a situation. This kind of thing simply doesn't happen to men like me. Perhaps that in itself should be a cause for concern. Is this simply good fortune or could there be some ramifications I haven't considered?

I run through the possible consequences as I towel myself dry.

Neither of us are married and we are both consenting adults. We are not doing anything even remotely scandalous, let alone illegal. What possible harm could come of any liaison?

"How are you getting on in there?" Gabby calls from the bedroom.

"Nearly there," I reply, my voice an octave higher than I anticipated.

I hang the towel up and draw a conclusion. I may never have this chance again and it would be foolish not to take it. And besides, who is to say this is a one-off event. Perhaps this might be the start of something — is that so impossible to believe?

For once in your life, William, follow your heart.

It is not my heart that leads me from the bathroom, to find Gabby lying naked on the bed.

"Come. Lie down," she orders.

I am more than happy to take her lead, and do as instructed.

Before I have time to consider any moves, Gabby takes the initiative and pushes me onto my back. In the same fluid movement, she straddles my thighs and grabs my phallus. That indescribable noise escapes the back of my throat once more.

Before the first shock wave ebbs away, she shuffles forward and lowers herself onto me, inducing a second, more intense reaction.

She stares down at me and begins to slowly grind her hips back and forth. The sensation, coupled with the view of her perfect body, is almost too much. My senses overload and I'm forced to close my eyes.

The grinding continues, although I'm relieved the intensity doesn't. With every thrust, Gabby emits a slight noise; somewhere between a mew and a groan. Assuming she isn't in pain, I would hope it suggests she's enjoying the ride, and that only serves to heighten my own excitement.

Time passes, although I have no idea how long. I do know it could never be long enough, though. And then without warning, she stops and dismounts. I open my eyes.

Gabby is on her knees next to me. She grabs my wrists, pulls me upright, and whispers in my ear. "Take me from behind."

Before I can question her on the mechanics, she turns, and assumes a position on all fours; her peach-like backside raised in readiness.

She might be ready. I might be willing. Being able is the issue that now concerns me.

I have only ever had sexual congress with two women. The first was in my final month of university and was as brief as it was unrewarding. A drunken fumble in the dark followed by seconds of penetrative sex. It was a performance so woeful, I never got the opportunity to try again with the same girl.

The second occasion, I'm ashamed to say, was nine years ago. I had a brief relationship with Melanie Dawson; a quiet, unassuming girl who worked in Marshburton library. We dated for six months and practised sexual congress on seven occasions. Despite having the opportunity to improve my skills, I was never convinced Melanie's heart was in it, and the missionary position was as far as we advanced.

After Melanie, I came to the conclusion that perhaps I was just naturally inept at sex. I took solace in the fact some people are hopeless when it comes to learning to drive, failing test after test after test. In some way, I have the same issue with the multi-tasking required for love making — too many things to simultaneously poke, lick, grasp, and flick. I am, alas, a sexual car crash waiting to happen.

But now it seems I have little choice but to learn on the job, so to speak.

Getting to my knees, I shuffle towards Gabby's raised posterior. I understand the theory behind this position, and the canine-inspired name if memory serves, but I'm less well versed in the practical.

I position myself between her legs and grasp her hips. My phallus doesn't appear to be at the correct level for entry, although I'm not entirely sure where that entry point is. Not wishing to keep the lady waiting, I throw caution to the wind and guide my phallus towards what I hope is the point of entry. My first attempt is a clear miss but the boat finds the harbour on the second attempt.

I tentatively move my hips back and forth. trying to keep the movements minimal for fear I might reverse too far and have to begin the docking procedure again. Slowly but surely I find some rhythm and increase the frequency of the thrusts. I assume Gabby finds my technique agreeable as she becomes more vocal, occasionally murmuring a profanity.

However, my confidence is put to the test when Gabby begins barking instructions.

"Harder!"

I comply and add a little more gusto to each inbound thrust.

"Oh, yeah. That's good," she groans.

I am only too pleased to have obliged.

"Slap my arse," comes the next command.

"I beg your pardon."

"Slap my arse. Now!"

"But…"

"Do it!"

Beyond the fact I have never struck a lady before, I'm unsure how much force to apply. She does seem very insistent though so I comply, but my effort is more of a pat than a slap.

"Harder!"

Is this what people do these days? Is this even normal? I try again with a little more force.

"Keep doing it," she screams back.

I administer a series of slaps until her left buttock glows pink.

"Now, fuck me hard."

Relieved the slapping is over, I return to my thrusting duties.

"Shout my name," comes the next instruction. "It turns me on."

Good grief.

"Gabby," I timidly venture.

"Louder."

"Gabby," I repeat with a little more volume. I feel ridiculous although Gabby appears to appreciate my efforts.

I press on, but despite the humiliating sideshow, I know the finale is fast approaching. Equally, Gabby is making some fairly encouraging noises so perhaps I might be able to coincide our arrival time.

Clearly she's partial to a more vigorous thrust so I up my intensity. She responds with loud groans. As the pinnacle of our love making approaches, I suddenly feel a sense of complete abandon. I enter the spirit of the moment and slap her backside while simultaneously shouting her name.

"More! More!" she shrieks in response.

The louder she shrieks and groans and squeals, the more intoxicated I become, and the less I feel like William Huxley. I am another man, about to enter some sexual Nirvana. I've never indulged, but I'd imagine this must be what a drugs high feels like, and I can now see the appeal.

I slap her backside hard, and her response is enough to tip me over the edge. I explode, and bellow a primordial noise which is part word, part throaty gurgle, or possibly Welsh.

As the final traces of my climax ebb away, Gabby wiggles her backside from my grasp, leaving behind a pool of bodily fluids on the bed sheet. I experience an overwhelming urge to hold her but she edges away, leaving me kneeling in the centre of the bed.

"Drink?" she asks, a little dispassionately, as she moves across the room.

I nod, and position myself so I'm leant against the headboard. I watch on as Gabby kneels down and pulls more bottles from the mini-bar. A wave of contentment crashes over me and I close my eyes; happy to bask in a cosy glow.

"William."

I open my eyes and Gabby is stood next to the bed, holding out a glass. I take it and thank her.

"That was fun," she adds. "Let's drink to the next time."

The fact she suggested there will be a second instalment causes my heart to flutter. I smile and raise my glass.

"To the next time."

Gabby, clearly thirsty, necks her drink in a second. I take a sip and follow her example, gulping down the cold liquid.

She takes my empty glass. "I'm just going to freshen up. Make yourself comfortable."

I watch her as she returns the glasses to the dresser. She then picks up the leather holdall and heads into the bathroom. A tiredness, unlike any I have ever experienced, descends upon me and I close my eyes again.

Before I have time to consciously fight it, I pass out.

8.

A shard of light bursts beyond the edge of the window frame — morning has arrived, apparently.

I open my eyes, squint, and immediately close them again. It is sufficient time to establish I am in unfamiliar surroundings — the only reason I'm able to confirm last night wasn't a dream. The conclusion is bolstered as my fuddled mind confirms I am naked, and my head is throbbing.

Did I really drink that much?

I roll over so I can safely open my eyes. A quick check of my watch and I'm relieved to see it's not quite seven yet.

Gingerly, I sit up and assess my surroundings. The room is silent, the bed empty.

"Gabby?" I call out, my voice scratchy, throat dry.

No response.

I swing my legs off the bed and tentatively get to my feet. It brings nausea and a coughing fit. The wall provides support as I take a few deep breaths.

Water. So thirsty.

Keeping one hand against the wall, I edge my way along the side of the bed and around the corner towards the bathroom. The door is open and I thump the light switch, keeping my head low to avoid the bright spotlights in the ceiling. Besides my clothes in a crumpled pile on the floor, there are no other signs of recent occupancy.

I stagger over to the sink and fill a plastic cup from the cold tap, trying to avoid my naked reflection in the mirror behind. I gulp it down and repeat.

Thirst sated, I splash my face with water before retrieving my clothes from the floor. I get dressed and return to the bedroom, stopping when I pass the wardrobe. I open the door to find my jacket on a hanger, but nothing else. After checking my keys, wallet, and mobile phone are still present, I slip the jacket on and close the door.

The rest of the room offers no further clues to Gabby's whereabouts. The leather holdall is gone, as is everything else of hers for that matter. I take a seat on the edge of the bed and process the possible reasons for her absence.

The last thing I recall, post coitus, was having a drink and Gabby heading to the bathroom. She seemed perfectly happy, and if memory serves, even implied there might be a repeat of our liaison. Did I offend her by falling asleep? Or did she have second thoughts in the night and creep out under the cover of darkness, just to avoid any awkwardness?

Questions I can't answer.

The only thing I know with absolute certainty is that she's gone, and there is no point me sitting here speculating on the reason.

I locate a notepad and pen on the dresser and scribble a note with my phone number, asking Gabby to call me. I suspect she'll never see it but I might as well cover that base while I'm here.

After a final glance around the room, I leave.

By the time the lift reaches the foyer, my curiosity has become a niggling itch. I cross the polished floor towards the reception desk where a young woman with prominent cheekbones is stationed.

"Good morning. I stayed in room 904 last night with a…friend, but she seems to have checked out. Can you confirm if she has, please?"

The young woman smiles and taps away at a keyboard.

"She has, sir. Yes."

"Right. Can I ask when?"

Her eyes drop to the screen. "Last night."

"Last night?"

"Yes, sir. Late last night."

I toy with the idea of asking the receptionist if she'll let me have Gabby's phone number or email address but I know she'll decline. Hotels are the last bastions of discretion and privacy.

"Thank you."

As I make my way out of the foyer and onto The Strand, I consider the legitimate reasons Gabby may have had for leaving the hotel so late. Perhaps she had a family emergency and didn't want to wake me. That seems perfectly plausible but why didn't she leave a note?

My frustration is stoked by the fact I never had the foresight to ask for her contact details; possibly because events proceeded at such a pace. Foolishly, I didn't even establish her surname, despite it being emblazoned across a badge around her neck as we sat in the hotel auditorium.

It then strikes me — I could contact the event organisers. They would obviously have a list of attendees and Gabby is a fairly uncommon name. However, I need to get back home and sort myself out before any further investigations can begin.

With my flat in Blackfriars only a mile away, I decide a brisk walk will do me some good.

Fifteen minutes later I turn into Temple Avenue and approach the imposing Edwardian building in which my flat is situated. I unlock the main door and enter the communal hallway. The lift is on the fifth floor so I press the call button and wait.

Like Hansworth Hall, the flat on Temple Avenue once belonged to my father and bequeathed to me in his will. He purchased it back in the eighties and I have fond memories of spending occasional weekends here as a child. Me, my mother, and my father — one happy family enjoying our glorious capital. Every visit was an adventure as we explored all the famous sights.

Now it is my home for four or five days a week, and I'm extremely fortunate to call it such. Being ideally situated for Westminster, the City, and the West End, there is no way I could afford such a property on my parliamentary salary. I can only imagine the value must now be well into the millions, not that I anticipate ever selling it. Like Hansworth Hall, it is one of the few connections I have to the family I once had. And perhaps optimistically, I still haven't given up hope of one day having children myself, and both properties will be theirs when my time is over.

For one brief moment last night, I thought I might have taken the first tentative step to realising my dream. Now I'm not so sure.

The lift arrives and transports me up to the top floor.

Although the flat itself is impressive, the furnishings and decor are less so. I have no interest in such things so the interior of the flat is best described as functional. The guest bedroom, dining room, and balcony are all devoid of furniture because I have no real use for them.

I head into the bathroom and take a long shower.

The simple act of showering and donning fresh clothes aids my wellbeing. I allocate six minutes for a breakfast of tea and toast before heading out the door.

I'm tempted to walk to work but I'm already ten minutes behind schedule so I follow the crowds into Blackfriars tube station and endure the six minute journey to Westminster. By the time I step into the office, Rosa is already at her desk.

"Morning, William."

"Morning," I mumble back.

"Tea?"

"Please."

I sit down at my desk and boot up the computer. It's still going through the motions by the time Rosa returns with a cup of tea.

"Are you ready to go through the diary and today's correspondence?" she asks.

I confirm, more reluctantly than usual, I am, and Rosa takes a seat in front of my desk.

"Are you okay, William?" she asks while sorting through the folders on her lap. "You look a little tired, if you don't mind me saying."

"Observant as always, Rosa. Yesterday was a long day."

"Of course, you had that event in the evening. How did it go?"

"Don't ask, but while we're on the subject, could you email the organisers and ask them for a list of the delegates. Tell them it's urgent, please."

She scribbles on her notepad before confirming I'm ready to get the day organised. Thankfully, my diary is looking lean today, and there isn't the same backlog of correspondence we have to wade through on a Monday morning. It takes ten minutes to cover everything before Rosa returns to her desk.

Before I do anything, I finish my tea and ponder the next move once I've established Gabby's full name. Assuming her profession will have created some footprint online, it shouldn't be too difficult to track her down. I can only hope her surname isn't something common like Smith or Brown.

But finding her is not really my primary concern — it's whether she even wants to be found. I have no wish to act like some lovesick teenager and stalk the poor woman, but I would like to establish why she bailed on me. It's a well-worn term, but I suppose I'd like some form of closure.

For now though, I have other matters to attend to, not least my never ending list of people to call.

I pick up the phone and call the first name on the list.

My initial impetus is exhausted by the fifth call, and a pounding headache is doing nothing to aid motivation. At ten thirty, my need for tea, aspirin, and a little peace, is overwhelming. I clamber from behind my desk and ask Rosa if she'd like tea. Just as she confirms she doesn't, and poses a question on a non-related matter, her phone rings. I wave a hand to suggest she should answer it and turn away. I cover eight feet of carpet before Rosa calls my name.

"Yes?"

Rosa has the receiver to her ear but her hand is covering the mouthpiece. The look on her face suggests my morning is about to be ruined.

"Apparently there are two police officers in the lobby, and they want to talk to you."

"What about?"

"They wouldn't say. Shall I ask Debbie to send them up?"

I scour my mind in search of any good reason why two members of the Metropolitan Police would want to talk to me. Nothing comes to mind.

"No. Tell her I'm on my way down."

It seems I'll have to wait a little longer for tea and aspirin.

I make my way down to the central lobby reception. On arrival, Debbie doesn't introduce me to two uniformed police officers but two serious looking detectives.

"William, these gents are from Charing Cross Police Station."

I nod at the two detectives. One is fairly young, and tall, with a mop of sandy hair. The second is a much older man, balding, with a ruddy complexion and bloodshot eyes.

They flash their identification.

"I'm Detective Sergeant Barker," the older man grunts; a slight Mancunian lilt to his accent.

"Detective Constable Perry," the younger detective adds; his accent of the nondescript, home counties variety.

"What can I do for you, gentlemen?"

"We were hoping you'd accompany us back to the station so we can have a chat," Sergeant Barker replies.

"A chat? About what?"

The two men glance around the lobby and Sergeant Barker shuffles towards me. "For the sake of discretion, I think it would be better if we discussed that at the station."

"You're not going to tell me?"

"No, Sir. That's not what I'm saying. I'm trying to be discreet so you're not tabloid news tomorrow."

I'm torn between standing my ground and protecting my reputation. Quite what I'm supposed to have done that would warrant press interest is beyond me but even a totally innocent visit from the police can set the parliamentary rumour machine into overdrive. Perhaps the detective is doing me a favour by not making a scene.

"Fine," I sigh. "As long as it doesn't take too long. I've got a meeting at one."

"Thank you, Sir. Follow us."

I ask Debbie to inform Rosa I'll be out for a while and follow the detectives down to the visitor's car park where I'm offered a seat in the back of a blue saloon car.

The journey to Charing Cross Police Station is only a couple of miles but in the London traffic, it takes twenty minutes. After my initial questions were rebutted, neither detective uttered another word so I spent my time trying to think of any indiscretions I may have inadvertently committed.

I'm none the wiser by the time we pass through a barrier and enter the station car park.

The two detectives then lead me through a series of security doors and once we're in the inner sanctum of the station, I'm offered a seat in an interview room. Constable Perry asks if I'd like a cup of tea while his older colleague heads off elsewhere. Seeing as I was pulled away before I had the chance to make one myself, I accept the offer of tea and the young detective also disappears. Five minutes later, the two men convene in the interview room, taking their seats opposite me.

"Right," begins Sergeant Barker. "This is just an informal chat and you're not under arrest."

"Do I need a lawyer?"

"Not for me to say, Sir. It's your right."

"Well, perhaps if you told me why I'm here, I could make that call."

He nods to his younger colleague who opens a folder on the desk and scans something inside. I take the opportunity for a sip of tea. Unsurprisingly, it's from a machine, and awful.

"Okay. Can you confirm your whereabouts yesterday evening?"

"I went to an event at the Montgomery Hotel."

"And how long were you there for?"

"Initially about an hour or so."

"And then?"

I start to feel a little uncomfortable with the direction of travel.

"I went for a drink with one of the delegates."

There's a brief pause before the next question is fired at me.

"And did you then return to the hotel with that delegate?"

"Yes. She invited me to her room for supper."

"You accepted that invitation?"

"I did."

"So you admit you went back to a room at the Montgomery Hotel?"

I can feel frustration bubbling away already. "That's what I said," I snap. "Look, what's going on here?"

"An allegation has been made against you," the sergeant intervenes.

"An allegation of what? And by who?"

"Theft," Perry replies.

"Theft?"

"It has been alleged that a sum of money was stolen from a handbag in room 904."

"What?" I scoff. "By Gabby? I don't believe it."

Sergeant Barker puffs his cheeks and sits back in his chair. "Look, Mr Huxley, an allegation has been made and we're duty-bound to investigate. All I need to know is if you took the money."

"Of course I didn't," I bark at the detective. "Why would I?"

The two detectives swap glances and Perry closes the folder. "Okay. That's it then," he says matter-of-factly. "Thank you for your assistance."

"What do you mean, that's it? You drag me down here, accuse me of theft, and that's it?"

"Nobody accused you of anything," Barker replies. "We received an allegation and you denied it. It's your word against hers, and with no evidence, there is nothing more we can do."

"Sorry. I don't understand. Why would she even make that allegation?"

"Who knows. Maybe she just lost the money and assumed you took it. In any event, there's no actual evidence of a crime having been committed, which is why we never arrested you. You do understand we have to follow-up on allegations, no matter how spurious."

I realise my frustration is being targeted in the wrong place.

"Fair enough. Could you tell me her name though; the woman who made the allegation?"

"I'm sure you know we can't do that."

I do know, but I'm struggling to think straight, such is my annoyance.

"Would you like a lift back?" Perry asks.

"No, thank you. I could do with a walk to clear my head."

I'm offered a half-hearted apology and led from the interview room by the young detective.

"Am I likely to hear anything further?" I ask as we walk back through the corridors.

"Very unlikely, unless of course you are guilty and some actual evidence comes to light."

"Well, I'm not, so I'll assume this is the end of it."

We reach the main entrance and he shakes my hand.

I leave Charing Cross Police Station, with more unanswered questions than when I arrived.

9.

I cross The Strand and cut through a series of back roads until I reach the north bank of the Thames. I stop for a moment to survey the London skyline and gather my thoughts, most of which are spiked with irritation and disappointment.

Simmering at the surface is Gabby's attempt to sully my good name. How dare she cast such aspersions when it was her who skulked away in the night.

But then, the disappointment. I have never understood how some people can engage in an act so intimate yet treat it with such wanton detachment, as if meaningless. Then again, I engaged in that act with somebody I barely knew and gave scant thought to the consequences. A victim of my own lustful hubris.

I have to accept disappointment in myself as much as Gabby. The difference is that she is gone and I have to live with myself. I should really try and put this tawdry affair behind me and move on — sometimes it's better to have unanswered questions than unpalatable answers. I text Rosa to say I'm on my way back, and with a bracing autumnal wind behind me, I set off under the Golden Jubilee Bridge towards Westminster.

By the time I arrive back at the office, it's lunchtime and Rosa isn't at her desk. I have little appetite so settle for a cup of tea and two long-overdue aspirin. I check my emails and reply to half a dozen before Rosa returns.

She hurries over to my desk, still decked in her grey tailored overcoat.

"Is everything okay, William?" she asks, clearly concerned. "Debbie said you went to Charing Cross Police Station."

"Just a misunderstanding. It's dealt with now."

"Right. Have you eaten?"

"No."

She undoes the clasp on her handbag and withdraws a paper bag. "Chicken salad with Dijon mustard," she says, handing it to me.

In one second, all my pent up irritation dissipates.

"How did you know?"

"Jake in the sandwich shop. He said you always order the same thing."

"Of course," I chuckle. "Thank you, Rosa."

"It's no trouble," she replies coyly. "I better get on."

She hangs up her coat and returns to her desk.

Despite my lack of appetite, I don't want to appear ungrateful so I eat the sandwich at my desk. Every mouthful tastes bitter; tainted with guilt. Would Rosa have been so kind, so considerate, if she knew of my shameful behaviour last night? A ridiculous notion but it almost feels like I cheated on her in some way.

What was I thinking?

I conclude I'd rather live with the unrealistic dream that is Rosa rather than the nightmare which was Gabby.

I call across the office. "Have you heard anything from the event organisers about that list of delegates?"

"Not yet. Do you want me to chase them up?"

"No. Email them again and say we no longer need it."

That, as far as I am concerned, is that. Back to reality. Back to my blissfully mundane life.

Two lengthy meetings fill my afternoon, followed by a concerted effort to clear the telephone list. By the time Rosa leaves I've dealt with all but one caller.

I shut my computer down and check tomorrow's diary; more meetings and a debate on immigration which is bound to attract a full house considering the current Brexit sensitivities. My party opened Pandora's Box with the decision to hold a referendum and I know many of my colleagues now wish we could slam the lid shut and hide it in the back of a cupboard. The United Kingdom is now anything but united.

I switch the lights off and leave the office.

More often than not, I prefer to walk back to Blackfriars at the end of the working day. A brisk walk under dusky skies is not only good exercise, but offers a rare chance to think. There is much to think about this evening; mostly an introspection of my life.

If I've learnt anything from last night, it's that I long for companionship more than I realised. It is the only explanation why I acted so out of character. I believe it was John Donne who said no man is an island, and like many quotes, there has to be some truth in it. What I can do about my isolation is another matter.

A colleague once suggested I should try online dating, and I did briefly consider it. However, I have always held the view that fate will intervene, and one day I will meet my soul mate. There is little appeal in allowing a computer algorithm to usurp fate and I've always been content to carry that belief. Last night's events have brought home just how long I've been waiting and my belief has been somewhat undermined.

As I turn from the bustle of Holborn into the quieter backwaters of Furnival Street, I consider whether it's maybe time to be proactive. For this evening at least though, I will continue my single life in the sanctuary of Fitzgerald's bar.

I push open the door and pause for a moment to sniff the air. The scent of home cooked food and ale greets me. Fitzgerald's first opened just over a century ago and has probably provided a place of refuge for thousands of men like me over the decades. Without question, its heyday was during the sixties and seventies when it was a fashionable members club. Nowadays, the backstreet location dictates a more flexible policy on who they allow in. Thankfully, that same location also ensures tourists, city types, and most of my colleagues aren't aware Fitzgerald's even exists.

I approach the bar and perch on a stool while I wait to be served. At the far end sits Stephen; an actor who, to the best of my knowledge, hasn't worked since the nineties. He always takes great pride in his appearance although he seems hell bent on destroying his once handsome features with excessive alcohol consumption. I don't know how he earns a living as he seems to spend every waking hour in Fitzgerald's — always the first in at opening time and the last to be ushered out before the doors close at night.

"Evening, William" he slurs, waving an errant hand in my direction.

He's already quite intoxicated it seems, and I'd rather avoid a conversation. I reply with a nod and then cast my gaze across the room as if I'm looking for someone.

It's a quiet night and only five of the two dozen tables are occupied. Beyond the hushed chatter from the tables, Elton John's *Rocket Man* is playing on the juke box in the corner. The juke box, an old Rock-Ola model, is full of vinyl from the seventies and embodies the spirit of Fitzgerald's to a tee — stuck in the past. The landlord for the last twelve years, Frank, has something of an obsession with the bar's glorious past, although his thirst to protect that heritage borders on neglect.

"Alright, William. Usual?"

I turn back to the bar where Frank is already pulling a pint of Old Speckled Hen.

"Evening, Frank. What's the special tonight?"

"Braised beef casserole. Bloody lovely it is," he replies, his jowly chops wobbling as he speaks. I suspect Frank's face has always looked older than his years — it's grizzly and furrowed, and not improved by his lack of hair. Yet despite the looks of a bulldog, Frank possesses the friendly nature of a Golden Retriever, albeit a bald, overweight Golden Retriever.

"Splendid. I'll take one of those too."

One of the main attractions of Fitzgerald's is the food. The menu consists almost entirely of British classics, lovingly cooked from scratch by Frank's wife, Jeanie. Unlike most of London's eateries, they don't call gravy, jus, and chips are served in a bowl rather than arranged in some Jenga-like formation. Some might call it old fashioned but I prefer authentic, unpretentious.

I hand Frank a twenty pound note and as he jabs away at the till, the door to the kitchen swings open behind him. I would have expected to see Jeanie emerge, carrying plates laden with food. However, the man stood in the doorway could not be more different from the landlord's diminutive wife.

"Oi, Frank," the man grunts. "Where's the bleedin' key for the cellar?"

Frank slaps my change on the bar and waddles over to the man. I think it would be fair to say Frank is of average height yet he's at least six inches shorter than the hulking brute by the doorway. The two men converse for a second before the big man disappears back through the door.

Frank returns to the bar and offers an apologetic smile. "Sorry about that, William. We're still working on his front of house skills."

"Clearly. I hope he's not your new chef."

"No, Jeanie is still in charge of the kitchen," he chuckles. "He's just helping us out, doing a few odd jobs and the like. Apparently he used to work here before, as security."

"Really? I don't recall ever seeing him, and he's not the sort of chap you'd forget in a hurry."

"You wouldn't have. It was before my time, so a good few years back. Interesting bloke though; he knows more about the history of this place than anyone I've ever met. And don't go telling anyone, but he's happy to work for a decent meal, free beer, and a few quid here and there."

"Rest assured, Frank, I won't be reporting him to the Work & Pensions Minister. I quite like the way my facial features are currently arranged."

"Probably wise," he replies before he waddles back down the bar to serve Stephen his umpteenth drink of the day.

I grab my pint and wander over to my usual table in the corner, opposite the juke box. I like to eat my meal alone and then I usually return to the bar and chat with Frank and a few of the regulars for an hour or so. It's not much of a social life but it does help to keep loneliness at bay during the long evenings.

I take a seat, facing across the room, and pluck an abandoned copy of *The Times* from the adjacent table. I scan the main headline with little interest and flick through to the inner pages. Unsurprisingly, the news is almost exclusively negative. Not what I need this evening.

I drop the paper on the table and sip my pint as the juke box emits a series of clunks and whirs. Seconds pass and the gentle crackle of a needle on vinyl leaks from the speaker. I am by no means an expert on seventies popular music, but I instantly recognise the record, *Baker Street*, for one simple reason — my mother played it a lot when I was a child. In fact, the juke box is stocked with dozens of records I recall from my childhood, before I started school. I wasn't consciously aware of what I was listening to at the time but the voices and the rhythms became indelibly ingrained in my young mind. Perhaps the home cooked food and music from my childhood is why I feel so at ease here. There is comfort in familiarity.

Time passes and I'm quite happy just to sit back, sip my ale, and listen to the eclectic sounds of Rod Stewart, Suzi Quatro, and Wings.

I'm just about to fetch another pint when Frank appears with a tray containing an oversized bowl.

"Enjoy," he says, placing the bowl in front of me. It smells divine and only then do I realise just how hungry I am.

"Thank you, Frank. Looks delicious, as always."

"Tell Jeanie when you've finished, unless you don't enjoy it, in which case I'd keep quiet."

"Noted."

Frank leaves me to eat and within the first few mouthfuls, I'm confident I'll have no cause for complaint; not that I ever have.

I read the sports pages of *The Times* as I eat. Typically the news is less depressing, assuming England haven't played rugby, cricket, or football in the proceeding twenty four hours.

The juke box continues to play suitable background music and I enter a semi-conscious state as I read the paper and savour Jeanie's home-cooked fayre. I'm halfway through reading an interesting article on grass roots football when I catch a flicker of movement from the corner of my eye. I drop the paper and almost choke on a mouthful of braised beef. It seems I have an uninvited dinner guest.

"Good evening, William."

I swallow hard and try to regain my composure.

"What are you doing here, Gabby?"

10.

There is no immediate answer to my question as she sips from a glass of white wine. Her navy business suit has been replaced with jeans and a brown leather jacket, and her dark hair styled differently. It irritates me to admit it, but the more casual look only enhances her physical appeal.

She puts her glass down and unzips her jacket to reveal a low-cut blouse.

"How are you?" she asks.

"How am I? How do you think I am?"

"I don't know. That's why I asked."

I realise my fork is still in my hand. I toss it into the bowl and wipe my mouth with a napkin.

"Let me see," I eventually reply, my voice dripping with indignation. "I was abandoned in a hotel room last night, and this morning I was escorted to Charing Cross Police Station where I was accused of theft. So please, take a guess how I am."

"Oh, yes, that," she replies in a dismissive tone. "Still, I knew they wouldn't press charges so no real harm, eh?"

Her casual manner is unsettling but I want answers.

"If you knew they wouldn't press charges, why bother? Did you even lose any money?"

"Actually, no, I didn't, but on an unrelated matter, did you sleep well?"

"What?"

"Last night. You were out like a light when I left — snoring away in the altogether."

I feel my cheeks redden. "Why did you leave like that?" I snap back.

"Well, you were dead to the world so I didn't see much point in hanging around."

I reach for my pint and swallow the last mouthful.

"Same again?" she asks.

I throw her a look which I hope makes my position clear. Whatever her game, I have no interest in playing it.

"Don't be like that, William. Let me get you a drink — I suspect you're going to need it."

Before I can respond she gets up and saunters over to the bar. I consider leaving but my pride won't tolerate being chased away.

Gabby returns and places a full pint in front of me. She sits down and takes a quick sip of wine.

"So, William. Shall we get down to business."

"Business? What business?"

"Hansworth Hall. I'd like to buy it."

I stare at her, open mouthed. Of all the things I might have expected her to say, an offer to buy my family home would not have figured highly.

"What? It's not for sale, and even if it were, I doubt very much you could afford it."

A thin smile crosses her lips as she dips a hand in her jacket pocket. A pound coin is extracted and placed on the table in front of me.

"See. I can afford it. You're going to sell Hansworth Hall to me…for a pound."

Despite the thin smile, there is enough conviction in her voice to suggest she isn't joking. I can only therefore conclude she's mentally unhinged.

I fight to keep my voice level. "You're insane, woman. I'd like you to leave now, please."

Her face twists into a picture of mock indignation. "But what about our deal?"

"I'm not going to justify that with an answer. Leave. Please."

Much to my surprise, she plucks the pound from the table and gets up. Just when I think she's about to turn and walk away, she leans over the table.

"Here's the situation, William," she spits. "You are going to sell Hansworth Hall to me, and I am going to pay a pound for it. Today's events were simply an aperitif to whet your appetite. I guarantee you'll be begging me to buy that house once the main course arrives."

I don't appreciate either her trite analogy or threats. Something inside my head snaps and before I can stop myself, my hand is gripping her wrist.

"Listen to me you stupid woman. I don't know who you are or what's going on in your head, but if I hear from you again, you'll regret it. Clear?"

"I'd let go if I were you," she replies, her voice level, measured.

I stare up at her, seething, my hand locked around her wrist, grip tightening. She remains calm and glances towards the bar. "See that big guy over there," she says, nodding towards Frank's odd job man, leant up against the bar. "When I bought your drink, I told him we were splitting up because you're prone to violent outbursts. If I were to scream now, he'd be over here in a shot, and I don't think that would end well for you."

I release my grip. "Go. Now," I growl through gritted teeth.

She winks at me. "I'll be in touch, real soon."

With a flick of her hair, she walks away. The odd job man at the bar watches her leave before returning his attention to his half empty glass.

I take a second to calm myself and reach for my own glass. It's only then I realise my hand is shaking, such is my anger. A deep breath helps to alleviate the excess adrenaline and I gulp down half the content of my glass. The ale lacks sufficient alcohol to really take the edge of my agitation — I need something stronger. I neck the rest of the pint and head to the bar.

I get within ten feet when the odd job man suddenly turns around and stares at me. I catch his eye for a split second and drop my head.

By the time I reach the bar I'm feeling decidedly uncomfortable. It seems this already awful day still has the potential to deteriorate further if the odd job man chooses to fight Gabby's fallacious cause. I keep my attention locked on the wall behind the bar while I nervously wait for Frank to appear. Seconds pass and I can almost feel the man's stare. Perhaps I'm being paranoid but it might be a good idea to leave now.

Before I can make that decision, the odd job man wanders behind the bar and stands directly in front of me.

"I reckon Frank is busy. What can I get you?"

I look up at him. His meaty arms are folded across his chest, his expression unreadable.

"Large brandy, please."

He grabs a tumbler and holds it under an optic for a few seconds before placing it on the bar in front of me.

"On me," he says, returning his arms to a folded position.

I look up at him again, daring to hold my gaze for more than a second. "Thank you."

His cold blue eyes stare back at me, and continue to do so as I take a gulp of brandy. The dark brown liquid brings a welcome burn, although not as intense as the burn of the big man's gaze. I place the tumbler back on the bar and chance another look. Still, he continues to stare down at me. The silence is intolerable and I can't bear it any longer.

"Whatever she told you, it was a lie."

"Who?"

"The woman who just left. She said she told you something about me."

"She didn't say anything to me, mate."

I shake my head. *Gullible fool*.

"I'll tell you something for nothing, though," he adds. "She's a wrong'un."

As I look up, he's stroking his moustache; some sort of retro affair framing his mouth like a horseshoe, and sandwiched between expansive sideburns. Coupled with his denim waistcoat, his general appearance seems to fit perfectly with the dated decor in Fitzgerald's.

"What makes you say that?" I hesitantly ask.

"Just a little voice in my head," he replies, absolutely dead pan.

I don't know whether he's being serious or pulling my leg so I decide not to react and take another gulp of brandy, emptying the tumbler.

"Same again," he asks.

As tempting as it is, something about the man makes me feel uneasy, and besides, I just want to go home, climb into bed, and try to forget about the last twenty-four hours.

"No, thank you, but please, let me buy you one."

His lips curl into a slight smile. "Nah, you're alright mate. Cheers for offering though."

I nod, and as I turn to leave, he holds out a pan-like hand.

"Clement."

I shake his hand and for the first time, realise what it must feel like for a child to shake an adult's hand.

"William. William Huxley."

He releases my hand from his grip and fixes his blue eyes on me again. "I'll see you around, Bill."

If anyone else had called me Bill, I'd have immediately corrected them. In this case, I think it would be wise to let it pass.

"Goodnight…Clement."

He never clarified if Clement was his first or last name. I'm relieved when he nods at my assumption.

I can feel his stare all the way to the door.

The two-minute walk back to the flat provides a woefully inadequate window to assess the evening's events. My mind is still ablaze with questions by the time I step through the front door. As tired as I am, sleep seems unlikely so I pour myself a brandy and slump down on the sofa.

The room is as silent as any city dwelling is ever likely to be. The triple glazed windows do a decent job of keeping the worst of London at bay but there is always a faint background hum, occasionally pierced by the sirens of emergency vehicles.

I sip at the brandy and try to untangle the nest of questions, searching for a loose end to grasp. Two questions eventually present themselves: who is Gabby and how did she know about Hansworth Hall?

The first question is the same question I had this morning, and I might now have an answer if I hadn't told Rosa not to bother with that delegates list. With little else to go on, I'll have to ask her to go back to the event organisers tomorrow. As for her knowledge of Hansworth Hall, that's an easier question to answer as I have a fairly visible profile online and there are several Wikipedia pages with information about the house and my family. It wouldn't take Sherlock Holmes to establish my ownership of the house, or indeed the value.

I take another sip of brandy and let my thoughts continue on their path.

Although I might have partially answered the two most pertinent questions, they both lead to another: why is Gabby so certain I'd entertain such a ridiculous proposition as selling my family home for a pound?

I can only assume today's allegations to the police were meant to unsettle me, and a more serious allegation will soon be lodged, but what? There are no skeletons in my closet and I've always been extremely careful to avoid potentially compromising situations. As tawdry as it may have been, the fact we had sex in a hotel room is hardly tabloid gold — I doubt anyone could care less that an insignificant backbench politician had a one-night stand.

As I let that fact settle, I feel slightly more confident Gabby's gun has no bullets. In fact, there is something vaguely familiar about this whole set up.

I seem to recall, some years ago, one of my colleagues becoming embroiled in a rather sordid affair after he slept with a woman at a conference. Unfortunately for him, he was married and therefore his blackmailer had leverage. I think his indiscretion only came to light after he tried to remortgage the marital home and his wife found out. I believe the term the newspapers used was *honey trap*.

It now seems I am the intended victim of a similar plot. As distasteful as it might be, I suspect Gabby only slept with me in order to create leverage, in the hope I'd be stupid enough to sell a multi-million-pound property for a pound. If I don't play ball, which clearly I won't, I'm guessing her next move will be a threat to sell her story to the newspapers. I'll give her some credit in that she probably thinks this is a win-win situation. Either I concede to her blackmail, or she sells her story to the newspapers in return for a sizeable cheque. What she has failed to realise is that no newspaper would pay anything for her non-story.

I think it's safe to say Gabby has overplayed her hand on this occasion. I'm no gambler, but even I know bluffing will only take you so far.

Satisfied I've thwarted Gabby's plan before it's even been properly deployed, I down the remaining brandy in my glass and head to the bedroom. Tomorrow will be the last day I ever have to consider that damn woman.

11.

There is no place of greater sanctuary than one's own bed, and I awake feeling significantly better than when I awoke yesterday.

My morning ablutions are promptly completed and I take thirty minutes to prepare and consume a hearty breakfast of scrambled eggs on toast with button mushrooms and grilled tomatoes. By the time I leave the flat, I feel positively chipper.

Today will be the day I put that heinous woman in her place, and perhaps give fate a nudge to ensure I don't find myself in a similar situation again.

A threat to my buoyant mood arrives as I step out of the lift. My new phone hails the arrival of a text message with a cheerful, and annoyingly loud tone…

Ready to do that deal? Gabby x

I allow myself a wry smile. She has no idea I'm one step ahead of her. I intend to establish her surname with that delegate list, and then I will be the one making allegations to the police. I'll let her sweat for now, though. I tuck my phone back in my pocket, her text unanswered.

I arrive at the office before Rosa and in lieu of her kindness yesterday lunchtime, I make us both a cup of tea. She arrives just as I'm placing the cup on her desk.

"Morning, Rosa."

She stares at the cup and then at me. "I hope that isn't a sweetener, William. The first thing people do when there's bad news is make tea."

"There's no bad news this morning. Well, apart from the fact I need you to email those event organisers again."

"Again?"

"I need that list of delegates after all. Sorry."

She doesn't complain and dutifully makes a note on her pad. "Leave it with me."

We go through our morning routine and once I have my to-do list, Rosa returns to her desk. I have an hour before my first meeting and one pressing task to perform before I get down to my parliamentary work. I open Gabby's message on my phone and compose a reply…

No deal. And rest assured, your plan is going to backfire. Watch this space…

I send it and sit back in my chair, content I now have the upper hand. My only disappointment is I won't be able to see her face when she receives the text message. I place my phone on the desk, just in case she decides to promptly concede defeat, and get on with the planning for my meeting.

The next hour passes quickly and as ten o'clock approaches, I gather up my files and folders.

"Right. I'm off. I shouldn't be more than an hour or so."

Rosa glances up from her monitor and acknowledges me with a nod; her elegant fingers continuing their dance across the keyboard.

I leave the office and check my phone as I hurry through the corridors. My text to Gabby remains unanswered which I hope is a good thing. I don't think she anticipated resistance and clearly there is no plan-B. I can almost imagine her frantically calling every newspaper editor and receiving short shrift from all of them. It's a thought that amuses me somewhat.

Unfortunately, my amusement is short-lived once the meeting begins and the committee chairman commences his Powerpoint presentation — over fifty slides containing an unfathomable series of charts, diagrams, and corporate jargon about core competences and untapped personnel streams. It is, to coin a phrase muttered by the chap sat next to me, "complete and utter bollocks."

The tedium eventually draws to a close as I mourn seventy minutes of my life I'll never get back. Beyond the fact my brain aches, the meeting over-ran which will have a knock on effect for the rest of my day. I'm the first to leave the room once the meeting concludes.

As I wander back to the office, I switch my phone back on and check for messages. Still nothing from Gabby but there is one unexpected message from Fiona Hewitt, the Parliamentary Commissioner for Standards. Six years my senior, I know Fiona well as we both entered office the same year, although her career path has followed an upward trajectory while mine has flatlined.

She is, however, somebody I would class as much a friend as a colleague.

Curious, I open her message…

William — come to my office the second you get this. It's urgent.

My curiosity remains piqued. The Commissioner's role is to regulate the conduct of all serving members of parliament, and any request for a meeting would usually be greeted with abject fear. However, my conduct is beyond reproach so I hold no such fear. It is most likely to discuss one of my colleagues — a few of whom continue to push the regulatory boundaries. I have no desire to play snitch, but I will certainly offer Fiona any assistance I can, especially if rules have been broken.

I change course and head up to Fiona's office.

When I arrive, her secretary greets me with more a smirk than a smile. "Good morning, Mr Huxley. Please, go on in — she's expecting you."

I ignore her odd reception and rap on the door to Fiona's office, just out of politeness, and push it open. Fiona is stood behind her desk, as if awaiting my arrival. "Thank heavens you're here," she blurts. "Please take a seat, William."

Whatever crisis is behind my summoning, it has clearly flustered the usually unflappable Commissioner. Fiona continues to stand, even after I've taken a seat in front of her desk. She fingers a strand of grey hair while staring at the ceiling, as if deep in thought.

"Fiona?"

Seconds pass before she regains her focus and sits down. Her behaviour is now becoming a concern and I'm about to enquire about her wellbeing when she sits forward.

"William. We have something of a problem."

"Right."

"And when I say *we* have a problem, what I mean is *you* have a problem."

"Do I?"

Her eyebrows arch. "You don't know what I'm referring to, do you?"

"I don't have the first clue, no."

"Oh dear, this is incredibly awkward. I'm not sure where to start."

"I usually find the beginning works."

I've always admired Fiona's diplomacy skills but it appears she's struggling to find the right words on this occasion.

"I do have another meeting in an hour," I add, hoping to add some urgency to proceedings.

She sits back and puffs out her cheeks. "There's no way to sugar-coat this, William, so I might as well get straight to it."

"Appreciated."

"Forty minutes ago, an email was sent to every recipient on the general communications list."

"The general communications list?"

"Yes. Our IT department created scores of segmented lists, each containing various recipients for email correspondence. The general communications list contains the email address of everyone who works in the Palace of Westminster. It's used for things like safety notices, security briefings, and any information we need everyone to see."

"Right."

"So, the email sent to the list was formatted in such a way it managed to bypass our spam filters. As best we can tell, everyone who works in this building would have received it."

"This is all very interesting, Fiona, but I fail to see how that is my problem."

"You clearly haven't seen it, so let me show you the email."

She twists her computer monitor so we can both view the screen and then clicks her mouse a few times. An email pops up, containing just a single line of text...

It is imperative that ALL parliamentary staff view this video — this is a matter of national security. CLICK HERE.

The last two words are blue, indicating a link to a website.

"Are you going to click the link then?" I ask.

"I don't think that's a good idea, William. I can tell you what's at the end of that link; there's no need for you to see it."

"Well, if everyone received a copy of the email, I can easily check myself so you might as well click it."

She pauses for a moment but clicks the link, and immediately turns away from the screen.

A browser window opens up to display a video player on a black background. A spinning disc whirls over the video player while it buffers. I glance across at Fiona but her attention is firmly fixed on the wall.

I turn back to the screen just in time to see the start of the video.

For the first few seconds I struggle to determine what I'm looking at. I lean forward to get a better view, and once I establish the *what*, the utter horror of the *who* hits home.

From the centre of the eight-inch video screen, a familiar face stares straight down the camera lens — Gabby's. The fact she is naked, and on all fours, is only the tip of the abominable iceberg. The intended star of this particular show is positioned beyond Gabby; on his knees, clasping her waist, and thrusting back and forth in a mechanical manner.

Words finally escape. "Oh…Christ!"

Already wishing the earth would swallow me whole, the action intensifies. My right hand slaps Gabby's bare backside. Then again, and again. If the imagery wasn't bad enough, the soundtrack completes my shame as I can clearly be heard braying Gabby's name between breathless grunts.

The browser window suddenly closes.

I turn my head to find Fiona's hand on the mouse. "I think that's enough, don't you?"

Elbows on the desk, my head falls into my hands — partly in despair, partly so I don't have to look at Fiona.

"I'm sorry. I did warn you," she says, her voice firm but sympathetic.

Her words fall away as my mind closes in on itself, much like it did after my mother passed. At this precise moment I would willingly join her. Without hesitation, I would grasp Death's cold hand if it was accompanied by a promise to take me away from the living hell which awaits.

Sadly, it is not Death who calls my name, but Fiona.

"William. Are you okay?"

I feel a hand on my shoulder as, one by one, my senses tune in to the world beyond my mind.

"William?" she repeats.

I look up. Fiona has moved from her chair and is now perched on the desk beside me.

"I shouldn't have let you see that," she says. "I'm so sorry."

In a desperate search for composure, I squeeze my eyes shut and suck long breaths over gritted teeth. Seconds pass and the tightening knot of shame in my chest finally snaps, giving way to anger. I welcome it, embrace it. Anger can be controlled, funnelled, but shame knows no master.

I swallow hard. "Fiona. The fact I saw it is inconsequential. What concerns me…no…what horrifies me, is who else has seen it."

"I know, and there is nothing you or I can do about that. We need to focus on damage limitation."

The anger continues to boil and it takes some effort not to vent at Fiona. "Damage limitation? Seriously? Don't you think it's a bit late for that?"

"Not at all. Our IT guys managed to pull it from the server as soon as we realised what it was, and I've already sent out a warning to every member of staff, stating that the email should be deleted immediately. I also made it clear that anyone found to have forwarded it will face disciplinary action."

I shake my head. "How many people were on the original distribution list?"

"Less than a thousand," she replies, trying her best to underplay the significance. "And less than a hundred opened the email before we removed it. We've also been advised by the hosting company they'll take the video down within the hour."

It's cold comfort.

"I'm not going to lie to you, William," she adds "It's going to be tough for a few days, but this will blow over and people will soon forget about it."

"And in the meantime?"

"Maybe it would be sensible to spend some time in your constituency."

"Run away you mean?"

"No, that's not what I mean. You're a victim of a criminal act, William. Your welfare is paramount."

I suppose Fiona is right. I am now a victim of what is commonly known as revenge porn. It only became a criminal offence a few years ago and I distinctly remember voting in favour of the new legislation. Little did I know.

"Have the police been informed?" I ask.

"Not yet."

"In which case, please don't."

"Why not?"

"Because, Fiona, getting the police involved will only increase the chances of this spreading. Once it breaches the walls of Westminster, there will be no escaping it."

She gets up from the desk and returns to her chair.

"I'm not sure, William. You're asking me to turn a blind eye to a crime."

"No. I'm asking you to protect my reputation. What's done is done and I just want this buried as deep as possible."

"Can I think about it?"

"Think all you like but be warned, I won't cooperate or bring charges if you do inform the police."

"But, William…"

"I mean it, Fiona," I interrupt. "You have my word this won't happen again but *I* need to deal with it, not the police."

She drums her fingers on the desk and puffs a resigned sigh.

"Fine, no police. There will be an internal investigation though. We need to establish how somebody got hold of that list."

"Thank you."

An uncomfortable silence hangs in the air. I suspect Fiona has more questions she daren't ask, and I don't want to leave the sanctuary of her office and face the inevitable humiliation.

"Did you know?" Fiona suddenly asks, breaking the silence.

"Know what?"

"That you were being filmed."

"Of course not."

"It could have been worse, though."

"I fail to see how."

"Well, it's not as though you were doing anything weird or, God-forbid, illegal. It was just sex."

"So you'd be okay having your most intimate moments shared with your colleagues?"

"Of course not. I'm just saying, it's not a bad as it probably seems. We all have sex, William — well, we did, before we had careers. And I have to say, she was a very attractive young lady."

As Fiona reflects on that fact, her expression suddenly changes.

"William, please tell me she wasn't…"

"No, she was not," I interject. "It was entirely consensual and no money changed hands. But thank you for thinking the only way I might sleep with an attractive woman is by paying her."

"Um…no…that's not what I meant."

I can't blame her for thinking that, and I suspect she won't be the only one.

"Forget it."

"Anyway, as I was saying. It really isn't as bad as it might appear, if you handle it correctly."

"Correctly?"

"In hindsight, perhaps going back to your constituency is a bad idea."

"Your bad idea. Not mine."

"Accepted, but it might be better to simply front this out. You'll probably get a bit of ribbing but I suspect most of the male staff will slap you on the back and congratulate you. You know what men are like."

"You say that like I'm a different species."

"A bit of male bravado," she says, ignoring my point. "And I think people will react differently. You never know, it might actually enhance your reputation."

It dawns on me I've just borne witness to Fiona's deft political skills. Within seconds, she has spun the situation into one that might somehow benefit me.

I manage a weak smile. "You were always so much better at this than me."

"This?"

"Politics. Making the unpalatable palatable."

"You know me, William — always been a glass-half-full kind of girl."

On that positive note, we conclude our meeting by agreeing an action plan; one that doesn't involve the police but does involve an internal investigation, which I agree to cooperate fully with.

As I'm about to leave, Fiona receives an email to confirm the hosting company have removed the video. Too late for the hundred people who've already seen it, but with Fiona's advice ringing in my ears, I hope it's a number I can contend with.

I thank her and steel myself. Time to face the shame.

12.

I clear two corridors, passing only four people — not so much as a glance in my direction. The gent's toilets offer a suitable stopping point to gather my thoughts before I complete my journey. I open the door and listen for signs of life. Other than a dripping tap and the hum of the florescent lights, all is quiet. I enter the furthest cubicle and the two most pressing concerns come to the fore before my backside touches the seat.

Firstly, is whether Rosa saw the video. Buoyed by Fiona's advice, I think I can just about handle the fact virtual strangers have witnessed my embarrassing bedroom antics, but Rosa is a different story. Even if she hasn't seen it, I can't avoid discussing it with her. This place is a hotbed of gossip at the best of times so there's no way she won't hear about it. I don't think I have any choice other than to warn her, and that is going to be as shameful as it will be humiliating.

The other concern is Gabby. How she managed to get hold of the email list is a question somebody else will hopefully answer, but more worrying is why she even did it at all. Could it be she tried to sell the video, and with no takers, sent it out of pure spite? That seems the most plausible reason but still, something doesn't feel right. She must have known her actions were illegal and no matter how annoyed she might have been, surely the threat of jail time was a risk too far.

I consider sending her another text message, but seeing as my earlier message was probably the catalyst for her actions this morning, I decide not to provoke her any further. She's done her worst, and with nothing further to gain, hopefully she'll now move on to her next victim. And besides, I should be grateful she never posted the video on social media or any number of porn websites where it could sit forever in public view.

No, it's best to leave Gabby well alone and hope she's sated her thirst for revenge. On the upside, she gets to keep her pound.

I exit the cubicle and head over to the sinks. After a splash of cold water on my face and a quick check of my tie, I look at the dour man in the mirror and assure him we're ready to face Rosa — he doesn't look convinced.

Sadly, I can't hide in the toilet forever. I reluctantly venture back into the corridor and make my way to the office.

I step back through the door to find Rosa at her desk, still furiously typing away.

"Everything okay?" she chirps.

"Why do you ask?"

"You said you'd only be an hour."

"Oh, yes. Right. I did."

She continues with her typing — her behaviour suggesting she hasn't seen the video. That might be a blessing but it doesn't excuse me from the humiliation I know has to come. I slink behind my desk and try to look busy while I consider how to broach the subject.

Every minute that ticks by is a minute somebody could call or text her to share the gossip. I can't put it off any longer.

"Can I have a word please, Rosa?"

"Erm, sure."

She steps from behind her desk and takes a seat in front of mine. There is more than a hint of concern in her face.

"Don't panic. You're not in trouble."

"Okay, that's a relief."

"It's a bit…delicate."

"What is?"

"What I'm about to tell you."

"Oh."

Despite her tough veneer, necessary for her role, Rosa is a kind, sensitive soul. Endearing qualities, but it makes what I'm about to say even more difficult. That task isn't helped when the concern returns to her face at the exact same moment my brain takes a leave of absence. I stare at her, lost for words. She stares back, perplexed.

"Um, is this about the video?" she suddenly pipes up.

My expression switches to one of slack jawed shock.

"You've…seen it?" I gasp.

"No. Somebody told me about it."

"Did they say anything about the content of the video?"

After a slight grimace, she nods.

"I feel I should explain, Rosa."

"Really, there's no need."

"There is. You're my personal assistant so whatever affects me, affects you. And to be frank, I'd rather you heard the truth than the twisted version I'm sure will already be doing the rounds."

She shuffles uncomfortably in her seat. "As you wish."

It's clear she doesn't want to discuss it but I don't want it hanging over us, like some pornographic albatross.

"Honestly, Rosa, this is a conversation I'd rather not have. But if I'm to retain even a scrap of your respect, I have to explain."

"You have my respect, William."

"Maybe now, but give it a few days, and enough poisonous rumours, and that might change. At least let me set the record straight."

"Fair enough."

"Thank you."

I consider offering to make tea. Everything seems more civilised with a cup of tea in hand, but time is not on my side.

"Okay. I'm assuming I can rely upon your discretion with what I'm about to tell you? I haven't discussed this with anyone, and I'd like it to remain between us."

"You have my word. I won't repeat it to another living soul."

"Good. Now, have you ever heard the term, honey trap?"

"I think so, in a book I once read. It's basically blackmail isn't it?"

"Exactly. Well, it appears I have been the victim of such a trap. Without going into the sordid details, a woman tried to blackmail me into selling her Hansworth Hall for a nominal fee, and when I refused, she released that video."

"Oh, William. That's awful."

"Indeed. Obviously I wasn't aware our…meeting was being filmed and I'm beyond mortified it was shared amongst my colleagues. But I want you to know I had no part in it."

She offers a sympathetic smile. "For what it's worth, I hope she gets locked up for a long time. What a despicable thing to do."

"To be honest with you, Rosa, I just want to forget the whole thing. I thought she was bluffing and I was wrong. The damage is done so there's precious little point in seeking retribution."

"That's a very magnanimous stance, William. I'm not sure I'd be so forgiving."

"I'll put it down to experience and hope it blows over soon enough. You know what this place is like — there's bound to be another scandal around the corner to keep the gossips busy."

"I'm sure you're right."

With the air cleared and a total humiliation avoided, Rosa returns to her duties. Now all I have to contend with are the whispers and sniggers beyond my office. It then dawns on me that Prime Minister's questions are about to start in the House of Commons. It's a thirty-minute session attended by almost all members and I don't think I have the fortitude to face them just yet. Like a truanting schoolboy, I decide to skip it and head out for some lunch.

I sneak back forty minutes later but with a meeting scheduled and a session in the house later this afternoon, I can't avoid my colleagues forever.

However, I am nothing if not a pragmatist. In the grand scheme of things, there are far worse situations to be in. I've seen enough poverty during my time in Africa to appreciate the difference between my embarrassment and real suffering. I might have to endure a few uncomfortable moments, but I won't be going to bed hungry tonight. It is always wise to keep a little perspective in one's life.

With that thought, I pull myself together and head for the meeting.

The journey to the meeting room is uneventful but the moment I walk through the door, the eager chatter suddenly descends into silence. A dozen or so faces turn in my direction.

"Don't stop on my account," I bark.

The dozen faces swap embarrassed glances and the silence continues, until a lone voice booms from the far end of the conference table.

"Everything okay, William?"

Adrian Lowe is a fellow backbencher with lofty ambitions. Young, arrogant, and boorish, I despise everything about the man.

"Fine, thank you, Adrian," I reply, taking my seat.

"Glad to see you weathering the storm," he adds. "I think I speak on behalf of everyone here when I say you have our full support."

Nods and murmurs spread across the table.

"I appreciate it."

"Nobody deserves that," he continues. "I mean, it was a real slap in the face for personal privacy."

His deliberate emphasis on the word *slap* draws stifled laughter from several of my colleagues. He then sits back in his chair with a self-satisfied smirk plastered across his face.

"Thank you, Adrian. And yes, I get the joke. Very droll. Now, if you've all finished behaving like adolescents, perhaps we can get down to parliamentary business?"

"Ooh, or what? Are you going to slap us too?" Adrian chirps.

There is less effort to stifle the laughter on his second jibe. I take a second to let it die down.

"Considering your face is eminently more slappable than an arse, Adrian, I wouldn't discount it."

Another round of laughter ensues, but at Adrian's expense this time. He slumps back in his chair and spends the rest of the meeting being deliberately obstructive. As irksome as it is, it's preferable to further discussion of slapped backsides.

With one meeting out of the way, and less fallout than I envisaged, I head to my next appointment with manageable apprehension. However, that appointment is in the House of Commons where I'll be amongst hundreds of my colleagues. Trying to put a positive spin on it, I suppose it's an opportunity for everyone to have a dig in one fell swoop. Death by guillotine rather than death from a thousand cuts.

I can, however, minimise my exposure by ensuring I arrive at the very last minute, before the Speaker silences the house. Another trip to the gent's toilets is in order.

At two minutes to three, I exit the cubicle and make my way towards the House of Commons.

I scurry through the commons corridor with seconds to spare, and enter the house just as the doors are about to close. My timing, it seems, is perfect. I'm greeted by the sound of a hundred conversations from colleagues on the tiered leather benches either side of the house. It looks like everyone has found time in their diary for the immigration debate.

Keeping my head down, I turn left and skirt the periphery of the hall. My seat is on the second to last bench from the back. I reach the row without incident but I need to squeeze past several colleagues. It's at that point I'm most exposed.

It doesn't take long before I'm spotted, and my journey along the bench is accompanied by an ever growing chorus of jeers and wolf whistles, interspersed with a few back slaps as I pass male colleagues. By the time I reach my seat, it feels like every set of eyes is upon me. If there was ever an opportunity to put a lid on this, now is it. I do the one and only thing that comes to mind — I perform an overly theatrical bow.

It works better than I expected and laugher peals across the house, together with cheers from my side of the chamber. It is with some relief when I finally take my seat and the Speaker calls order.

For three long hours, an impassioned debate ensures my folly is quickly forgotten. And with a much needed drink awaiting me at Fitzgerald's, I don't hang around afterwards to prompt any further discussion on the subject. By tomorrow, I will hopefully be yesterday's news.

My walk to Blackfriars is spent in a contemplative mood. It would be fair to say it's been an eventful day but I've come through it relatively unscathed. As bad as it's been at times, it could have been so much worse. If nothing else, I've learnt a valuable lesson.

I turn into Furnival Street just after seven o'clock and as I approach Fitzgerald's, there appears to be some commotion at the door. A suited man is hurling expletives at Frank, who in turn is wildly gesticulating back at him. I get within twenty yards when Frank is joined by Clement. The situation takes on a new dynamic as he confronts the suited man. The expletives stop as Clement grabs him by the lapels and pins him against the wall, his feet dangling a several inches from the floor.

I approach Frank. "Everything okay?" I ask.

"Found that bloke snorting coke in the gents. Clement was just updating him on our drugs policy."

The man pinned to the wall is still mumbling an apology as Clement turns to confirm further instructions with Frank.

"Alright, Bill," he says as he spots me. His manner is fairly relaxed, considering the circumstances.

"Erm…evening, Clement."

Frank then nods at Clement and the suited man is unceremoniously hurled halfway across the street. He quickly clambers to his feet and scuttles away.

"Usual, William?" Frank says before heading back into the bar. Clement lights a cigarette and I decide not to hang around.

Once inside, I position myself on a stool while Frank pulls my pint.

"Frank, I thought you said that Clement chap was an odd job man?"

"He is."

"But based upon what I just witnessed, his role clearly extends beyond putting up shelves and serving occasional drinks. You do realise door staff require a licence?"

"I do."

"And is Clement licenced?"

"Do you want to ask him?"

"Um, not really."

"Very wise. Tonight's special is sausage and mash."

A pint is placed in front of me.

"Right. I'll take one of those too, please."

I pay Frank and retreat to my table in the corner. Seated, I take a long gulp of ale and slump back in my chair. For the first time today, I can take a moment to wallow in nothingness, while Frank Sinatra croons *My Way* from the juke box. I close my eyes and block out everything except Sinatra's melodic voice. Tiredness descends, aided by the fact I haven't eaten since breakfast. My hellish day hasn't exactly stoked my appetite but now the worst is behind me, pangs of hunger make their presence felt.

I choose to ignore them in lieu of slipping towards a semi-serene doze. That is until a voice suddenly pulls me back to consciousness.

"Evening, William."

Startled, I snap my head forward and open my eyes.

"What the hell?"

"I thought you'd be pleased to see me," Gabby replies.

13.

For a second I dismiss her presence as a bad dream. When she drags a chair across the floorboards and takes a seat, I realise my nightmare is real.

"How was your day?" she asks.

"Go. Away." I snarl.

"Don't worry. It's just a flying visit."

I can only assume she's here to gloat — misguided creature. She may have won a minor victory, but ultimately, she lost the war. That fact helps to bring some composure.

"Flying or otherwise, I have no interest in any more of your little visits. Now, kindly go away."

"Aww, did you not like your starter?"

"What?"

"The video was only a starter, William. The main course is still to be served."

Here we go again.

"You are seriously beginning to get on my nerves. What will it take for you to leave me alone?"

"Ohh, you know the answer to that, and my offer still stands."

"You're deluded, and wasting your time."

"Maybe. But I've got a little gift for you — *this* is the main course."

She delves into her handbag and withdraws a silver box. Slowly, deliberately, she places it on the table and sits back in her chair.

"And why would I want that piece of tat?" I huff, shrugging my shoulders.

"If I'm honest, it's more a bargaining chip than a gift. I'll leave it with you for twenty four hours and hopefully you'll then be willing to accept my offer. If not, my terms will increase."

My confused expression prompts her to expand on the threat.

"In twenty-four hours' time, you'll agree to sell Hansworth Hall for a pound. If not, my offer will double to two pounds, but I'll also want your flat in Temple Avenue."

"What? How did you know about my flat?"

"I have sources."

I'm not, by nature, an aggressive man but this bloody woman is testing my patience.

"No. Damn. Way," I growl. "I'd rather give my properties away then sell them to you, at any price."

She gets up and taps the top of the box with a manicured fingernail. "I'd look at what's in there before you make any rash decisions. See you tomorrow."

A final glare and she walks away before I have chance to offer a riposte.

I gulp down more ale and steady my breathing. As I wait for my pulse to slow, my gaze falls to the box on the table. Roughly the size of a paperback book, it's possibly silver but more likely pewter, judging by the patina. The lid has a machine engraved decorative design which dates it to the post-war period, and therefore it holds little value. Whatever is inside clearly has some value to Gabby, though.

As I stare at it, not daring to open the lid, my supper arrives. I'm grateful for the distraction.

"You order bangers and mash?"

I look up at my hulking waiter. "Frank's got you waiting tables too?"

"Keeps me busy," Clement replies, placing the tray down next to the box.

I thank him, and just as I expect him to stride away, he bends over the table and studies the box.

"*Be who you are,*" he mumbles to himself.

"Sorry?"

"The inscription. Latin ain't it?"

I lean forward and study the lid. Amongst the engraved decorative swirls, the words *Qui Estis* are just about visible in the dim light.

"Yes it is," I reply, trying to suppress my surprise. "Are you conversant with Latin?"

"Nah, don't understand a bleedin' word of it."

"But…"

"Don't ask. What is it, anyway, the box?"

"I have no idea. Remember that woman who came in last night?"

"The wrong'un?"

"Yes, that one. She gave it to me."

Rather than pressing me further, he slowly runs his finger over the lid while staring at the box intently. Seconds pass, and despite the slight awkwardness of the silence, I have no desire to question his motive.

He eventually snaps back to reality and turns to me. "If you need anything else, you just ask."

"Thank you. I will."

He turns to walk away but stops in his tracks. "I mean it, Bill — anything. Just ask, alright?"

Something in his tone suggests an offer beyond fetching condiments, but I'm not quite sure what. He's already gone before I'm minded to ask.

I decide I'm not ready to open the box and spend five minutes picking at my food. Distracted, all I can do is stare at the box with a growing sense of dread. That dread quickly stifles whatever appetite I had after Gabby's visit. I give up, and arrange my knife and fork next to the mound of food.

Another sup of ale and another glance at the box. It is, in every literal sense, Pandora's Box.

You can't fight blind, William.

Whatever Gabby has up her sleeve, there is nothing to be gained by remaining ignorant. I open the lid.

I don't know what I expected to find, but it probably wasn't a cream coloured envelope with my name scrawled on the front. That is though, precisely what I do find. My immediate conclusion is the letter is from Gabby, but why deliver it in a pewter trinket box?

I snatch the envelope and take a second to study it. The thick, quality paper suggests the sender had an eye for premium stationary. But if this is a formal notice of intended blackmail, why not just use run-of-the-mill stationery that is near impossible to trace?

Something tells me the letter isn't from Gabby.

The flap of the envelope is folded inside rather than stuck down. I prise it open and extract a single sheet of equally expensive writing paper, before slowly unfolding it.

"Good God!"

It takes a moment to fully absorb what I'm looking at — my father's headed stationery with his title and Hansworth Hall address embossed at the top in gold leaf. Below the header are six paragraphs of hand-written text, and the date the letter was penned.

"21st November, 1999," I whisper to myself.

The date is relevant because it was the day before my father died. Suddenly, the significance of what I'm holding in my hand becomes obvious. Whatever the six paragraphs reveal, the lines of scrawled text are some of my father's final thoughts.

I carefully place the letter on the table and begin to read...

My Dearest William,

There is much to say but little time to say it. I'm afraid my mind is now fading but I'll try to make some sense. My son, I am sorry to say my time is nearly over and while I hold no fear of death, the fact I may never see you again makes that hard to bear. Even in poor health, if I knew your whereabouts I would be with you tomorrow. I would gladly travel the world to spend a final day in your company. And I would beg your forgiveness for the way I failed you, and the way I failed your mother. Sadly, it is not to be and I must therefore confess to those failings on paper.

You will never know just how much I loved your mother. She was my world and perhaps when she left, some part of me left with her. That is not to excuse the dreadful way I treated you. I pushed you away when you needed me most. I would never seek forgiveness because my actions were unforgivable, but I now carry the burden of that behaviour. It weighs heavy, and of that I am glad — it is no less than I deserve.

More than anything, I wish I could end this letter now, but I must now write what must be read. My sin is great and if I am to find peace, I have to pray you can help me find it. There are no words to truly convey, nor excuse, the shame of what I'm about to tell you. Please be prepared.

Some years ago, I made a mistake. I let lust and alcohol cloud my judgement. It was for one night, and it was a decision I came to rue. You may recall my assistant, Susan Davies. We were at the party conference, in Bournemouth, and I am ashamed to say I shared my bed with Susan on the final night.

If my shameful behaviour had ended there, perhaps I might not be telling you this, but it did not. Nine months after our night together, Susan gave birth. To even acknowledge the existence of the child would have ended my marriage and ended my career. I chose not to lose either. I provided financial support but that was all I provided. I never felt worthy of your mother's love ever again.

It is too late for me, but I needed you to know — you are not alone in this world, and the Huxley bloodline does not end with you. I understand this must be a shock, and for that, know I am so very, very sorry.

I cannot tell if it was prompted by sadness or anger, but a single tear rolls across my cheeks and falls on the paper. I read the letter again, and again. More tears follow and with them, a dull ache forms in the pit of my stomach; the like I have never felt before. That ache is joined by a stabbing truth. To learn my father betrayed my mother is difficult enough to bear, but his astonishing revelation that I have a sibling is the cruellest of twists.

All these years I've been alone — an only child with no parents; an orphan, or, so I thought. Somewhere I have a brother or sister who almost certainly doesn't know I exist. How could he have kept that from me?

As an entire inquisition of questions pummel my mind, and two in particular hit hardest — where has the letter been all these years and how did Gabby get hold of it? If, as my father clearly intended, I had seen it in the weeks after his death, I might already have some kind of relationship with my estranged sibling. So many wasted years have passed, so much time lost.

Long minutes slip by as I sit alone in the darkened corner of Fitzgerald's — confounded, shocked, saddened. But beyond any other emotion, my anger is so intense it's near paralysing. That anger is not towards my father, although God knows he deserves it. No, my anger is focused on the woman who has not only kept this secret from me, but chosen to use it as in instrument for blackmail.

I pull my phone from my pocket and curse the unfamiliar screen layout. Frustration mounts as I try to extract Gabby's phone number from her text message. Twice I have to stop and calm myself. A third attempt and I finally manage to call the number. It rings four times before she answers.

"That was quick. Ready to do that deal?"

"Where did you get it," I growl.

"Get what? The letter?"

"Don't mess me around, or so help me God I'll swing for you. Where did you get it?"

"Doesn't matter where I got it. What matters, William, is where it goes next."

"What's that supposed to mean?"

"I gave you my terms. You agree to sell me the house tomorrow. If you don't, the terms change and I'll want the flat too. The alternative is I go to the press and daddy's little secret becomes public knowledge. Be warned, William, I'm not messing around here."

She hangs up. I redial the number but it goes straight to a generic voicemail.

I slap the phone on the table and press my fingertips into my temples in an attempt to quell my rage. Anger is such a debilitating emotion — it's impossible to think rationally, to find any sense of clarity. All I want to do is upend the table and scream. Mercifully, there remains enough of my rational mind I don't, and stare at the letter instead, all the while pulling deep breaths.

"Bill?"

I look up to find Clement stood over me.

"You finished with your plate?" he asks.

I nod and return my gaze to the letter.

"You alright, mate? You look like you've seen a ghost."

As much as I'd rather not antagonise Clement, his interference is the last thing I need.

"If it's all the same with you, I'd rather be left alone."

Ignoring my protest, he pulls up a chair.

"Can't do that, Bill. Goes against my terms of employment."

I shoot him a puzzled look.

"It's complicated," he adds.

I drop my head and hope my silence will be enough for him to get the message.

"You gonna tell me what's up then?"

Just go away.

"Something to do with this?" he asks, tapping the letter.

I snatch the letter from the table and stuff it in my jacket pocket.

"For a politician, you ain't got much to say."

My head snaps up. "Who told you I was a politician?" I bark, paranoia fuelling my aggression.

"Frank."

"Right. Of course."

Silence descends over the table as the juke box loads another record. Clement appears comfortable waiting for me to break. It doesn't take long.

"With respect, Clement," I sigh. "I don't think you can help."

He sits forward and rests his elbows on the table.

"Maybe. Maybe not. Either way, I can't say if I don't know what's pissed you off."

Up until I met Gabby, I always considered myself an excellent judge of character. A decade working in politics exposes you to the very best and the very worst of people. But looking at Clement, all I see is a conundrum — a man who looks the very personification of trouble, yet there's an almost inescapable gravity about him; his gravelly voice and blunt tone feel assuring, genuine.

Without thinking, I blurt a response. "I'm being blackmailed.

His blue eyes widen a fraction, their cold edge softening.

"That woman?"

"Yes."

"Something to do with that letter?"

"Yes."

"Bleedin' hell, Bill. You wanna stop playing twenty questions and give me something to go on?"

As much as I might welcome the opportunity to offload, I'm not sure Clement is the man I should be offloading to.

"Don't get me wrong, Clement, I appreciate your good intentions, but I really don't think you can help. In fact, I think it's time I spoke to the police."

"You *think*? Why ain't you already been on the blower to them then?"

It's a good question.

"Because I was hoping not to. She has…certain information that I really don't want in the public domain. The moment I invite the police in, there is every chance that information will leak — there's always somebody willing to sell their soul when a politician is involved. To be frank, it's looking like a choice of lesser evils at the moment."

"And I'm guessing that letter is part of her blackmail plot?"

"It is. I can't even begin to consider the consequences if it were made public."

He sits back and strokes his moustache, seemingly deep in thought. Seconds tick by before a conclusion is returned.

"Well, Bill. I can't fix stupid, but I think I can show it the door."

"I beg your pardon."

"No offence, mate, but I thought you politicians were supposed to be bright."

"I…what?"

"The letter," he groans. "It didn't look like a photocopy."

"No, the gold leaf in the letterhead is…"

I fear my initial anger might have clouded the obvious.

"It's...it's the original," I splutter.

"Yeah, and I'm no lawyer but I doubt a newspaper will run a story on the back of photocopy cos' it ain't worth shit in court. You sue for libel and they ain't got a leg to stand on. So, what's she gonna do without the original?"

It seems Gabby has dropped the ball. She must have known a photocopied version of my father's letter wouldn't be anywhere near convincing enough for me to believe it was genuine, so her only option was to give me the original.

"Clement, if I didn't think it would end in violence, I could kiss you."

"Yeah, you're not my type, Bill."

"Thank you so much. I can't believe I didn't realise it myself."

He gets up. "Anytime. Need anything else?"

"No, thank you. But, please, let me buy you a drink."

"Nah, you're alright, mate. I've got shit to be getting on with."

He picks up my tray and with a parting nod, he ambles away.

I watch him go and finish my drink. The temptation to have another one is great, but I need a clear head. Perhaps Clement's observation is enough to thwart Gabby for now but if I've learnt anything about her, it's that she doesn't easily give up. Even so, her plot is no longer my primary concern.

Those six paragraphs of scrawled text have undermined everything I knew to be true. They have created a new truth; that my father was a cheat and a coward, and my poor mother oblivious to the most despicable of betrayals. And what of my forgotten sibling? Where are they? Who are they? Do they know the truth about their father?

There is however, one overriding question to be asked before any answers will be forthcoming — what do I do next?

14.

Sleep is elusive and I eventually give up trying to find it despite dawn still being an hour away.

I clamber from my bed and head to the kitchen. Tea won't deliver sufficient caffeine so I make a cup of strong coffee and retire to the lounge. Beyond the windows, London slumbers the way it always does — never quite silent, never quite still. It mirrors my mind ever since I left Fitzgerald's last night.

The dark, bitter coffee proves a fitting analogy for my mood. The anger has given way to brooding resentment, laced with something that feels too much like grief. I suppose it could be grief. Perhaps I'm subconsciously mourning the memory of the father I knew, rather than the one who, as it turns out, was a complete bastard. Or perhaps I'm mourning the lost years with my sibling. My brother, my sister — hidden away from me like the dirty secret they were.

And in amongst everything, I now question my own life. My choice of career was not my career of choice, but a means to fulfil the wishes of a man no longer alive to see those wishes fulfilled. Through nothing other than a blind sense of duty, of obligation, I have given a decade of my life to a cause now tarnished, tainted.

Knowing what I now know, my father's shadow has grown longer, darker, and that poses a hypothetical question: given the chance, would I have preferred his secret to remain exactly that? I conclude I would not. The truth, however unpalatable, is the truth. And no matter how belated, perhaps I still have the opportunity to do something meaningful with it. I must step beyond the shadow.

Caffeine provides a welcome boost to my morale and I accept there is nothing to be gained by wallowing in self-pity. It is not in my nature to simply sit and lick my wounds. If they are ever to heal, I need to administer a remedy. A second cup of coffee provides the impetus and as dawn arrives, I think I have something approaching a strategy in mind. As my father used to say, *doing nothing mends nothing*.

I force down some breakfast and leave the flat just before eight o'clock.

The short tube journey takes on a different perspective as I stare at strangers, knowing any one of them could be my sibling. Despite the statistical improbability, I find myself appraising each of my fellow commuters for physical similarities. I quickly accept I'm more likely to experience a punch in the face than a family reunion.

The train arrives at Westminster and I disembark with the huddled masses. Despite the crush, I quickly weave through the crowds, keen to get to my desk.

Fifteen minutes later my resolve encounters the first hurdle of the day, in the form of my computer. I vow to one day throw the damn thing off Westminster Bridge. If Bill Gates happens to be passing on a boat underneath, and it floors him, I'll consider justice served.

Eventually the computer splutters into life and I can finally enact the first part of my strategy — finding the one woman who can give me answers — Susan Davies.

I start by searching on Facebook and it doesn't take long to establish the magnitude of my task. My father could not have chosen a more commonly named woman to enjoy a dalliance with. My search for people with the name Susan Davies delivers hundreds upon hundreds of results. And with nothing other than her name and approximate age to go on, frustration quickly mounts. I give up and try Google, then Twitter. The same problem, the same frustration.

I sit back in my chair and cuss.

"Language, William."

I spin around to find Rosa in the process of hanging her coat up.

"Sorry, Rosa. You didn't hear that."

"Of course not," she smiles. "Tea?"

With Rosa on tea making duties, I stare into space, hoping for inspiration. With all the technology we have at our disposal in this day and age, it can't be that hard to find somebody, surely?

I then spot something in my in-tray which sparks a thought. I lean forward to closer inspect a reminder letter regarding Rosa's probation period, which ends soon. However, it isn't the content of the letter itself which triggers optimism; it's the sender's name: Judith Dixon.

Judith is a freelance recruitment and human resources consultant; a role she's held for almost four decades. Most people aren't aware that every member of parliament is technically an employer, and we're responsible for recruiting and managing our own staff. As most of us don't have the first clue about recruitment or human resources, it's quite common for us to use the services of consultants such as Judith. In my case, she ensures I follow all the correct procedures and contractual obligations that come with employing staff.

And the very reason I use Judith's service is because she also worked for my father. If I frame it correctly, I might well be able to call in a favour. I scribble down her name and email address.

"Are you ready to go through the diary," Rosa asks as she places a cup on my desk.

"Sure."

Two minutes in, my plans are thwarted as Rosa reminds me I have to attend a select committee hearing at nine thirty. One of my female colleagues once remarked that select committee hearings were longer and more painful than childbirth. I can't vouch for the latter but she was certainly right on the former. It's the last thing I need today but there's no getting out of it.

I'm not known for my patience, and having already lost so many years, I'm desperate to speak with Susan Davies. I need to set my plan in motion before I leave.

"Rosa, I need you to do something for me."

"Sure."

I hand her the slip of paper with Judith's email address.

"Can you email Judith Dixon and ask her a favour on my behalf. I need the last address she has on file for my father's former PA, Susan Davies."

"Isn't that information confidential?"

"It would be if Susan Davies still worked for my father. Tell Judith I found some old photos of Susan amongst my father's possessions that I'd like her to have. I'm sure she'll be happy to oblige."

"Okay, I'll get onto it."

"Make it a priority, please. I'd like that address by the time we break for lunch."

I feel a little guilty for my subterfuge but I think the end justifies the means. My father might have turned his back on Susan but I have no such intention now I know the truth.

With Rosa confirming she'll prioritise my request, we finish our planning for the day and I head to the committee room. I had hoped yesterday's nonsense with the video might be forgotten but I'm greeted by a sudden silence. I'm really beyond caring and pay no attention, choosing instead to chat with a couple of my more mature colleagues. The whispers, the nudges, and the smirks soon peter out.

The hearing doesn't start well by virtue of the fact it doesn't actually start. We're forced to wait for the chairwoman who is apparently stuck in a taxi somewhere several miles west of Westminster.

Half an hour passes before she finally appears and we can get going. Fortunately, the delay turns out to be a blessing as we rattle through proceedings at an unusually efficient pace. By late morning we've made sufficient progress to call the session to an end. On any other day I might have felt some sense of accomplishment with my morning's work, but this is no ordinary day. For once, my own needs outweigh those of the nation.

I arrive back in the office just after noon.

"Did you get that address?" I ask Rosa.

"I did. Susan Davies moved home after leaving her job here but Judith managed to get her current address from the pension records."

"Excellent. You're an absolute star, Rosa."

She hands me a slip of paper as her cheeks flush pink; often the case when I compliment her work. The slip of paper reveals Susan's address, and the fact it's not exactly local.

"She lives in Sandown?" I groan. "On the Isle of Wight?"

"She does."

"I don't suppose you happened to look for her phone number?"

"I assumed you'd ask and I did check. I'm afraid she's either ex-directory or doesn't have a landline."

Not ideal, but considering the possibilities after more than thirty years, it's as good a result as I could have hoped for.

"Never mind. Thanks, Rosa."

I retreat to my desk and consider my next move. The lack of a phone number means I only have one option and that's to pay Susan Davies a visit. Thankfully, I'm due back in my constituency tomorrow and there's not a great deal in my diary I can't postpone. I can get the train down to Portsmouth in the morning and hop on the ferry to the island. All being well, I could be in Sandown before lunch.

"Rosa, can you reschedule whatever commitments I have for tomorrow, please?"

"Sure."

With my plan set, it dawns on me I'm less than twenty-four hours away from an answer that could have huge implications. Beyond my brother or sister, I could have nieces and nephews — a whole family I never knew existed. Is it too much to hope?

I shouldn't get too carried away. And for now, I have more pressing matters to attend to; namely lunch.

"I'm just popping out for a sandwich. I'll be half an hour or so."

Rosa looks up from her screen and nods. For a second I consider asking her to join me but that nagging fear of rejection quickly puts pay to it. Maybe once I've dealt with Susan I'll invite Rosa out for supper, under the pretence of celebrating the end of her probation period. We'll see.

I head to the sandwich shop for my usual order and then on to St James's park. The mild weather is still holding out and the park is busier than one would expect for late October. I eventually locate an empty bench and sit down to eat.

As I tuck into my sandwich, a chap walks past with a handsome chocolate Labrador. The dog catches scent of my sandwich and lollops over. Clearly an optimist, he sits down at my feet in anticipation of a lunchtime snack.

"I'm so sorry," the man says as he approaches. "He's like a dustbin when it comes to food."

"It's quite alright. Does he like chicken salad?"

"Benson likes anything and everything," he chuckles.

I tear a small portion from my sandwich and offer it to Benson. He takes the food with surprising gentleness which I reward with a pat on the head. The man thanks me and calls his dog away. The two of them continue on their walk; Benson no doubt hoping to find other generous bench dwellers.

I finish my sandwich while daydreaming of one day owning a dog myself. Perhaps when I give up my political career, if you can call it that, I might take a trip to the local pound and find my own Benson. Yes, I think I'd like that.

I'm dragged from my thoughts as somebody joins me on the bench.

"Afternoon, William."

The voice is so ingrained in my memory I don't have to turn my head to know who it belongs to.

"Has anyone ever told you, Gabby, you're quite the proverbial bad smell?"

"Charmed, I'm sure."

"Have you been following me?"

"Not exactly hard, is it? You visit the same sandwich shop almost every day."

"What do you want?"

She shuffles along the bench until only a foot separates us.

"Your memory is terrible, William. Today's the day we conclude our deal."

"I don't think so."

"You know what will happen if you don't."

I'm so tired of her games I get straight to the point.

"Do whatever you like. I really couldn't care less."

"You don't care about your father's reputation, or the damage his dirty little secret will do to that reputation?"

Clement's words of wisdom float through my mind, fuelling my resolve. Even if she could find a newspaper willing to publish a story based on photocopied evidence, I will have already spoken to Susan Davies before Gabby's claims ever make it to print. My only interest is in repairing my father's mistakes, not burying them.

"With fear of repeating myself, I don't care."

She remains silent for several seconds; perhaps, I hope, because I've called her bluff. She then dips her hand into the inside pocket of her jacket and withdraws an envelope.

"Take a look at what's inside," she says, offering it to me.

I stare at the envelope but resist the urge to take it from her.

She leans across and whispers. "We never got around to dessert so here you go. And trust me — it's bittersweet."

Every part of me wants to get up and walk away but curiosity is a demanding maiden. I snatch the envelope from her hand and tear it open.

The first thing I find is a grainy black and white photo of a sleeping infant; swathed in a blanket and lying in a Moses basket. The child can't be more than a few months old I'd guess.

"Who is this?" I snap.

"It's your little sister. Cute isn't she…for a bastard child?"

My anger dissolves in an instant as my focus returns to the photo. I wish I could say the child had some distinguishing feature to identify her as a Huxley, but to me, all babies look the same. Nevertheless, gazing at a photo of my tiny sister brings a lump to my throat.

I turn to Gabby and attempt to keep my voice level. "Where did you get this?"

"There's something else in the envelope that will answer your question."

I prise it open and remove a piece of folded, cream-coloured paper. With my pulse quickening, I carefully open it.

"A birth certificate?" I mumble to myself.

"A copy of your sister's birth certificate, to be precise."

I now know my sister's name — Gabrielle Anne Davies. The certificate confirms her date of birth, putting her just over thirty years of age now. It further confirms her mother's name as Susan Veronica Davies, and her father's name as Charles Augustus Huxley.

My arm falls to my lap as I try to take it all in. Suddenly, I have supporting evidence of not only my father's infidelity, but the existence of his lovechild — my sister. What I don't have is an explanation as to why this information will assist her blackmail plot.

She clears her throat, seemingly about to answer that question.

"Joined up the dots yet?" she asks.

I turn to her, confused.

"I...what?"

"Let me give you a clue. What's a shortened version of the name Gabrielle."

As her eyes lock onto mine, my mind flashes back to the moment we first met in the auditorium at the Montgomery Hotel. That spark of familiarity I couldn't quite place is now a raging fire.

No...no way...it can't...

"What's the matter, William?" she coos. "I thought you'd be pleased to finally meet your little sister."

15.

Like the punchline of a convoluted joke, my mind struggles to comprehend the seemingly obvious. In this case, there is no spontaneous laughter as the pieces fall into place. There is only shock. A shock so abhorrent it soon gives way to denial.

"What? No…this is…you're insane. How dare you say such a thing."

She rests her hand on my shoulder and calmly continues. "Let me just clarify the facts for you: Susan Davies is my mother, Charles Huxley was my father, and you, dear William, are therefore my brother." Her smile widens. "Oh, and as I'm sure you recall, you were also briefly my lover."

Bile begins to burn at the back of my throat as my stomach heaves. I try to gulp air but the recently consumed sandwich and remnants of my breakfast are already making their return. I turn to the side a split second before an explosion of vomit escapes my mouth. Another wave of nausea quickly follows, and more retching. Only when there is nothing left in my stomach do the convulsions finally end.

"You're lying," I spit between ragged breaths.

She reaches into her pocket and pulls out a passport; flipping it open right in front of my face. The photo is unmistakably her and the name is there in clear black print — *Gabrielle Anne Davies*.

"Satisfied?" she snipes before whipping the passport away.

I pull a handkerchief from my pocket and dab my mouth before asking the only question I can muster.

"Why?"

"I thought I was very clear about my motives. I want Hansworth Hall and the flat."

"But why did you…what sort of sick mind…"

"If you're referring to our evening at the hotel," she interjects. "That was my insurance policy."

"Insurance policy? We had sex for God's sake."

"I agree it was a bit nasty, but necessary. You could have avoided this unpleasantness if you'd been a good boy and buckled to my earlier threats. But you didn't, so you've nobody to blame but yourself."

That picture of a happy family I had in my head is now in a hundred fractured pieces — smashed with the most depraved of hammers.

Never in my life have I ever wanted to be further away from another human. I get to my feet and stumble away.

"Where are you going?"

"Away from you. I don't ever want to see or hear from you again."

"Sit down, William."

I ignore her.

"I wouldn't leave if I were you," she calls after me. "Don't you think my revelation puts a new slant on that video?"

Her words are like a lasso. I stop dead in my tracks and slowly turn around.

"What?"

"A seedy video is one thing," she adds. "But a video of you having sex with your sister is something else."

I glance around nervously, hoping nobody is within earshot. "Why would you tell anyone?" I hiss. "It's your sordid secret as much as it is mine."

"The difference is, I didn't know we were siblings. But you did, and you fucked me anyway, didn't you, William?"

"What? You lying piece of…"

"Who are people going to believe? A politician, or a poor innocent girl with a sob story. Abandoned by her rich, cabinet minister father at birth, and humiliated by a deranged brother who clearly has relationship issues. Past forty and still a bachelor — that's going to look bad. It'll be front page news, for sure, and you can't prove I knew a thing."

I have never intentionally inflicted pain on anyone, let alone a woman, but the compulsion to throttle Gabby is overwhelming. Tempting as it is, it won't solve anything. If ever there was a time to be the diplomat, now is it.

I swallow my rage and try a different angle. "Why are you doing this to me?"

"Sit down and I'll tell you."

She looks at me, expectant, innocent — a face that would fool anyone.

I weigh up my options and accept they're limited. Reluctantly, I return to the bench and slump down.

"You've got two minutes."

She shifts her position, twisting to the right so she can look me in the eye.

"Your father abandoned my mother, and he abandoned me."

"I know, and I can't excuse his behaviour, but that doesn't come close to justifying your actions."

"Doesn't it?"

"For crying out loud, Gabby — you tricked me into sleeping with you. We can talk about my father's negligence…"

"*Our* father's negligence," she interjects, correcting me.

"Either way, what you've done is beyond the pale. There is no justification."

For once, there is no immediate rebuttal as she turns away and stares off into the distance. Seconds pass before she speaks again.

"What was your childhood like, William?"

"What?"

"Simple enough question. What was it like attending those expensive private schools, living in that huge house, with money no object for the spoilt little rich kid?"

"It wasn't like that," I protest.

"Wasn't it? Sure looks like it from what I've read about your family."

"I was an only child. I was lonely."

"Aww, poor William," she mocks. "Must have been awful."

"It was."

"Fuck you," she barks. My throwaway response appears to have struck a nerve and her tone becomes aggressive.

"You want to know how I grew up? How we moved from one grotty flat to another, from shitty school to shitty school? How I was picked on for wearing charity shop clothes, and how many times I went to bed on an empty stomach?"

"But, the letter — I thought my father provided financial support?"

"Yeah, right. Like politicians never lie. If he did pay my mother anything, it wasn't anywhere near enough."

I suspect I've just uncovered the root of her anger. Her actions have been deplorable but her motives appear genuine. If I were in her shoes, having grown up in poverty while her half-brother enjoys all the trappings of wealth, I suspect I'd be equally bitter.

"So this is about revenge is it? Seeing what I'm prepared to give you as penance for my father's behaviour?"

A snort builds into maniacal laughter. Then, just as quickly as it started, it ends.

"Oh, William," she sighs. "You really are a dim-witted idiot."

"I beg your pardon."

"This was never about what you're willing to *give* me; it's about what I can *take*."

"I don't understand."

"I'm going to take Hansworth Hall and your flat, but that's just about money. Now, if you'd played ball in the first place, I might have been happy with that, but you chose to do what all rich people do and shirk your moral responsibilities. So now I don't just want the properties; I want to take everything your father took from us: our pride, our self-respect, and our dignity."

There doesn't appear to be much room for negotiation.

"And if I refuse?"

"My story would be worth a fortune to the newspapers. I'll sell it and you'll go to prison."

It's my turn to snort laughter. "Prison? I don't think so."

"Don't you? I think you'll find incest is illegal, and my understanding is that you can serve up to two years if found guilty."

"Good luck with that," I sneer. "You'd have to prove I knew who you were."

"Yes, William, you're right. But as you were yelling my name while you screwed me, I don't think a jury will need much more evidence than that."

Another part of her trap I'd walked straight into.

She leans towards me, close enough I can see the hatred in her eyes.

"I planned this down to the finest detail, William, and I guarantee there are only two choices open to you: I take your properties and leave you to wallow in shame for the rest of your days, or I sell my story to the papers and you go to prison. If you choose that option, I'll then go through the courts to get my fair share of your father's inheritance and you'll still spend the rest of your days living in shame, only it'll be far, far worse because everyone will know exactly what you did."

The end game has been reached — she has me completely cornered. If it were not for the fact my life is about to be destroyed, I might admire her cunning. Now all I can do is try to appeal to her better nature. I'm not hopeful.

"Look, Gabby, I understand you're angry and you have every right to be, but can't we find another way through this?"

"Another way?"

"I'm happy to give you the flat in Blackfriars because, believe it or not, the money is not important to me. Can we then not try and forge some sort of relationship? Maybe, in time, I can prove I'm a better man than my father and I can repair the damage he caused."

"You want to give me the flat?"

"Willingly."

"And then play happy families?"

"Yes, why not?"

Her ensuing laughter does not bode well.

"You're priceless," she chuckles. "Deluded, put priceless. I want nothing to do with you, other than to see you suffer. And I certainly don't want a constant reminder of what happened in that hotel room. It makes my skin crawl even thinking about it."

My humiliation is complete. Nothing else left but to beg.

"Gabby, please…"

"You're wasting your breath and my time," she snaps, her smile long gone. "You know my terms and they're non-negotiable. I want both properties signed over to me within seven days."

"Seven days? How the hell am I supposed to do that? It's not like selling a bloody car you know."

"I'm sure you must know a friendly solicitor. Just get it done."

"It's impossible."

She stands up and hands me a slip of paper. "Those are my solicitor's details. I'm not bluffing, William. I've already spoken to an editor of a national newspaper and given him the gist of my story — he's desperate to know names and willing to pay big bucks for an exclusive. If those properties aren't in my possession by Friday of next week, you'll be front page news on Saturday, but not before I've given a statement to the police about how you tricked me into an incestuous relationship."

Just before she turns to walk away, her coup de grâce is delivered.

"Your turn to be badly fucked…brother."

16.

Time passes by as I sit and stare into space. I'm only torn from my malaise when an elderly man passes and remarks what a lovely afternoon it is. I may have told him to fuck off — I can't recall. Like a man jilted at the altar, my thoughts are torn between the immediate humiliation and the impending fallout. Unlike a man jilted at the altar, the evil bitch in my life is coming back — in just seven days.

During my decade in politics, many times I have stood by and watched some poor unfortunate colleague manipulated into a corner. Intelligent men and women, deftly turned in any direction the party so chooses, typically without said individual realising until it's too late. By comparison, Gabby's conniving makes the Chief Whip look like a rank amateur. I have been royally stitched up.

Perhaps I shouldn't be surprised. My father fought his way to the top table in politics through fair means and foul. Now I can see Gabby is her father's daughter alright. Devious genes, for sure, but Gabby has plumbed the depths of absolute depravity to get what she wants. She stands alone.

My assessment might be complete but no solutions are forthcoming. I fear there are no solutions. A quick search on my phone confirms my worst fears — I have broken the law and that particular infringement carries a two-year sentence. Even if I thought I could handle prison, which I most certainly don't, conviction for such a deplorable crime would consign me to a lifetime of abject shame. I would be a social pariah, but worse; a social pariah with little prospect of employment or forging a meaningful relationship. Friends and colleagues would shun me, and my crime would follow me around for the rest of my days. I would be forever defined as that politician who knowingly had sex with his own sister.

To use Clement's term, Gabby might be a wrong'un, but she is right in that I only have two choices; one of which simply isn't worthy of consideration.

As it stands, there is no bluff I can play, no ace up my sleeve, and no hope of walking away from the table. Beyond those facts, the only other conclusions I can draw are that I can't face the prospect of going back to work, and I desperately need a stiff drink.

I call Rosa and tell her I'm not feeling well, and to cancel all my appointments for the afternoon. I doubt anyone will really miss me. Despite her obvious concern for my wellbeing, I reassure her I'm probably just suffering one of those twenty-four-hour bugs and I'll be back at work on Monday.

With Rosa dealt with, my attention turns to that stiff drink and I make my way on foot towards Blackfriars. I can't risk another wave of nausea descending upon me whilst stood in a packed tube carriage. There is only so much humiliation one man can stand.

I traipse through the streets of London in a near-catatonic daze. Horns blaze and cyclists hurl expletives as I cross roads with no consideration to my personal safety. While I have no wish to end my life, that doesn't mean I would be sorry if it happened; not that anyone can rue their decisions while lying cold on a mortuary slab. I could argue that in some way my life is already over, and my continued existence will be worse than an eternity of feeling nothing. A fate worse than death or actual death — a dilemma only alcohol can resolve.

Thankfully or otherwise, I make it to Furnival Street in one piece. I rarely ever visit Fitzgerald's during the day but today is an exception due to exceptional circumstances. Besides a few suited office workers having lunch, and Stephen the ever-present barfly, the place is quiet.

"Hello, William," Frank beams. "What brings you here of an afternoon?"

"Brandy. Doubles thereof."

"Oh, one of those days is it?"

"It's *the* day, Frank. The absolute worst."

It must be a skill honed over decades but Frank seems to know precisely when to chat and when to shut up. He hands my drink over and confirms I'll be needing a tab this afternoon. Oblivion beckons.

The brandy doesn't touch the sides and sixty seconds after ordering the first, my second drink is placed on the bar. I quickly down that too, and on a now-empty stomach, it doesn't take long for the fuzzy hue of tipsiness to arrive. At this rate I'll be legless within the hour or, God forbid, engaged in conversation with Stephen. I order a single and consume it with a little less vigour.

As I sip away, a voice booms from behind me. "Pint, Frank."

I turn to find Clement ambling up to the bar.

"Alright, Bill."

"Clement."

As Frank pulls Clement's pint, I ask him to put it on my tab. I still owe him a drink in return for the one he bought me on Tuesday. I might not have a great memory but I never forget a debt, especially when owed to a man of Clement's imposing stature.

"Good of you, Bill. Ta."

Frank disappears into the kitchen and the three of us are left stood at the bar: me, Stephen, and Clement. I'd rather not engage in any conversation but if I don't, the choice will be removed and I risk enduring Stephen's drunken nonsense for the duration of my stay.

As it transpires, it is Clement who engages first.

"How did it go then, with the letter and that woman?" he asks.

"Not well."

"Shit. I thought you had it covered."

"So did I, but I may have grossly underestimated her deviancy."

"Well, my offer still stands."

"Your offer?"

"Yeah. I said I'd help if you need it."

"Ah, yes. I don't suppose you know a reliable hitman?"

"Probably, but surely things ain't that bad?"

"Worse, and for the record, I was joking."

I'm ashamed to say that my thoughts do then turn to murdering Gabby, but are quickly dismissed. I could never take another life, and even if I were to pay somebody to take Gabby out, I'm sure she's got a contingency plan in place that would reveal my secret regardless. Rather than two years in prison, I could end up spending a few decades there.

"You wanna grab a seat?" Clement asks.

I don't want to put any unnecessary distance between myself and the bar, but equally, I don't want to offend the big man.

"Erm, sure."

He leads me over to a table in the corner and we sit.

"Come on then, what's she done now?"

Do I tell him? As much as it might be beneficial to share my woes, I don't know this man from Adam.

Detecting my hesitancy, he throws me a question. "Did Frank tell you what I used to do for a living?"

"He mentioned something about security work."

"Yeah, sort of. I was a fixer."

"A fixer?"

"People had problems and I helped fix them. Sometimes they were legit problems, but mostly not. I also did a bit of minding amongst other things."

"But now you're an odd job man?"

"Things change. Times change."

Beyond his tenuous qualifications, I am reluctant to get him involved, primarily because I don't know why he'd want to get involved.

"Forgive me for asking, Clement, but why would you offer to help me?"

"You wouldn't believe me if I told you."

"You'd be surprised what I'm willing to believe."

He takes a long gulp of lager and stares off into the distance for a few seconds.

"I'm a lost soul," he eventually murmurs.

I assume he means figuratively rather than literally.

"Right. And how does helping me solve that?"

"Let's just say I owe a debt to society. I need to make penance."

Overlooking his vague answers, he does at least appear sincere. Nevertheless, I know there's a world of difference between sincere words and sincere acts.

"I'm not sure, Clement."

"Look, Bill. You've got a problem and all I'm offering to do is help fix it. If you reckon you can sort it yourself, why are you here in the middle of the day, getting pissed?"

"I didn't say I can fix it. Quite the opposite in fact."

"So why are you here? It ain't gonna go away is it?"

I sip my brandy, fully aware of my situation. "No. It isn't."

"Exactly. Doing nothing mends nothing?"

I almost choke. "What…what did you say?" I ask, almost in disbelief.

"Doing nothing mends nothing."

Besides my father, I have never heard anyone quote that phrase.

"Where did you hear that?" I ask.

"Dunno," he replies, shrugging his broad shoulders. "Stuff just floats in and out of my head."

If I did believe in such things, I could almost accept his random use of my father's phrase as a sign. Poppycock obviously, but simply hearing those words does reinforce the absurdity of sitting here and doing nothing.

I have reached the point of no return — I either put my trust in him or I don't. I'm not sure sharing my tawdry secret with anyone is a good idea but in lieu of any actual good ideas, perhaps there's some merit. I suppose if he were to double cross me, anything I tell him would be of little value without Gabby's testimony. It comes down to a multi-million-pound gamble, albeit a gamble which I'm absolutely going to lose anyway.

Truth be told, I can't see any way out of my fix so the risk is minimal. However, I want his help to be proffered on my terms.

"If, hypothetically, you were able to help me, I'd want to pay you."

"No need, Bill, apart from expenses."

"I absolutely insist. If I'm going to take advantage of your…expertise, I don't want to be in your debt. Shall we say two hundred a day, plus a five-thousand-pound bonus if you get that damn woman to go away for good?"

"I don't need your money."

"Whether you need it or not, I wouldn't feel comfortable unless you were financially compensated for your time and trouble. It's only fair, and the only way I'm willing to proceed."

He holds out a hand. "Fair, enough. Looks like you've got yourself a fixer."

I shake his hand and offer a silent prayer, to a God who doesn't exist that I've made the right call.

Then comes an uncomfortable discussion as I bring him up to speed on the week's sorry events. I save the part about Gabby's bombshell right until the last moment.

"And she turned up in the park at lunchtime today."

"Right."

"And told me something."

"Go on."

I shuffle uncomfortably in my chair, and have to physically force the words out.

"She told me… she's my sister."

His face puckers as if he's caught wind of a bad smell. "Fuck."

"Quite."

He repeatedly shakes his head. "Jesus, Bill. You knobbed your own sister?"

"Well, yes, but she's only my half-sister, and I didn't know it at the time."

"I knew you politicians were into some dark shit, but that's off the scale."

"Just to be perfectly clear, I didn't know, so can we please not mention it again?"

"Was she any good?"

"Clement!"

"Alright," he says with a wink. "I won't say another word."

"Good, and now you know pretty much all there is to know. The question is: what can I do to stop her?"

"Do you know where she lives?"

"Afraid not."

"Where she works?"

"Sorry, no."

"Hangs out?"

"Um, no."

He lets out a long sigh and strokes his moustache a few times. Seconds tick by as I await a plan I fear isn't going to come. After what feels like an age, he finally clears his throat and delivers his verdict.

"You're in deep shit, mate."

"That much I do know. Care to suggest how I get out of it?"

"Well, it strikes me we ain't gonna get anywhere trying to track her down. And if we can't find her, we can't have a cosy chat and point out the error of her ways."

I get the impression a chat with Clement would be anything but cosy.

"So what do we do?"

"I reckon the mother is the next best bet. She's got the biggest axe to grind but ain't caused a fuss in all these years. She's probably forgiven your old man and might be able talk some sense into that loony daughter of hers."

It's a sound point and I'm slightly miffed I never thought of it. Susan Davies is probably unaware of Gabby's scheme, and assuming she's not as demented as her daughter, she might be horrified enough to intervene.

"That's a good point. And as luck would have it, I have her mother's address."

"Shall we head round there then?"

"Hold on. Firstly, Gabby's mother isn't exactly local; she lives on the Isle of Wight. And secondly, don't you think it'd be better if I saw her alone?"

"Depends."

"On what?"

"If she's prepared to do anything. I know you politicians think you can charm the birds from the trees but sometimes it takes more than words."

"I hope you're not suggesting we give Susan Davies a good kicking."

"Nah, leave it out. I ain't gonna hit any bird, let alone an old one. All I'm saying is that just the threat of things turning ugly can focus the mind."

"You mean threaten her? I'm sorry, but I wouldn't want any part in that."

"I'm not saying I'll threaten the old woman, Bill. We just need to sew a few seeds — I doubt she'll want a bloke like me going after her daughter. We just need her to realise it's a possibility if she doesn't do something. She doesn't know we ain't got the first clue where this Gabby bird is."

"Right. I see."

I'm not convinced. If I am to find a way out of Gabby's clutches, I'd rather do it with my integrity and reputation still intact. Intimidating old women is not what I had in mind when I agreed to Clement's help.

"Just trust me, Bill. I've been doing this a long time. I'll play nicely — you have my word."

As things stand, Clement's word is all I do have. It'll have to suffice.

"Alright, I'll take you at your word," I sigh. "When do you want to go?"

"Seeing as it's gonna take nearly all day to get there and back, we'll have to leave it until tomorrow. I told Frank I'd help out behind the bar later."

"Okay. I can meet you at Waterloo around, say nine thirty?"

"Sorted. You want another drink?"

If I thought I could sit quietly and wallow in self-pity, I might be tempted. However, accepting another drink would mean engaging in small talk I'm just not in the mood for.

"No, thank you. I think tomorrow might be a long day so I'm going to head home."

"Fair enough," he replies, getting to his feet. "I'll see you in the morning then."

Before he goes, I hand him two twenty-pound notes. "Could you settle my tab while you're at the bar? And get yourself a few pints with the change."

He grunts what I assume is an affirmative response and strides off to the bar. As I watch him go, the juke box starts playing *No Regrets* by The Walker Brothers.

Possibly a little late, I think.

17.

Seven in the morning and Friday's sky is a palette of dark greys. As I stare out of the window, the first droplets of rain splatter against the glass. It appears our unseasonably mild weather is no more and normal service has resumed. The view does little to lift my already sombre mood.

I spent what remained of yesterday nursing half a bottle of whisky and over-analysing the meeting with Gabby.

One long, tortuous afternoon leading to more of the same in the evening.

Much of that time was spent in denial. I was sure, given sufficient time to think about it, I'd find a chink in her plot. I almost found one when it crossed my mind the birth certificate she showed me might be a forgery. I called in a favour with an acquaintance at the records office, and after an agonising two-hour wait, he confirmed my worst fears — Gabby and I both have the same father.

My final hope extinguished, I slipped into a semi-drunken coma from which I awoke an hour ago, on the sofa. I was greeted by a text from Gabby, reminding me that her solicitors were expecting contact from mine today. I need to buy some time so at the very least I'll have to instruct them to send a letter out.

Now my anger has subsided, the cold reality of her demands has sunk in. Both the properties are far more than just bricks and mortar; they're the only link I have to my parents — and in the case of Hansworth Hall, my ancestors. As if I don't feel enough shame, I will be the Huxley who finally breaks generations of ownership. One might argue that Gabby is part of our bloodline, but I have no doubt she'll put the house up for sale the moment the ink dries on the contract. It sickens me to think that next week, our family home will become the grand prize in Gabby's twisted game.

That is of course, unless today's quest bears results.

I pour myself another coffee and return my thoughts to the trip, or more specifically, my travel companion. I've asked myself over and over again, why I'm even taking Clement with me. If somebody had told me last week I'd be staking everything I own on the assistance of a virtual stranger, particularly one as odd as Clement, I'd have given them short shrift. Yet that is exactly what I'm about to do. Am I being monumentally naive, or is this just the act of a desperate man. I suspect it's a little of both.

I suppose there are more reasons to take him than not. It's hard to see how my situation could get any worse; with or without Clement's assistance. And to coin an old adage: two heads are better than one, even if one of those heads isn't wired correctly.

I waste an hour on breakfast and a long shower before assessing the contents of my wardrobe. I sift through my limited options and choose a pair of tan cords and a sweater over a checked shirt. As I stand in front of the mirror, I can't help but despair at my drab, conservative attire. It's no wonder I have trouble attracting a partner when I dress like a retired accountant. No point fretting over the least of my current concerns, I suppose.

Hoping to have missed the worst of the rush hour stampede, I leave the flat just before nine and make my way to the tube station. The journey to Waterloo is only eighteen minutes and one change, and I'm afforded the luxury of a seat on both legs. I arrive on the platform of Waterloo Station eight minutes before I'm due to meet Clement. He finds me before I even think to look for him.

"Mornin', Bill."

As I look him up and down, concerns for my own attire fade. Seeing him for the first time in broad daylight, I get to fully appreciate his retro ensemble. He's still wearing his denim waistcoat, over a navy sweater which looks a couple of sizes too small. Faded, bell-bottom jeans drop to a pair of Chelsea boots which have seen better days. Overall, his style is reminiscent of a roadie from a seventies rock group.

"Morning, Clement. I wasn't sure you'd turn up."

Perhaps part of me was hoping he wouldn't.

"As I said, you can rely on me."

"I really hope so."

We head to the departure board and our day gets off to a positive start. Our earlier than planned arrival at Waterloo allows us to catch the nine thirty to Portsmouth Harbour. With a minute to spare, we take our seats in an almost empty carriage towards the front of the train. All being well, we should be at the ferry terminal just after eleven o'clock.

The train sets off and slowly clacks out to a monochrome vista of wide skies and grey buildings. The thing about travelling through central London is you lose all sense of proportion. You're either contained in the claustrophobic womb of the Underground or hemmed in by tall buildings. It's only when you depart by train do you get a real sense of the sprawling scale of the city.

It is a view that Clement appears to appreciate as he stares out of the window.

"I assume you live in London, Clement?"

"Yeah, all my days. Born and bred."

"Which part?"

"Grew up in Kentish Town. Worked all over."

Beyond the Westminster bubble and the centre of London, my geographical knowledge of the wider city is limited.

"Kentish Town. That's north London isn't it?"

"Yeah."

"And where do you live now?"

"Stepney. Got a room there."

"Right. And what did you do before you started working at Fitzgerald's?"

For the first time since we boarded, he turns his head from the window and looks directly at me.

"What's this, Bill? A job interview?"

"Of course not," I chuckle nervously. "Just making conversation."

"I'm not that interesting, mate. You are though."

"I'm really not."

"Nah, I don't buy that. What's it like then; being a politician?"

"Overrated."

"You don't like it?"

"Not really. It's a job, I suppose."

He returns his attention to the view beyond the window before responding.

"Why do you do it then?"

"It's a long story."

"As we're stuck on this bleedin' train for the next hour and a half, you might as well tell it."

Boring him with my life story is preferable to making small talk so I spend ten minutes explaining the former. Much to my surprise, he seems genuinely interested and asks several questions during my monologue, particularly about my father.

"So it's cos' of your old man you're now a politician?"

"In a way. I felt I'd let him down. After I left university, he set me up with an internship at party headquarters, but I had no interest in politics. I turned it down and went to work for an aid charity in Africa. I don't think he ever forgave me and I only entered politics to make amends. Stupid really, considering he was long dead by the time I was appointed."

"Guilty conscience?"

"Something like that."

"What about your old dear?"

"My mother? What about her?"

"What did she think about your choice of career?"

"Not much, considering she died when I was fourteen."

"That's kinda shitty."

"Indeed. She was almost twenty years younger than my father and I always assumed he'd go first. I suppose he did too."

"So there's just you now?"

"Just me, if you exclude my new-found sister, who I suspect isn't big on families."

"I sorta got that."

With little else to say on the matter, we fall into a comfortable silence as we pass through Woking, and then Guildford. Clement appears content just staring out of the window and I'm equally content reflecting on our journey thus far.

I must confess that beneath his gruff exterior and industrial language, there appears to be some semblance of a decent man lurking beneath. It was actually quite cathartic chatting about my life and family. I don't think we're likely to become life-long friends but I feel less concerned about Clement than I did back at the flat. However, he was never my primary concern.

As we pass through Haslemere, I decide maybe it's time we discussed strategy.

"How do you think we best approach Susan Davies then?"

"I'm guessing you don't want the police involved?"

"Absolutely not. Why would you say that?"

"Because we need to know how hard to push her."

"Push her?"

He sits forward, resting his elbows on his thighs.

"You ain't going to the police because you know it'll make things worse for you. Right?"

"Yes."

"We need her to think the same thing."

"By threatening her?"

"Not exactly."

"How then?"

"Just leave it with me."

"I'm not comfortable with that, Clement. I'd rather know in advance what you're planning."

He sits back in his seat and for a moment I don't think I'm going to get my answer.

"Word of advice," he finally says. "Never pick a fight with a homeless man."

"Not that I was planning to, but why not?"

"He's got sod all to lose."

"Right. I'm not sure I get your point."

"We're not gonna threaten her, but we are gonna make it clear you've got sod all to lose."

"And how does that help?"

"Folks who are cornered fight dirty and fight hard, and that's what we've gotta get across. Not a threat, just a statement of fact."

"That still sounds like a threat to me."

He shakes his head. "Don't get it, do you, Bill?"

"Get what?"

"You're fighting for your life here, mate, and there's no room to pussyfoot around. This Gabby has you by the balls and you're worried about being polite to her old dear?"

"I'm worried about making the situation worse."

"Bill, you're being blackmailed cos' you knobbed your own sister. You're gonna lose everything or spend a few years doing bird, so how much worse can it get?"

I have no answer because Clement's blunt assessment is a stark reminder things can't get much worse. Perhaps there is some merit to his advice. I'm not visiting one of my constituents to discuss local bus services over tea and biscuits — I'm visiting the mother of a woman who is doing everything to destroy my life.

"Okay," I sigh. "Perhaps you're right."

"I usually am."

"But I want you to promise me one thing. If I think things are going too far, we leave when I say. Scaring an old woman senseless doesn't sit well with me."

"I don't do promises, Bill, but stop worrying. I know where to draw the line."

Our tenuous strategy sorted, we settle back while the rural scenery rolls past the window. The heavy rain has followed us south, and judging by the way the trackside trees are swaying to and fro, it's brought strong winds with it. Another week and those trees will be stripped of their leaves, much like I'll be stripped of my assets if Hurricane Gabby continues on the same path.

Soon enough, the rural scenery gives way to urban sprawl as we reach the outskirts of Portsmouth. With the first leg of our journey nearly over, a knot of apprehension tightens in my stomach. For the first time since agreeing to his offer, I'm willing to accept that perhaps Clement's company is no bad thing. Conversation is preferable to stewing in my own thoughts.

"Have you been to the Isle of Wight before, Clement?"

"Never set foot off the mainland."

"You've never been abroad?"

"Been to Wales. Long time ago."

Not exactly what I'd classify as abroad, but I suppose Wales is another country.

"Right. Any plans to travel?"

"Don't have a passport."

"Well, that's easily remedied. You can apply online these days."

"The Internet thing?"

"Yes."

"Dunno how to use it."

It's a surprising revelation, even for a relative technophobe such as me. Considering the Internet is so ingrained in our lives, it's hard to see how anyone could function without it. Saying that, perhaps Clement is better off without the constant intrusion of Facebook, Twitter, and email in his life.

"Maybe once we've got through this mess I can show you how to use it. You know, just the basics."

"We'll see," he grunts with a distinct lack of enthusiasm.

We make one more stop at central Portsmouth. Four minutes later the train slows to a halt at our destination.

"All set?" I chirp, offering my best impression of positive.

Clement gives me a thumbs up as the doors hiss open. We step down to the platform and follow the signs to the adjacent ferry terminal.

"Never been on a ferry before," Clement remarks.

Considering he's never been abroad, it's not exactly an earth shattering revelation.

"Unless you count the boats on the Thames," he adds.

I leave him staring out of the window and head over to the ticket office.

"Can I have two adult return tickets, please?" I ask the young man behind the counter.

He taps away at a screen and prints out our tickets. I pay with a card and enquire about the departure time of the next ferry.

"It's your lucky day," he chirps.

It most certainly is not.

"The eleven fifteen sailing has been delayed due to high winds. If you're quick, you should just catch it."

I thank him and beckon Clement to hurry. We then stride down a ramp to a set of gates where we're ushered on board by a windswept chap in a hi-viz jacket. We're fortunate to be on the catamaran service which only takes twenty minutes to cross the

Solent. The downside is the catamaran bounces over the choppy waters rather than cutting a smooth path like a traditional ferry.

Consequently, Clement is looking decidedly green around the gills barely ten minutes into our journey.

"Are you okay?"

"I'll live. Where's the bog?"

I point him in the direction of the toilets and he hurries off. He returns just as we enter the calmer waters near Ryde.

"Bleedin' ferries. Never again," he grumbles, falling into his seat.

"Are you intending to walk back later then?"

His frown is answer enough.

Having made this trip several times over the years, I'm used to the unusual docking arrangements at Ryde, whereby the ferry docks at the end of a long wooden pier rather than a harbour. The other quirky feature of the island's transport system is the trains, one of which is awaiting us at the end of the pier.

"I don't bloody believe it," Clement gasps. "Is that what I think it is?"

"Yes it is."

The rolling stock on the island consists of pre-war London Underground trains. It amazes me how they keep them running, or why, but they have become something of a tourist attraction in their own right.

Clement approaches one of the carriages and gently runs his hand across the battered red paint.

"Alright old girl," he says under his breath.

I'm somewhat taken aback by his reverence towards the tatty old train. I don't like to pre-judge people but there's no way I would have taken Clement for a train enthusiast.

"You obviously know what this is." I remark.

"Yeah, I do," he replies, still eyeing the outside of the carriage with obvious interest. "This old girl used to run under the streets of London."

"Are you an enthusiast?"

He ducks through the open door into the carriage without a reply. I shake my head and follow him in.

The inside of the carriage is in better condition than the outside but still a world away from the interior of modern trains. The window frames are in varnished wood and the seats heavily sprung like an old sofa. I take one of those seats while Clement continues his inspection.

He eventually joins me as the trains sets off. As we reach speed, the carriage fills with a cacophony of whines and clickety clacks, reminiscent of today's London Underground. Close your eyes and you could just as easily be on the Bakerloo Line.

Clement appears mesmerised but it's too noisy in the carriage to question his reasons. I turn my attention to the darkening view outside, leaving him to indulge whatever trainspotter fantasy he's engaged in.

We stop at four stations, too briefly to allow any meaningful conversation, and arrive in Sandown a little after twelve. Thankfully our arrival coincides with a break in the rain. As we stand outside the station, Clement returns his attention to the matter in hand.

"How far is her gaff from here then?"

I extract my phone and waste a minute familiarising myself with the map function.

"A ten minute walk."

"Good. You ready for this?"

I'm not sure I am. The journey here has provided a welcome distraction from the purpose, but with just a short walk to our final destination there is nothing to focus on other than the imminent challenge.

A ten-minute walk followed by either a constructive discussion, or a door slammed in our faces.

Soon enough I'll know which.

18.

The Isle of Wight is just twenty-five miles across, and thirteen miles north to south. Clement's long strides make it feel even smaller as the duration of our walk turns out to be less than seven minutes. The blusterous tail wind probably helped.

Too soon, we're stood in front of a semi-detached bungalow in a quiet cul-de-sac.

"Ready, Bill? Now or never."

Never would be my preference but I have no choice. With Clement at my heels, I make my way up the path to the front door.

I ring the bell.

Seconds pass and the knot in my stomach returns with an ever-tightening vengeance.

The door opens.

"Yes?" comes the curt greeting.

A woman, who I assume to be Susan Davies, stands in the doorway. The years don't appear to have been kind and it's hard to imagine this frumpy, grey haired woman was once the object of my father's desires; for one night at least.

"Susan Davies?"

She eyes me suspiciously. "Who are you?"

"We're looking for Susan Davies," I repeat. "Would that be you?"

"Tell me who you are and I'll answer your question."

"I'm, William, and this is my friend, Clement…"

I don't want to offer my surname yet for fear she'll slam the door in my face, and I'm suddenly minded I don't even know Clement's surname.

"And what do you want?" she asks, her tone spiky.

"Well, assuming you are Susan Davies, I was hoping we could have a chat."

"About what?"

"It's a bit sensitive and I'd rather not discuss it on your doorstep."

She sighs but finally relents. "Yes, I'm Susan Davies. And you've got five minutes."

I wasn't sure what to expect but I hoped Susan might be a little more friendly than this frosty harridan. Nevertheless, I follow her into the hallway and through to a twelve-foot square lounge. The tight space is crammed with mismatched furniture including two armchairs, a small sofa, three overstocked bookcases, and several wall-mounted shelves laden with cheap ornaments.

"Take a seat," she mumbles, waving a hand at the sofa.

I do as instructed while Clement stands in the doorway. Susan glances in his direction but seems indifferent to his presence as she lowers her plump frame into one of the armchairs.

"Come on then. What is it you want?" she mumbles.

"It's a long story."

"Well make it short," she snaps back.

"Fair enough. I'll get straight to the point — Charles Huxley was my father."

I wait for a reaction but other than a slight twitch in her left cheek, she doesn't erupt as I feared she might. I press on.

"And your daughter, Gabby, is…how can I put this…blackmailing me."

Her eyes narrow but there's no immediate response to my bombshell. I expected something more than the stony glare she's offering.

"Did you hear me, Susan. Your daughter has recently discovered who her father is, and she's using that fact to blackmail me."

A clock ticks somewhere in the room but otherwise silence fills the air.

"So?" she eventually grunts.

"So I was hoping you would talk to her."

"And say what?"

Agitation prickles but I try to keep my voice calm. "I'd like her to stop, obviously, and I assumed she might listen to you."

Susan shrugs her shoulders. "Nothing to do with me."

"What do you mean it has nothing to do with you? It has everything to do with you. I assume it was you who gave her the birth certificate and my father's letter which, I might add, was not yours to share. How did you even get hold of it?"

She shuffles in her chair but doesn't answer.

"Well?" I bark, my patience wearing thin.

"I'd like you to leave now."

"Hold on a second. I've just told you that your daughter is blackmailing me and you couldn't be less interested. You do realise blackmail is a serious crime."

"You better call the police then," she snipes.

An obvious suggestion but not an option.

"And that's okay with you, Susan? You don't mind if Gabby is sent to prison for blackmail?"

"She's bloody minded, that one — always has been. She won't listen to me even if I wanted to intervene."

I'm about to try pleading when Clement steps across the room and stands next to the sofa.

"Oi. Look at me," he growls at Susan.

She looks up at him but remains impassive. The tone of his voice is far from friendly but as Susan appears unwilling to listen to reason, I'm prepared to let Clement try his approach, to a point.

"Do you know what the mad bitch did?" he says.

Another shrug of the shoulders.

"She slept with Bill here, and then told the poor bloke she's his sister. What sort of fucked up chick does something like that?"

I stare up at Clement, horrified he chose to reveal the specifics of my tawdry secret. However, when I turn back to Susan, it's her expression that stuns me. There's not even a hint of shock or disgust. In fact, it appears the old woman is not to be intimidated and she glares back at Clement.

"Good on her," she spits.

She then fixes her glare on me. "The way your father treated us, I hope Gabby takes your every last penny. She's entitled to it as far as I'm concerned."

"I'm not debating the fact she's entitled to something," I plea. "I offered her my flat in London, and if you need money I'm willing to help. What my father did was totally wrong but what Gabby is doing is wrong too. Can't you see that?"

Oddly, she begins to chuckle. "You're a chip off the old block, aren't you?"

"Sorry?"

"Throw us a few crumbs and expect gratitude. Typical of your sort."

"I hardly think a two-million-pound flat in central London is a few crumbs," I scoff. "And whatever sort you think I am, you couldn't be more wrong."

We reach an impasse. The clock ticks away while both sides assess their next move. I'm out of ideas. Thankfully, Clement intervenes again.

"Let me ask you something old woman. Do you think Bill here is just gonna roll over and give her everything?"

"He will if he's got any sense."

"Oh, he's got sense alright. Trouble is, I ain't."

The twitch in her cheek becomes a spasm, flickering rapidly. "What's that supposed to mean?"

"It means I don't roll over for no one. I suggest you and your daughter take Bill's generous offer while it's on the table."

"Or what?"

Clement leans forward and looks Susan straight in the eye. "Or, sweetheart, there won't be an offer, and I'll take over proceedings."

Her expression changes and the defiance withers. But as much as I might find some hope in Susan's sudden change in demeanour, I really hope I haven't misjudged Clement's temperament.

"You've got till Monday to call the dogs off," he adds. "Otherwise the rules change. That nutter might think she's got Bill in a corner, but he ain't alone, and I'm no stranger to helping people out of corners. It's what I do...by any means."

His final three words are delivered with enough intonation to make his position clear. I'm pretty sure he's strayed beyond our agreed strategy but for the first time since Gabby delivered her ultimatum, the balance of power appears to have swung a few degrees in my direction.

"I think we're done here," I say. "But as Clement says, Gabby has until five o'clock on Monday and then my offer of the London flat will be withdrawn. I think that's more than fair, considering the circumstances. Don't you?"

She doesn't answer.

"Goodbye, Susan. We'll see ourselves out."

We leave her sitting shell shocked in the armchair.

Once we're the other side of the front door, I release a sigh of relief almost as strong as the gusting winds that greet us.

"That went better than I expected."

"She knew we were coming."

"You think so?"

"Yeah. She didn't bat an eyelid when I said what her daughter had been up to."

On reflection, I shouldn't be surprised Gabby covered all her bases, and it's not unreasonable to think her mother was in on it. It seems sick that she would condone Gabby's tactics, but I'm seldom surprised by how low some people are prepared to sink to get what they want.

"Anyway, I thought the way you handled her was superb. It never crossed my mind to counter her threat with one of my own."

"Just common sense, Bill. Dunno why you're offering her your bleedin' flat though."

"Because, Clement, she grew up with nothing, and that no doubt contributed to her angst. No matter what the flat is worth, it's a small price to pay to settle my father's debt and get Gabby off my back."

"If you say so. Your money, mate."

"It is, and if Mrs Davies tells Gabby we're serious about pulling that offer, she'd be mad not to accept."

"Trouble is, Bill, we know she is mad."

I don't share Clement's reticence at the outcome. While there's no doubting Gabby is quite deranged, only a fool would chance losing two million pounds whilst risking the wrath of a man like Clement. I'm not sure what we're to do if she passes on my offer, but I'm quietly confident she won't.

"Well, I think we've put a pretty compelling case forward. I wouldn't be surprised if I receive a text from Gabby in the next few hours, accepting the offer."

"Hope you're right, Bill."

We make our way back along the cul-de-sac.

"To be honest with you, Clement, I had reservations about today, but I'm both glad and grateful you came along. Thank you."

"Thank me when we know for sure she's done with you."

"Of course, but I didn't want you to think I don't appreciate your input."

"It's alright. You can buy me lunch to show your appreciation."

"It would be my pleasure, although I'm not sure what the restaurants are like in Sandown."

"Do I look like the sort of bloke who eats in restaurants?"

"Um…"

"Let's just find a cafe where I can get a mug of tea and a fry-up. That'll do me."

"A fry-up sounds perfect. I'm pretty sure there are a few cafes towards the front."

After a quick check of the location on my phone, we head towards the sea front.

What we find as we turn onto the esplanade, a few minutes later, is a depressing view of a typically downtrodden seaside town in October.

"Shit. What happened here?" Clement remarks.

"What do you mean?"

"Look at the place. I know it's October but this ain't like any seaside town I remember."

His observation is valid. It's a bleak scene of boarded-up amusement arcades, empty shops, and once-grand hotels entombed in wire fencing; prepped for demolition.

"It's a similar story in many seaside towns, I'm afraid. When was the last time you visited one?"

"Clacton-on-Sea. A long time ago."

"It must have been a long time ago because the rot set in several decades back. A consequence of cheap overseas holidays with guaranteed sunshine — hard to compete with."

If the sorry view wasn't depressing enough, the backdrop of black clouds does little to improve it. Coupled with the bitter wind rolling off an angry sea and I can quite see why people would rather spend their autumn break in the Mediterranean.

With fear of being blown from the promenade, we retreat to a side street. Good fortune favours us when we stumble across a small cafe, still open.

As we step through the door we immediately double their customer count; an elderly couple, seated by the window their only other patrons.

We take a seat and a middle-aged woman gratefully takes our order. As she returns to the kitchen, I can't help but feel sympathy. Chances are, this little cafe is hanging on by the skin of its teeth and I'd be surprised if it sees another summer.

The woman returns after ten minutes with two enormous plates. Spain may have its tapas, Italy its pasta dishes, but nowhere in the world can you enjoy an all-day breakfast quite like those served in a British seaside cafe. Clement destroys his in minutes.

"Hungry were we?" I comment.

He stretches his arms before patting his belly in appreciation. "Peckish, mate, and that was good."

Such is the generous portion size, I can't quite finish mine.

I pay the bill and leave a generous tip. As we ready ourselves to leave, the black clouds offload and fat droplets of rain pepper the windows.

"I don't fancy a soaking. Maybe we should get a cab to the station," I suggest.

Clement nods and I ask the waitress if she knows a local cab number. She goes one better and calls a cab for us.

Two minutes later, we depart the cafe and hurry through the torrential rain into the back of a waiting saloon. The car is in almost as sorry a state as the town in which it operates. The driver asks if we're on holiday. I'm not sure if he's being sarcastic or he's a deluded optimist, but a glare from Clement makes it clear we're not looking for a conversation.

With the windscreen wipers going full tilt, we make the short journey to the station, arriving minutes later. Another dart through the rain and we reach the ticket hall at Sandown station.

Much like the town itself, the place is deserted apart from a weary looking chap at the ticket kiosk. I enquire about the departure time for the next train to Ryde.

"Twenty minutes," he replies.

"Thank you."

"Are you heading back to the mainland?"

"We are."

"Were," he replies with a smirk.

"I beg your pardon."

"All the ferries have been cancelled due to the weather."

"Seriously? Until when?"

"Tomorrow morning at the earliest. They reckon this storm is set to stay for the next twelve hours."

"There must be another way back to the mainland, surely?"

"You might be able to charter a boat from Cowes, if you can find a skipper stupid or desperate enough. Won't come cheap, mind."

I relay the news to Clement. It's not well received.

"I ain't getting on no boat to be tossed around like a bleedin' cork."

"It'll only be for forty minutes or so."

"Listen, Bill. I could just about stomach the ferry but I ain't getting on a tiny boat. It ain't happening."

"I don't see what the big deal is, Clement. I'm sure it's perfectly safe, even in this weather."

"Yeah. Perfectly safe, right up until it capsizes."

His stern glare tells me this is not an argument I'm likely to win.

"Fine. Looks like we've no choice but to stay here for the night."

I reluctantly refer to my phone and search for local hotels. Google return a selection of grim, two and three-star establishments in Sandown. I search in Ryde and it's even worse so I return to the Sandown search. The only saving grace is they're all fairly inexpensive and rooms are, unsurprisingly, in plentiful supply.

"There's a hotel a few streets away."

We both look towards the glass doors we just entered. On cue, wind whistles past the frame as a curtain of rain sweeps across the pavement.

"Taxi?" Clement suggests.

"Agreed."

I find a number for a local cab firm. Seconds later a familiar battered saloon pulls up by the doors.

"I think he was still parked outside," I surmise.

Two minutes and five pounds later, we arrive at the Sandown Bay Hotel. Our third dash through the wind and rain leaves my corduroy trousers feeling decidedly damp and my usually neat hair in something of a state.

I catch a glance of the hotel's facade on the way in and it doesn't inspire confidence in my choice of accommodation. The picture on the website was of a bright white building set against a cloudless blue sky, with hanging baskets full of colourful flowers either side of the door. Today, it looks like a Victorian sanatorium.

By the time we reach the gloomy reception area, I have already decided to call the cab firm again. Alas, we're spotted by the receptionist before that call can be made.

"Good afternoon, gents," she chimes. "I just heard about the ferries. Are you after a room?"

I turn to face a woman with auburn hair and piercing green eyes. She has the same look on her face as the waitress in the cafe — like Benson the Labrador; grateful for whatever scraps are offered, no matter how meagre.

Clement answers before I have the opportunity to discuss my reservations. "Yeah."

Her face lights up and my hopes of going elsewhere suddenly feel like a guilty secret. Resigned, I approach the reception desk.

"A twin room, please. One night."

She jots down my details and confirms her name as Emma. It turns out she's the co-owner of the Sandown Bay Hotel, together with her elderly mother who used to run the place with her late father. I don't make a habit of chatting to hotel receptionists but Emma is a friendly soul and I suspect, glad of the conversation.

"If you need anything just call down to reception."

"Right. Thank you.

"I'll show you up to your room."

She leads us along a corridor and up a flight of stairs. As I suspected, the place is in a fairly poor state of repair but I don't voice my opinion. As we navigate the final corridor, I take the opportunity to check my phone, just in case Gabby has texted me to accept the offer. Nothing.

"Here we are. This is our best twin room."

She opens the door and invites us to enter; the same hopeful look on her face.

I take four steps beyond the door and as many decades into the past; such are the aged furnishings and decor. I remind myself we're only here for the night and confirm to Emma the room is lovely. It is not. She hands me the key and hurries away, presumably before we change our minds.

"What a dump," I grumble to myself while inspecting a shabby chest of drawers.

"You said it was lovely," Clement remarks.

"I was being polite. It's as grim as the weather."

He flops down on one of the single beds. The springs groan and twang at the sudden load.

"I like it."

Considering his attire is rooted in the seventies, I shouldn't be surprised.

"Well, we're here now so it'll have to do, I suppose."

"What's the time?"

"Two thirty."

"What do you wanna do then?"

"Do?"

"Yeah. I ain't sitting here till tomorrow morning."

To say we have limited options would be an understatement. What does anyone do in a near-deserted seaside town in October, in the midst of a storm?

"Pub?"

He sits up. "Good call."

I'm not sure it is.

19.

We return to the reception and find Emma staring into space. She snaps to attention upon spotting us.

"Off out are we gents?"

"We are," I reply. "Assuming the crazy golf isn't open, can you recommend any decent pubs in the area."

She chuckles at my quip and steps beyond the reception desk.

"I know a nice place a few minutes away. I'll run you down there."

"Honestly, there's really no need."

"It's no trouble. I could do with getting out for ten minutes."

"If you're sure."

Her smile confirms she is and we follow her out to the small car park fronting the hotel. As soon as we clap eyes on the tiny hatchback, it's clear I'll be sitting in the rear seats. I clamber in and Clement shoehorns himself into the passenger seat. Once we're all secured, Emma revs the weedy engine and pulls onto the main road. If not for our combined weight, I'm almost certain the car would be blown from the road like a paper bag.

"So, what do you chaps do when you're not stranded in Sandown?" Emma asks.

Clement remains mute so I feel compelled to answer.

"I work at Westminster."

"Oh, how fascinating. Doing what?"

When people ask what you do for a living, generally it's just small talk and they have no real interest in what you actually do. Not Emma, apparently.

"I'm a member of parliament."

She turns to face me; a concern, considering we're travelling at thirty miles per hour.

"I should be honoured you're staying with us then," she chuckles.

I offer an embarrassed smile and mercifully, Emma returns her attention to the road.

"I'd love to see Westminster Palace one day," she says wistfully. "Such incredible architecture."

I'm slightly taken aback by her statement. Usually when I tell people my profession, they almost always ask if I know the Prime Minister and what she's really like.

"You should. It's the most remarkable building."

"I'll get there at some point. What with running the hotel and looking after Mum, there aren't enough hours in the day."

"Surely it's quiet enough in the winter months for you to take a day trip to London?"

"Deathly quiet, but the bills still need to be paid. From November through to March I work as a seamstress making curtains for a company on the mainland, just to make ends meet."

That would explain why the hotel is in such a poor state of repair. My derogatory comments may, in hindsight, have been a little harsh.

"Well, if you ever do get the chance, I'd be more than happy to show you around."

Emma glances at me in the rear-view mirror. Despite the smile, her expression suggests she doesn't expect to visit anytime soon.

A silent minute passes until we pull up outside a double-fronted pub.

"Here we are gents. The Bay View Inn."

"Can I give you something towards petrol?" I ask.

"Don't be silly. And if you need a lift back later, just call the hotel."

I withdraw a ten pound note from my wallet. "If you don't take this, Emma, I will be mortally offended."

She pauses for a second but relents and takes the note. "Thank you."

Once we've contorted our way onto the pavement, we wave her off and the tiny car disappears back down the road. Hopefully it won't be blown into the sea.

"She's very pleasant," I casually remark.

"Word of advice," Clement shouts above the howling wind. "Check you're not related before you make a move."

Before I can offer a defence, he turns and makes a beeline for the front door of the pub. I shake my head and follow.

The Bay View Inn turns out to be a very pleasant establishment. We opt for the saloon bar where a log fire crackles away in an inglenook fireplace. Unlike many modern pubs, there is nothing fake about the interior; the oak beams and exposed brick form the very fabric of the building. Even the handful of customers appear part of the furniture, and accordingly eye us with suspicion as the obvious non-locals we are.

As there is every chance we could be holed up in here for some time, I order just half a pint for myself. Clement requests a pint of lager.

Furnished with drinks, we take a seat at a table near the fireplace. I check my phone but still nothing from Gabby.

"Nice boozer," Clement remarks.

"Yes, it's very pleasant. I can certainly think of worse places to spend an afternoon."

He nods in reply.

We take occasional sips of our drinks in silence, but there is only so long you can gaze around a room and avoid conversation.

"So, tell me a bit about yourself, Clement. I'm intrigued about your previous career."

"Not much to tell."

"You must have a few interesting tales, surely?"

"A few."

"Care to share any?"

He takes a gulp of lager before answering. "Do you read much, Bill?"

"A little. Why?"

"Ever heard of the author, Beth Baxter?"

"I think I've seen posters on the tube, promoting one of her books."

"My last job was helping her out of a hole."

It seems an odd combination; a successful author and a man like Clement. Then again, it's probably no odder than the predicament which has thrown us together.

"Okay, now I'm more than intrigued. Tell me more."

"Read her book, *The Angel of Camden*."

"Are you not going to tell me anything."

"Just read the book, Bill. Everything will make sense."

That line of conversation is now closed, apparently.

After another round of drinks, we venture into the public bar to find a pool table and a juke box. I've only ever played pool a handful of times but I'm grateful of having something to do other than sit and force conversation.

As it transpires, even if I was any good at pool I'm certain I'd have still lost eight consecutive games, such is Clement's skill with a cue.

Five thirty rolls around and I'm about to rack up the ninth game when the barman interrupts. "Sorry gents. We've got to move the pool table so can you make that your last game."

"Move it where?" Clement replies.

"Out back. We've got to clear this bar for tonight."

"Tonight?"

The barman looks at him, puzzled. "Err, yes. Tonight."

Clement returns an equally puzzled look so the barman points at a poster, fixed to the wall behind the bar.

The big man's face lights up. "A seventies night?"

"Yes, with a prize for the best fancy dress. Sorry mate, I assumed you knew, what with your…outfit."

I have a horrible feeling I know precisely what Clement is about to say next.

"Cool. Give us two tickets, mate."

The barman confirms we're in luck as there are only a handful left, and Clement pays him. He then strides over to me, apparently keen to share our new plans for the evening.

"Sounds like it'll be a cracking night, Bill."

I am far from convinced. I was hoping for a quiet meal and an early night.

"I'm not sure it's really my cup of tea."

"Shut up. You could do with letting your hair down after all the shit you've been through."

It is illegal to drive having consumed more than two pints, and for good reason — it severely impairs one's judgement. I have had the equivalent of three pints, and therefore I really shouldn't rely upon my own judgement, let alone Clement's.

Inevitably, alcohol wins the argument. "Oh, what the heck. Okay."

"Good man. We'll have a right laugh — few beers, bit of dancing, checking out the local talent."

He playfully digs his elbow into my ribs. I try to hide a wince behind a thin smile.

"Well, I'm not so sure about two of those suggestions, but a few beers, certainly."

Decision made and my fate sealed, we return to the other bar. Despite our sizable lunch, additional food is required to further line my stomach. I order a few rounds of sandwiches which we consume as the bar begins to fill.

By seven o'clock, Clement's attire is no longer the oddest in the room as dozens of people mill around in excited anticipation of the night's entertainment. Just my luck I happen to be in the only place on the island where my conservative attire looks out of place. Still, at least I'm not wearing a fire hazard, unlike the army of polyester-clad revellers.

Clement, though, doesn't appear to appreciate the fancy dress efforts.

"That lot are taking the piss," he complains, nodding at one particular group decked in bushy wigs and flared trousers.

"In what way?"

"Nobody dressed like that in the seventies. They look right clowns."

"I don't think they're trying for an authentic representation, Clement. Anyway, what makes you an authority on seventies fashion?"

"Experience."

"Right," I reply with some hesitation. "Is that why you dress like…that?"

"That?"

"Your style is very much rooted in the past, wouldn't you say?"

"This is designer garb, Bill. Got it from one of the best outfitters on Carnaby Street."

"I'm sure it is designer, or was…four decades ago," I chuckle.

Having spent some time in his company, and bolstered by alcohol, I hope I've got the measure of his humour correct.

"Cheeky git," he replies with a grin. I breathe a sigh of relief.

By seven o'clock, the room is rammed and we can barely hear ourselves over the chatter. Clement seems to be revelling in the atmosphere though, and twice he disappears outside for a cigarette, returning on each occasion with a different woman in tow. I watch him as he stands at the bar, engaged in conversation with the second woman; a blonde with an inappropriately short dress, giggling, and overly tactile. Men like Clement appear able to turn on the charm whenever the need arises, and I hate to admit it, but it's a skill of which I'm deeply envious.

He eventually extracts himself from the blonde woman's clutches and returns to our table.

"You alright, Bill? Not mingling?"

"I'm not really the mingling type."

"No better time to try. There's some cracking birds in here."

"Birds?"

"Yeah, you know. Chicks."

"I understand the reference, Clement, I just don't think it's an appropriate label in this day and age."

He shrugs his shoulder. "You need to lighten up, mate."

"I'm sorry."

"Ever wonder why you're still single?"

"Frequently."

"It's all well and good being a gent, mate, but women like a bloke with a bit of an edge. You know, unpredictable, fun."

"I can be fun," I reply with little conviction.

"Not with that rod stuck up your arse, you can't. I'll get another round in; see if that helps to shift it."

He heads back to the bar, leaving me to consider his advice.

I should be offended but if anything, I appreciate his candour. Life, alas, does not come with an instruction manual, and few people have the self-awareness to realise where they're going wrong. However, knowing I need to remove that theoretical rod from my posterior doesn't make the task any easier.

Clement returns and hands me a pint, rather than the half I wanted. I decide to pick up the conversation from where we left it.

"How do you do it then, Clement?"

"Do what?"

"Interact with females."

He shakes his head. "For starters, stop using terms like, 'interact with females'. You make it sound like a scientific experiment."

"Okay. How do you chat up women?"

"You don't."

"Sorry. I don't understand."

I wait for him to expand on his answer.

"Well? What's the secret?" I ask again, losing patience.

"There's no secret, Bill, and chat up lines are bullshit. You just gotta do what it said on that silver box."

At first I don't quite comprehend what he's referring to. Then, memories of Wednesday evening return, and the pewter box Gabby delivered to my table in Fitzgerald's.

"Qui Estis — be who you are," I mumble to myself.

"You reckon that box belonged to your old man?" Clement asks.

"I'm not sure. Maybe. Probably."

He leans across the table and fixes his blue eyes on mine. "Maybe he was trying to tell you something?"

"I doubt it," I scoff. "It's just a worthless bit of mass produced tat. I don't know how it came into his possession but I think you might be reading too much into it."

"You said it yourself, though, Bill. You fell out, and you've spent the last ten years trying to be the bloke he wanted you to be."

I stare back at him, incredulous. "And you seriously think my father's dying wishes were to let me know I should just be myself? Come off it, Clement."

"Who knows? But I'd bet my last fiver you don't even know who you are. Work that out, mate, and you might find it easier chatting to women."

"Well, thank you for the counselling," I reply dismissively. "But I know precisely who I am."

"Tell me then — who are you? Politician? Bachelor? Loner? Strikes me you're all those things but don't wanna be any of them."

Without waiting for my answer, he gets up and pulls a cigarette packet from his pocket. "Think on, Bill. I'm going for a smoke."

I watch him make his way through the crowd towards the beer garden, from where he'll no doubt return with another woman in toe. Seconds later, the door to the other bar is opened and the revellers are invited in. Quickly, the room empties, leaving myself and a handful of other patrons in relative peace.

Perhaps it's just the alcohol, but Clement's words sit heavy. Notwithstanding the fact his assessment is worryingly accurate, what troubles me to a greater degree is that I'm so obviously transparent. Either that, or Clement has an almost uncanny gift for reading people. I only armed him with minimal information about my life, yet he's pasted together a perfectly reasonable theorem; a theorem which is as reassuring as it is unsettling.

Something tells me there is more to my denim-clad friend than meets the eye.

20.

I had hoped to sit in the quiet bar and reflect. I'd have been quite happy to do that for an hour or two, in lieu of attending a noisy, boisterous seventies party.

Clement ensured it was never an option.

Nine o'clock and the party is in full swing, although I'm reluctant to participate. I have secured a table in a dark corner where I can watch the evening unfold and remain anonymous. It suits me just fine.

There must be over a hundred people crammed in the public bar. A mobile disco has been set up in the opposite corner from my table, and the space where the pool table stood is now a makeshift dance floor. The disc jockey's voice is loud and irritating, as are the tracks he deems suitable to play.

As I watch the ever-growing number of people attempting to dance, Clement returns, holding a tray.

"These should liven things up," he says, placing the tray on the table.

Laid out are ten small glasses, each containing a clear liquid.

"Ten shots for a tenner," Clement beams. "Couldn't resist it."

"Ten shots of what exactly?"

"Dunno. I think the barman said Sambuca or something like that."

"I don't even know what that is."

"Who cares. Ready?"

"Ready for what?"

He plucks two of the miniature glasses from the tray and places one in front of me.

"Down in one. Then we move on to the next."

"This seems highly irresponsible, Clement."

"Exactly. Grab your glass."

Despite my reticence, I surmise it would be ill mannered, and probably futile, to decline his generosity. I tentatively take the glass between my thumb and forefinger, and raise it to my nose. There's a strong scent of something familiar but I can't quite place it.

"Ready?" Clement booms. "Three...two...one..."

I tip the clear liquid into my mouth and swallow. The taste is not unpleasant, nor as harsh as whisky or brandy.

"Next one."

I am aware of the concept of downing shots but I don't understand the reasoning behind it. Surely if one wanted to consume a drink in such quantities, why not simply order one large glass? It would make far more sense.

Nevertheless, I down the second shot.

"Again."

The third, fourth, and fifth drinks are subsequently dispatched in a timely manner. I am none the wiser to the appeal.

"Your round," Clement orders. "Same again."

"What? You want more?"

"It's only fair, Bill."

"I really..."

"Go on, get 'em in."

I slope over to the bar and return five minutes later with another tray of glasses.

"Do you think we should pace ourselves this time?" I ask.

"Nah, think of it as Dutch courage. By the time you down these, you'll be chattin' with the chicks in no time."

It feels a hollow claim, but as Clement already has his sixth glass at the ready I don't appear to have much say in the matter. Five more shots are quickly dispatched.

So much alcohol consumed in such a short space of time — surely not a good idea. Clement disappears for his umpteenth cigarette of the evening, leaving me to ponder my reckless actions. Minutes pass and a melancholy haze descends; not unpleasant but I fear it's the calm before the storm. I decide to switch my phone off, for fear I might send a drunken text to Gabby, or even worse, one of my colleagues.

I stare at the dance floor which is now heaving with revellers. I've always considered dancing to be a peculiar pastime, and one I've never had cause to participate in. Is it a function we're able to instinctively execute, like walking, or must it be learnt, like swimming?

I watch on with mild fascination.

The record ends and the disc jockey introduces *Mamma Mia* by ABBA. His choice of track is met with an enthusiastic cheer. As the music begins, bodies bob up and down, and arms sway. Feet shuffle left and right, back and forth. It's an unsynchronised melee of obvious joy.

It looks enticing.

I tap my feet beneath the table. Somewhere from the deepest recesses of my mind, the words to the chorus spring forth. The foot tapping increases in intensity as I find myself singing along; substituting the words I don't know with alternatives unlikely to be found in the Oxford Dictionary.

Probably the Sambuca, but an inner-glow develops.

All too soon the record ends. I'm disappointed. The disc jockey announces the next record to an even louder cheer — *Tiger Feet* by Mud. I know the tune but the words are a mystery.

Clearly a popular choice, the crowd swells. Then I spot him; stood on the very edge of the dance floor.

"What are you doing, Clement?" I slur to myself.

It soon becomes clear this particular piece of music has an accompanying set of dance moves. With legs astride, thumbs are tucked into trouser pockets, elbows pointed out. The actual move involves bending forward with alternate thrusts of each shoulder. This is followed by a series of steps where the back leg crosses over the front in an approximation of stepping backwards and forwards.

Despite the apparent simplicity of the moves, many on the dance floor appear unable to master them. One man has them down to a tee though.

I have no idea if Clement's moves are correct, but they certainly have a fluidity to them. He moves with surprising grace for such a big man; a fact not lost on the gathered crowd as some try to copy him while others simply stand and watch, clapping in time to the music. Unsurprisingly, many of the gathered crowd, and the most engaged, are female. How does he do it?

The track comes to an end with a raucous cheer and more clapping. Half a dozen women buzz around Clement but he waves them away and barrels through the crowd towards the disc jockey. Words are exchanged and Clement makes his way back to the centre of the dance floor.

The disc jockey's voice booms from the speakers.

"You wanna do that again?" he roars.

The crowd cheers to confirm they do.

"This time we've got a request for somebody to join us on the dance floor," the disc jockey continues. "Where are you, Bill? Come on!"

The crowd turns and faces scan the room in search of Bill so they can get on with enjoying themselves. All those people waiting for him — poor Bill has my sympathy.

What occurs next is the stuff of nightmares. Clement points in my direction and every face in the crowd follows his finger. Realisation dawns.

I'm Bill. Shit.

This can't be happening. I can't dance. I don't even know if I'm capable of standing unaided.

"Bill! Bill! Bill!" chant the crowd as they clap in time. Stood in the centre of the braying masses is Clement — a broad grin on his face.

There is one door out of the public bar and it's situated the other side of the dance floor. I am trapped, again.

You utter bastard, Clement.

The chanting becomes louder, the clapping more intense. In my drunken mind, a plan forms. I'll go over there, and once the music starts and their attention is elsewhere, I'll make my escape. Simple, but hopefully effective.

I stand up and the crowd cheer. As excruciatingly embarrassing as the situation is, I find a smile and even a timid wave as I shuffle slowly towards them. As I get within fifteen feet, Clement breaks through the crowd and steps towards me. He reaches out a hand and clasps my upper arm like a vice.

"Come on then, Billy Boy," he yells.

I'm unceremoniously pulled into the very centre of the dance floor. It appears my plan is about to be stamped upon by dozens of feet; primarily of the tiger variety.

The music begins and another cheer goes up. The crowd tightens around me, closing off any hope of escape.

As the guitar riff builds, Clement leans forward and shouts instructions in my ear. "Just copy me. You'll be fine."

I stare up at him in much the same way I might if Usain Bolt had suggested I could be a world-class athlete just by copying him. Before I can argue, I'm taken through the moves which I attempt to replicate, each with toe-curling awkwardness.

Further advice is proffered. "Nobody gives a shit if you can't dance, Bill. Just relax and enjoy yourself."

With little alternative, I try.

Then, a minute into the song, something remarkable happens. No doubt aided by the sheer volume of alcohol in my bloodstream, I actually start to get some rhythm going. My movements are still jerky, and several times I step when I'm supposed to thrust, but there is definite progress.

Against all expectations, I feel a sudden rush of euphoria. I'm actually dancing and nobody is staring at me, nobody laughing at me. It is an intoxicating sensation unlike anything I've felt before. It engulfs me and thoughts of Gabby, of my father's infidelity, and my tedious career are all lost in the moment.

All too soon, the track ends and the disc jockey's shrill voice bursts my bubble. He declares the buffet open and a stampede ensues; the dance floor left empty besides myself and Clement, and two middle-aged women.

"Bill, this is Jackie and…"

"Sandra," one of the two women shrieks.

I look up at Clement and he winks. "These two lovely ladies are gonna join us for a drink."

Lovely is pushing it. *Ladies* a blatant mis-description. Jackie is the same short-dressed woman I spotted with Clement earlier, and she appears to have claimed him now; her arm locked around his. Sandra must be close to fifty; her dress too short and makeup too heavy. Still, I suppose it might be nice to have some female company.

"Right. Great," the new carefree, drunk version of me replies.

Our odd foursome heads back to the table in the corner.

"You make yourselves comfortable, girls. We'll get the drinks in," Clement says. "What's your poison?"

"Bacardi and coke, doubles," Jackie replies.

Clement nods towards the bar and I take his lead. As we wait to be served, he offers his insight on our new friends.

"Got ourselves a couple of right sorts, Bill. Play your cards right and I reckon you're in there."

Under any other circumstance, I'd already be assessing the practicalities of such an endeavour, and the morality. And given my recent experience, it is also beyond foolish to even consider such a liaison. However, my drunken self appears less concerned.

"Oh. How lovely."

Armed with two pints and drinks for the apparent ladies, we return to the table. They are, if nothing else, grateful. As soon as Clement takes his seat, Jackie sits on his lap and drapes an arm around his shoulder. For one horrifying moment, I fear Sandra might do the same. I cross my legs, just in case.

My lap out of bounds, Sandra leans in and attempts conversation.

"Thanks for the drink, darling," she slurs. Incredibly, I suspect she's even more intoxicated than I am.

"You're most welcome."

She leans in further. "You're really posh."

"Am I?"

"Yeah. You got manners like a proper gent."

"Thank you."

"I love your voice. Like those blokes from Downton Abbey."

I look beyond her shoulder where Jackie is attempting to eat Clement's face. I need to keep Sandra talking, should I befall the same fate.

"Never watched Downton Abbey, I'm afraid. What other shows do you like?"

While I wait for her to answer, I keep my mouth protected by sipping my ale. I really shouldn't be consuming more alcohol but I'm not taking any chances.

"Ooo…lots of things," she purrs. "I love watching porn, too."

I almost choke. "Oh, that's…nice."

I suddenly feel a hand on my knee. Sandra stares at me with what I assume is supposed to be an alluring smile. The hand then moves up my thigh. If she thinks anything is likely to stir, she's much mistaken.

Before I can return to my pint, it happens. Her mouth engulfs mine and a squid-like tongue invades.

Shocked into inaction, I consider how best to react? My sober self would immediately pull away, but I find myself strangely flattered by Sandra's attention. She's no oil painting, but then again, neither am I. Clement's words of advice return. He was right on that occasion so maybe I should just relax and enjoy myself.

To hell with it. I embrace Sandra's probing tongue as her hand unzips my fly.

"What the fuck?" a voice suddenly roars.

I pull away.

Two men are stood to the side of Sandra. Both have receding hairlines and jowly faces. Neither looks happy.

"Can I help you?" I enquire.

"That's my ex you're fucking around with," the one on the left replies.

"Ex? Ex what?"

"Girlfriend, you muppet."

I stare up at him, annoyed as much as confused. "If you're no longer in a relationship with Sandra, I fail to see why our liaison is any of your concern."

Judging by his deepening scowl, I fear my statement has not clarified the situation. He takes a step forward.

"No, Barry," Sandra pleads. "Leave him alone."

Barry chooses not to heed Sandra's advice and steps even closer.

"Get up," he orders.

"Why?"

"I'm not gonna punch a man sat down."

"I'll stay here then, thanks."

It seems Barry won't take no for an answer as he moves towards me. He grabs a handful of my pullover, and before my brain can engage a reaction, pulls me to my feet. One of his hands releases the hold on my pullover and a fist is formed. I'm pretty certain I know what's coming next.

As Barry's arm winds up to deliver a punch, a voice pulls his attention momentarily.

"Oi! Dickhead."

Clement unleashes a ferocious jab into Barry's ribs. He instantly collapses to the floor and assumes the foetal position, clutching his stomach. I turn to his companion, and not unsurprisingly, he's already scampering away, leaving Barry to suffer on his own. Some friend.

Clement nods in my direction before returning to his chair. "Where were we?" he says to Jackie, matter-of-factly.

It appears Sandra is more concerned with Barry's welfare than continuing our petting, so I console myself with a large gulp of ale. As I drink, I spot a troubling sight from the corner of my eye.

Barry's companion has returned with reinforcements — four of them to be precise.

"Shit. Clement!" I yell.

He turns to the cause of my panic. "For fucks sake," he grumbles.

Jackie is unceremoniously removed from his lap before he clambers back to his feet.

Faced with five men intent on causing harm, my own expression would be one of abject fear. Clement on the other hand, appears mildly irritated at the interruption. As the group of men edge ever closer, Clement picks up the chair and raises it above his head, as if weightless. The unfortunate chair is then slammed into the floor with brutal force, splintering into a dozen pieces. The leg remains in Clement's hand; a club-like weapon.

The five men converge around us.

I have never been involved in a physical altercation. Not even close. I am no coward though and despite my inebriated state, or possibly because of it, I get to my feet and stand next to Clement.

"What you doing, Bill?"

"There's five of them. I'm not going to stand by and watch you get battered."

"Sit down you soppy git," he snorts.

"Absolutely not."

Barry's companion steps forward. "You two are gonna get the kicking of your lives."

Clement turns to me, any hint of humour now gone. "Don't get in my way, Bill. I'm going for shock and awe."

Before I can object, he pushes me backwards with such force, I fall flat on my backside. In the very same second, Clement enacts his battle plan.

His use of the chair leg is devastating. Barry's companion is the first to go as Clement ducks down to evade a punch and cracks his makeshift weapon across the man's kneecap. Two of the men then try to take Clement from either side. The first is instantly floored as the chair leg meets his testicles. Every man in the room, myself included, winces. The second man fares no better as Clement straightens up from his crouched position while simultaneously delivering an uppercut to the man's jaw.

If I thought he was graceful on the dance floor, it was nothing in comparison to his prowess while fighting.

One of the two men still standing tries to catch Clement off guard by throwing a punch from the side. The big man must have seen it coming though, and stoops just in time. He retaliates with a vicious haymaker that connects with the assailant's cheek. The final man spots an opportunity and decides a swift kick might succeed where punches have failed. His left leg swings towards Clement's nether regions but fails to reach the target. Clement grabs his foot and lifts it a few inches higher. The helpless man is forced to hop on his standing leg while Clement smiles at him.

"An eye for an eye," he growls before promptly kicking the man in his now woefully exposed testicles.

More wincing ensues.

At some point during the fracas the disc jockey must have fled his post. The silence in the room is absolute for a moment, eventually punctuated by the sound of gasps and shocked mumblings, not to mention the groans of the five incapacitated men.

Clement drops the chair leg and helps me to my feet.

"Think the party might be over, Bill."

The sheer unadulterated violence I've just witnessed doesn't tally with his casual manner. I look across the bloody scene. The five assailants are now in various states of suffering and strewn across the floor like fallen soldiers on a battlefield; their wailing and groaning now the only sound in the quiet bar.

"I think you're right."

We step over one of the groaning men and the crowd parts like the Red Sea. Nobody says a word as we leave.

Back outside, beyond the killing fields of the public bar, we're greeted by two sounds: the howling wind, and the distant wail of sirens.

"Old Bill," Clement suggests.

"Could just be an ambulance. You did go a tad overboard in there."

"Dunno about you, but I'd rather not hang around to find out. Think we better head down towards the front and make our way from there."

I concur with a nod, and in near darkness, we make our way down a grassy bank towards the beach. By the time we reach the footpath at the bottom, which I hope leads us back to the hotel, the fresh air and exertion of jellied legs has exasperated my drunken stupor. With the waves crashing on my left and the footpath bathed in the orange light of street lamps, I enter a surreal world a million miles away from sobriety.

I stumble twice, find some balance, then stumble again. On the third attempt, I fail to hold my balance and end up sprawling across the pavement.

Clement offers me a hand up, together with his prognosis. "I think you're wankered, mate."

My mouth moves but nothing intelligible comes out. With Clement's assistance, I get to my feet and take a few steps forward; holding onto the big man's shoulder for support. Slow progress is made but I somehow manage to stay upright.

After a hundred yards I attempt speech again. "You're a good man, Clement," I slur.

"Yeah."

"And you're a brilliant…punchy man…fighting."

"Whatever you say, Bill."

"You really gave them what for…buggers and bastards."

"Cheers."

"Have you…hic…have you ever…lost a fight?"

"Once."

"No! Don't believe it…someone beat you?"

"Sort of. Got hit from behind with a cricket bat."

"Bloody coward. I hope…hic…I hope you got them back."

"Nope."

"No? Why not?"

"Cos' I died."

"That's…awful. I'm so sorry…my condo…my commis…I'm…"

Going to pass out?

And I do.

21.

Three times I was woken in the night: once by the wind outside and twice by the wind emanating from the adjacent single bed.

It's not quite eight o'clock and it's all I can do to lie here and stare at the ceiling. Even blinking hurts. To make matters worse, the air is laced with a stench so foul it would make a billy goat puke.

Clement grunts, rolls over, and breaks wind again.

What have I done to deserve this?

I doze for another half hour but the constant fear of suffocation proves a barrier to actual sleep. I have two choices: endure the pain of getting out of bed or stay put and suffer more of Clement's rancid flatulence.

I attempt to sit up. Every slight movement causes my brain to shift and thump against the inside of my skull — unlikely, but certainly how it feels. That same brain then provides vague flashbacks of last night. Little by little, those flashbacks all come together into one horrendous show reel, ending at the moment we left the pub. The journey back to the hotel is lost, though, and I have no recollection of how I managed it.

It's scant consolation, but I suspect six unfortunate men are feeling far worse than I do this morning.

I stumble to the bathroom and collapse in front of the toilet bowl. After several minutes of dry heaving, I clamber to my feet and lean against the sink. The view in the mirror only adds to my suffering. A face suddenly appears, reflected from the doorway beyond my shoulder.

"Morning, Bill. Sleep well?"

Dressed only in his socks and a pair of unflattering underpants, Clement ambles over to the toilet. Unabashed, he empties his bladder and breaks wind.

"Jesus, Clement. Must you?" I groan.

"What's the matter? You feeling a bit delicate?"

"I feel like death."

"You'll be fine," he chirps, still urinating. "Nothing a cooked breakfast won't sort out."

Even the thought of food induces more dry heaving.

Clement shakes himself, and just when I think he's about to leave me in peace, he pauses. Without warning, he drops his underpants and sits on the toilet.

I stare at him, open mouthed. In hindsight, I should have kept my mouth closed.

"What?" he says, staring up at me. "I need a shit."

I find a surprising turn of speed and hurry from the bathroom, closing the door on the way. To a soundtrack of grunts and groans, I locate my discarded trousers and pullover. It is with some relief I find both my phone and wallet still in my trouser pockets.

It takes several minutes to get dressed and put my shoes on. By the time I've finished, Clement has returned from the bathroom and is in the process of getting dressed himself.

"Cracking night weren't it?" he says.

"It was…eventful."

"Did you get anywhere with that Sandra bird?"

I inwardly cringe. "No, not really."

"Never mind. Plenty more fish in the sea."

Once we're both dressed, Clement insists we take advantage of the hotel catering and frog marches me down to the dining room. I have no appetite but I'm in desperate need of fluids. We arrive to find Emma setting a single table.

"Morning gents."

She invites us to take a seat and we're handed a menu each. Clement orders a pot of tea and a full English breakfast while I opt for dry toast and orange juice. Emma heads off to fulfil her role as cook, leaving us alone in the empty dining room.

"She ain't a bad sort," Clement remarks.

I nod.

"You should get her number."

"I think I have enough complications in my life at the moment, don't you?"

For the first time this morning, Gabby crosses my mind. In truth, I haven't given her a great deal of thought since we left Susan's place, but the fact I haven't heard from her is troubling. Has she called my bluff on this occasion?

Before I can give the matter further thought, Emma returns, carrying a tray.

"Here we are. One pot of tea and one glass of orange juice."

I smile politely as cutlery and condiments are decanted to the table.

"How was the pub?" she asks casually. "I don't suppose you saw what happened last night?"

I stare at Clement but he appears preoccupied pouring his tea.

"No. What happened?"

"I'm not sure. There was some vague post on Facebook about a fight."

"Oh, it must have happened after we left. Just our luck to miss the excitement," I chuckle nervously.

She returns my smile and heads back to the kitchen.

"Did you hear that, Clement?" I hiss. "People are talking about the fight on Facebook."

"On what?" he replies before slurping his tea.

"Facebook."

He stares at me blankly.

"Never mind. The point is, we need to get out of town before the police get involved."

"Why?"

"Because you assaulted five, or was it six men last night? You do actually remember?"

"Unlike you Bill, I remember everything that happened last night. Anyway, it was self-defence."

"That's as maybe, but I doubt they'll consider your retaliation reasonable force. One of those men will be walking with a limp for the rest of his life."

"Yeah," he replies with a chuckle. "And two of them are probably still looking for their bollocks."

I have to fight back a smirk. I really shouldn't encourage him but I have to admit, recollecting what happened does trigger a frisson of excitement. It was certainly more eventful than my average Friday evening.

"I think we should catch the ferry back to the mainland at Yarmouth, just in case the police are keeping an eye out for us at Ryde."

"Great idea, Bill. Let's hope they haven't informed Interpol yet," he replies, his tone sarcastic.

Beyond my paranoia, there is some logic in getting the ferry from Yarmouth as it sails into Lymington which isn't far from my country home in Marshburton. I can leave Clement at the train station and recover at the cottage in peace.

"No matter. We'll go from Yarmouth," I confirm, just as Emma arrives with our breakfast.

Five minutes later, I'm still struggling with my second slice of dry toast. Clement's plate is empty. I give up on breakfast and we make our way to the reception and ask Emma to call a cab. She does offer to drive us to Yarmouth but as it's the opposite side of the island, it doesn't seem fair. Besides, I need to travel in a car that would allow a quick escape, such are my levels of nausea.

I settle the bill and leave a generous tip. I also hand Emma my business card, just in case she ever wants that guided tour of the Palace of Westminster.

By the time we head out to the car park, our cab is already waiting.

Lymington is only eighteen miles from Sandown. However, the island's roads are not designed for speedy transit and the cross-country journey takes almost fifty minutes. Our journey time is further extended by the fact there's a forty-five-minute wait until the next ferry departure. The only saving grace is the weather, with the return of clear blue skies and a gentle breeze. I suggest a wander around Yarmouth's quaint shops but Clement decides he'd rather sit on a bench by the quay and watch the world go by.

I while away the time mindlessly staring in shop windows, happy just to be breathing the crisp sea air. On the way back to the quay, mindful the ferry takes three times as long to cross the Solent from Yarmouth, I pop into a newsagents and buy a paper.

I return to find Clement eyeing up the various yachts moored in the marina.

"Thinking of buying one?" I joke.

"Not unless you're paying."

I join Clement in gazing at the expensive yachts. Some of my previous trips to the Isle of Wight have been as a guest at Cowes Week — the island's world-famous regatta. I'm no sailor but Cowes Week is as much about the accompanying social scene as the sailing. That said, I can appreciate the sense of freedom that must come with owning a yacht; able to dock whenever and wherever the fancy takes you. There is a certain appeal to that lifestyle.

As much as I could happily remain on the bench, romanticising about life on the ocean wave, a trip on a much larger vessel beckons.

"We better get going, Clement."

We head to the ticket office and make our way on board the ferry. There's no sign of any police or Interpol detectives, as Clement repeatedly points out.

Fifteen minutes later, we depart the island; a day later than we envisaged and with one or two stories to tell.

The sea is far less choppy than our outbound journey, and coupled with comfortable seats, Clement decides to take a nap. As tired as I am, I've never been able to sleep on public transport. I glance enviously at my snoozing companion and resort to reading my newspaper. The first four pages are full of the usual fayre: depressing forecasts about the economy and Brexit, thinly disguised as news. I keep turning pages, hoping to find something worthy of my interest.

On page eight, I spot a headline which is not so much interesting as it is alarming — *Tory MP in Sex Tape Leak.*

I read the headline again, barely able to bring myself to read the article. What are the chances one of my colleagues has been involved in a sex tape leak? At best, the chances are remote. This can only mean one thing. My mouth now bone dry, I swallow hard and begin to read.

It was only ever going to be about one Tory MP; the same Tory MP currently on a ferry, and about to suffer a seizure.

"Clement!" I gasp. "Wake up."

He slowly comes around. I fold the paper over and hold the page in front of his face.

"Look what that bitch has done now."

Bleary eyed, he studies the article. Seconds pass, and as his eyes dart left and right, the crease in his forehead deepens.

"Shit," he growls.

If there's any consolation, it's that the article doesn't mention the minor fact the two people involved are siblings. If it had, I doubt very much it would be buried at the bottom of page eight.

"I don't get it," Clement adds.

"Get what?"

"Why she went to the papers with this. Apart from making you look like a dickhead in public, how does it help her?"

Whether I look like a dickhead or not is immaterial. However, his point about her motive is salient.

"I don't know how it helps her."

He strokes his moustache a couple of times. "Maybe she's pissed off cos' we paid her old dear a visit."

I'm not convinced. Thus far, Gabby's scheme has been enacted with clinical planning. Everything she's done has been for a reason and a retaliatory strike feels too impulsive, too unplanned. There has to be more to it.

"It's not her style, Clement. She's done this for a specific reason."

We both sit and frown at the newspaper for a long minute. A theory eventually breaks through the fog in my head.

"Christ," I mumble. "I think this is a precursor."

"A what?"

I sit forward, conscious of nearby passengers eavesdropping.

"Okay. Ask yourself a question: why would a national newspaper have any interest in an illegally filmed video of a backbench MP having sex?"

"Gotta fill their pages with something."

"Yes, but I have no public profile. This isn't a newsworthy story, otherwise they wouldn't have buried it on page eight."

"So why did they print it then?"

"I can only think of two reasons and they both fit with Gabby's threat."

"Go on."

"This is just a teaser. I reckon Gabby convinced them to print it on the understanding they'd get an exclusive when the real story breaks."

"The whole brother knobs his sister story?"

My stomach churns, and not because of the hangover. "Precisely."

"So she's only done this to pile on the pressure?"

"Yes, and I suspect, in reaction to our ultimatum. I think it's fair to say she won't be accepting my counter offer."

"Bollocks," he groans. "That's us back to the drawing board then."

I slump back in my chair and shake my head. Whichever way you look at it, this entire trip has been nothing but a monumental waste of time.

22.

In need of fresh air and time to think, I head out to the deck. I grip the handrail and squeeze it until my knuckles turn white. The sun might be shining but there's a distinct chill to the breeze whipping off the Solent. It does nothing to cool my growing anger.

How could I have been so stupid, so reckless?

Granted, the fact I spent an entire day on the island was beyond my control, but I should have stayed at the hotel and formed a contingency plan. But no; I allowed myself to become distracted. Rather than thinking of all possible outcomes, I had to act the fool and get blind drunk.

I have nobody to blame but myself.

And now it's over. I've lost. It's time to do what I should have done in the first place.

I head back inside and find a quiet corner to stand; away from the other passengers and away from Clement. With no more time to waste, I pull out my phone. It's still switched off from last night. I turn it on and it immediately chimes the arrival of a text message. I'm not surprised to see Fiona Hewitt's name as the sender. The video was one thing, but now I've been named and shamed in the press, the Parliamentary Commissioner for Standards is duty-bound to intervene.

I open the message — *Call me. It's urgent.*

Fiona will have to wait. I've a more pressing call to make.

I scroll through my contacts until I find Rupert Franklin's details. I call my solicitor's number and he answers on the fifth ring.

"Sorry to call on a Saturday, Rupert, but it's a matter of some urgency."

"It usually is," he chuckles. "What can I do for you, William?"

"I'm selling Hansworth Hall and the flat in Blackfriars."

"Really? I must say, I'm surprised to hear that."

"It's a long story and unfortunately time is not on my side. I need both sales to be completed by Friday."

"Which Friday?"

"This coming Friday."

"Very funny, William. This is obviously a joke, right?"

"I wish it were but I'm serious."

The line goes quiet for a few seconds. "I'm not sure what's behind this, but it's not possible anyway."

"Why not?"

"Well, firstly there's all the information your buyer's solicitor will require: local authority searches, leasehold information, energy performance certificates, and not to mention surveys. All of that will take weeks to organise."

"They won't need any of that."

"Don't be ridiculous. There isn't a solicitor in the land who would allow their client to purchase a property without it."

"They would if they were only paying a pound for the property."

The line goes quiet again. I can only begin to imagine the thoughts going through Rupert's mind. It doesn't take long for him to air them.

"I simply can't allow you to do this, William. It's madness on every level."

"I appreciate your concern but my mind is made up. I'll sign whatever disclaimer you require but the sales have to be completed by Friday. If you won't do it, I'll simply find another solicitor who will."

We spend another ten minutes going backwards and forwards. In the end, he reluctantly agrees to send the contract out first thing on Monday morning. I thank him and hang up before he makes another attempt to change my mind.

One call down. One to go. I ring Fiona.

"At last," she blusters, bypassing any greeting. "Where have you been?"

"Don't ask, but I assume you wanted to talk to me about the newspaper article?"

"You've seen it then?"

"I have."

"And you know we have to open a file on it?"

"I do."

"I'm not suggesting you're to blame, William, but we have to follow procedure just in case there's more to it. You do understand that?"

"I'll save you the bother, Fiona. I'm thinking about resigning."

"I beg your pardon."

"I'm thinking about resigning. This whole mess has taken its toll and I can't stand the added pressure of being under scrutiny by all and sundry."

Much like Rupert, I suspect Fiona has been stunned into silence.

"Why though?" she eventually sighs. "You told me there was nothing to this stupid video."

"There isn't. To be honest, it's just made me realise how little I want to remain a politician."

"But you're a damn fine politician, William."

"Right," I snort. "I think we both know that's not true."

Before Fiona can mount a defence, I tell her it would be better to discuss my plans on Monday morning. She agrees to meet with me and the weak mobile signal brings the call to a premature end. In truth, I have no idea if I do want to resign but hopefully the threat alone will keep Fiona off my back while I consider my next move.

I return to my seat where I find Clement gazing out of the window.

"Alright," he mumbles.

"Depends what you mean by alright?" I reply, retaking my seat.

"Like, are you gonna throw up again?"

"No. But I have thrown something — the towel in."

He shoots me a look to suggest he's not in the mood for puzzles.

"I've instructed my solicitor to sell both my properties to Gabby."

"You've done what?" he growls. "What the bleedin' hell for?"

"I'm done, Clement. She's won, and I just want this over with."

"Nah, that ain't happening," he snaps back.

"I appreciate all your help but this is my decision and it's made."

Worryingly, he looks more agitated than he did last night before taking on those men.

"I ain't done here, Bill. You might wanna give up but I sure as fuck don't."

"What's to give up? She's won."

He suddenly leans forward and jabs his finger in my chest with more force than is necessary. I'm not sure why but he seems incensed at my decision.

"She ain't won, not by a long chalk. And you need to grow a pair."

If I wasn't so concerned he might jab his finger through my chest, I might have offered a sterner defence. As it is, I try to placate him.

"Look, Clement. I really do appreciate all your help but you have to understand it's my future at stake here. If the truth about Gabby comes out, I'll be ruined. It's just too great a risk."

"And you reckon she'll keep shtum once she's got what she wants?"

"I hope so."

"Hope? Do me a favour, Bill. She ain't exactly played by the rules so far, has she?"

"What else can I do?"

"You could at least put up a fight. For crying out loud, we've still got six days to come up with something."

Perhaps I might have been a tad defeatist, but I can't see any way forward. And why Clement is so clearly upset by my decision is anyone's guess.

"Forgive me for asking, but why is this so important to you?"

"Cos' it just is, alright," he huffs, finally sitting back in his seat.

He appears to have blown himself out. Mumbling a couple of expletives, he returns his gaze to the view beyond the window. I really don't know what to say and an uncomfortable silence sets in.

Long minutes pass and the tension hangs. I can't stand it and decide to head back to the deck. Just as I'm about to get up, Clement suddenly sits forward and throws me a proposition.

"Tell you what, answer me a question and I'll walk away without another word."

"Okay," I reply with some hesitancy.

"But if you can't answer it, I want you to rethink where you're heading. Deal?"

On the face of it, I have nothing to lose. "Deal."

He looks me straight in the eye. "My question is: why now?"

I'm not sure I understand and my furrowed brow says as much.

"Why is she doing this *now*?" he clarifies.

"I'm not with you."

Clearly frustrated, he kneads his temple with a knuckle.

"How old is that Gabby bird?"

I think back to the birth certificate she took so much pleasure in showing me. "About thirty, give or take a year."

"Right, so that Susan woman has sat on this secret for thirty years. She clearly hated your old man so why is her daughter suddenly blackmailing you after years of doing nothing?"

It's a good question but I can only guess at an answer.

"I don't know. Maybe Gabby has only just found out who her father is. Maybe she stumbled across the trinket box by accident and her mother had to confess the truth."

"Nah, I don't buy that. That was one bitter old woman we met and she's had years to get her revenge without her daughter getting involved. Any newspaper would have paid a decent chunk of change for your old man's confession letter so why didn't she sell her story years ago?"

"Perhaps she wanted to protect her young daughter from the fallout."

"So I'll ask you again: why now?"

"I honestly don't know," I sigh. "But I don't see how it helps one way or another."

"Because it means something ain't right about all this."

"And what is that *something*?"

"If I knew that, I'd know how to fix it."

"Marvellous," I groan. "We know something isn't right but we don't know what it is, or what we can do about it."

"So we find out."

"How?"

"We start with the one man who created this bleedin' mess — your old man."

"Unless you have a Ouija board to contact the dead, I'm not sure he'll be much help."

"You'd be surprised," he mumbles.

"Sorry?"

"Look, I know he's dead," he says, returning to the subject. "But we can still dig into his past. He must have left paperwork and stuff from that time?"

"Well, yes. There's a dozen boxes of his paperwork in my loft. I meant to send it to one of those paper shredding companies but never got around to it."

"Gotta be worth a look ain't it? There might be something in there for us to work with."

I try my hardest to portray some semblance of optimism. Not so easy while contending with a pounding head, sleep deprivation, mild nausea, and the minor fact I'm about to be financially ruined.

"If you've got nothing better to do then I suppose so. I'm not sure what you think we'll find though."

"Who knows. Just call it a hunch."

I let out a sigh and confirm my acceptance with a nod. Content to have won the battle, Clement settles back in his chair and closes his eyes. I wish I shared his faith but I'm already consigned to defeat. All we're likely to do is waste several hours and what remains of my patience. Still, I owe him the chance to check, if for no other reason than to put his mind at rest.

As Clement dozes, I stare out the window and watch the mainland edge ever closer.

With a little over ten minutes before we dock, I turn my thoughts to my immediate future. In exactly one week from now, I'll no longer own the flat in Blackfriars or Hansworth Hall. By default, the cottage I rent in Marshburton will become my home. Perhaps it might be a fitting time to end my political career too, although paying rent on the cottage could be problematic without any income. They say that money can't buy happiness but it certainly buys you options. And despite my spur of the moment threat to quit, I fear it's not a realistic option. It would be an inadvertent twist of Gabby's knife if her actions consign me to a job I have no heart for.

Thankfully, the ferry docks at Lymington before I can depress myself any further. I nudge Clement awake and we disembark.

After a short walk from the ferry terminal to the station, I'm relieved we only have a five minute wait for the train to Marshburton. It promptly arrives and we take our seats in an empty carriage. Seconds later, it departs Lymington and we begin the final leg of our journey.

On any other morning I'd sit back and enjoy the views of rural Hampshire rolling by, but not even the combination of autumnal colours and bright blue sky can lift my mood. If Clement has any apprehension about my predicament, it doesn't show on his face as he dozes once more.

He wakes up a minute before we arrive at Marshburton.

We're the only passengers to get off at an otherwise deserted station, as it is most Saturday mornings. We cross a footbridge which puts us outside the station entrance. Besides the wind rustling through the trees lining the front of the station, there isn't a sound to be heard.

"Fuck me," Clement mutters, coming to a halt. "You live here?"

"Yes, and I happen to like the fact it's quiet."

"Too quiet, like the *Village of the Damned*. Makes my balls itch."

"How pleasant. Now, if you've quite finished insulting my village, shall we get going?"

He looks off to the distance, frowning. "Before the locals arrive with pitchforks?"

I shake my head and set off down the lane towards my cottage. After catching up with me, Clement spends the whole five minute walk grumbling about it being too quiet for his liking. I suspect he'll have more to grumble about a few hours from now; once we've wasted the afternoon pointlessly sifting through boxes of paperwork.

23.

According to an article I once read, there are over eleven thousand properties in the country named Rose Cottage. My rented home is one of them. I believe it once provided a home for the workers who tended the hop fields surrounding the village. It's a bitter irony that such desirable rural dwellings are now beyond the means of all but the most affluent.

While the rent of Rose Cottage might be high, the door frames are not, much to Clement's annoyance. He stoops past the front door and follows me into the kitchen where my most pressing task is to consume strong coffee.

"Coffee, Clement?"

"Tea."

I scrap the idea of using the percolator and grab a jar of instant coffee. Today is not a day for appearances so I extract two large mugs from the cupboard, in lieu of the usual china cups and saucers.

"I'm afraid I don't have any fresh milk in. Black okay?"

Presented with Hobson's choice, he half shrugs.

Once we're both furnished with caffeine-laden beverages, we head upstairs to the landing.

"It's a little cramped up in the loft so shall I pass the boxes down to you, and we can go through them in the spare bedroom?"

I point out the room to my right.

"Yeah, whatever."

I open the loft hatch and pull the ladder down. After a nervous climb up the rickety steps, I switch the light on and clamber in. It must be five or six years since I last stepped foot in the loft; a fact affirmed by the pungent smell of stale air that greets me.

I let my eyes adjust to the dim light and shuffle over to the pile of boxes. This is their second home after spending eight years in a storage facility, after my father passed away. I leased the cottage when I returned from my second stint in Africa, only ever intending to stay here for six months. Little did I know that within a few months of my return, I'd be elected as a member of parliament and it would remain my home for the next decade. So, rather than continuing to pay for storage, I had a removal firm deliver the boxes to my loft. With my father's solicitor having dealt with his estate and all the accompanying paperwork, I had no real urgency to sort through the boxes before their ultimate disposal — until now.

I grab the first box and carry it back to the loft hatch where Clement is waiting. I pass it down to him and he carries it off to the spare bedroom while I return for the next box. Working together, it takes only minutes to move all fourteen boxes. I switch the light off and climb back down the ladder. By the time I enter the spare bedroom, Clement already has the lid off one of the boxes.

"Shit," he groans.

"I did warn you. My father was a stickler for paperwork and kept everything."

Clement returns the lid and we both stare at the boxes, hands on hips.

Detecting his reluctance, I throw him a lifeline. "We don't have to do this, Clement. There must be over ten thousand individual documents to sort through, and we don't even know what we're looking for. Perhaps we should just leave it."

He puffs his cheeks and turns to me. "Nah. There's gotta be something in this lot — I can feel it in my bones."

I remind myself I did agree to this. It feels such a pointless task, though. I take a large gulp of coffee in the hope it will boost my enthusiasm for the task ahead. I fear it will take more than a cup of coffee.

"What year was she born?" Clement asks.

"Gabby? Err…1987, I think. Why?"

"Cos' if we are gonna find anything, it'll be around the time she was born. I reckon the year before and the year after."

"Makes sense, although it doesn't make our job any easier."

A thought occurs. I pull the lid from the nearest box and check the dates on a dozen documents.

"These are all from 1995."

"How does that help?"

Ignoring his question, I pull the lid from another box. I'm hoping for two things: firstly, that my father had a chronological filing system, and secondly, whoever transferred the paperwork from his study to these boxes did so in the same order.

I randomly pluck six documents from the box. "Thank heavens," I sigh, seeing they're all dated 1991. "It looks like each box covers a specific period of time so hopefully we can narrow our search to three or four boxes."

Thanks to Clement's pragmatism and my father's fastidious filing system, we're quickly able to locate three boxes containing documents from 1986 through to 1988; a year before Gabby was born and the year after. If there is anything to be found, which I still doubt, it's unlikely to be anywhere else. We shift all the other boxes to the landing and Clement drops the first box on the unmade double bed, ready for us to sort through.

We start at opposite ends of the box and scan every document. Tedious doesn't cover it.

Fifty minutes later, it's clear 1986 was an uneventful year in my father's life, overlooking the one night he spent with Susan Davies, and my sister's conception. Despite sifting through countless bank statements, tax notices, utility bills, and dozens of benign letters, we find nothing of significance. The only thing of interest I find is a receipt from Curry's for a Commodore 64 computer — a present for my eleventh birthday. Perhaps my parents never considered it, but it made the ideal gift for a solitary child. I appreciated it nonetheless and it filled many a lonely hour.

"What's that?" Clement asks as I mindlessly stare at the receipt, reminiscing about my childhood.

"Oh, just a receipt for a birthday present; an old computer. Did you have one back in the eighties?"

"Nah."

"Really? Were you not into computers back then?"

"Wasn't really into anything in the eighties. I was somewhere else at the time, and there weren't much of anything there."

Based on last night's events, I suspect he may well be referring to a young offender's institute, or possibly prison, depending how old he is. Either way, I think I'd rather not know.

"Anyway, 1986 was always gonna be a long shot," he remarks, swapping the box for the next. "I reckon we'll have more luck with this one."

And so we begin sifting through 1987. We get ten minutes into it when Clement asks where the toilet is.

"Turn left and it's the first door."

He ambles off while I offer a silent prayer he doesn't need to evacuate his bowels again. I draw breath and continue plucking documents from the box. It's all much of the same and reveals nothing untoward. Every paper cut brings more annoyance and more frustration. This feels such a waste of time.

Clement returns within two minutes — hopefully not long enough to have contaminated my bathroom. Having made slightly more headway than Clement, I slow down slightly to ensure we meet in the middle of the box. It's a lazy move that immediately summons guilt so I move on with a little more enthusiasm.

Time drags and my eyelids get heavier with every document I scan. I still have at least two more inches of paperwork to check when Clement suddenly gets to his feet.

"You're not skiving off to the toilet again?"

"Not yet," he mumbles, his attention fixed on a single sheet of paper in his hand.

"When was that mad cow born?" he asks.

"Gabby?"

"Who else?"

"Gosh, I can't recall the exact month but if my father and Susan Davies got together at the conference, that would have been in October. Nine months on from there would put her birth around July I guess."

His eyes narrow as he studies the document in more detail.

I get to my feet. "Why do you ask?"

"Look at this," he replies.

I sidle up to him. It turns out he's clutching a statement from one of my father's three bank accounts, dated August 1987. At first, I don't see why Clement's interest was piqued, until my eyes scan halfway down the list of transactions.

"Twenty-five thousand pounds," I murmur.

"Yeah, and look who it was paid to."

My eyes dart across the page to see who benefited from such a sizeable payment. In bold type are the names of the recipients — Mr Kenneth Davies & Mrs Susan Davies.

"Bloody hell," I gasp. "Susan Davies was married."

"Yeah, and so much for her bullshit about not getting any money from your old man."

Stunned, I sit down on the edge of the bed and attempt to work out the implications of this revelation.

"So both Gabby and Susan lied to us. They both said they were living in poverty because my father never gave them a penny, and neither mentioned this Kenneth character."

Clement flops down next to me. "And if they're lying about the money, what else are they lying about, and why?"

I stare at the bank statement in Clement's meaty hand. It is quite a revelation but my addled brain can't fathom out what we do with this new information.

As if reading my mind, Clement makes a suggestion. "We need to find this Kenneth bloke."

"Why?"

"He was the only one involved who ain't trying to blackmail you. And cos' he's a bloke, I can beat the shit out of him if he don't answer our questions."

I'd rather not consider how well versed Clement is in the art of torture, but he does have a point about Kenneth being our best bet for answers.

"So the question is," he adds. "How do we find the bloke?"

I rummage in my pocket and pull out my phone. "I think I might know somebody who can help."

"Who?"

"Judith Dixon. She looked after my father's personnel needs and this Kenneth guy might be listed as Susan's next of kin on her old work records. If he is, there should also be an address."

I scan the contacts in my phone.

"You know it's Saturday, right?" Clement says.

Such is my excitement at our discovery, I hadn't even stopped to think what day it is.

"Dammit. Of course."

"Afraid you're gonna have to wait until Monday, Bill."

I sit and tap my phone screen. I can't sit on this until Monday so I need another angle.

"I'm going to call her anyway."

"And say what?"

"It's only been a few days since Judith dug out Susan's record so it might still be fresh in her mind."

I don't hold out much hope but it beats doing nothing. I continue to scroll through my contacts until Judith's number pops up. It rings for what feels like an age.

"Hello, William," she eventually chirps.

"Morning, Judith. I'm so sorry to call you on a Saturday. I hope I've not caught you at a bad moment?"

"Not at all. I've just got back from walking the dog."

I'm forced to swap small talk for a few minutes before I can broach the reason for my call.

"Do you remember Rosa asking for some information from a personnel file the other day? It was for my father's former personal assistant, Susan Davies. I was going to send her some photographs."

"Oh, yes. I do recall."

"Great. I know this is an odd question, and it's probably a long shot, but I don't suppose you recall who Susan's next of kin is?"

"I'm afraid my memory isn't what it once was. Sorry, William."

"I understand, Judith, and there's no need to apologise."

That's plan-A derailed. Time to move on to plan-B.

"Do you remember Susan at all?"

"Vaguely, and the only reason I do is because I got into a bit of an argument with your father about her."

"Really? Why was that?"

"Susan left without giving notice. Apparently your father was perfectly willing to let her go but it was a breach of contract and he should have consulted with me first."

Her revelation comes as no surprise. I bet my father wanted rid of Susan the moment she dropped her pregnancy bombshell.

"Sounds like my father. He never was one for following rules."

We swap a few anecdotes about my father before I decide there is nothing further to be gleaned from Judith today. I apologise again for interrupting her weekend and make one final request.

"Would you mind looking up Susan's next of kin when you get back to the office on Monday?"

"Of course. I'll get on to it first thing."

"Thank you, Judith."

"And I'm sorry Susan never got to see those photographs. Such a tragedy."

I only half catch her comment as it was delivered in such a throwaway manner.

"Sorry, Judith...what was a tragedy?"

The line goes quiet.

"Judith?"

"You don't know?" she finally replies in hushed voice.

"Know what?"

"I'm sorry, William. I thought you knew, and that's why you wanted details of her next of kin."

I draw a deep breath in an attempt to contain my frustration. "Judith. Whatever it is you think I know about Susan, I'm afraid I don't."

Another pause, followed by a long sigh. "I'm sorry, William, but Susan Davies died in a car crash twelve years ago."

24.

My backside meets the edge of the bed again; more a shocked stumble on this occasion.

"Susan Davies is dead?" I reply in disbelief.

I glance across at Clement to check he heard. His expression is what I'd expect from someone who has just returned from visiting an apparently dead woman.

"Yes, I'm afraid she is," Judith confirms.

"Are you sure?"

"We sent flowers to her funeral, so yes, I'm sure."

I struggle to keep my voice level. "So why on earth did you tell Rosa she was happily living on the Isle of Wight?"

"I beg your pardon?"

"Rosa asked for Susan's address and you emailed her an address in Sandown, on the Isle of Wight."

"Yes, William," she replies, her tone now defensive. "I know where Sandown is, thank you. But I can assure you I did no such thing."

"Wait. You never emailed Rosa?"

"No, I did, but not with an address. My email pretty much said what I just told you; that Susan Davies died twelve years ago."

My head pounds with confused thoughts, to the point where it's no longer possible to simultaneously hold a conversation and think clearly.

"I…err…I'm sorry, Judith. Clearly there's been a mix up my end so I'll give you a call on Monday when you're back in the office."

I say goodbye and end the call.

"Did I hear that right?" Clement asks before I have chance to catch my breath.

I nod.

"So that woman we went to see ain't Susan Davies?"

"Apparently not."

"Interesting," he mutters while stroking his moustache.

Silence descends while we process Judith's revelation.

Clement is the first to break it. "Who's Rosa?"

"She's my PA."

"Your what?"

"Personal assistant, like a secretary."

"And what's she got to do with all of this?"

The fact I'm unsure how to frame my answer, is telling. "I don't know."

"Tell me what you do know then."

I think back to my conversation with Rosa and attempt to relay as much as I can recall.

"I asked Rosa to email Judith in order to find out Susan's address. When I got back from a meeting, she gave me a slip of paper with the address in Sandown."

"Right."

"But Judith was very insistent she told Rosa that Susan had died."

"So why would this Rosa woman give you some bullshit address if she knew Susan was dead?"

I don't have an answer and my expression says as much. Clement wanders over to the window and stares out. Silent seconds pass before he turns around and leans against the ledge.

"You reckon she's working with Gabby?"

It's a reasonable conclusion but not one I can readily accept.

"I know it looks bad but she could just as easily have made a mistake."

There is a distinct lack of conviction in my reply and Clement immediately picks up on it.

"I'm guessing she's good at her job?"

"Very."

"That's one hell of a fuck up then, Bill. I might believe it was a mistake if she'd got an address wrong, but she was told the bloody woman was dead."

"I know, I know. It doesn't make any sense."

After a brief pause, he continues the interrogation. "How long has she worked for you?"

"Less than three months."

He shakes his head. "Jesus."

I can guess at what he's thinking and suspect we're drawing the same conclusions, albeit mine are more informed. The fact my previous PA left in such a hurry, with no real explanation yet able to recommend Rosa, suddenly feels like another part of Gabby's grand plan.

It doesn't take much imagination to guess why she'd want somebody in my office. One by one, the dominoes topple.

Firstly, there was Rosa's insistence on delaying the new lease on Hansworth Hall, which ensured it could be sold without complications. Then there was the mix up with my arrival time for the speech which put me in a chair next to Gabby for over an hour. And then that damn video, which could have only been emailed to my colleagues by someone who knew how our email system works.

But as damning as the evidence might be, I simply can't correlate Rosa's actions with her overall demeanour. If it does transpire she's been working with Gabby, there has to be an explanation.

That assumption points my train of thought in a different direction.

"Perhaps Gabby is blackmailing Rosa too."

"Wouldn't put it past her. Seems a bit over the top though."

"We're talking about Gabby here, and she's planned everything else so meticulously. Blackmailing Rosa would allow her access to information she couldn't otherwise get. It does make sense."

I'm not sure if he's convinced but it appears his thoughts are already heading off on another tangent.

"What about the woman in Sandown?" he asks.

"The woman who definitely isn't Susan Davies?"

"Yeah."

"What about her?"

"Who the hell is she, and why was she happy playing the part?"

"I'm guessing she's some stooge Gabby hired. If you think about it, it's pretty obvious our first move would be to speak to her mother."

Clement nods in agreement.

"But why bother sending us to the Isle of Wight?" I add. "What possible reason would Gabby have for pretending her mother is still alive?"

"Buggered if I know, but maybe she's just messing with us so we waste time. You know, like a distraction."

"Perhaps."

"But, thinking about it, she's given us a lead."

"How so?"

"The problem is, we know bugger all about Gabby. We don't know where she lives, where she works, who her friends are, or anything really."

"Agreed."

"So we don't have any leverage. We can't fight back cos' it's like trying to punch a shadow."

"Right. And what leverage do we have that we didn't have twenty minutes ago?"

"The woman pretending to be her old dear. She's obviously in cahoots with Gabby and we know where she lives — that's our best point of attack."

"Please don't tell me you want to go back to Sandown."

"We need to know who that woman really is. Once we know that, we've got leverage on Gabby."

There are many reasons I don't want to go back to the Isle of Wight, not least because I feel like death. Thankfully, my desire not to return does serve up an alternative solution.

"I've got a better idea. Come with me."

I lead Clement downstairs to the dining room which serves as a home office.

"Grab a chair."

He does as instructed and we sit side-by-side at my desk. I switch on a computer almost as archaic as the one in my office.

"What's this idea then?" Clement asks.

"Rather than asking her who she really is, we check her electoral roll entry online. That'll give us her full name."

"How does that help? We need more than her bleedin' name."

"Once we know who she is, we can search for her on the social media platforms and on Google. Very few people can avoid leaving a digital footprint of some sort online. We just need to find that one piece of information that connects her to Gabby."

He stares at me blankly. "I have no idea what most of that means."

I return his blank stare. "You really are a technophobe, aren't you?"

"Again, no idea."

"Honestly, Clement. I thought I was a dinosaur when it came to technology but I'm virtually Steve Jobs compared to you."

"Steve who?"

"Steve Jobs, the founder of Apple?"

"I thought The Beatles founded Apple."

"No…what? They did, but that was a different company called Apple."

"So what's so special about this Steve Jobs fella?"

"Good grief," I groan. "I was just making a point. All you need to know is he was very clever, and now he's very dead."

"I know the feeling," Clement mutters in reply.

I roll my eyes and count to five in my head in an attempt to quell my annoyance. "What is it with you and all these odd comments?"

"What odd comments?"

"About death and such like? You've made several throwaway comments on the subject."

"Nothing. Forget it."

"No, Clement," I snap. "Quite frankly, it's becoming more than a little disturbing. Is there something I should know?"

"Like what?"

"Like, are you on the run for murder or something? You keep mentioning death as if you're overly familiar with the subject."

"Just forget it, Bill. And for the record, I'm not on the run."

The computer finally boots up, sparking a reminder I have more pressing questions that need answers.

"Anyway, let's get back to Susan Davies shall we?"

I conduct a search on Google for electoral roll records and click through to a website which allows users to search by either name or property address. I enter fake Susan's Sandown address and strike the enter key.

As much as I love living in the country, the one downside is the woefully slow broadband connection. It takes an age for the next page to load but I'm relieved it shows the address we're after. Annoyingly, I have to register to view the occupant's name, and that involves a tedious process of entering my details and making a payment.

Fifteen minutes later, I'm returned to the home page where I have to search the Sandown address again. More single finger strokes are applied to the keyboard before I strike the enter key again.

"Here we go."

We both stare at the screen as a spinning disc indicates the information is loading. The home page goes blank while the browser waits for the results page to load.

"Bloody broadband."

Slowly but surely, the real name of the woman from Sandown is revealed.

"Barbara Jones," Clement mumbles.

"Oh dear."

"What? Does that name mean something to you."

"It might just be a coincidence. It's a very common surname."

"Bill?"

"Rosa's surname is Jones."

"Bloody hell. And you reckon it's a coincidence?"

The tone of his voice suggests he doesn't.

"I don't know what to think, Clement."

The evidence against Rosa is stacking up. I picture her face, in all its beauty, and then compare it to the woman we met in Sandown. The eyes, the nose, the shape of the brow — if you stood the two women side by side and asked ten strangers if they were related, I'd wager eight of those strangers would say they were.

"I think you need to face facts, Bill. Your girl is up to her neck in this."

Even if I could explain away her involvement this week, which I can't, knowing the two women share a surname and similar facial features eliminates any lingering doubt. They have to be related, which means Rosa has to be involved in Gabby's plot.

The nausea returns.

"I need water."

I get up and stagger through to the kitchen. Leaning against the sink, I turn the tap on and scoop handful after handful of water towards my mouth. I gulp down seven or eight mouthfuls before I stop. It succeeds in flushing the bile but a bitter taste remains.

How could I have been so stupid, so blind?

Those little signals Rosa gave me; the ones I foolishly misinterpreted as signs of affection, were simply wicked lures. The technique might have been more subtle but she played me in much the same way Gabby did. The worst of it is, I allowed them both to do it. So desperate for companionship, I made it easy for them to exploit my loneliness, and they did so with cold indifference.

"You alright, Bill?"

I turn around. Clement is stood in the doorway.

"Not really. I've been a bloody fool."

"We've all been there, mate."

Well intended as his words are, they offer little in the way of consolation.

"No point beating yourself up about it, though," he adds, stepping into the kitchen. "The only way you're gonna feel better is if we stick it to that bitch."

I suppose he's right. No good dwelling on the symptoms when I need to find a cure. Not for the first time, I consider how things might pan out if I involve the police. Not for the first time, I conclude it's a non-option.

"How do I stick it to her then?"

"First, we need to lay a trap for your girl, to make sure she's definitely involved."

"You suspect she might not be?" I ask hopefully.

"Nah, I reckon she's bent as a nine-bob note, mate. We just need to be sure."

Hope thwarted, I decide our planning needs an injection of caffeine. I put the kettle on while Clement takes a seat at the kitchen table.

"You any good at acting?" he asks.

"Can't say I've ever tried. Why?"

"Cos' Monday morning, you're gonna need to pretend you don't know anything about that Rosa's involvement."

"But surely we should be confronting her with our allegations?"

"And then what? She goes to ground and we lose our closest tie to Gabby."

The thought of going through the motions with Rosa, like it's just another day, fills me with dread.

"I'm not sure, Clement. At this precise moment I want to scream at the woman. I really don't know if I'll be able to act as if nothing has happened."

"Well, you're gonna have to. Get it right and this could all be over within a few days. Get it wrong and it could well blow up."

"Blow up?"

"If Rosa suspects you know anything, she'll tell Gabby. And that crazy sister of yours is likely to either tell the world about your dirty secret or turn the screw tighter."

To use Clement's own turn of phrase, hearing the words *sister* and *screw* in the same sentence makes my balls itch.

"I'm not sure how much tighter she can…I mean, make matters worse."

"I bet you said that a few days ago, just before things got worse."

"Fair point."

"So like it or not, Bill, you've gotta go to work on Monday and act cool. I've got an idea how we can flush Gabby out so you just need to play the game for one day."

We sit at the kitchen table and Clement reveals what I have to do. It's a simple enough plan that, if executed properly, could give us some leverage against Gabby. But one thing I've learn about my new-found sister is to expect the unexpected, so I mindlessly stir my coffee while contemplating the ways it could backfire.

To quote the Boomtown Rats, I don't like Mondays, and I fear this coming Monday is going to be particularly unlikeable.

25.

The 06:33 service to London Waterloo rattles through the Hampshire countryside. I check the weather app on my phone to keep my mind distracted from what lies ahead this morning. It forecasts a cold, bleak day. How fitting.

We've yet to stop at any of the larger stations en-route so the carriage is sparsely populated. I suspect it was equally quiet on Clement's returns to London Saturday afternoon. I hate to admit it, but I was disappointed he declined my invitation to stay for the weekend. Apparently he promised Frank he'd work on Saturday night so I was left to stew in my lonesome juices. For all his weirdness, his propensity for violence, and obscene flatulence, he's the closest thing I have to a friend and ally at the moment.

With little else to do, or perhaps to avoid dwelling on today, I spent much of the weekend either asleep or tending the garden. Typically, I would visit the village pub on a Saturday evening but I was in no mood for idle chit-chat with the locals, or alcohol. This morning, however, a nip or two of brandy would be most welcome — purely for Dutch courage.

The train continues onward, stopping at Southampton and Winchester. A handful of commuters get off but more get on; resulting in a frenzied game of musical chairs. Every seat is eventually taken with a few dozen poor souls left to stand in the gangway. It's best to avoid eye contact as they glare resentfully at those fortunate enough to have secured a seat.

The rural scenery of Hampshire is long forgotten by the time we pass through Clapham Junction. My anxiety levels are now too high to pay much attention to the urban scenery as I go over my plan for the umpteenth time. It is not so much the implementation that worries me; more the fact I have to pretend my trusted PA is not colluding with my sister in an attempt to ruin me. I'm still not convinced Rosa isn't also being blackmailed by Gabby but that theory is immaterial at the moment. Perhaps, if things go according to plan, I might be able to establish her motives. Until then, I have to assume she's a voluntary participant, and that stings.

With my mind elsewhere, the final leg of my journey passes in an instant. Before I know it, the platform at Waterloo fills the window and my fellow commuters bustle towards the doors. I remain seated; content to stay where I am until the last possible minute. If I could stay here all day, and pretend my life was as mundane as it was when I made this journey a week ago, I would.

If only.

When all but the most reluctant of commuters have left the carriage, I get to my feet and check my watch — quarter past eight. For once, the train has arrived on time and in a little under fifteen minutes I'll be in the same office as Rosa.

I step from the carriage and remind myself that fortune favours the brave. I need to be the latter if I'm to avoid losing the former.

A minute later, I enter the raging mass of humans that is Waterloo station during rush hour. It's no place for the meek; more a place where good manners and patience are forgotten concepts. I head towards the Underground entrance where I'm absorbed into a tightly packed shoal of commuters.

After an arduous shuffle to the platform and a brief train ride, I'm spat onto the platform at Westminster.

Nerves jangling, I dart down the walkway towards the Palace of Westminster, passing the bored policeman. I'm so focused on my role I forget my customary nod in his direction. I doubt his day will be any the worse for it.

Much to my relief, I arrive at the office before Rosa. It affords me the opportunity to settle in and look busy, which in turn will feel more like a typical Monday morning. Once she's made the tea and we sit down to go through the diary, it'll be the moment to enact Clement's plan. It'll also be the moment I'm most likely to mess that plan up if I can't maintain my composure.

I open a random folder on my desk and stare at the first page of a report. I'm greeted by blocks of words my brain can't decipher. Nevertheless, I continue to stare at the page as the seconds tick by and the growls from my churning stomach grow louder.

"Morning, William."

"Morning," I rasp, my mouth dry.

Rosa smiles at me while removing her coat. "Sounds like someone needs a cup of tea."

Without waiting for an answer she heads off to the kitchen. I watch her shimmy away; her curvaceous shape captured by the clingy two-piece suit — my beautiful deceiver.

I stare into space and reassure myself Clement's plan is the only way out of this. To show our hand at this stage could push Gabby towards the worst possible outcome; an outcome where my antics are not buried on page eight but make front page news. I can almost feel the big man in the room, willing me to keep my nerve and follow his plan to the letter. As much as anything, I don't want to report back to him that I made a mess of it. I doubt he takes bad news well.

"All set to go through the diary?" Rosa asks as she places a cup on my desk.

It's just another Monday morning, William.

"Sure," I reply. "And thank you."

Rosa pads over to her desk and returns with her notepad. She sits in her usual chair on the opposite side of my desk and crosses her legs.

This is it.

"We might need to switch a few things around today, Rosa."

"Oh, okay."

"Yes, I've got a meeting with Fiona Hewitt at nine."

She studies the planner on her phone. "It's not on my schedule."

"No. She called me over the weekend and wants to talk through a few things. Probably wants to close the file on last week's…unpleasant episode."

"Right. No problem."

"And while I'm with Fiona, I need you to do a couple of urgent tasks for me."

"Sure."

"Firstly, I want you to contact the estate agents in Hampshire. Ask them if the tenants are willing to renew the lease on Hansworth Hall on the same terms as before."

Please, Rosa. Just agree without complaint.

A crease forms on her forehead. "But I thought we agreed I could handle the lease?"

Her spiky tone confirms my fears.

"I did, but circumstances have changed."

"How have they changed?"

"With respect, Rosa, that's my business."

Her cheeks adopt a ruddy hue as she glares at me. "Is it because you don't think I'm capable?"

"No, it's because I want to know if the tenants are willing to renew the lease," I reply firmly. "I simply want to keep my options open."

"But, William…"

"It's not up for discussion, Rosa."

I pick up my teacup and take a long sip, hoping she takes the hint. As I look over my cup, our eyes meet. Both her expression and body language are taut, but not quite enough you could say she was angry. Simmering, definitely, but not angry.

I put the teacup down.

"And when you've done that, can you contact an estate agent in the Blackfriars area to arrange a valuation of my flat."

If I wasn't looking for signs, I probably wouldn't have noticed her eyes narrow a fraction.

"Are you thinking of moving then?" she replies, her voice calmer than I expected.

"Possibly."

"But why? It's in such a great location, perfect for work."

"I know, but I won't be here forever, and besides, it's ridiculous having all that money tied up in property when it could be put to good use."

"Good use?" she replies, her expression now puzzled.

"I'm thinking of investing in a charitable venture. I can rent a flat for the foreseeable."

Her silence tells me she has no way of countering my idea without blowing her cover. With the worst of the lies behind me, I take an exaggerated glance at my watch.

"If you could get on with that for me, we'll deal with everything else when I return from my meeting with Fiona."

Before she can question me any further, I get to my feet and neck the remains of my tea.

"I'll be about half an hour."

I turn and leave without another word. The bait has been set so all I need to do is wait.

Feelings of relief and monumental disappointment follow me on the walk to Fiona's office. I'm relieved the first part of our plan went off without any obvious suspicions being raised, but

Rosa's reaction quashed any lingering doubts about her involvement. My thoughts turn to her motivation and a few quick sums give me the answer — almost seven million pounds. I doubt Gabby is offering a fifty percent split but even so, there's enough value in my properties for her to make Rosa a millionaire. I don't suppose you need to look much further than money for her motive.

I reach Fiona's office and her secretary shows me in.

"Morning, William. Please, take a seat."

The last time I sat in front of Fiona's desk, it was to watch a pornographic video in which I was the male lead. I'll take some comfort in knowing that whatever happens in today's meeting, it couldn't possibly be as bad as the last.

As I sit, Fiona asks for a moment to finish sending an urgent email. I nod and watch on as her fingers furiously tap the keyboard. Whatever she's typing, it summons a deep furrow to form across her already lined forehead. Fiona might be just six years older than me, but the responsibility of office has added at least another decade. It prompts concern I might be staring at the Ghost of Christmas Yet to Come.

"Sorry, William."

"No peace for the wicked?"

"Quite," she replies with a strained smile. "And I must have been bloody wicked at some point."

She looks as tired as I felt on Saturday morning.

"Are you okay, Fiona? I can reschedule if it's not a good time."

"Truth be told, there's never a good time but needs must."

"Right. If you're sure."

She nods and opens a folder on her desk.

"So, we were talking about that newspaper article, if I'm not mistaken?"

"Indeed."

"If it's any consolation, there hasn't been much in the way of fallout. I've received a few emails from opposition members; the usual faux outrage, but that was to be expected. Other than that, your non-story appears to have died the death it deserved. You've been very fortunate, I must say — these things have a nasty habit of escalating."

If only you knew, Fiona.

"Good to know."

"However," she continues. "I'm hoping we don't witness a second coming. Is there anything else I should know?"

I shift awkwardly in my chair. "All you need to know is that the situation is in hand."

"Meaning?"

"Meaning, I'm dealing with it. Suffice to say, somebody had it in for me, but I'm confident we've found a resolution."

"Good. I trust you, William, so please don't give me any cause to regret that trust."

"You have my word I'll do whatever is necessary."

Seemingly content, she scribbles a few notes and closes the folder. "I've done what I'm compelled to do. I've opened a file, and now it's closed. Let's hope it stays that way."

It's a sticking plaster on a gaping wound but one less thing to worry about, I suppose. I take a quick glance at my watch and ready myself to leave when Fiona moves the conversation along.

"But what I really wanted to talk to you about was the other thing we discussed."

"Oh, that."

"Yes, that. Are you seriously thinking about resigning?"

"Thinking about it? Yes. Seriously? I'm not sure."

She leans forward, resting her elbows on the desk. "You want my advice?"

"I always value your advice. You know that."

Her once lustrous eyes fix on mine. "Do it, William. Do it."

Not what I was expecting.

"Sorry? Aren't you supposed to talk me out of it?"

"Would you like me to?"

"I…I'm not sure."

"Look at me. This is what's in store if you don't get out while you're still relatively young."

"I don't understand. You've reached a position of great responsibility. You've got respect, authority, a distinguished career."

"Yes, but do you know what I haven't got?"

I shake my head.

"A bloody life."

Somehow, her confession seems to have aged her a few more years.

275

"To get this office," she continues. "I've sacrificed relationships, marriage, children, my family. And do you know what's waiting for me when I retire?"

"A sizable pension?" I offer in an attempt to lighten her gloomy outlook.

"Yes, a sizable pension I can spend on furnishing an empty house. Or on dining alone in the best restaurants. Or travelling the world while staying in single rooms."

She reaches across the desk and clasps my hand.

"You'll never be your father, and I mean that in a positive sense, but there is still time for you to be William Huxley. If you've got even the slightest inkling you don't want to be here, please don't make the same mistake I did. Get out while you still can."

It's not often I get to hear somebody speak with total sincerity in this building. This is one such occasion.

"Bubbles within a bubble," I reply. "I didn't know you were so unhappy in yours, Fiona."

She finds a half-smile. "My choice, and I have to live with it. I'm sorry to vent in your direction but I wouldn't be much of a friend if I didn't tell you how I really feel. I'm not looking for sympathy; I just wanted to give you the benefit of my experience."

"I appreciate it, but is it really too late for you?"

"Sadly, it is. I've passed the point of no return, so I might as well stay on the Westminster treadmill. You, on the other hand, still have options."

I have no doubt Fiona is right, and I should consider a life beyond Westminster. Ultimately though, I will only have options if I can meet the challenge still waiting for me beyond the door of this office.

"As always, Fiona, I appreciate your candid advice."

We both stand, and just as I expect her to shake my hand, she steps around the desk and embraces me.

"You're a good man, William," She whispers in my ear. "Too good for this place."

I leave her to deal with her unenviable workload and head back through the corridors. As I walk, I check my phone for messages. If Clement's theory is sound, there should be one from Gabby. As relieved as I am to see there is, and even without reading it, Rosa's involvement is now proven beyond all refutable doubt.

Now all I can hope is that we haven't overplayed our hand.

I stop, draw a deep breath, and read the message.

26.

I'll give Gabby credit for getting straight to the point...

Call me within the hour or I give the newspaper your name.

It's as much as I could have hoped for. When I discussed this plan with Clement, I feared it was too risky. Telling Rosa that I'm considering renewing the lease on Hansworth Hall, and I might wish to sell the flat, could have pushed Gabby over the edge rather than into the open, where we need her. It seems Clement was right, though.

I head to the gents toilets and check none of the cubicles are occupied. Satisfied I have the place to myself, I call Gabby's number.

"Morning, brother."

"What do you want, Gabby?"

"I'll tell you what I don't want, and that's to be messed around."

An ironic accusation, considering I was the one sent on a wild goose chase across the Isle of Wight. And as tempting as it is to divulge that we know about her mother's death, Clement rightly suggested we keep that information to ourselves in case we need it down the line. With his instructions in mind, I steer the conversation in another direction.

"You're the one who's messing around, with that bloody newspaper. Why did you do that, Gabby?"

"That was just a taster of what's to come if you don't play ball."

"I am playing ball."

"Why don't I believe you?"

"Believe what you like."

I can imagine her on the other end of the phone, struggling to hide what Rosa told her this morning. One slip of the tongue and her mole will be compromised.

"So, where are the contracts?" she snaps.

"I spoke to my solicitor on Saturday morning and he assured me they'd be sent out today."

I can almost hear the cogs whirring. "You better not be lying."

"I gave him your solicitor's details. Rather than harassing me, you should be checking in with your solicitor."

After a brief pause, she returns to type and issues another threat.

"If I find out you're up to something, William, I'll give the newspaper your name in a heartbeat. And you know what happens after that, don't you?"

I can sense the dynamic shifting, and her usually calm, controlled voice has a strained undercurrent. I might have wrestled control of this conversation, but she still has me cornered in every other respect. I need to keep that in mind.

"Everything is in hand, Gabby. Just leave me alone and you'll get what's yours."

I hang up.

With one more fact to check before we can move forward, I call another number.

"Good morning. Hassard & Partners," a female voice answers.

I ask to be put through to the senior partner, Dominic Hassard. After a short rendition of *Greensleeves*, I'm connected to the man I originally instructed to handle the lease on Hansworth Hall.

"Ah, Mr Huxley. I'm so glad you called. It's been a while."

"Yes, my apologies I've been a little tardy. I understand my PA has been dealing with the lease renewal?"

"Um, yes, she has," he replies a little hesitantly.

"Can you just bring me up to speed on where we are please, Dominic?"

"Well, your PA gave strict instructions not to renew the lease, or to bother you with the matter for the next few weeks. She said you have some major parliamentary situation to deal with and shouldn't be disturbed under any circumstances."

"Right. And has she contacted you this morning?"

"I'm pretty sure she hasn't, but if you can give me a moment I'll check."

I'm treated to more *Greensleeves* while he checks.

"We've not heard anything this morning, Mr Huxley."

"Are you absolutely sure?"

"We're not a large firm and there are only four of us in the office. Nobody has received an email or telephone call from your PA."

"Okay, thank you, Dominic. Can I ask a favour?"

"Ask away."

"Can you advise your staff not to accept instructions from anyone other than myself. If they receive any emails, just acknowledge receipt and forward them to my private email account. The same goes for any future communications from your office — everything must be sent to my private email account."

"Of course. And can I ask, what is the situation with Hansworth Hall? The tenants are getting a little anxious and want to know if they should start looking for alternative premises."

"Can you pass on my apologies and advise them I'll be in a position to offer a definitive decision by the end of the week. Ideally, I'd like them to stay but there are a few issues beyond my control I need to address first."

"I'm sure they'll welcome that news. I'll pass it on."

I end the call.

As angry as I am with Rosa for her now obvious duplicity, I'm just as angry with myself for allowing it to happen right under my nose. There is a fine line between trust and naivety, and I've inadvertently wandered beyond that line.

I return to the office.

Rosa is sat at her desk and stops typing the moment I step through the door.

"Everything okay?" she asks, smiling up at me.

The nerve of the woman.

"Fine, thanks."

I sit at my desk and sort through a random pile of paperwork in an attempt to portray normality.

"Did you email the estate agents in Hampshire for me?" I casually ask.

"I did, within five minutes of you leaving for your meeting."

Her lie is faultlessly delivered. Cold comfort, but I doubt many would be able to see beyond her confident smile.

"Good. And the valuation on the flat?"

"All in hand. I asked an agent to pop round next Tuesday evening at six if that's okay?"

"Oh, they couldn't fit me in this week?"

"Apparently it's a very busy time of the year."

Another lie I'm sure, but it's of little consequence. I really don't wish to know the true value of the flat in case Gabby's plot succeeds. Losing a home is one thing; knowing the exact monetary value of that loss is quite another.

She returns to her typing and I return to my paper shuffling. Just a typical Monday morning — two colleagues going about their business, with one of them involved in a multi-million-pound blackmail plot against the other. All perfectly normal.

I can't bear it.

Every fibre of my being wants to confront her. I want her to know just how much suffering she's brought to my door. I want to unleash the bitterness, the resentment, and the anxiety I've carried since Gabby entered my life. Why should I have to suppress my rage when one of the architects is just across the room from me?

I can scarcely bring myself to breathe the same air as the woman, let alone continue this charade of normality all day.

"I'm really not feeling too well. I think I might have to go home."

"Oh dear," Rosa replies with mock concern. "What's wrong?"

"I suspect that bug is still lingering. Can you cope on your own for the rest of the day?"

"Of course," she coos, perhaps equally relieved she won't have to keep up the pretence either.

I collect my things and tell her to call me if there are any major problems. She looks up at me from her desk and assures me everything will be fine. Her expression, so angelic, so innocent, yet it's just a mask. I can see that now.

I force a smile and leave.

Even though I'm greeted by a skyline of low black clouds outside the palace, it is a preferable view to Rosa's lying face. I make my way on foot towards Blackfriars to meet with Clement. I assumed, like virtually every adult in the country, he would own a mobile phone and I'd be able to call him when I'd completed the first phase of our plan. I should have known better. When I asked for his number, I was greeted by a puzzled face and negative grunts. In lieu of no other practical option, I agreed to meet him at Fitzgerald's at lunchtime. Seeing as it's only mid-morning I'll have to keep myself occupied for another hour or so.

I traipse through the streets until I find a quiet coffee shop. My timing is perfect as the first few drops of rain splatter on the pavement as I enter.

There is no queue and within minutes I'm furnished with a double espresso and a croissant. I place my late breakfast on a table near the window and take a seat. Beyond the glass, the rain is now teeming down. Some pedestrians had the foresight to carry an umbrella and those that didn't are now scampering for cover in doorways. I sip my coffee, happy to be in the cosy confines of a coffee shop rather than just about anywhere else, but particularly outside.

Not wishing to dwell on Rosa, my thoughts turn to Fiona and her heartfelt advice earlier. I have always been slightly envious of her career; not because I had any personal aspirations for higher office, but more the fact she's always had a clear ambition — and was willing to pay the price for it. I've never really questioned why I'm ambivalent to career advancement but I suppose it's because I've always had financial security and I have no thirst for power or recognition.

However, Fiona might have achieved her career goals but in order to do so, she has sacrificed the very same things I've always craved — a meaningful relationship and a family. The difference is, I have sacrificed nothing and still achieved nothing.

What a waste.

My mind turns to Clement, in the hope I can draw some consolation from his seemingly humble existence. I'm not sure I can.

The fact he lives in a rented bedsit and works as a low paid odd job man suggests he isn't motivated by money. Indeed, he hasn't once mentioned my offer of payment or when it might be forthcoming. He is clearly intelligent, although he does a good job of hiding it sometimes, and possesses a certain charisma that particularly appeals to women, yet he's obviously still single. And beyond all of that, I still don't understand why he's even helping me.

More than any man I've ever met, he is proving to be quite the enigma. Whether I ever get to decode him remains to be seen, but I must confess he has proven himself invaluable on more than one occasion. I hope that value ultimately bears a positive result.

Fuelled by two further double espressos, I spend an hour mindlessly wallowing in my own thoughts. I conclude it's hard to determine the right path when every one of them has a Gabby-shaped roadblock in the way. No option other than to deal with her before I can deal with the rest of my life.

Conveniently, I finish my third coffee a few minutes before Fitzgerald's is due to open and after the rain has stopped. I leave a tip at the counter and make my way towards Furnival Street.

I arrive just as Frank is unlocking the front door.

"Bloody hell, William. You're keen."

"Remember that bad day I had last week?"

"Yeah."

"It turned into a bad week."

"Sorry to hear that, mate. I'm sure a few drinks will make the world a better place."

He serves me half an ale and continues with his opening duties while I wait at the bar. Five minutes later, Clement arrives. He has a brief conversation with Frank before lumbering over.

"Alright, Bill."

"I am now."

He pulls up a stool and sits next to me.

"Well? How did it go?"

He listens intently as I give him chapter and verse on Rosa's behaviour, and my conversation with Gabby.

"That's that then," he concludes. "We know for sure the two of them are working together."

"As much as it kills me to say it, there can be no doubt."

He nods in agreement. "So, you know what comes next."

As uncomfortable as this morning was, the next part of Clement's plan doesn't sit well.

"Is there no other way?"

"Nope."

"Fine," I sigh. "But you're just going to follow her, right?"

"Yeah, yeah. Trust me, Bill."

Once we'd established Rosa's involvement, we concluded the best hope of establishing some leverage against Gabby was through her. And that meant following Rosa from work in the hope she'd lead us to my sister. Obviously I couldn't do it, even if I wanted to, so that left Clement as the only option.

"What concerns me, Clement, is you're probably the most distinguishable man I've ever met."

"I'm what?"

"You stick out like a sore thumb."

"Yeah, but this is London. Probably the easiest place on the planet to hide in a crowd."

"I guess I'll have to trust you on that, but I want your word you won't do anything other than follow her, even if she does lead you to Gabby."

"Scout's honour."

"You were a scout?"

"Not gonna lie to you, Bill."

I roll my eyes. "Just…please stay out of trouble. It's my head on the chopping block here."

I suspect the reason for my concern is because I'll have to sit at home and sweat while Clement does my bidding. I'm no control freak, but this plan involves placing a huge amount of trust in a man I only met last week.

"I'm going to head home once I've finished my drink. Let's meet back here at half four…"

The ringing of my phone interrupts me. I glance at the screen and scramble to think of an excuse when I see the caller is Judith Dixon.

I answer the call. "My humble apologies, Judith. I've been meaning to call you all morning but it's been frenetic."

"No need to apologise, William. You're the one paying my bill."

"I know, but that's no excuse for my call Saturday. I hope you weren't offended."

"Not offended, just puzzled."

"Really? Why puzzled?"

"I know you recruited Rosa yourself, but you know I have high standards and I like to look out for my clients. I was concerned how a seemingly competent PA could make such a glaring mistake."

"Right, well, let's just say her employment is under review."

"In which case, I suspect my call might help with that review."

"Go on."

"The reference from her previous employer came in last week, and at first glance, it looked perfectly fine, albeit fairly brief. I was all set to file it until we had our chat on Saturday."

"Okay."

"Maybe I was just annoyed she'd messed up my message, but I thought I'd double check with her previous employer if there'd been any major issues. So I googled her previous company,

Stephens & Marland, to find the email address for their personnel department."

I'm only half listening to Judith while trying to sup my drink. A suspect reference is of little consequence compared to Rosa's other indiscretions.

"The thing is, William," she continues. "There's no record of them anywhere online: no website, no social media profiles, no Companies House records, nothing."

I put my glass on the bar. "Really? That's highly unusual, wouldn't you say?"

"I would, so I checked their address, thinking I might be able to pop in to their offices."

"And?"

"The address is on a housing estate in Hounslow. As far as I can ascertain, Rosa's previous employer doesn't exist and the reference I sent out went to a private address."

Judith now has my complete attention. I click my fingers in Clement's direction and make a sign of a pen scribbling in the air. He reaches over the bar and grabs a pad and a pen.

"Can I have that address please?"

I scribble it down on the pad and assure Judith I'll deal with Rosa. I hang up and turn to Clement.

"We might have an alternative to following Rosa."

I open the electoral roll website on my phone and enter the address in Hounslow. The result comes up almost immediately.

"What you got?" Clement replies.

"An address in Hounslow Rosa used for a fake reference. I know she lives in Islington so it's not hers."

"Who lives there then?"

"A Miss E. Douglas."

"And who's she?"

"No idea, but this might offer us another route to Gabby. You never know, she might be staying there and that's why she had Rosa's reference sent to that address."

It would be too much to ask, but it feels a better option than tailing Rosa around the city.

"What do you wanna do then?" Clement asks.

"I think we should hop on the tube and head to Hounslow."

27.

Twenty minutes after leaving Fitzgerald's, we find ourselves back at Waterloo station. With time to kill before the next train to Hounslow, we pop in to Costa.

"What do you fancy, Clement?"

"Eh?" he mumbles, distracted. "Tea."

"Something on your mind?"

"Nah, just thinking back to the last time I was in this place."

"I didn't think you drank coffee."

"I don't. A friend dragged me in here once."

The chap behind the counter coughs to attract my attention. I order two teas.

"Do you want to grab a seat upstairs?" I ask.

"Nah. I'm gonna wait outside."

He ambles away before I can ask why.

Two minutes later, I exit Costa and find Clement leant up against a wall. I hand him a cup and nod towards an empty bench.

"I'm going to grab a seat."

He follows me over to the bench and we sit quietly, sipping our drinks as the world passes by. I've always held a mild fascination with the transience of train stations. When I'm not in any hurry, I'm actually quite content to sit and watch people heading in every possible direction for every possible reason: to visit loved ones, to say a final goodbye, to start anew, to escape.

So many people with so many stories. I wonder how many of them are travelling with a heart as heavy as mine.

As I turn my thoughts back to our quest, I can't help but breathe a resigned sigh.

"You know, Clement, I've still got a major concern about this plan of ours."

"Go on."

"What are we going to do?"

"Do?"

"If…when we find Gabby."

"Depends."

"On?"

"It's not up to us what happens when we find her — it's up to her."

"We're going to threaten her?"

"Call it what you like, Bill, but if you're gonna blackmail someone, you've gotta take the risk with the reward."

"That's what worries me. There doesn't seem to be much at risk for Gabby."

"Oh, there is," he replies, confidently.

"What?"

He turns to face me. "Pissing me off."

I take a sip of tea and ponder his response. A week ago, I would have vehemently objected to any sort of threat, even towards a woman as twisted as Gabby. But desperate times call for desperate measures. My sister has absolutely no scruples and if she wants to fight dirty, why shouldn't I? However, my fear is that Clement's brand of retaliation will involve physical violence.

"I'm not sure I want to know, but you're not going to…hurt her, are you?"

"In my world, Bill, we have an unwritten rule; we don't hit women."

"So, in your world, how do you deal with women like Gabby?"

"Everyone has a weakness. A five-minute chat and I'll know hers."

"That sounds very much like you're going to hurt her."

"Nah. I'm just gonna make her think that I *might* hurt her. That's usually enough to convince most people."

"And if that doesn't work."

"It will, Bill. It will."

I picture a situation where Clement might be threatening me. Would I offer any resistance? Would I risk enduring the full force of his wrath? I conclude only an idiot would ignore the obvious threat he poses. Gabby might be many things, but an idiot isn't one of them.

I check my watch. "Fifteen minutes. Shall we take a slow walk to the platform?"

He necks the remains of his tea. "Yeah."

As we stand, a woman passes by in front of us, some twenty feet away. She casually glances in our direction and does a double take before coming to an abrupt halt.

"Going for a piss," Clement suddenly blurts.

Before I can tell him not to be too long, he's already striding away. I turn around and the woman is still stood in the same position, staring across the concourse towards Clement as he disappears into the crowd. I watch her with growing curiosity as she taps her forehead and chest in the sign of a cross. Her eyes remain transfixed at the crowd, her mouth agape.

I step across to her. "Are you okay, Madam?"

She turns to face me. Despite the heavy application of makeup, there is no hiding the fact she's well beyond state pension age. Her long hair has clearly been dyed blonde and set in a style far from age appropriate.

"Sorry, sweetheart?" she replies in a raspy voice, her accent suggesting East London roots.

"I was just checking you're okay. You look a little lost."

"I'm…um…yeah, fine sweetheart. It's just…that friend of yours is the spit of a bloke I used to know. Spooked me for a moment."

I know so little about Clement, I'm intrigued enough to pursue the conversation.

"You know him?"

"Him?"

"Yes, the man I was with."

"Course I don't."

"You're sure he's not the man you used to know?"

"Bloody right I am," she scoffs.

"But my friend looks like him?"

"Yeah."

"He's quite…distinctive, isn't he?"

"I know, and that's what made me stop. Thought I'd seen a ghost."

"And you're absolutely sure he's not the man you knew?"

"I went to his funeral, back in the mid-seventies, so yeah, I'm sure."

"Right, um, sorry for your loss."

"Long time ago sweetheart but I still think about him every now and then. We were close for a while, if you know what I mean."

She winks at me. I inwardly shudder.

It appears our conversation has descended into pointlessness. I have neither the time nor the patience to continue it.

"Well, it was nice meeting you."

She returns a smile, revealing a row of yellowed teeth. "And you sweetheart."

As I edge backward towards the bench, the woman looks to the skies. "God bless you, Clement," she mumbles, and promptly scuttles away into the crowd.

It's my turn to stand motionless, mouth agape. Did I just hear what I thought I heard? Did she say Clement?

I return to the bench and try to process what just occurred. Logic quickly dictates there can only be two possible conclusions: either I misheard her, or it's pure coincidence her now-dead friend looked like Clement and shared his name. My mind starts running through the alphabet, formulating names that might rhyme with Clement, like perhaps, hearing the name Tim instead of Jim. Nothing comes even remotely close to the name Clement. I don't think I misheard the woman.

That leaves only one other explanation — coincidence.

"You ready?"

Clement has returned from the toilets.

"What? Right, yes."

We make our way to the platform without conversation. I've now established Clement only talks when he has something worth saying, while I have nothing I feel ready to say.

Our train is already waiting and we wander to the far end of the platform where the carriages are less crowded. We take our seats, facing one another, and wait in silence as the seconds tick by to departure.

No matter how hard I try, the conversation with the woman remains an itch I can't scratch. I can't resist.

"Did you by any chance see that woman who walked past?"

"Where?"

"On the concourse, by the bench. Blonde hair, probably in her seventies."

"Nope."

"Right."

The train edges away while I carefully consider my next words.

"I had a chat with her while you were in the toilets."

"Triffic. Get her number did you?"

"Not that kind of chat. She was a little shaken so I just checked if she was okay."

He puffs his cheeks. "Is there a point to this, Bill?"

"She said…she recognised you, or at least thought she recognised you."

"Good for her."

"But as it turns out, she mistook you for an old friend who died in the seventies."

A shrug of the shoulders and he turns his attention to the window.

"I mean, that in itself isn't particularly strange, but she said a little prayer for her friend as she left. And what was strange, is that her friend happened to be called Clement."

Another disinterested shrug.

"What are the chances, eh? A man who apparently looked exactly like you, and with the same unusual name. That's quite some coincidence, wouldn't you say?

He shakes his head. "Alright, Bill. You got me," he says, his hands raised in mock surrender. "Her name is Marion and I shagged her a few times back in the day, but then I carked it. Now, I'm back from the dead, and for some bleedin' reason I'm stuck helping idiots sort out their problems."

His voice is laced with sarcasm and annoyance; enough to rein in my questioning.

"Okay, I was only saying, that's all."

"Yeah, well," he grumbles. "I don't know what you expect me to say to something like that."

It's a fair point and on reflection, what did I expect him to say? Coincidences, no matter how unlikely, happen every day. Perhaps it would be best to change the subject.

"If you don't mind me bringing it up, you never clarified if Clement was your first name or surname."

"Take your pick. I'm not fussed."

"What does that mean?"

"It means you can call me Clement or Mr Clement. I don't give a shit either way."

I choose neither option, and keep quiet. Enough conversations have now ended the same way and it's clear Clement is at his most prickly whenever I ask personal questions.

I make a few half-hearted attempts at conversation over the remaining thirty minutes of our journey but Clement's mind appears elsewhere.

We eventually pull into Hounslow station and make our way out onto the street. I pull my phone from my coat pocket and check the directions to the address Judith found.

"It's a ten-minute walk away."

Before Clement can reply, the sound of jet engines roar above us. I look up to see the huge and distinctive silhouette of an Airbus A380, almost hanging in the mottled grey sky. London's busiest airport, Heathrow, is located in the borough of Hounslow and for all the commercial benefits, it must be one of the noisiest places in the country to live.

I gesture with a nod to the right and set off. Clement follows, his attention split between the pavement and the aircraft above us. It's afforded the same level of fascination as the old underground train on the Isle of Wight. Perhaps he spots planes as well as trains? I don't ask.

The navigation app leads us through a series of streets lined with scruffy terraced houses and takeaways of every kind. We turn a corner, to be greeted by the sight of three tower blocks on the opposite side of a busy dual-carriageway.

"There should be an underpass that way," I say, gesturing down the road. "And it looks like we're heading towards those tower blocks."

Clement nods and a minute later we descend into the dimly lit tunnel beneath the road. The smell of stale urine, and graffiti-ridden walls are a stark reminder I'm a long way from the sanctuary of my cosseted world. If I wasn't with my intimidating companion, there is no way I'd walk this route on my own.

With some relief, we exit the underpass and continue along a path bordered both sides by low concrete walls and scrubby patches of grass.

"Might wanna stop waving that thing around," Clement suggests, nodding towards my phone.

Sage advice. I memorise the remaining three hundred yards to our destination, and tuck the phone into my pocket.

"I can quite see why Judith was suspicious," I remark as we close in on the nearest block. "It's not exactly the kind of place a law firm would operate."

"I doubt they care too much for the law around here."

"Quite."

We pass three youths sat on a wall; all dressed in the customary attire of hooded tops and baggy jeans. Suspicious eyes watch our every step but a glare from Clement prevents their intimidation going any further than unintelligible mumblings.

The path leads us out onto a narrow road, running along the front of all three tower blocks; the first of which is directly in front of us.

"We're looking for flat ten, Derwent House."

I assumed each block would be clearly signposted. If ever there were any signs, they're long gone. It takes five minutes of searching stairwells and landings to establish the first block is not Derwent House, courtesy of a young woman waiting at the lift with a pushchair.

"Nah, bruv," she says. "Derwent is next along, innit. This is Orwell."

I resist asking if it was named after the author, George Orwell. I doubt the young woman knows or cares.

"Thank you for your help."

"Gotta be worth a smoke, ain't it, bruv?"

Clement furnishes her with a cigarette. She takes a puff and throws a question at me.

"What are you then?" she asks. "Debt collectors?"

"No. We're just here to have a chat with someone."

I realise my casual reply sounds more sinister than I intended.

"Don't matter if you are. Nobody got nothing round here."

She then turns her attention to the lift, and thumps the control panel with frustration. "Pissin' lift never works."

"Would you like us to help you down the stairs?" I ask.

She eyes me suspiciously then glances at her watch. "Yeah, but don't try nothin'."

I don't know quite what she thinks we'll try but Clement picks up the pushchair and carries it down the two flights of stairs. As we descend, the young woman checks her watch again and tuts.

"Are you late for something?" I ask.

"Food bank closes in fifteen minutes."

"Oh."

We reach the narrow road outside the block and Clement carefully lowers the pushchair to the pavement. The young woman nods at him and zips her coat up. She sets off without another word.

"Wait," I call after her.

She stops and looks back at me. "What do you want now?"

I scoot over to her and pull out my wallet. "Here," I say, handing her a twenty-pound note. "Just in case you don't make it in time."

She looks around and eyes the note, still in my fingers. "You ain't one of those old man pervs are you? I ain't into that shit, bruv. Got my boy to think of."

"Um, no. I'm not."

"What you giving me cash for then?"

"We held you up so it only seems fair to recompense you for your trouble."

"I ain't no charity case."

"I'm sure you're not. If it makes you feel any better, consider it a loan. You can pay me back when that young man of yours graduates university."

For the first time since we bumped into the young woman, something of a smile creeps across her face.

"You reckon he could go to university?"

"He can do anything. His life is a blank canvas."

She takes the note and tucks it in her coat pocket. "Thank you."

I stand and watch her hurry off along the pavement. I know the statistics are not in that young child's favour, and at best, there's only a ten percent chance he'll secure a degree, but the opportunity is there.

"Never thought I'd see the day," Clement crows from behind me.

I spin around. "What?"

"A politician doing someone a favour. Gotta be a first."

"We're not all expense-swindling narcissists," I bark back. "Some of us do actually care about other people."

"Alright, Bill. Calm down. If I didn't think you were a decent bloke, I wouldn't be here."

Sadly, Clement is not alone in the misconception us politicians are out of touch with people's everyday issues. That's the inherent problem with running a country; while trying to help the many, people like that young woman slip between the cracks. No parent should have to resort to using food banks and it fills me with shame that they clearly need to.

"What's up?" Clement asks.

"Oh, nothing. I was just thinking some of my colleagues would benefit from visiting this place. Might make them realise that not everyone is enjoying the prosperity we preach about."

"Amen to that," he replies. "But ain't we got something else to be dealing with first?"

Somehow my own troubles don't feel quite so significant. Nevertheless, if I don't deal with Gabby then I won't be in a position to help anyone.

"Come on then."

28.

Derwent House is a carbon copy of Orwell House, and flat ten is on the first floor. An open landing gives access to eight front doors; all in a varying state of neglect. Somebody's idea of music blares from a flat at the far end of the landing. There's no discernible tune, just a throbbing bassline.

We reach flat ten and stand side by side in front of the door. A patch of bare wood on the frame suggests there might have once been a doorbell. As Clement reaches for the knocker, I hold my hand up to intimate he should wait.

"What?" he asks.

"What exactly are we going to say?" I reply in a hushed voice.

"Depends who answers the door."

"Well, what if this Miss Douglas answers? It is her flat."

"I reckon that girl had the right idea. We'll say we're debt collectors, looking for Gabby Davies."

"Right, but her name isn't Gabby."

"Eh?"

"It's Gabrielle. Gabby is a shortened version."

"Whatever."

He raps the door knocker and we both take a step backwards. Seconds pass and there's no obvious sign anyone is about to answer. Clement raps the knocker again, only harder.

A voice echoes along the landing. "She ain't there no more."

We turn to our right to see an elderly man poking his head around the door of the adjacent flat.

"Oh, right," I reply.

"Are you the filth?" he spits.

"The what?"

"No mate," Clement interjects. "We're old friends. We were in the area and thought we'd pop by to say hello."

"Not very good friends, are you" the old man snipes.

"What?"

"She had a stroke. Social services moved her out, back in the summer."

"Do you know which month?"

The old man scratches a stubbly chin. "Let me think. Must have been early June cos' I went into hospital for a week at the end of the month, and she was gone before then."

"Right. Don't suppose you know where they moved her?"

"That care home on Adam Street. Personally, I'd rather die at home caked in my own shit than end up in one of those places."

"Good for you, mate. Have you seen anyone coming or going from this place?"

His eyes narrow as he glares at Clement. "You sure you're not the Old Bill?"

"Do I look like Old Bill?"

"Nah, you don't. But your mate there does."

"Trust me. He ain't a copper."

"Can't abide the tossers," the old man continues. "Never around when you need 'em, always around when you don't."

"Tell me about it," Clement replies. "But as we're not the police, you mind telling us if you've seen anyone?"

"Nah, not seen a soul but I've heard some noises though, so somebody's been in there. Probably the family fighting over her stuff, the thieving bastards."

"When did you last hear anything?"

"Can't be sure, what with the fucking noise around this place all hours, but maybe a few days ago."

"Right. Cheers, fella."

The old man and Clement swap nods before the curmudgeonly pensioner disappears back inside his flat.

"Interesting," Clement mumbles.

"Is it? I'd say we've just lost the only lead we had."

The moustache receives a customary stroke.

"You said letters were being sent here?"

"Yes. Rosa's reference letter."

"And when was that sent?"

"Roughly eight or nine weeks ago."

"Sometime in August then?"

I catch up with Clement's train of thought.

"Ah, right. Somebody received and replied to the reference letter some two months after this Miss Douglas moved out."

"Exactly. And who was here a few days ago?"

"Could have been Rosa."

"Why her?"

"Maybe, like the old man said, she's slowly clearing the place. I'm sure the council are keen to have their property back."

Clement steps across to the large window on the left of the door and tries to peek inside.

"It's the kitchen but I can't see much beyond the net curtains."

"So, what do we do now?"

"We could have a look inside? There might be something in there that leads us to Gabby."

"And how do we do that without a key?"

He returns to the door and shakes the handle. "This thing won't put up much resistance. A firm shove and the catch should pop."

"Absolutely not," I hiss. "We're not breaking in."

"Suit yourself. We'll just head back and sit on our arses till Friday then."

"I'm not saying we should do nothing, but I can't be involved in a criminal act."

"Right. So knobbing your own sister is perfectly legal then?"

"I thought we'd agreed never to mention that?"

"I agreed nothing."

We reach an impasse, but every minute we stand here doing nothing only wastes precious time. We either walk away or I let Clement break in, and hope there is something in the flat to justify breaking the law.

No hope or a vague hope?

"Just do it then. But keep the noise down."

Clement turns to the side and lines his shoulder up against the edge of the door. A quick check to ensure we're not being watched and he thrusts his entire body weight against the wood. The feeble lock never stood a chance against his bulk and the door springs open.

"Come on," he orders, stepping across the threshold.

I take a nervous glance up and down the landing and follow him in. Once we're in the hallway, Clement closes the door and fiddles with the now-crooked locking mechanism.

"Think it might be a bit fucked," he mumbles. "But it sorta works."

I suppose I should be grateful the door is still on its hinges and not lying in the middle of the hallway, such was the force Clement exerted upon it. Ideally, I'd rather we walk away without anyone knowing we'd been here, but a wonky lock seems a reasonable compromise.

"We'll go room by room," Clement whispers.

I nod and follow him through the first door on the left.

The kitchen offers little of interest until we open the fridge and find a carton of milk and a stack of ready meals. I check the best-before date on the milk.

"This must have been bought within the last day or so. It's still in date for another three days."

"Someone is obviously staying here then," Clement acknowledges.

My money is still on Rosa. With a full-time job there would only be a limited amount of hours in the evenings and weekends to clear the flat, so it makes sense she'd need provisions.

We systematically check all the cupboards and drawers, finding nothing untoward, or any clues as to who intends to eat the ready meals.

With the kitchen searched, we turn our attention to the room opposite; a poky bathroom containing a dated avocado suite. There are three plastic bottles lined up on the edge of the bath: shampoo, conditioner, and shower gel. Their presence proves nothing but Clement has the foresight to check the towel, hanging over a radiator next to the sink.

"Feels a bit damp."

Further evidence somebody is using the flat but not who.

We return to the hallway and the two remaining rooms behind closed doors. Clement decides to investigate the room on the left and I follow him into the lounge. The furniture extends to a stained coffee table, a threadbare couch, a foldaway dining table with two chairs, and a sideboard with an old television on top. A few pictures are hung on the wall but the room appears to have been stripped of personal possessions.

"Not much to show for a life," I comment.

"You ain't seen my room," Clement replies. "This is the bleedin' Ritz compared to my hovel."

"If we deal with Gabby, I'll book you a suite at the Ritz."

We inspect the sideboard but it's been emptied. There is nothing else in the lounge worthy of our attention. With only one room left to inspect, we return to the hall and open the door to the bedroom.

The moment I step foot inside, a familiar smell greets me — patchouli.

"Can you smell that, Clement?"

"Perfume?"

"Yes, and if I'm not mistaken, the same perfume Gabby wears."

The bedroom is even more sparsely furnished than the lounge. There's an unmade double bed with a small table next to it, a chest of drawers, and what looks like a built-in wardrobe behind a pair of louvre doors. As I step closer, the patchouli scent intensifies.

I open one of the doors to find a dozen garments hanging on the rail. It only takes a second of searching to find a navy business suit and a sleeveless white blouse.

"These are her clothes."

"You sure?"

"She wore this suit and blouse on…that night. I'm positive."

I turn to face Clement. "I think we've found her hideout."

A frantic ten minutes of searching ensues. We cover every corner of the room, even searching through the pockets of clothes in the wardrobe and under the mattress.

We find no clues to Gabby's life beyond the flat.

"Now what?" I ask, exasperated.

"She's obviously staying here so we just wait for her to come back."

Part of me doesn't fancy the idea of hanging around for what could be hours. However, a more significant part relishes the thought of Gabby walking in and finding us waiting. I can almost picture her face as I introduce her to Clement.

"Better makes ourselves comfortable then."

We decide to hole out in the bedroom. Clement theorises that if we sit on the floor, a few feet left of the door, our position will be obscured when it's opened. By the time Gabby steps into the room and our position is visible, we'll be able to leap up and block her only exit.

The trap has been set. All we can do now is wait.

And wait some more.

We take turns in standing up and shuffling on the spot. Backs and buttocks ache, and the music from the neighbouring flat becomes a form of torture. Eventually the sun sets and the room becomes bathed in orange light from a streetlight outside the window. The lack of light isn't the biggest issue, though.

"I wish I'd worn a thicker coat," I complain.

"Bit parky ain't it."

I check my watch for the umpteenth time. If I didn't know any better, I'd swear it had stopped, such is the painstaking crawl of the minute hand around the dial.

"Do you think she has a job?" I ask.

"Dunno. Why?"

"If she does, it's nearly half five so she could be on her way home by now."

"Let's hope she ain't a nurse. We could be waiting all night."

"I don't think she's a nurse."

We fall into a pattern of talking about nothing for a few minutes, followed by prolonged periods of silence. Despite the tedium and plunging temperature, Clement doesn't complain. I get the impression he is used to waiting around and doing nothing.

"You don't have to tell me, but have you ever been in prison, Clement?"

"Why do you ask?"

"Well, I just assumed it was an occupational hazard in your line of work."

"And it ain't in yours?"

"Fair point."

"But since you ask, no I ain't."

"Right, it's just you seem content with all this waiting around and doing nothing. Personally, I'm losing the will to live."

"Yeah, well, where I come from, doing nothing is about all there is to do."

"I thought you were from London."

"I am. Just not…forget it."

"Come on, Clement" I plead. "I'm genuinely interested."

"Nah, leave it, Bill. Last person I told thought I was insane. Tried setting me up with a shrink, so I ain't gonna make that mistake again."

"Why would somebody consider you insane?"

He turns to face me. If he didn't look sinister enough in daylight, the orange light casts an eerie shadow across his features, making him look almost demonic.

"Drop it."

I oblige without question.

Another hour passes, as does my theory that Gabby might return now the working day is over. It is now so cold I can see my own breath, and coupled with the oppressive darkness, despondency quickly descends.

"How much longer should we give it?"

"What's the time now?"

"Nearly seven."

"Couple more hours."

A punch in the face would have been more welcome than his answer. I let out a long sigh and get to my feet.

"If we're going to be stuck here for another two hours, we need to keep warm. I can't feel my fingers."

I traipse over to the bed and grab the duvet. It feels damp to the touch, although it could just be the cold. I drag it over to the wall and sit down, a foot away from Clement.

"Do you want to share this?"

"Not really," he replies. "But seeing as my knackers feel like frozen spuds, I suppose I'm gonna have to."

He takes one edge of the duvet and pulls it across him. I do the same with the other end, pulling it tight to my chest.

And there we sit, in the dark beneath a musty duvet, like a couple married too long; wishing they were somewhere else. The only saving grace is that we're no longer at risk from hypothermia.

Now all I have to contend with is boredom and hunger. For a second I contemplate heading into the kitchen and liberating one of the ready meals from the fridge, but it would be my luck for Gabby to return and spot the light from the microwave.

Seeing as there is no practical way to deal with my hunger, I turn my attention to the boredom.

"Can I ask you a question, Clement?"

"If it involves you snuggling up any closer, you can fuck right off."

"No, I'm quite close enough, thank you. I was going to ask what your plans are?"

"Plans?"

"Yes, once this is all over. Are you intending to work at Fitzgerald's for the foreseeable future?"

"Foreseeable future," he snorts. "What a crock of shit that phrase is."

"Why do you say that?"

"Did you see this mess with your sister coming? Was it part of your *foreseeable future*?"

"Well, no, of course not. But some parts of our lives we can predict with a degree of certainty."

He shakes his head. "There's only one thing you can be certain of, Bill."

"What's that?"

"When the Grim Reaper comes calling, you'll be on your own and all those plans will count for nothing."

"Well, thank you, Clement," I huff. "That's cheered me up no end."

"Wasn't supposed to cheer you up. I'm just saying people would be better off if they just lived their lives with that in mind. Trying to predict what's gonna happen next week, next month, or next year, is just bullshit."

"And is that how you live your life? For the moment?"

"I did, a long time ago," he says wistfully. "Now I just…exist."

I'm wary of straying onto personal matters as Clement has shut me down on every previous attempt. But seeing as we're stuck here with little else to do, I take a risk.

"You say exist, like you don't have much of a life."

"I don't," he sighs. "Not anymore."

For a moment I almost forget where I am and why I'm here, such is my surprise at the vulnerability in his voice. I decide to push a little further.

"What's so wrong with your life?"

As I wait for him to reply, I realise the music from the neighbouring flat has stopped. For the first time since we arrived, complete silence envelops the bedroom.

"Things ain't the same," he finally mumbles. "People, places, everything I knew — all gone."

He exhales a deep breath and turns to face me. "We ain't so different, Bill. And I know this better than anyone — you're lonely cos' you're living the wrong life."

I'm not sure how this has suddenly become about me, but I can't argue with his insight.

"The wrong life?"

"Yeah. You're no more a politician than I am."

"Um, right."

"And don't think I'm being a bender or anything, but you're not such a bad bloke. I saw what you did for that young girl, and I also saw the look on your face after."

I decide to overlook his inappropriate language. "I didn't realise I had a look on my face."

"You did, and you need to think about being that bloke full time; not the dickhead in a suit who turns up for work every day just cos' he thinks it's what his old man wanted."

Harshly put, but a reasonable point.

"Perhaps you're right," I concede. "But for now, it's semantics."

"It's what?"

"If Gabby fails to turn up before we starve to death, I might not have much of a future to ponder over."

On cue, the thumping music starts again, even louder than before.

"Fucking noise," Clement grumbles.

"Indeed."

We sit for what feels like a lifetime, but turns out to be ninety minutes. The only noise more unbearable than the music is that from our grumbling stomachs.

"Okay, that's it, Clement," I eventually announce. "I think we should call it a night. We can always come back tomorrow."

"Yeah, I suppose so."

With unbridled relief Clement is in agreement, we put the duvet back on the bed and check all the rooms are how we found them. We invest a couple of minutes ensuring the lock on the front door doesn't show any obvious signs of forced entry, and leave.

As we retrace our steps through the estate, my thoughts turn to tomorrow.

"You can stay at my place tonight, if you like? We can make an early start in the morning and perhaps catch Gabby before she leaves the flat."

"You got any booze in?"

"Plenty."

"And food?"

"There's an excellent Chinese takeaway near my flat."

"Then I accept."

Cold, tired, hungry, and dejected, we trudge back to the train station. By the time we arrive, I've concluded that today has been another groundhog day; another chance to derail Gabby's plans, thwarted. It's beginning to feel like the gods are conspiring against me. So, as I sit in a poorly heated waiting room at Hounslow train station, I resort to something I last tried thirty years ago, and I offer a silent prayer. With time and options running out, I have little else to try.

29.

A bowl of Singapore noodles and three shots of brandy finished me off. I retired to bed, so exhausted I didn't hear Clement's snoring, or flatulent backside as he slept on the sofa.

I open the curtains to the same black sky I said goodnight to. It's just turned five thirty as I stare out of my bedroom window at the street below. Even at this early hour, people are out and about; some suffering the cold on foot and others cocooned in cars. We'll be joining the frozen pedestrians within the hour.

I put the kettle on and grab a quick shower while it boils. If I've learnt anything about my snoozing friend, it's to get in the bathroom before he contaminates it.

Keen to avoid another session beneath Gabby's musty duvet, I dress in appropriately warm clothes and return to the kitchen to make tea. Presumably having heard the kettle, Clement appears, yawning in the doorway.

"You done in the bathroom?" he grunts.

"It's all yours," I reply, passing him a mug of tea.

"What time is it?"

"Nearly six."

"We got time for breakfast?"

"We have, if you're happy with toast or cereal."

"Toast, ta. Four slices, buttered."

I wasn't actually offering to prepare his breakfast but it's too early for a debate on the subject.

"I've gotta grab some fags. Where's the nearest newsagents?"

"Turn left out of the door and there's one just around the corner. Don't be long."

He takes a couple of sips of tea and places the mug on the side.

"I'll be five minutes."

I throw him my keys. "You'll need those to get back in."

He disappears, and five seconds later I hear the front door slam shut.

Our plan is to get to Hounslow before half seven which means leaving the flat within the next thirty minutes. We'll be arriving a little more prepared this morning as I equipped Clement with a screwdriver and a handful of paperclips. He assured me he'd be able to pick the lock with those modest tools; preferable to yesterday's assault on the door and necessary if we're to catch Gabby by surprise.

However, if Gabby isn't there, our plan is to hang around the flat until lunchtime, just in case she returns. If we have no luck, our next option is to pay Miss Douglas a visit to see what she has to say about her guest. Beyond that, our plans are sketchy at best. Clement is still keen to tail Rosa in the hope she leads us to Gabby. I remain reluctant but if we have no luck with plan-A or plan-B, it might be the only option left on the table.

Thinking of Rosa, I send her a text to say I won't be in again today as I'm still unwell. She's still way ahead of me in the lying stakes so I feel no guilt.

I turn my attention to Clement's breakfast order and slide four slices of bread into the toaster. With my anxiety levels already building, I can't stomach much more than cereal and grab a box of muesli from the cupboard.

Seated at the kitchen table, I'm about to tuck into my bland breakfast when I hear the front door slam shut again. Heavy boots stomp across the tiled hallway floor before Clement bursts into the kitchen. I look up at him. His scowl does not bode well.

"You want the good news or the bad news?" he asks.

I'm not in the mood for games but indulge him. "Go on," I sigh. "I could do with some good news."

"Alright. The good news is I found a fiver on the way to the newsagents."

"I'm thrilled for you. Shall we put up some bunting to celebrate?"

"Not yet. Here's the bad news."

He pulls a rolled-up newspaper from his back pocket and slaps it on the table.

"Front page," he adds.

An immediate sense of foreboding destroys what little appetite I had. With hands that have suddenly developed a tremble, I unfurl the newspaper and lay it flat on the table.

"Oh, fuck," I gasp. "What the…?"

"That's bad," Clement blurts, pointing out the obvious. "But it gets worse."

I look up at him, and then back at the headline dominating the front page of a national newspaper — *Perverted MP in Incestuous Sex Tape Scandal.*

"Worse? How the hell can this get any worse?" I yell.

"There's already a dozen journalists waiting outside the building."

I can't find words. My mind collapses in on itself as if I'd just been told by a doctor I have a terminal illness. There is no way out, no solution, no plan left to enact. Three days ahead of her deadline, Gabrielle Davies, my own sister, has destroyed my life in the most abhorrent manner possible.

End game has been reached. It's over. I am ruined.

"Bill. Bill."

I hear Clement's voice but it can't penetrate my conscious mind. My senses lose all definition as I stare into space; shocked, mortified, inert.

"Bill? Can you hear me?"

I'm suddenly aware of a heavy weight on my shoulder. My upper body sways as the weight shifts back and forth. Focus finally arrives when a stinging sensation explodes across my right cheek. Like a drowning man breaking the water's surface, I gasp for air.

"Bloody hell, Bill. Thought you were gonna pass out on me there."

I wasn't even aware he'd moved, but Clement is now on the chair next to me.

"You…you slapped me."

"Listen," he orders. "We ain't got time for this shit. Pull yourself together."

What was the term Rosa used last week? Tea and sympathy? Clement might have a mug of tea in his hand but there's precious little sympathy in his voice.

"It's over, Clement," I murmur. "I'm done for."

"No it ain't. Not till I say it is."

My gaze falls to the table and the taunting headline. I turn the paper over and stare blankly at the back page. England lost at cricket. Again.

"Why do you reckon she's done this now?" Clement asks. "Don't make no sense."

"Doesn't matter. All that matters is that she's done it."

Even in my own head, my voice sounds feeble, broken.

"Course it bleedin' matters," he booms. "Three more days and she stood to make millions, yet she settled for what? Fifty grand? A hundred? There's no way the paper would pay more than that."

He leans across the table. "I reckon we've spooked her. That Rosa must have told her you left work early yesterday and she probably thought you were up to something. Maybe she didn't think it was worth the risk holding out for the big pay day on Friday."

"With fear of repeating myself, so what? The damage has already been done."

"For fuck's sake, Bill. You're not getting it are you?"

"Getting what?"

"She took the money because she couldn't risk waiting until Friday, so the question is: what is it she couldn't risk?"

I offer a half-shrug.

"We need to find out."

"And how do we do that exactly?"

"We stick to the plan, well, the second part anyway. We head to Hounslow and visit that care home."

Self-pity gives way to anger and the need to vent becomes too great. "For God's sake, man," I blast. "There's no damn point."

To enforce my stance, I turn the newspaper over and slap my hand across the headline. "It's all there in black and white. Nothing is going to change that."

The chair legs scrape across the floor as Clement suddenly gets to his feet.

"Fine. You stay here and sulk then. No wonder you got yourself in this mess — you're a fucking drip, Bill."

"I beg your pardon."

"You heard me," he growls. "You're just like all the other gutless tossers in Westminster. You ain't got the balls to make the hard choices."

"I…what?"

He rests his hands on the table and looms over me. For one horrible moment I fear I've pushed too far, such is the rage in his eyes.

"You're a smart bloke, Bill, so don't pretend you don't know. When the shit hits the fan in life, people tend to do one of two things: face up or fuck off, and you ain't done much facing up."

He shakes his head and glares at me; his disdain obvious.

"When are you gonna stop ducking and deal with your shit?"

His eyes bore into me as the question hangs unanswered. It shames me to admit it, but perhaps there is some truth in his accusation. I've never had to make any tough decisions in my life because money has always provided the route to an easy escape. And now, I've arrived at a terrible place as an incestuous deviant; a shamed politician of the very worst kind. There is only one way out — to run away.

"You might be right, but it doesn't change anything. I need to focus on damage limitation now."

"How?"

"I don't know. If there's any silver lining to this whole sorry episode, at least I still have both properties and therefore, options."

"What options?"

"I could move abroad and start a new life."

"Right, and spend the rest of your days hiding on the Costa Del Nonce with all the other pervs? Do me a favour, Bill."

It's clear we're going around in circles. I know there will be no hiding from my crime wherever I go in the world, but I'm too tired and too battle-weary to continue such a senseless argument.

"Please, Clement," I whisper, my head bowed. "Just leave it be."

He mumbles an expletive and just as I expect him to storm out, he sits back down.

"I'll leave it, but first, answer me a question."

"Go on," I sigh.

"Are you a religious man?"

I look up. "Don't try to sway me with some religious platitudes about faith and belief."

"I'm not, and you didn't answer my question."

"No, not since my mother passed."

"So, if I said I was told to help you by…a voice in my head, you'd think I was insane?"

"Very much so. Why?"

"Cos' that's why I'm here, to help you. Believe it or not, it's the truth."

He sits back in the chair and folds his arms as if he's just told me the time.

"Sorry…what?" I splutter. "You do realise how ridiculous that sounds?"

"Yeah, don't I know it. That's why I never told you."

"And what exactly am I supposed to do with that information?"

"What do you wanna do?"

"At this precise moment, throwing myself out of the window seems an attractive proposition."

"You wouldn't be the first."

"Jesus wept," I murmur, kneading my temples in slow circular movements. "Why are you doing this to me? Haven't I got enough to contend with?"

"I'm doing it cos' you didn't leave me any other choice. You might be able to give up, but I can't."

"Why not?"

"Cos' I'm tired, Bill, and I'm sick of being on my own in a place I don't belong. This ain't where I'm supposed to be and if I don't see this thing through, that ain't gonna change."

Some years ago, one of my colleagues suffered a nervous breakdown. Nobody spotted the signs until it was too late, and he made a crude attempt to end his own life. Fortunately, the poor fellow failed, and eventually sought treatment. Is Clement going through some sort of breakdown himself? Should I treat his delusional claim with the disdain it deserves, or play along for fear of tipping him over the edge?

"I honestly don't know what to say, Clement."

"Course you do," he snorts. "You wanna tell me I'm a nutter and I should see a shrink."

"Well, that isn't quite how I'd put it, but yes, maybe you should."

"Alright, I will, but on one condition."

"And that is?"

"Give me today."

"Today?"

"Yeah. I've got this itch I can't scratch but if we go and see that woman in Hounslow, I reckon that'll sort it. Give me to the end of today."

"And if we do, you promise to seek help with your…condition?"

"I don't do promises, Bill, but yeah, I will."

I can't believe I'm even considering a deal with a man who is taking advice from a voice in his head. Would that make me equally as crazy?

"Look, Clement. I want to help but there's no need for us to go on some wild goose chase first."

"You owe me, Bill. I've not asked anything from you — now I am."

Every part of me wants to run away from this madness, but the one thing keeping me rooted to my chair is a sense of debt. He's right. I do owe him.

"Okay" I sigh with a shake of my head. "Four o'clock."

"What about it?"

"I'll come with you to Hounslow and we'll see that woman, but if we haven't scratched whatever itch you have by four o'clock, we'll go and see my doctor and then I'm going to hand myself in at the police station. Fair enough?"

"Fair enough. And one other thing."

"What now?"

"I need you to have a bit of faith."

"In what?" I huff. "That all my troubles will miraculously disappear after chatting with a stroke victim in Hounslow?"

"I don't know what we're gonna find but whatever it is, this is for your benefit, remember?"

"Fine. I'll embrace this madness if it makes you happy."

"Good man."

I clamber to my feet, still unconvinced I'm doing the right thing. For now though, I'd rather focus on more mundane matters.

"Do you still want toast?"

"Yeah."

On still shaky legs, I switch the toaster on and lean against the counter.

As the bread browns I use the opportunity to collate my thoughts. Notwithstanding Clement's ridiculous claim, I do wonder if there is even the slightest slither of merit to his insistence we visit Miss Douglas. And before his ludicrous confession, he did raise a salient point about Gabby not waiting until Friday.

Why?

Suddenly, I have my own itch to scratch.

I think back to the moment in the park when Gabby first told me the truth about her identity. What was it she said? So much of that conversation passed in a haze I struggle to remember the specifics, but I vaguely recall she mentioned a claim for my father's inheritance. I have no idea if she has any legal right, but with all the blame on my shoulders, and coupled with Gabby's ability to spin lies, it's not inconceivable she could mount a strong case.

Has Gabby really delivered the final blow or is the newspaper article just an opening salvo? Was my reputation her first target, and now that's been sullied beyond repair, will she now pursue me through the courts to compound my shame and strip me financially bare?

Even now, all I can do is second guess the damn woman. Perhaps Clement's suggestion isn't as pointless as I first thought.

And so, it has come to this — a trip to Hounslow to visit a stroke victim on the advice of a mentally unstable man, and the voice in his head.

"God help me," I mumble to myself.

I guess the only silver lining is I can delay facing the impending shit storm about to hit Westminster, and the police. I know I can't hide forever but that doesn't mean I'm quite ready to face my punishment.

Nor, as it happens, can I face the remains of my cereal. Clement, however, destroys his four slices of toast within a few minutes.

Fed and watered, at just after seven o'clock we're all set.

"I just need to grab my phone."

I scoot to the bedroom and pluck the phone from the bedside table. It's still on silent mode and my stomach turns when I see the worrying number of missed calls, voicemails, and unanswered text messages. No doubt Fiona Hewitt will be amongst them, and I dread to think who the others are from. One thing is for sure though: the calls and messages aren't going to stop arriving anytime soon. I leave the phone on silent mode and slip it in my pocket.

I return to the hall where Clement is waiting.

"Is there another way out of here?" he asks. "Don't fancy your chances against that mob down there."

"There's a service yard at the back where they collect the bins. We can get out that way."

"Lead on."

Rather than taking the lift, we descend the building via a service stairwell meant only for use in emergencies. I consider my plight worthy of such status. It leads us down to a utilitarian corridor at the back of the building.

"This way."

We exit through a fire door into a yard, hemmed in by tall brick walls and a cobalt blue sky. Besides the door we just passed through, a set of iron gates are the only other way in or out.

"Just gonna take a quick reccie," Clement says before marching up to the gates and peering left and right.

"All clear," he calls.

We slip out of the gates and dart down a side road away from the flat.

"It's too risky getting the train," I comment as we walk. "Let's just hop in a cab."

A minute later we're in the back of a black cab; driven by a cheerless man who either doesn't read the papers or doesn't care who he ferries across the city.

Once we've navigated through the streets of central London, the cab picks up pace. Fortunately, all the traffic is heading into the city while we're heading out.

We reach the M4 motorway and the thrum of the diesel engine settles at a steady tone. With every passing mile the darkness fades to a brighter shade of blue, promising a cold, crisp start to the day for those fortunate to still be at home. I wonder if Gabby is still tucked up beneath her musty duvet, or, as is more likely, she's heading in the same direction as our cab. While we're heading towards a care home in Hounslow, she's probably heading across town to the departure lounge at Heathrow Airport; ready to jet off to sunnier climes, courtesy of her ill-gotten gains.

It is a thought that bolsters my decision to make this journey.

Besides the thrum of the engine, I'm accompanied by the soundtrack of Clement gently snoring. Not quite the guttural noises I had to endure in Sandown, but loud enough to be irritating. If only that was all I had to worry about.

I close my eyes and focus on the many ways a conversation with Miss Douglas might pan out. It's hard to see how anything she says will help, but it certainly can't hurt to ask a few questions, I suppose. The reality is, my very liberty now hinges on a woman who has recently had a stroke, who may or may not know my sister is staying at her flat, and a delusional man in double denim, snoring beside me.

If there really is a God, he has a twisted sense of humour.

30.

With only a twenty-pound note left in my wallet, it's fortunate cab drivers now accept credit cards. I pay the man and begrudgingly give him a small tip for not crashing on the way.

Not knowing the precise location of the care home, or even the name, I asked the driver to drop us at the entrance to Adam Street. Little did I know it's almost a mile long.

"I guess we just walk until we find it. There can't be more than one care home on the street."

With Clement once again grumbling about his frozen knackers, we set off with hands tucked firmly in pockets to stave off the cold. We make our way past an eclectic mix of residential properties from every era, and the frigid air soon becomes choked with fumes as vehicles crawl past on both sides of the road; going nowhere in a hurry.

As we walk, my attention turns to what we're going to do once we find the care home. Like most of our plans thus far, we haven't exactly focused on the details.

"Any idea what we're going to say to her?" I ask.

"We're not gonna say anything. You are."

"Why me?"

"Cos', Bill, you're the one with the plummy voice and polite manner. I don't think the old bird is gonna appreciate my style of questioning."

"Okay. Agreed. But what exactly do I ask her?"

"Simple. Where is Gabby and why was she staying at the flat?"

"And what if we get the same reaction as that woman in Sandown?"

"We rough her up a bit."

"What?"

"I'm kidding. Let's just see what she has to say, then we'll decide how to play it."

Once again we'll be making it up as we go along. It doesn't fill me with confidence.

"I'm sorry, Clement. With fear of sounding negative, it does feel like we're clutching at straws."

"We are."

"Splendid," I groan. "You weren't quite so pessimistic back at the flat. Why do I feel like I've been played?"

"It's a hunch, Bill. Nothing more. If you've got a better idea, I'm all ears."

I don't and my desperation morphs into frustration.

"This is bloody ridiculous," I mumble. "Dragged halfway across London on the back of a mere hunch."

"Three things you should never underestimate: a pissed off woman, a good hunch, and me."

I can't argue with his first assumption and can only hope he's right about the other two.

We walk on and a hundred yards later, we find what we're looking for. Orchard Lodge is an imposing block of brick and tile; featureless and stern. It could just as easily be a library or a community centre, such is the utilitarian architecture. Only the sign at the head of the driveway tells of its function.

"Grim," Clement remarks as we make our way to the entrance.

As we approach, a pair of automatic doors part and a waft of warm air greets us. We step inside an entrance lobby and push through another set of glazed doors to the reception area. The air is warmer still, and laced with the scent of disinfectant; barely masking a heady blend of odours I'd rather not decipher.

The reception area itself is relatively small, with a desk at the far end, half-a-dozen chairs, and two corridors leading to the left and right. I approach the desk, and the forty-something woman in a blue uniform, stood behind.

I hastily prepare my pre-concocted white lies.

"Good morning. I was wondering if you could help me?"

"Good morning," she replies in a strong eastern European accent. "I'll try."

I fish my wallet out and present the woman with my parliament identification card.

"My name is William Huxley and I'm a member of parliament."

The woman leans forward and studies the card. For a second I fear she might recognise my name from the newspaper, but she smiles and seems happy with who I am.

"You are here for inspection?" she asks.

"Not quite. I've been asked to visit a Miss Douglas. I work with a member of her family and they've asked me to see if there's any way I can help with her situation."

"Ahh, government is going to give us more money, yes?"

I wish. If ever a sector needed better funding, it's social care. Still, why waste taxpayer's money on the sick and needy when we have a pointless nuclear deterrent to fund.

"I can't make any promises, but I would like to chat with Miss Douglas. Is that possible?"

The woman's smile dissolves as she points to a sign fixed on the wall behind her.

"I'm sorry. Visiting hours don't start until eleven o'clock."

Almost three hours away. Time I can ill-afford to waste.

"Unfortunately, I have a meeting with the Prime Minister at eleven, which is why I'm here so early."

The lie flows effortlessly. If I am to have a meeting with the PM today, I suspect it will involve my very public sacking.

"You know the Prime Minister?" she asks, seemingly impressed.

"Well, yes. She's my boss."

Some sort of thought process appears to take place as the woman stares off into the distance.

Her attention eventually returns to me. "Can you ask the Prime Minister to pay us more money? London is too expensive."

"I can ask."

"You definitely ask?"

"Definitely."

"Okay. You come back in thirty minutes. Miss Douglas will be with her carer now but you can see her later."

"Thank you, and will you be here?"

"Yes, I'm always here," she huffs. "Too many hours."

"Right, yes, and your name?"

"Anna."

"Thank you, Anna. I'll pop back in half an hour."

Seeing as I couldn't think of a reasonable explanation for a giant man in retro clothing accompanying me, Clement wisely chose to sit in one of the chairs while I spun my lies. As I walk back towards the doors, he gets up and follows a few seconds later. We don't exchange words until we're back on the street.

"How did it go?" he asks.

"We can see her in half an hour."

"Cool. Let's go grab a cuppa then."

We wander back up Adam Street and find a grotty little cafe that Clement decides will do. Despite the greasy table and questionable hygiene standards, at least it's warm, and virtually empty.

Twenty minutes are wasted as we drink insipid tea and avoid the elephant in the room. Inevitably, it proves too large.

"This voice of yours? How often do you hear it?"

"Haven't heard it for best part of a year. Then, it came back last week at Fitzgerald's, when you were first there with that Gabby bird. Since then, I hear it…I dunno…maybe once or twice a day."

"Right. And what does it say?"

"It's hard to explain, Bill. It's not as if it speaks to me like you are now. I can't make out clear sentences…it's just a faint whisper in your ear, you know?"

"Not really, no."

"You ever play hide and seek as a kid?"

"Considering I was an only child with no real friends, no, I did not."

"But you know how it works, right? The one who has to do the seeking, you tell them they're getting hot if they're close, or cold if they ain't."

"Okay, I get it."

"That's how it feels. I don't get directions — just a sense if I'm going the right way, and the odd word which don't often make sense."

"But it's telling you to help me?"

"Kind of."

"Kind of? It either is or it isn't, surely?"

"Look, Bill, I can't explain any more than I have. I don't know why the bleedin' voice is there, or why I'm supposed to help you — I just know I do. But I'll tell you something for nothing: I could do without it."

His claim, if you discount what he actually said, appears sincere; almost believable. Then again, I've witnessed people make equally sincere declarations at work. They truly believe they are right about a particular subject and it becomes their truth. In essence, that is the very heart of politics: trying to persuade others that your version of the truth is the correct version.

It follows that perhaps Clement is simply hearing his own version of a truth; concocted in a broken mind.

"Do you know who's voice it is you're hearing?"

"Fucked if I know."

"Alright, but why did you ask if I'm religious? What does that have to do with anything?"

He plays with his empty cup for a few seconds, either avoiding my question or trying to conjure a plausible answer. My money would be on the latter.

"I don't think we should go there."

"Why not?"

"You think the voice in my head is hard to believe? If I told you the full story, you'd have the men in white coats here in a flash."

"Try me."

"Nah, Bill. I ain't gonna take that risk."

"What happened to trust?"

"Nothing to do with trust — this is about getting the job done. If I go spooking you now, there's every chance the job could go tits up. Can't let that happen."

"Is that what this is then? A job?"

"Yeah, of sorts. S'pose it's more like a test, though."

"And what happens if you pass the test?"

He stares directly at me, and delivers his reply completely dead pan. "Redemption."

I'm no expert on mental health, but clearly Clement is dealing with some serious internal issues. If it were not for the fact I have my own issues to contend with right now, I might well be suggesting he seeks immediate medical assistance.

"Okay then," I hesitantly reply. "I think perhaps we'll leave it there."

He shrugs his shoulders and returns to his usual self. "Shall we go then? I need a fag."

A minute later we're ambling back along the road; Clement with a cigarette in hand, acting as if our conversation had never taken place. If indeed he is suffering a mental illness, he's done a remarkable job of hiding it up until this morning.

I just hope his delusions return to wherever they came from, for now.

31.

We return to Orchard Lodge to find Anna still at her station. I approach the desk and deal with the first issue: introducing Clement and explaining his presence.

"This is Mr Clement. He's my security detail."

"Like a bodyguard, yes?" she replies.

"I'm afraid we live in troubled times, so yes, he's like a bodyguard."

Anna looks Clement up and down. Sensing her concern, I intervene.

"I apologise for my colleague's attire. The public don't want to see members of parliament with bodyguards as it undermines their sense of security. For that reason, they wear clothes to blend into the background as required."

Convinced or otherwise, she nods and hands us visitor badges. "Okay. Come this way please."

We follow Anna down a corridor past a series of numbered doors like a hotel. The drab magnolia walls, vinyl flooring, and cold lighting suggest this is not a place people stay of their own choosing.

"Miss Douglas is not a well lady," she remarks as we walk. "Her stroke was very bad."

"I'm sorry to hear that."

"She cannot speak much, and very little movement in her body."

I shake my head and shoot Clement a frown to confirm I'm not happy harassing the poor woman.

Anna comes to a stop and raps her knuckle on door number sixteen. Without waiting for an answer, she half opens the door and pokes her head through the gap.

"I have a visitor for you, Miss Douglas. A man from Westminster," she states in a slow monotone voice. "Are you okay for him to come in?"

After a brief pause, Anna turns and beckons us in. I lead and Clement follows behind.

Within seconds of stepping into the room, I want to leave. A frail bag of bones is seated in an armchair near the window. Her silver-grey hair is a tousled mess and she's wearing what I assume is a standard issue nightgown.

Besides the chair in which Miss Douglas is seated, the cramped room is furnished with a single bed, over which a hoist is fixed, a wardrobe, two plastic guest chairs, a chest of drawers, and a commode. Beyond the single window, a slither of blue sky is just about visible beyond a brick wall, with more vinyl flooring and magnolia walls completing the drab accommodation.

"I have to go back to reception," Anna says. "You must check out when you leave. Not more than fifteen minutes, please."

I nod and watch her close the door on the way out, wishing I could follow.

Once Anna has left, there is no option other than to face Miss Douglas.

"Good morning," I chime, trying to offer some semblance of cheer.

She stares up at me through widening green eyes and grunts a series of sounds that might have been words.

"I'm sorry? I didn't catch that," I reply, trying to mimic Anna's monotone voice.

"I don't think she's deaf, Bill."

"What?"

"You don't have to shout."

"Right. Of course."

Clement drags the two plastic chairs across the floor and positions them in front of Miss Douglas. We sit, and she continues to stare at me, as if I'm the oversized oddball wearing seventies attire.

"I'm William Huxley and this is my associate, Clement."

Whatever mobility Miss Douglas possesses, it appears she's trying to communicate by waving her left hand as her bottom lip moves frantically up and down.

"Chaa," she eventually blurts.

I look at Clement and he shakes his head.

"Sorry?"

"Chaa," she repeats.

"Chair?"

A deep furrow creases her forehead and the left hand is waved dismissively.

Clearly frustrated at our inability to understand, she tries again and a different sound comes out. "Chars."

Again I look at Clement. Again he shakes his head. This is ridiculous. I decide to ignore whatever it is she's trying to say and move the conversation along.

"Miss Douglas. I'm here regarding a recent security breach at Westminster. There's nothing for you to worry about but the address of your flat came up during the investigation. I was hoping you might be able to answer some questions if that's okay?""

I can't tell if her shaking head is a nod or just an involuntary movement. I need a more robust system if this isn't to become the pointless exercise I feared.

"Miss Douglas. Are you able to make a thumb sign?"

I demonstrate by giving her a thumbs-up sign.

"This is yes," I say, before turning my hand over so my thumb is pointing to the floor. "And this is no."

With an unsteady hand, she slowly replicates the thumbs-up sign.

"Excellent. And are you able to do the thumb-down sign?"

With a concentrated turn of the wrist, she copies my action.

"That's great. Thank you."

Now we have a rudimentary form of communication, I can at least ask her some questions.

"Okay. First question: Do you know somebody called Rosa Jones?"

Her hand twist and she give me a thumbs-up.

That explains why Rosa used the flat address for her reference.

"And is she related to you?"

The thumb remains up.

"Is she your niece?"

Thumb down.

"Daughter?"

Thumb up.

Surprising, considering they have different surnames.

"Great. So Rosa Jones is your daughter. That's the first answer established."

"Now, do you know a woman called Gabby?"

Thumb down.

"Perhaps you know her as Gabrielle Davies?"

The thumb remains in the down position.

Damn it.

Detecting my annoyance, Clement steps in with a question of his own.

"Alright, darlin'. Did you know somebody was staying in your flat?"

Thumb down.

Clement sits back in his chair and strokes his moustache. I have no idea what else there is to ask so offer a feeble smile. Seconds tick by and the silence becomes awkward. There doesn't appear to be any good reason to continue this farce.

"I think we should leave Miss Douglas in peace now, Clement."

He ignores me and leans forward. With his elbows resting on his thighs, he addresses her again. "You were trying to say something a minute ago. Was it a name?"

Thumb up.

I turn to Clement. "How did you know that?"

"Lucky guess," he replies before posing another question to Miss Douglas. "That name you were trying to say. Was it Charles?"

Thumb up.

"Like his dad?" Clement adds, nodding in my direction.

Thumb up.

"Wait a minute," I interject. "How on earth would she know my father's name?"

"Dunno," Clement replies. "Why don't you ask her?"

Puzzled, I follow his suggestion. "Miss Douglas. Did you by any chance know my father?"

Again the thumb is pointed upward.

I'm taken aback at her revelation. And although her positive response might explain why she was staring at me when I first stepped into the room, it also opens up an entirely new set of questions. However, I can't think of a single one with a simple yes or no answer.

Perhaps noting my quizzical expression, Miss Douglas becomes as animated as a person with limited movement can be. She points across the room towards the chest of draws. Her pointing is accompanied by a series of frantic grunts.

"Is there something in the chest of drawers?" I ask.

Thumb up.

"Did you want me to look for it?"

Thumb up.

I get up, cross the floor, and stand in front of the chest of drawers. Facing Miss Douglas, I point at the top drawer like an amateur furniture salesman.

"This one?"

Thumb up.

Without any clue what I'm even looking for, I open the drawer. On first glance, it looks like it contains nothing other than clothing.

"Pus," Miss Douglas grunts.

I look in the draw, hoping to spot something that connects with her sound. Nothing.

"Purs. Purs."

"I think she's saying purse," Clement suggests. Miss Douglas gives him a thumbs-up.

I move a few of the folded garments and find a black leather purse.

"This?" I ask, holding the purse aloft.

Thumb up.

After closing the drawer, I return to my chair and place the purse on Miss Douglas's lap. With her one good hand, she tries to undo the clasp.

"You wanna hand there, darlin'?" Clement asks.

Perhaps I should have considered her lack of dexterity before dropping the purse on her lap. Clement flicks the catch open and passes it back to Miss Douglas as I watch on; curious what she's so keen to show us.

The purse flops open. The inside flap has a row of credit cards one side and a photo behind a transparent plastic window on the other. Miss Douglas jabs at the photo with a spindly finger.

Clement and I both lean forward to take a closer look, but the photo is upside down and obscured by light reflecting off the plastic window.

"May I take a closer look?" I ask.

She gives me the thumbs-up.

I pluck the purse from her lap and turn it around. The photo is small and faded with age. But it's not the condition that prompts my reaction; more the subject of the photo.

"Good Lord," I gasp.

"What is it?" Clement asks.

"It's Hansworth Hall," I reply, holding the purse up for him to take a closer look.

"And who's that?" he adds.

The photo is of a middle-aged woman stood on the gravel driveway outside my family home. Whoever took the photo must have been some distance away as the face lacks much in the way of definition. However, there's enough to determine a similarity with the woman now seated a few feet away.

"Is…is this you?" I ask, pointing at the photo.

She gives me a thumbs-up.

I squint at the photo again; more perplexed than ever. Dozens of questions pepper my mind, and that's where they'll stay because Miss Douglas can't answer any of them. All I know is that this frail woman once visited my family home, and somehow she knew my father. And then, many years on from that visit, her daughter teamed up with my sister to blackmail me. Are these events connected? If they are, the lines are simply too faint to follow.

A toxic combination of frustration and irritation bubble beneath my calm exterior.

The smile fades.

"Miss Douglas. Did you know your daughter is involved in a plot to blackmail me?"

Her hand drops to her lap, her expression confused.

"Bill? What you doing?" Clement asks.

"Getting answers," I spit back at him. "That's what we're here for, isn't it?"

"Yeah, but…"

I turn back to Miss Douglas and continue to vent my irritation. "I'm going to assume you probably did know Rosa was involved. Now, I want to know where Gabby is?"

She makes another grunting sound and shakes her head.

"Oh, come on, Miss Douglas," I blast. "Where is she? Are you in on it too?"

"Bill. Cool it," Clement rumbles.

"Like hell I will."

I lean forward and stare straight into the woman's eyes. "I've had just about enough lies from you and your daughter. You know who Gabby is, don't you? She was staying in your damn flat, for crying out loud."

Her eyes tell me nothing and the irritation boils over. I stand up and kick the chair away.

"Damn you woman," I roar, jabbing my finger towards her. "Answer my questions."

"William!" a voice screams from behind me. "Stop it."

I spin around to find Rosa stood in the doorway. With no point in hiding the fact we know of her subterfuge, I now have a new target to aim my rage at.

"Welcome to the den of liars, Rosa. So glad you could make it."

"Please, William. Calm down," she pleads. "You're scaring my mother."

I step towards her, my fists balled and every sinew strained; such is the effort to curb my anger.

"Don't you dare tell me to calm down," I bark. "Not after what you've done."

Her gaze drops to the floor and she swallows hard. No denial, no defence. "I'm sorry," she whispers.

"You're sorry?"

Her feeble apology is the spark to the gunpowder. I take six steps towards her, and without consciously giving instructions, my arm swings through the air in her direction. While I have no control over my action, there is no part of me that would consciously strike a woman; a fact born out as my fist connects with the plasterboard wall, three feet to the left of Rosa's face. Pain crackles across my hand.

I fall to my knees.

With ragged breath, I look up at Rosa and spit the final remnants of rage. "With every ounce of my being, I hate you for what you've done to me."

A stunned silence falls across the room, broken only by the sound of heavy boots across the vinyl floor. Clement stands over me.

"You alright?" he asks.

I shake my head. I have never felt less right in my life.

He helps me to my feet and then turns his attention to Rosa. "If you don't want us chatting to your old girl, get in here and close the door."

She does as instructed without complaint.

"Sit down," Clement orders, pointing to the chair he occupied a few seconds earlier.

Rosa takes a seat next to her mother and Clement picks up the chair I kicked across the room, placing it a few feet from Rosa's.

"You and me are gonna have a little chat," he says, his tone firm but calm.

Rosa nods as she grasps her mother's hand. Now my anger has subsided, a growing sense of shame blossoms. Whatever Rosa has done, her mother is a frail invalid and didn't deserve to witness my outburst. I stand in the corner and deal with my shame, content to let Clement ask the questions.

"I'm guessing you're supposed to be at work about now?" he confirms. "How did you know we were here?"

"William's phone," she murmurs. "I put a tracking app on it."

"You did what?" I blurt.

"Bill. Let me handle this," Clement orders. "You're gonna lose your shit again."

I stare daggers at Rosa but don't argue.

"And I reckon we already know the answer, but have you been feeding Gabby info about Bill?"

She looks up at Clement, puzzled.

"Have you been feeding Gabby info about William?" he asks again, correcting my name.

No reply other than a faint nod.

"Alright. Now we've established that, you wanna tell me why?"

Silence.

The need to grab Rosa and shake the answer from her is almost overwhelming. It is just as well Clement has taken over the questioning as I don't think I'd be able to control myself. I bite my lip and slowly count backwards from ten to calm myself down.

"Come on girl," Clement prompts. "It ain't a tricky question. Why have you been feeding info to Bill's sister?"

Frustration mounts and I restart my count.

"She's…," Rosa eventually whispers

Seconds pass but the rest of her answer isn't forthcoming.

"She's what?" Clement asks. "Speak up, girl."

"She's not William's sister. She's my sister."

32.

I can't speak, and I can barely see through the tears welling in my eyes. Clement looks up at me; possibly to check I haven't fainted. He nods before returning his attention to Rosa.

"What? Gabby ain't his sister?"

"Gabby…Gabrielle…*is* his sister," Rosa stammers. "But she's not the woman who's been blackmailing him. That's my sister, Amy."

"Eh? I don't get it."

"Amy was pretending to be Gabby."

Clement sits back in his chair and scratches his head. Rosa turns to me, her eyes pleading for a release of some kind.

"I'm so sorry, William. I never wanted any of this."

I swallow hard and blink to clear the tears. Beyond confused, my addled brain can only muster three words.

"Not my sister?"

"No, she's not.

"But…the passport, and the birth certificate…and the photo?"

"The passport was fake — good enough to fool most people but still a fake. The birth certificate and photo were real, but neither belonged to the person who showed them to you."

The quest for answers trumps confusion and I find a reply.

"How did you get them then?"

"I…we found that silver box when we were clearing Mum's flat back in the Summer."

"The box…with my father's letter?"

"Yes."

That explains how they got hold of it, but not how the box found its way from Hansworth Hall to Hounslow.

"Why was it in your mother's flat?"

Rosa turns to the frail woman and mouths an apology.

"Mum used to be your father's carer, right up until he died. She took the box because…," she stops and swallows hard. "Because she was desperate for money. She didn't know it was worthless until a few weeks after she took it."

Suddenly the photo of Miss Douglas outside Hansworth Hall makes sense, as does her motivation for stealing from my father.

"That box and the contents were meant for me," I growl in reply. "And your mother could have kept the damn box for all I would have cared. What was inside mattered, and she should have understood the significance."

Rosa takes another glance at her mother. A faint nod is returned.

"You've tried speaking to my mother, and you know she has limited speech, right?"

"Your point?"

"She explained to me what happened, as best she could."

"Go on."

"She did try to give you the letter back, about a month after your father's funeral, but apparently you'd left Hansworth Hall and were somewhere in Africa, I think. Knowing what the letter said, Mum didn't want to give it to anyone else so she just buried it in a drawer and pretended it never existed."

I stare at Miss Douglas and shake my head. She did far more than steal a worthless trinket box — she stole my sister from me, and the life we may have had together.

"I know it's no consolation," Rosa continues. "But she could have sold that letter to the papers for a lot of money, what with your father's confession. She didn't though, because she's a decent, honest woman who made a bad decision. She was desperate, William, but not so desperate she was prepared to destroy your father's reputation, or yours for that matter."

A valid, but now inconsequential point seeing as my name is already adorning the front page of a national newspaper.

Clement, having caught up with the conversation, poses a question of his own.

"So who's idea was it to blackmail Bill then?"

"Amy's."

"What sort of twisted mind comes up with a plot like that?" I abruptly interject. "For God's sake, Rosa. You stood by and let me think I'd had sex with my own sister."

"I honestly didn't know she was going to do that, otherwise I'd never have agreed to Amy's plan."

"But you did know she was going to blackmail me, didn't you? In fact, it's the only reason you started working for me, isn't it?"

She nods.

"How did you even engineer that?"

"Amy threatened your previous PA and forced her to resign."

"She threatened Joyce? How?"

"She befriended Joyce's grandson on Facebook. They chatted for a while and then she convinced him to send her…compromising photos. Amy told Joyce she'd share those photos with the lad's college tutors if she didn't resign and recommend I replace her."

"Devious bitch," Clement remarks.

"I didn't know any of this until afterwards," Rosa adds. "I swear."

She gets up from her chair and steps towards me.

"This is my fault, William. I was only supposed to be in your office for a week or two, just to make sure you didn't contact the police. The original plan was to sell you the box in return for enough money to put Mum in a decent care home, but during that first week I found the lease for Hansworth Hall and stupidly mentioned it to Amy. She said you deserved to be punished and we should take the house."

"Punished? For what exactly?"

"My sister isn't a well woman, William. She's had a tough life and has…issues, some of which she blames on you."

"Me? What the hell have I ever done to her?"

"You made us homeless."

"Eh? What are you talking about? I did no such thing."

"Perhaps not directly, but a few days after your father died, we were given a weeks' notice to leave the staff annexe at Hansworth Hall. That photo in my mother's purse was taken the day before we left — the day before we were made homeless."

"I...that was nothing to do with me. I didn't even know you were living there."

"Did you ever ask?"

"No. I left everything to my father's solicitor."

"You were never curious who looked after your father when he was ill?" she snaps, her apologetic tone no more. "Who cooked for him, helped him to bed, administered his medication, cleaned up after he soiled himself?"

Rosa turns and points at her mother. "There's the woman who did all that, and then you cast us out on the street with no thanks and nowhere to go."

Somewhere in our conversation, the shame and the anger have seamlessly switched between us.

"Then why didn't you just ask me for help? Surely you know me well enough now to know I would have done something?"

Her anger eases and her head drops. "I do now."

In truth, we could spend the entire morning batting blame back and forth. However, I'm too emotionally exhausted to punish myself any further. As far as I'm concerned, this is now a matter for the police and I have a genie I need to force back into its bottle.

Ignoring Rosa, I step across the room and sit back down in front of Miss Douglas. It's clear from her moist eyes and ghostly complexion she knew nothing of her daughter's plot.

"I'm sorry for what happened to you, Miss Douglas, and I'm sorry you had to hear all this. I'll ensure you receive the same level of care you gave my father — you have my word on that."

I take her hand a give it a gentle squeeze. "We'll leave you in peace now."

I get up and tell Rosa I want a word outside. As if taking her final walk on death row, she nods and shuffles after me, with Clement bringing up the rear. The drama may be over for her mother, but for Rosa it's only just beginning.

Once we're back in the corridor, I pull the door shut.

"No more lies, Rosa. Where's your sister now?"

Her eyes dart left and right, as if she's avoiding either my gaze or my question. I'm not sure which but I suspect both.

"Rosa, look at me."

She slowly turns her head to me.

"Despite what you've done to me, I'm going to help your mother, but only if you come clean and Gabb…Amy faces justice. Now, where is she?"

"She had a meeting with the newspaper at ten, to collect her payment."

I glance at my watch. Nine thirty-five.

"You need to put the brakes on that sharpish," Clement suggests.

"Keep an eye on her please, Clement. Don't let her leave — I'll be five minutes."

He nods and I hurry back to the reception where I waste no time calling my solicitor, Rupert.

"Thank God," he blurts after the third ring. "I've left four messages this morning."

"Sorry, Rupert, but I've been inundated with messages so I left my phone on silent. Anyway, I'm guessing you've seen the article?"

"I'm afraid I have."

"Good."

"Good?"

"Yes. I don't have to explain it."

"Um, okay, but I think we need to talk about how we're going to deal with it. The police will undoubtedly want to talk to you."

"Don't worry, Rupert. I'm keen to talk to the police because the woman is lying — she's not my sister."

"And you can prove that?" he asks with almost a hint of disbelief in his voice.

"Of course I can."

"Sorry, William. It's just that most national newspapers wouldn't print a story like that without concrete evidence."

"Up until ten minutes ago, I believed it myself so I know only too well how good she is at lying. But her real name is Amy Jones and you need to contact the newspaper now because she's due for a meeting in twenty minutes."

"And say what?"

"How the hell should I know? You're the solicitor so slap them with an injunction or something."

"Right, of course."

"And make sure they don't give her a penny. They're going to need it because I'm going to sue them till they squeak."

"I'll get straight onto it. Do you want me to issue a statement on your behalf, refuting her claim?"

"Yes, I damn well do."

I end the call and sit down for a moment. With no other distractions, the enormity of the last fifteen minutes swallows me up. There is no fitting analogy to describe the sense of relief as shame, guilt, and fear slowly ebb away. One emotion remains resolute though — desire for justice. It's a shame I won't be there when Amy Jones tries to collect her payment, and as much as I'd like to wallow in my antagonist's disappointment, there are more pressing issues that require my attention. Decisions must now be made.

I inform an obviously annoyed Anna we'll be leaving shortly and return to the corridor where Clement and Rosa are leant against the wall outside Miss Douglas's room.

"Right. I have some questions I'd like answering."

"I'll do my best," she replies in a low voice.

"Firstly, why the hell did your sister get the newspaper to print that garbage on their front page? I thought she had her eye on the bigger prize."

"She did, until yesterday."

"What happened yesterday?"

"You found Mum's flat. Amy knew you'd been there, and I guess she thought it wasn't worth the risk, waiting until Friday."

Precisely as Clement theorised.

"How did she know we'd been to your mother's flat?"

"Um, the tracking app," she replies sheepishly.

"What's a tracking app," Clement asks.

"It's exactly that," I reply. "Wherever my phone goes, I can be tracked."

"You mean we sat there freezing our knackers off and they knew we were there?" he groans.

"Apparently so," I confirm.

I make a mental note to remove the app and move to my next question.

"And the woman in Sandown pretending to be Susan Davies?"

"Oh," she sighs, visibly deflating. "You knew?"

"Yes, but not why you sent us on a wild goose chase to the Isle of Wight in the first place. Who was that woman?"

"Our aunt, on our father's side," she reluctantly confesses. "She had a debt to Amy, and went along with it to repay that debt. To be honest, it wasn't that hard convincing her — she knew the history after we were turfed out of Hansworth Hall."

No wonder fake Susan gave us such a frosty reception. But in the grand scheme of things, sending us on a pointless trip to the Isle of Wight sits pretty low on their list of deceptions.

"I thought it was a stupid move," she adds. "But once you decided to track down Susan Davies, Amy knew you'd discover she was dead, and you might start digging around trying to find other family members. There was too much at stake, so Amy decided to lead you up a blind alley instead."

"She did that alright," Clement mumbles.

"And why is you mother using the surname Douglas?" I ask.

"It's her maiden name. After our father…died…she wanted rid of his name."

Questions answered, a reflective silence descends; punctuated only by my own thoughts. The truth has finally prevailed, and what a truth it is. If it hadn't been for the circumstances, perhaps I could find a begrudging admiration for the lengths the sisters went to. As is often the case though, greed was their downfall. Maybe if they'd just tried to extort money for the contents of the trinket box, I might have succumbed, but Rosa will now pay the price for Amy's greed.

"I'll give you credit for flawless planning," I concede. "But now it's over, I need to decide what we're going to do with you."

Apparently Clement has his own suggestion. "Hand her over to the Old Bill and we'll make it to Fitzgerald's by opening time."

I quickly conclude both parts of his plan are eminently sensible.

"Agreed."

"Wait," Rosa interjects.

"Don't waste your breath. I'm not going to change my mind?"

"I know, and I'm not going to try. I deserve whatever punishment is coming my way, but can I ask you one question first?"

"Go on."

"Did you mean what you said in there, about helping Mum?"

"Whatever you and your sister have done, I owe your mother for looking after my father and in lieu of the way she left Hansworth Hall."

"Thank you," she replies with a weak smile. "And in return, I have something that's rightfully yours."

She opens her handbag and removes a white envelope.

"This was also in your father's box," she adds, handing the envelope to me.

Wary of more sordid revelations, I tentatively open it and extract a single sheet of familiar velum writing paper.

"There was a second page of the letter," Rosa explains. "Which Amy chose not to show you."

"Why?"

"Read it and you'll see why."

I unfold the letter to find another four paragraphs of my father's scrawled handwriting; written eighteen years ago…

The child, your sister, was christened Gabrielle Davies, and would be around twelve years of age by now. To the best of my knowledge, she still lives with Susan and her husband, Kenneth, at Brooke Cottage in a small village called Cranleigh, near Guildford.

Susan and Kenneth had been trying, unsuccessfully, for a child over many years. Kenneth, as it proves, was a better man and husband than I. Despite knowing of his wife's infidelity, he agreed to raise Gabrielle as his own. His only condition was that I had nothing to do with her. To my shame, I agreed without argument and paid a sum of money to unburden myself from the guilt. Besides the one photo (enclosed), I have never set eyes on your sister, and it pains me that I never will.

At the time, and you must believe me, Son, I thought I was doing what was best for all concerned. Time has taught me I was wrong. Sadly, there is no longer enough time for me to make amends. I hope you can find it in yourself to forgive me, and to seek forgiveness on my behalf. I would rest easy knowing perhaps one day, you and Gabrielle might forge the relationship I so readily gave away.

I am sorry to say I can already feel my mind fading, and I must leave now. There is so much still to say, but know that I always have, and always will be proud of you. Be strong and follow your own path, for mine is not worthy.

God bless you, Son

All my love - Father

For the third time this morning, tears well. Perhaps if this letter had reached me as a twenty-four-year-old, my life would be different now. I'll never know.

"What's it say, Bill?" Clement asks.

I hand the page to him. "See for yourself."

I turn my attention back to Rosa. "Why did you keep that page? You must have known it would undermine your sister's plot if it ever came to light?"

"Of course, which is why she threw that page in the bin. I removed it when she wasn't around."

"You didn't answer my question, Rosa? Why did you keep it?"

"Because I knew Amy's plot would never work in the long run, and I'd have to face you one day. It was all I had to prove to you I'm not her."

"Maybe not, but you were complicit."

"I know, and I'm not trying to shift the blame, but you have to understand Amy to appreciate how I got here."

"I'm not sure I ever want to understand your sister. She's pure evil."

"She's not evil, William — she's a victim too."

"Really?" I scoff. "I fail to see how."

There's no response but the body language suggests Rosa is holding back another revelation.

"Well?"

She squeezes her eyes shut and draws a long breath.

"Okay," she finally sighs, opening her eyes. "Before my mother worked at Hansworth Hall, we were a normal family living a normal life, or so I thought. Turned out my father had been sexually abusing Amy for years, and one day…she just snapped. He snuck into her bedroom one evening but on that occasion, Amy was waiting for him. She hid behind the door and stabbed him in the back with a carving knife, eleven times. He died before the ambulance arrived."

"Christ."

"And without his income, the house was repossessed and that's how Mum ended up caring for your father. We simply needed somewhere to live. Amy spent years undergoing treatment for her ordeal, but I guess it was too late — she was irreparably damaged. Both Mum and I learnt that life was easier if you went along with whatever Amy wanted. Sounds stupid, but we were…are, terrified of her."

I'm truly lost for words. Clement, it seems, is not.

"That's tragic. Fucked up, but tragic."

"As I said," Rosa adds. "It's not an excuse, just an explanation. I'm not condoning what Amy did...what we did."

Whatever sympathy I might now hold for Amy, and indeed Rosa, it isn't enough to stifle my need for justice. If it hadn't been for Clement's insistence we come back to Hounslow, and perhaps my willingness to ignore his ridiculous claims, I would probably be sitting in a police cell by now.

"I'm sorry, Rosa. What you've all been through sounds horrific, but you do realise I can't just ignore what's happened?"

"I know, and once I say goodbye to Mum, I'm going to hand myself in at the police station."

I look across at Clement and he returns a shrug.

"I'll give you until two o'clock. If you haven't been to the police and confessed by then, I'll review my decision to help your mother."

Rosa nods and gives me her word; not that it's worth much.

"I mean it, Rosa," I sternly warn. "I'll be telling the police the whole sorry tale and the first thing they'll do is come here to interview your mother. If you don't want to put her through that, I would strongly advise you keep your word."

"The only reason I agreed to any of this was to help Mum. I'll keep my word if you keep yours."

"Very well. And what about Amy?"

"I'll call and tell her it's over, but I can't promise she'll do the right thing."

"Well, I'm sure the police will catch up with her soon enough. I've got enough to deal with for the moment but I will talk to them later today. It would be in everyone's best interests if Amy also handed herself in."

"I can't promise she'll listen but I'll ask her. Thank you, William, and for what it's worth, I truly am sorry."

A frowning Anna suddenly appears at the end of the corridor and impatiently taps at her watch. "I said fifteen minutes. You finished now, yes?"

Clement slaps me on the back and smiles. "Yeah. We're all done, sweetheart," he calls back.

33.

I walked into Orchard Lodge as a condemned man.

I leave like a prisoner granted unexpected parole.

As we wander back up Adam Street, I try to process the morning's events. A raft of wildly different thoughts and emotions battle for attention; some positive, some negative. However, the one emotion I expected to feel is not there. There is no elation at finally closing this sorry chapter of my life. A chain of events, first triggered almost two decades ago, has reached a wholly unsatisfactory conclusion.

My father's letter, at least the concluding page, is the most unsatisfactory part. He might have hoped I connect with my estranged sister but he also inadvertently gave me good reason not to. Gabrielle is now thirty years of age and must know who her real father is, by virtue of the fact his name is on her birth certificate. Yet she has made no effort to contact me because, I suspect, she already has all the family she needs. The man who raised her deserves to be called a father and she probably doesn't need, or want, me turning up as a reminder that Kenneth isn't her biological parent.

No, I must accept I haven't found a sister — I've found a secret I must protect, for everyone's sake.

"Penny for them," Clement chirps as we reach the end of Adam Street.

"Sorry, I was just thinking."

"About what?"

"Doesn't matter."

"Sure? You don't seem pleased we've dealt with whatever her bleedin' name is."

"Oh, don't get me wrong. I'm more relieved than you'll ever know. It's just…I'm really back at square one. Nothing has changed."

"Something has."

"What?"

"Well, I can't rib you about knobbing your sister now."

"Every cloud, eh?" I chuckle.

We cross the road and make our way towards the train station. My thoughts turn to my companion, and the deal we struck back at the flat. After everything he's done for me, I need to put his welfare above mine for the moment. Whatever is going on in his head, it needs fixing.

"How's that itch of yours?" I ask.

"Scratched."

"Really? As simple as that?"

"Yeah. The jobs done."

"So is that it then? The voice just stops?"

"I reckon so. Can't say for sure."

"What will you do now?"

"Getting pissed feels appropriate."

"No, I didn't mean now, as in the next few hours. I mean, in the future."

"I ain't got a clue. I'll end up where I end up."

"But you don't know where?"

"Nope. Life's like a road trip, mate. We get to choose the route but not where or when it ends."

"That's rather profound, Clement, although I'm not sure I see your point."

"That's a shame, seeing as you've been on the wrong road most of your life."

"Wait…what? How is this suddenly about me?"

"It's always been about you, Bill."

"Now I'm officially confused."

"The only reason I'm here is because you needed help. You're part of my road trip, or I'm part of yours. Dunno for sure."

Frustrated, I conclude my mind is already cluttered enough without attempting to decipher whatever point he's trying to make.

"Have you ever considered a career in politics, Clement."

"Christ, no. Why?"

"Because whenever I ask you a straight question, you're rather adept at avoiding a straight answer, don't you think?"

"Not every question has an answer, Bill."

"I rest my case."

With very little progress made on Clement's mental health issue, we finally reach Hounslow train station. We head to the platform where our train is waiting to depart.

Once safely ensconced in our seats, I turn my attention back to my own issues; the first of which is dealing with the vast number of voicemail and text messages on my phone. I pull it out of my pocket and inwardly groan.

I decide to deal with the sixteen text messages first and scroll through them one by one.

Not unsurprisingly, there are three from Fiona Hewitt; each one conveying increasing irritation. Seeing as I assured her everything was under control during my last visit to her office, I suspect a pink fit was thrown when she woke up to that article this morning. Probably best I put her near the top of my call list.

Next up are Rupert's four texts, all of which I delete without reading. My solicitor knows what he has to do, and he better be getting on with it.

Four texts are from journalists asking for my comment on the allegations made against me. If Rupert is doing his job, they'll have a response via a press release within the next hour. I delete them.

There are five texts from my colleagues — four offering support, although my instinct tells me they're just glad it's not them in the firing line, and one from the boorish young backbencher, Adrian Lowe, which he'll rue sending once the truth is out.

The final text is from the deviant previously known as Gabby. Sent just after nine this morning, it simply reads…

Game over, brother. I win.

I allow myself a self-satisfied smile while typing a reply…

No, Amy. I know everything now, so I win. Enjoy prison.

"What's so amusing?" Clement asks.

"I'm just replying to our little friend, Amy. She sent me a taunting message this morning."

"What do you reckon will happen to her?"

"I don't know, nor do I really care. I understand she didn't have the best start in life but actions have consequences, and she has to pay for hers."

"Pretty bleedin' sick though, what her old man did to her?"

"Well, yes, I'm not saying it wasn't. I suppose, in some twisted way, maybe she'll now get the treatment she needs, albeit within the confines of a secure unit."

Clement doesn't reply and returns his attention to the urban scenery now zipping past the window. Perhaps I've touched a raw nerve with talk of treatment and secure units. Considering his propensity for extreme violence, any further discussion about his own mental wellbeing will need careful handling. A problem for another day perhaps. For now, it's probably best to leave him and his voice to their own devices.

Text messages dealt with, I call the voicemail number. I know this task will be far more unpleasant than reading text messages as I'll have to hear the raw emotions of nine callers who, when they rang, were under the assumption I had slept with my own sister.

The first two messages are from Fiona, and contain language not becoming of her position. I delete both, and in the same instant, confirm a decision I had already half-made. There are four messages from various journalists, including the one who wrote the article, and not unsurprisingly, one from the Prime Minister's personal secretary, suggesting I call her back as a matter of some urgency. I'll tell her the same thing I intend to tell Fiona — that I'm resigning.

Seven down. Two to go.

The eighth message is from Rupert, simply confirming he's spoken to the newspaper and they were currently in the process of pulling the article from various online media outlets and replacing it with a grovelling apology. Too little, too late. In their eagerness to besmirch me, they cut corners by not checking the facts thoroughly. I might have been fooled by Amy's fake passport but they should have spotted it. They'll pay handsomely for their tardiness, and that money will fund private care for Miss Douglas.

The last message was left at the same time Rupert called, while I was stood in the corridor at Orchard Lodge. It is from the very last person I expected to hear from...

Mr Huxley, this is Kenneth Davies. Can you call me urgently when you get this message, please.

"Good Lord," I murmur once the message ends.
"What's up?"

"I just received a message from Kenneth Davies."

"The bloke who brought up your sister?"

"The very one."

"What's he want?"

"I don't know. He just asked me to call him back."

I retrieve Kenneth's number from my list of missed calls and tap the phone icon. As it connects, I consider the possible reason for his call, and I quickly conclude he's probably furious his daughter's name appeared in the paper, albeit attached to a different woman.

"Hello," a frail voice answers.

"Mr Davies, it's William Huxley returning your call."

"Ahh, Mr Huxley, thank God."

"Please, call me William."

"Yes…right…I'm calling about an article I read in the newspaper this morning."

His voice is frantic but I don't detect any anger.

"Oh."

"Yes, and you should know the woman in the article — the one claiming to be Gabrielle Davies — is a fraud."

Do I tell him I already know? Probably best to stick to the truth.

"Thank you for letting me know, Mr Davies, and I was already aware. Unfortunately, I only found out this morning so it was too late to do anything about the newspaper but they are going to print a retraction and an apology."

"You know that woman isn't your sister?"

"Yes. It's a long story but that woman was pretending to be Gabrielle and blackmailing me. Up until last week, I wasn't even aware I had a sister."

"But now you know," he replies in a sombre tone.

"I know everything, Mr Davies."

The line goes quiet.

"Mr Davies?"

"Yes," he replies in almost a whisper. "I'm still here."

"Sorry, just out of curiosity, how did you get my phone number?"

"I got it from your website, about three years ago."

"Right. Why three years ago?"

I can only assume he's carefully considering his reply as the line goes quiet again.

"I had a health scare," he eventually says.

"I'm sorry to hear that. You obviously made a recovery though."

"A recovery of sorts, but really it was only prolonging the inevitable."

"The inevitable?"

"Yes," he replies after another pause. "But…oh dear…this is all a bit of a mess."

Clearly confused, I attempt to pull his thoughts in the right direction.

"I don't want to cause any upset, but why were you trying to contact me three years ago?"

Another period of silence ensues.

"Look, William," he sighs. "This is extremely difficult for me. I don't suppose you could come down to Surrey and we could discuss the matter face to face?"

"Of course. When did you have in mind?"

"With that newspaper article in circulation, I'd prefer it if we met sooner rather than later. Can you come down this afternoon?"

"I can be with you in an hour or two if that works?"

He agrees, and confirms the same address as the one in my father's letter. I end the call and check the location, only to find it's in the middle of nowhere, some forty miles south-west of London.

"Well?" Clement asks.

"He wants me to go down to Surrey and talk to him."

"What about?"

"I'm not sure, but I get the impression he's not a well man."

"You're going straight down there then?"

"Once I work out how. It doesn't appear there's a train station nearby."

"Surrey ain't far. Why not drive?"

"Because I don't drive."

"Shit. Really?"

"Never had any need to."

"You want me to run you down there?"

"Are you telling me we've been travelling everywhere by train when you could have driven?"

"No, cos' I ain't got a car."

"Good grief," I groan. "So, besides stealing a car, how are you going to drive me to Surrey?"

"I'll borrow Frank's. He's lent it to me a few times so he'll be cool about it."

"Oh, okay. You don't mind?"

"One condition."

"Not more toast?"

"Nah. When we get back, we get right royally pissed, and you're paying."

"You have a deal."

34.

"What is that?"

"It's a motor," Clement replies as we stand in front of a battered Ford of some kind.

I'm no expert, but even I can tell that Frank's car should have been consigned to a salvage yard some years ago.

"No wonder he doesn't mind you driving it. I've seen skips with better bodywork."

"You wanna walk?"

"No," I groan. "But I'd better check my tetanus jabs are up to date before I sit in the damn thing."

"Just quit your moaning and get in."

I open the door and flop into the passenger seat. The interior is no better and stinks of cigarette smoke, and more worryingly, petrol. It does at least start on the first turn of the key.

"She's no oil painting but reliable as clockwork."

A fair assessment.

Clement pulls out of the parking bay at the rear of Fitzgerald's and heads up Furnival Street. With Mr Davies' address plugged into the navigation app on my phone, a synthesised voice offers directions out of the city. Clement, like most people who drive in London, shows utter contempt for all other road users. Many, many expletives are hurled, and I get to enjoy his full repertoire of obscene hand gestures.

It is with some relief we finally escape central London and reach the A3. The synthesised voice falls silent as we have nothing but several miles of dual carriageway ahead of us.

With just the whistling of air through the ill-fitting windows for entertainment, Clement decides we need some music. He switches the radio on and tunes it to a crackly medium wave station playing seventies tunes.

"You nervous?" he asks, as the disc jockey introduces a track by Showaddywaddy.

"Just a bit."

"You reckon you'll get to meet your sister then?"

"I'm not sure. I got the impression Mr Davies has more to say before, or even if, I get the chance to meet Gabrielle."

"But you wanna?"

"Of course. It's not my decision though."

We listen to the rest of *Under The Moon of Love* before I reluctantly decide to return some calls. I call Fiona and listen to a five-minute rant about trust and standards before I can get a word in edgeways. She eventually runs out of steam and I offer my explanation. Once she's satisfied I've done no wrong, I tell her about my decision to quit politics — with much enthusiasm she congratulates me.

Next up is the Prime Minister's prissy personal secretary, Camilla. I've never liked her and I suspect the feeling is mutual. With no small talk offered or sought, I simply refer her to Rupert's statement, confirming my innocence. Not wishing to miss the opportunity to berate, she then launches into a tirade about letting the party down. With some degree of glee, I cut her short by confirming my resignation letter will be on her desk by tomorrow.

Those two sorted, I allow myself a moment to bask in self-satisfaction. It doesn't last long as Clement poses another question.

"Had enough?"

"Sorry?"

"You said you're resigning."

"Oh, right. Sort of. If this whole episode has taught me anything, it's that I need to re-evaluate my life choices."

"What you gonna do then, for a job?"

"I've got a few ideas, but I want to get away for a bit first. And before you say anything, I'm not running away — I simply need a little space to think."

"I wasn't gonna say that, but since you mention it, where you going?"

"Somewhere nobody knows me. Somewhere quiet, but not too far away."

"And that's where exactly?"

"The Isle of Wight."

"Christ, why there? It's bleedin' dead."

"Exactly. There's hardly a soul around this time of year and I quite like the idea of bracing walks along the sea front whenever the fancy takes me."

"Rather you than me."

"So I take it you won't be popping over to visit?"

"No offence, Bill, but I'd rather shag my own sister than spend another second over there."

"You couldn't resist one final dig, could you?"

"Sorry, mate," he replies with a grin.

"Anyway, shall we talk about your typically vague plans?"

"Not much to say."

"Are you going to continue working at Fitzgerald's?"

"Probably not, but it depends."

"On?"

"Let's just say I'm waiting for a call."

"A call from who?"

He taps the side of his nose with his finger to suggest it's none of my business. He then reaches across and turns up the volume on the radio.

"Love this track," he shouts over David Bowie's *Life on Mars*.

I know by now when he doesn't want to continue a conversation, so I settle back in my seat whilst we listen to a succession of seventies tracks in glorious mono. Thoughts of Clement's future give way to those of Kenneth Davies, and why he's so keen to meet with me. The fact he almost called three years ago raises more questions than answers.

By the time we approach Guildford, I conclude there is precious little point second guessing the man. I'll know precisely what he wants to talk about soon enough. And I certainly don't wish to tempt fate by hoping I might finally meet my sister.

The navigation app returns to service and directs us from the A3, through the centre of Guildford, and on towards the village of Cranleigh. Although the road itself is fairly busy with traffic, the scenery becomes more rural as we head into the Surrey countryside.

As my nerves begin to jangle, the app directs us from the main road up a single lane track bordered by hedgerows. Those nerves are not helped by Clement's aggressive driving style.

"Can you slow down?" I plead as he throws the car into a blind bend.

"Trust me, Bill. I've got it all under control."

"Today's newspaper article was bad enough. Let's try and avoid a follow-up in tomorrow's obituary column shall we."

Thankfully we have to slow down behind a tractor, much to Clement's annoyance.

"Before you even consider an impossible overtaking manoeuvre, Brooke Cottage is just up here on the right."

Fifty yards later, we pull into a shingle driveway fronting a double-fronted cottage. Clement switches off the engine while I breathe a heavy sigh of relief we made it in one piece.

"You go on in. I'll wait in the motor."

"Are you sure?"

"Yeah. You don't want me hanging around while you talk to the bloke."

"Thank you."

I clamber out and cross the driveway to the front door, passing an Audi four-wheel drive on the way. A few seconds to regain my composure and I ring the bell.

A moment later, a tall, gaunt man with wispy white hair opens the door.

"Mr Davies?"

"Yes, and you must be William. Come in."

I step into the hallway and he closes the door.

"Good trip?" he asks with no suggestion he really cares.

"Yes, thank you. A friend drove me down."

"This way."

He turns his back on me and strides down the hallway. I follow him into a farmhouse-style kitchen with a pine dining table and chairs in the centre.

"Take a seat," he says, waving an arm towards the table. "Can I get you a cup of tea?"

I sit down. "I'm fine, thank you."

He stops, and for a second appears unsure what to do now I've declined his offer of tea. He eventually turns around and shuffles over.

"Thank you for coming to see me," he rasps while gingerly lowering himself onto a chair. "I appreciate you must be a busy man."

"I'll be honest with you Mr Davies, I was intrigued why you wanted to have a chat."

A pair of frosty grey eyes peer over the top of his horn-rimmed spectacles.

"It's not a case of wanting to. I'm afraid it's a necessity."

His tone is as frosty as his eyes.

"Why is it a necessity?"

He sits back and scratches his scalp. "I'm guessing you're not married?" he asks.

"No."

"Never?"

"Unfortunately not."

"In which case, you won't know how it feels."

"Sorry? How what feels?"

"To know your wife slept with another man."

I had an inkling this might be the starting point of our conversation. And while I'm sympathetic, I can hardly be held responsible for my father's actions.

"No, I don't," I reply, standing my ground. "But it's not something I would ever condone or try to justify. I'm not my father, Mr Davies."

"I know precisely who you are, William. I've been following your career with some interest."

"Have you? Why?"

"To see what kind of man you are."

Agitation prickles. "Well, seeing as you've gone to so much trouble, perhaps you can tell me what kind of man I am."

"Don't be so defensive," he retorts. "Up until this morning, I was under the impression you were a veritable saint. Back when dinosaurs roamed the earth, I studied politics at university and I know nobody survives a decade in Westminster unless they're of good standing."

His expression softens slightly but I'm still no clearer to his motive for this line of questioning.

"I appreciate the reference, Mr Davies, but why is my reputation of any concern to you?"

My question is left hanging as his attention appears to drift off.

"Mr Davies?"

"Susan," he eventually sighs. "Did you ever meet her?"

"I don't think so."

"She was the love of my life."

I don't know what to say to the man. I try a sympathetic smile.

"And for that reason only, I agreed to bring up Gabrielle as if she were my own flesh and blood. We were never blessed with children, and I couldn't deny Susan the chance, no matter how sordid the conception might have been."

Still nothing. I try a slow nod.

"You're probably wondering why I'm telling you this."

"I, um…yes."

"Gabrielle might not be my flesh and blood, William, but I couldn't love her any more if she were. That girl is my world."

"Right."

He appears to steel himself with a deep breath.

"As I mentioned on the phone, my health isn't what it once was."

"You seem fairly fit, if you don't mind me saying."

"In mind and body perhaps, but not of heart — the old ticker has seen better days. I had major heart surgery three years ago and that's why I was going to contact you. I don't know how long I've got left. It could be six years, or six months, but either way I need to make plans."

"Forgive me, Mr Davies, but I'm still not clear why you were going to contact me then, or now for that matter."

"Because Gabrielle doesn't have any family, other than me. Susan, her mother, was killed in a road accident twelve years ago."

"Well, if it's of any comfort, I've managed to function without any family for the last eighteen years."

"That much I know, William, but Gabrielle isn't you."

He sits forward and tries several times to clear his throat; an action which clearly pains.

"Can I get you a glass of water?" I ask.

"No, no," he wheezes. "I'll be okay in a moment."

He takes a few deep breaths and regains his composure. "Where was I?" he mumbles to himself.

"Gabrielle. You said she's not me."

"No, she's not. My daughter…your sister…has Down's Syndrome."

Somewhere across the room a boiler fires up. It's the only sound in an otherwise silent kitchen.

"Down's Syndrome?" I parrot.

"I'm assuming you've heard of the condition?"

"Yes, of course, although I can't profess to know much about it."

"Let's not dwell on that for the moment. My concern is for Gabrielle's future — not her condition."

"Her future?"

"Yes, and whether I like it or not, you are her only blood relative."

The reason I'm here is now clear. I'm being interviewed for the position of Gabrielle's guardian, although I suspect Mr Davies is struggling to get past the fact I am my father's son.

"I think I understand."

"Do you? Gabrielle is an incredible young lady, William. She's kind, humorous, and loving, but I don't think she'd cope, living on her own. Don't get me wrong, her condition is immaterial inasmuch she lives a full life, but..."

His voice breaks. He swallows hard before continuing. "But she needs somebody to look out for her."

"Are you suggesting I care for her when you're…no longer around?"

"I'm not suggesting anything. Gabrielle is not an object, to be haggled over."

"No, of course not. I'm just not sure I understand what you're asking of me."

"Let me put it another way, William. Imagine if I died tomorrow — what would you do?"

"I, erm…"

"Before you answer," he interrupts. "Please don't tell me what you think I want to hear. I need you to be completely honest, even if you think the truth might offend me."

I don't need to think too long or too hard for an answer. "I'd want to care for my sister in any way I could."

"Even though you might find her a burden?"

"A burden?" I reply with some indignation. "Why on earth would I think that?"

"I don't know, William. You tell me."

I pause for a moment to gather my thoughts. If I've got any measure of Mr Davies, I need to make it abundantly clear I appreciate the magnitude of what he's asking me, and how difficult it must be to even ask it, considering the circumstances.

"May I ask you something, Mr Davies?"

"Ask away."

"When we first sat down, you asked me a question? Do you recall?"

"Remind me."

"You asked if I knew what it felt like: knowing another man had slept with your wife."

His eyes narrow a fraction. "I did. And your point?"

"I don't know what that feels like, but I'd imagine there must be a lot of anger, resentment, and jealousy?"

"Correct."

"And somewhere amongst all that, probably a fair amount of loneliness? It's a betrayal you'd rather suffer alone, I'd guess?"

"There is no lonelier place than being the wrong side of an infidelity."

"I'd beg to differ. I grew up in a house, not unlike this one, in the middle of nowhere and with no siblings for company. I lost my mother at fourteen and my father sent me off to boarding school. Trust me when I say I know what loneliness feels like."

"I…wasn't aware of that."

"No, you wouldn't be — it's not on my Wikipedia page. My point is: it's a feeling I wouldn't wish on my worst enemy, and certainly not something I would ever want my own sister to experience."

He appears to ponder my statement, and slowly nods. "I appreciate your candour, William."

"You're welcome, and perhaps you could answer my question as frankly: what is it you want from me?"

He drums his fingers on the table, perhaps stalling while he finds the right way to phrase his reply.

"When I'm gone, you'll be the only family Gabrielle has left. Is that a responsibility you'd embrace, assuming it's what she wants?"

I sit forward and look him in the eye. "Without question or condition."

The old man takes a moment to process my answer. We've taken the long way round but finally arrived — he now has a decision to make.

"Very well. That's all I needed to hear."

He checks his watch and slowly gets to his feet. I still don't know if I've passed his test.

"Of course, this is all hypothetical," he adds with the thinnest of smiles. "My daughter might think you're a tiresome bore and want nothing to do with you."

"She wouldn't be the first," I reply, returning his smile.

"But I guess there's only one way to find out," he adds. "Would you like to meet her?"

The one question I prayed I might hear but it still takes me by surprise.

"Sorry…really?" I splutter. "What, now?"

"Unless there's somewhere else you need to be?"

"No, definitely not."

"Okay, let's go then, before I change my mind. Gabrielle is down at the stables at the moment but I said I'd collect her about now. She's a keen rider and fanatical about her horse, Archie. Damn thing costs me a small fortune but he's worth every penny for the joy he brings to her life."

"Does she know who I am?"

"No, not yet, and perhaps it's best if I introduce you as an old friend, just until she gets to know you."

"Fine by me."

As Mr Davies puts his coat on, it dawns on me Clement has been waiting outside all this time.

"Would it be okay if my friend came along? He won't get in the way but I feel a bit guilty leaving him in the car all this time."

"If you like."

"Thank you."

We leave the house and as Mr Davies locks up, I scoot over to Frank's battered car. Clement winds down the window.

"How did it go?" he asks.

"A bit tense at times, but he's taking me to meet Gabrielle. Come on."

"You want me to come?"

"This is only happening because of you, Clement. Of course I'd like you to come."

He extracts himself from the car and I introduce him to Mr Davies.

"This is my friend, Clement. This is Mr Davies; Gabrielle's father."

"Alright, mate," Clement booms, extending one of his meaty hands.

Somewhat hesitantly, Mr Davies reciprocates. "Nice to meet you. I think you'd better sit in the front."

The three of us then get into the spacious Audi which, unlike Frank's Ford, is thankfully void of combustible fumes.

"Nice motor, Ken," Clement remarks as Mr Davies puts his seatbelt on.

I sink into my seat and inwardly cringe.

"Thank you. She's a bit thirsty, mind."

"What do you get from her?"

"No more than thirty a gallon."

"Still, I bet she pulls like a train."

For the entire ten-minute journey, Clement and Mr Davies wax lyrical about engines and horsepower and torque — all meaningless to a non-driver like me. By the time we pull into the car park at the stables, they're chuckling away like old friends. When he wants to, Clement can morph from a deranged oddball into the most affable of men. Another trait that would serve him well should he reconsider a career in politics.

We all climb out of the Audi and I survey the rural scenery. Beyond the three wooden buildings at the edge of the near-empty car park, which I assume are the stable blocks, a vista of open fields surrounds us.

"Where are the bogs, Ken?" Clement asks. "I missed my morning shit."

Horrified at Clement's statement, I turn to Mr Davies, expecting a similar reaction.

"Over there," he chuckles, pointing to the first wooden structure. "They're a bit basic, mind."

Relieved he didn't take offence, I breathe again.

"When you're done," Mr Davies adds. "Follow the path round to the paddock on the other side of the stables. I'm sure you'll find us."

Clement trudges off and Mr Davies places his hand on my shoulder.

"Ready?"

It's a good question.

Just one week ago I wasn't even aware I had a sister and now I'm seconds away from meeting her. I'd challenge anyone not to feel apprehensive in such circumstances, but after the week I've had, my emotions are already bruised. For Gabrielle's sake, I only hope I can hold it together. I'd hate her first impression to be one of a middle-aged, blubbering wreck.

I pull a deep breath and ready myself. "I'm good."

We follow a path between two of the wooden structures, leading out to a large paddock surrounded by railed fencing. The path splits left and right, fronting the stable blocks; each split into four stalls. At the far side of the paddock, a figure bobs up and down on a light grey horse as it canters along. The rider spots us and waves.

"That's Julie," Mr Davies says, waving back. "She spends more time here than Gabrielle."

Deciding it would be odd for me to wave at a woman I don't know, I simply nod at Mr Davies. He then turns and shuffles down the path towards one of the stable blocks.

Despite growing up in the countryside, I have never had much interest in the equestrian world; probably because horses intimidate me. Why anyone would choose to ride around on a creature with free will and no failsafe braking system, is beyond me. Nevertheless, they are handsome animals, and worthy of respect.

I follow Mr Davies towards the first stall where the door is split into two sections; the bottom half closed and the top half open. A black and white horse stands the other side of the door and sniffs at the air as we pass. The second stall is occupied by a seal-brown horse which tosses its head as we approach.

"Afternoon, Chester," Mr Davies chimes, stopping to stroke the horse's snout.

I decide not to interfere with Chester and keep my hands in my pockets.

"And here we have Archie," Mr Davies announces as we approach the third stall.

This is it. Presumably Gabrielle is inside the stall, doing whatever horsey types do to their animals when they're not careering around a field without brakes.

I take another deep breath as Mr Davies opens the bottom half of the door. Archie, obviously well trained, takes a step back to allow Mr Davies to enter. The chestnut coloured horse receives a pat and Mr Davies steps into the stall. I follow, keeping my distance from Archie as I close the door behind me.

"Gabrielle," Mr Davies says. "I've got somebody I'd like you to meet."

I stand a few feet behind the old man, with Archie to our left, and pause while my eyes adjust to the dark interior of the stall. The overpowering smell of hay and manure might take a little longer to adjust to.

"Gabrielle?" Mr Davies repeats.

It can't be easy playing hide and seek in a relatively confined space but it appears Gabrielle is having a go. I follow Mr Davies towards the rear, beyond Archie's hind quarters.

We discover two figures seated next to one another on a hay bale in the corner. Another scent immediately battles past the hay and the manure — patchouli.

"Hello, William," the nearest figure coos. "What kept you?"

It's a voice I know only too well.

I squint to confirm my worst fears. As my pupils widen sufficiently my heart stops.

Amy.

35.

My attention turns to the tiny figure next to Amy. A tear-stained face, capped in a riding hat, stares back; wide eyed, full of fear.

"Who are you?" Mr Davies blasts.

"Aren't you going to introduce us, William?" Amy sneers.

I turn to Mr Davies. "Go and call the police," I hiss.

"What? Why?"

"Just do it. Now."

"I'm not going anywhere without Gabrielle," he barks.

Mr Davies turns back to his daughter and holds out a hand. "Come with me, my darling."

The tiny figure omits a quiet sob but remains still.

"Gabrielle isn't going anywhere," Amy confirms, unfolding her arms to reveal a long, silvery object. She slowly turns it in her hand until it catches the light from the part-open door. "See, William — seems you didn't win after all."

"Mr Davies, she's got a knife. Go and call the police," I repeat with as much authority as I can muster.

The gravity of the situation finally strikes. "I'll be back in two ticks, my darling," he says gently to his daughter while backing towards the door.

With Mr Davies gone, the sole responsibility of Gabrielle's welfare falls in my lap. I squat down so I can look her in the eye.

"Hi, Gabrielle. I'm William."

A barely perceptible nod.

"I know you're frightened," I continue, trying to sound reassuring rather than patronising. "But everything is going to be just fine."

She nods again, but her eyes tell me I've done little to allay her fear. All I can do while we wait for the police is buy time.

I stand up and change my tone.

"How did you know…"

"Too easy," Amy interjects. "Gabrielle here is an avid Facebook user and kindly advertised where she spends most of her time."

"But…" I don't have to finish my own question before the answer dawns.

"I thought Rosa might have told you about the tracking app. Apparently not."

What an idiot. With the situation seemingly resolved, I didn't see any great urgency to delete the damn thing.

"So, here we all are for one final hurrah."

"I don't know if you've really thought this through, Amy, but the police will be on their way by now."

"The nearest station is miles away. Plenty of time for what I've got in mind."

While she's talking, I scan the stall for anything I can use as a weapon, should the need arise. To my right, a wooden divide separates Archie's stall from the one next door. In the four feet of open space above the divide, I can just see the shoulders of the two other horses we passed outside; both oblivious to the human drama unfolding only feet away. With nothing useful on the floor, unless I can weaponise a plastic bucket or a broom, options are limited to my own fists.

"And what exactly do you have in mind?" I reply.

"Just a dose of revenge. Nothing too heavy."

I know the answer but I ask anyway. "Revenge for what?"

"Let me see," she says, tapping her chin. "How about the fact you ruined my life?"

"So, you want to punish me?"

"Indeed I do."

"Fine. You can do what you like to me. There's no need for Gabrielle to be here."

"Oh, William," she chuckles. "I'm afraid there is. You see, I had to watch my family suffer because of your actions so it's only fair you suffer in the same way."

She's clearly unable to see past her own issues. Time to play the only card I have left.

"I struck a deal with Rosa."

"Did you?" she replies with disinterest.

"I agreed to pay for better care, for your mother. If anything happens to Gabrielle, or me, you can forget that offer."

She appears to ponder my revelation while running her finger along the shaft of the knife. What I wouldn't give to know what twisted thoughts are being processed. As it happens, I don't have long to wait.

"That's a kind offer," she purrs. "Very generous."

Something I've learnt about Amy is that her eyes are a better indicator of her true feelings. What comes out of her mouth is often the complete opposite of what those green eyes tell me. Her glare gives me reason for concern.

"But I'm really beyond caring now," she adds, her genial manner departing as quickly as it arrived. "And in some way, it's poetic justice."

"What?"

"My mother didn't protect me when I needed her, so why should I care if she's stuck in some shit-hole for the rest of her days?"

Last card played. What the hell do I do now? I return my attention to my sister.

"How are you doing down there, Gabrielle?"

"Okay," she replies in a voice barely a whisper. "Can I go home now?"

To hear a voice so helpless, and so desperate for a release, is heart-breaking.

"Soon. I promise."

I can now see why Clement isn't keen on making promises. At best mine is hollow. At worst it's a downright lie. But promises or not, the fact he isn't here only adds to my desperation. This is the one moment where I need him more than ever, and he's camped in the toilets, blissfully unaware of what's going on.

The reality is I'm helpless if Amy decides to do anything before the police arrive. I must keep her occupied.

As much as I want to scream at Gabrielle's captor, I try to remain calm. "Look, Amy. I know what happened to you and I can't begin to imagine how awful that must have been."

"Do you indeed? How?"

"Rosa told me."

"Ahh, my kid sister — always trying to fix me. What else did she tell you?"

"That this whole plot just spiralled out of control."

"For her maybe. I knew what I was doing from day one."

"I can't deny it; you've outwitted me all the way."

"Don't patronise me, William," she spits. "If I'd outwitted you then I wouldn't be here."

She turns, glares at Gabrielle, and then looks back at me. "Half an hour," she mumbles while shaking her head.

"What?"

"If you'd waited half a fucking hour longer, before getting your damn solicitor to call the newspaper, I'd be on my way somewhere hot by now."

"And your mother? I thought you were doing this for her?"

She shrugs her shoulders. "Nope."

It seems I wasn't the only one Amy duped.

"So this was only ever about you?"

"Fuck, yes," she snorts. "But you had to have the final say and steal the hard-earned fruits of my labour. That's why we're here, William — you, me, and Gabrielle. Basically, it's your fault."

"I'll give you the money," I blurt. "Whatever they were paying you, I'll give you double."

"Yeah, right," she sniggers. "I mean, politicians never lie, do they?"

"I promise."

"Shut up."

"I mean it. I'll give you whatever you want."

"We both know that isn't going to happen, William, so I'm afraid this ends here and now. There's no happy ending…for any of us."

"Please, Amy. Let's just talk this through."

I can hear desperation in my own voice, and I can hear Archie's heavy breathing next to me. What I can't hear are police sirens.

"Sorry, William, but I've already resigned myself to spending the rest of my days locked up. In a strange way, I'm almost looking forward to it. No bills, no responsibilities, no stupid do-gooders trying to rationalise the crap in my head. It'll be quite liberating, don't you think?"

As Clement suggested last week, you can't win a fight with someone who has nothing to lose. Her defeatism is a worrying sign.

"Anyway, I think the time for talking is over," she adds. "I just want one final thrill before they take me away."

"Thrill?"

"Yes. The thrill of seeing you suffer for throwing us onto the street as kids, but mainly for what you did this morning."

"I...please, Amy..."

"Ahh, that's what I wanted to see. A little begging."

"Okay, I'll beg if that's what you want."

"I do, and then I want to see your face as I slit your sister's throat."

Gabrielle's tiny frame stiffens, and her bottom lip bobs up and down. Fear robs her of any words.

And then, at last, I hear the sweetest of sounds. Distant, but unmistakable — police sirens.

"How's that for timing?" Amy taunts. "But just a little too late."

She gets to her feet, the knife held prominently in her right hand. Gabrielle's riding hat is plucked from her head and tossed to the floor.

"Jesus, Amy...please...you're terrifying her. Just let her go...please."

Never in my life have I felt so utterly helpless. I have to do something, anything.

I take one step towards her. "If you must hurt anyone, hurt me. This has nothing to do with my...Gabrielle."

"How noble of you. Pointless, but noble."

I hold my arms out in surrender. "Come on, Amy. It's me you really want to hurt, isn't it?"

"Yes it is, and that's exactly why I'm doing this."

I risk another step.

"That's far enough, William. Unless of course you really want a ringside view?"

"No. What I really want is for you to let Gabrielle go."

Amy smiles in response and kneels on the hay bale. She teases the tip of the knife along the zip of Gabrielle's jacket.

The poor girl finds her voice. "I'm frightened," she croaks.

I can't risk another step. The sirens now taunt — close, but not close enough.

"Stop!" a voice cries from behind me. Not wanting to take my eyes off Amy, I risk a glance over my shoulder. Mr Davies has returned and for some reason he's carrying a metal bucket.

"Put the knife down," he screeches at Amy.

Bemused, she relaxes her hand a little while assessing the threat — a frail old man carrying a bucket. She draws the same conclusion I do; he's no threat at all.

"Put the knife down or you'll get every drop," he wheezes, drawing level with me.

Amy notes an obvious flaw in his plan. "Whatever," she shrugs. "Damp clothes won't be much of a concern where I'm going."

Blinded by anger, Mr Davies isn't able to contain himself. Summoning every ounce of strength, he swings the bucket forward. The liquid content escapes and arcs towards Amy. Half of it doesn't reach her and splashes harmlessly across the floor, but a few litres slap against her upper body.

It takes but a second for the smell to register. Whatever Mr Davies hurled at Amy, it certainly wasn't water.

"What the fuck…" she screams, just before her gag reflex engages.

Even stood six feet away, the smell — a combination of ammonia and stale urine — is vile. But despite her gagging, and frantic attempts to wipe the toxic liquid from her eyes, she keeps the knife within striking distance of Gabrielle. As much as I admire his efforts, Mr Davies has bought us no more than a few seconds.

It then strikes me. Perhaps that was his sole intention — a distraction so I can attempt to disarm Amy. Without thinking, I risk two steps forward.

Despite the rapid blinking to ease her stinging eyes, Amy spots my advance and waves the knife in my direction. "Back the fuck off."

Another gag catches the end of her sentence and she bows forward. At the exact same moment I consider another step, I catch a flicker of movement at the top of the wooden divide separating the adjacent stall. Two hands appear at the top, and a split second later, Clement's head and shoulders follow. Realisation dawns — Mr Davies wasn't creating a diversion for my heroics.

In one fluid movement, Clement leaps over the wooden divide while Amy is still bent double, trying to fight another gag. It would be impossible not to notice Clement's huge frame in her peripheral vision, and Amy duly reacts. She spins around while adjusting the position of the knife. I can only assume she doesn't fancy her chances against the giant man approaching so she turns her attention back to Gabrielle.

With no time for finesse, Amy swings her arm in Gabrielle's direction; the tip of the knife flashing through the dim light like a shooting star. The horrific scene is compounded as my mind conjures up a vision of a pre-teen Amy stabbing her own father to death.

Her arm passes the midway point of its arc. My attention shifts from the knife to Gabrielle's face, and immediately I wish I could unsee the panic in her eyes.

The knife continues its rapid descent towards Gabrielle's chest with seemingly unstoppable momentum — too late for Clement's outstretched arm to intervene even if it were within grabbing distance.

And then, he appears to stumble.

Only when his entire bulk falls forward, uncontrolled, does it become clear he's deploying a last-ditch contingency plan. Again, it appears an attempt too late and the direction of the knife doesn't change. The tip reaches Gabrielle's jacket.

The police sirens are now deafening.

Definitely too late.

36.

If it wasn't for the cold weather, I fear my sister would already be dead. The tip of the knife must pass through multiple layers of thick clothing before it can penetrate flesh. The combination of materials offer almost negligible resistance to the steel blade, but miniscule fractions of time and distance are often the difference between life and death.

Eighteen stone of Clement finally connects with eight stone of Amy. The momentum of the man whips the knife away from Gabrielle's jacket, and not a heartbeat too soon.

There is, however, no control, and no direction to Clement's momentum. It's like watching a truck with no brakes slam into the side of a hatchback. There can be no second guessing how the carnage will unfold after the point of contact.

Two bodies become one as they fall — gravity pulling them towards the floor and kinetic energy shifting them horizontally. Inevitably, they sprawl across the hay and crash against the wooden divider on the other side of the stall.

Their journey ends with Amy almost buried beneath Clement's vast frame.

A shocked silence descends; only the police sirens audible. Even Archie appears stunned by what has just occurred, although he could just as easily be asleep.

However, it doesn't take long for the human shock to subside.

Mr Davies scuttles across to Gabrielle and throws his arms around her. Conscious this wasn't quite the introduction any of us wanted, I hold back while they sob into each other's arms. Perhaps if I were in the old man's shoes, I might reconsider whether William Huxley is a fit and proper person to care for my daughter. As for Gabrielle, it's likely she'll now associate my face with the attempt on her life. God only knows how much this ordeal has damaged her, or our chances of a relationship.

I turn my attention to Clement; on his haunches next to Amy, who herself looks to have been knocked unconscious. I watch for a second, expecting him to get to his feet, but suddenly he throws a fist towards the wooden divide. A loud crack explodes in the silence as the slat splinters.

"Fucking hell," he gasps. "No. No. No."

Judging by his display of mindless violence, I can't imagine he injured himself in the fall. Curious, I step past Archie's backside and stand over Clement. My new position affords a view of what prompted his reaction.

"Oh, my God," I splutter.

Clement looks up at me, wide eyed. "This weren't meant to happen, Bill."

Amy remains silent, almost certainly because the knife is now embedded in her chest to the hilt, just below the left breast. A flower of red blooms from the wound; absorbed into her pastel pink sweater.

"Is she…" I can't bring myself to finish the question.

"As a fucking doornail," Clement huffs.

The knife appears to have entered Amy's chest at an unfortunate angle. Perhaps unfortunate isn't the right word —

terminal might be more accurate as the blade tip must be dangerously close to her heart. Even so, I'd rather trust my basic first aid training than Clement's assessment.

I quickly kneel down next to Amy and feel her wrist for a pulse. I then check her neck before returning to her wrist. No pulse. The only other option is to listen for any signs of breathing. With my ear positioned within an inch of her mouth, I listen intently while trying to ignore the stench of whatever Mr Davies threw at her. Long seconds pass before I'm forced to concede the obvious.

"Not good news," I sigh. "No sign of life, I'm afraid."

"No shit, Dr Kildare."

I've lost count how many times I've wished Amy dead over the last week. Seeing her like this is a stark reminder to think more carefully about what I wish for. Looking at her face, it's hard not to see glimpses of a terrified young girl; abused to such a degree she had no choice but to inflict death on her own father. For that, I can find sympathy, but her retribution for an inadvertent eviction, all those years ago, really wasn't worth her vengeance. And now she's paid the ultimate price for clinging to that hatred.

Such a waste of life but my sympathy for a woman who tried to kill my sister, only seconds ago, is limited. Clement, on the other hand, seems particularly upset. Guilt maybe?

"It wasn't your fault, Clement. You weren't to know this would happen — it was an unfortunate accident."

"Don't matter. It's fucked everything."

"Don't say that. You saved Gabrielle's life. I'll be forever in your debt."

He clambers to his feet while mumbling another barrage of obscenities. Perhaps it's shock rather than guilt.

He stands over Amy's body and clamps his hands to his head.

"Clement? I think we should get you checked out. Shock can be nasty."

"Just leave me alone, Bill."

His tone is level but with enough intonation for me to back away. Whatever he's going through, I think it would be wise to let the medical experts deal with it.

With Clement lamenting over Amy's death, and Gabrielle and Mr Davies consoling one another, I'm left alone — the irony isn't lost on me. Just as I decide to exit the stall, the police finally arrive with two burly officers barging through the door.

"Nice of you to join us," I snap. "But you're too late."

"What's happened here?" one of the officers asks.

"Long story," I sigh "But nobody is in danger now, so come outside and I'll fill you in."

I edge past them without waiting for permission, and wander over to the railed fence. They follow, and as more officers descend on the stable block, I tell them the sorry tale of how we all ended up here on a cold October afternoon.

With notes taken, the two officers return to the stall while a young constable creates a cordon with striped tape. Standard crime scene procedure when a death has occurred, I'd imagine. I watch on from the fence as Gabrielle and her father are led out to an awaiting ambulance. A minute later, Clement appears; chased by a woman in civilian attire. I assume she's from CID and it's clear from his body language that Clement doesn't welcome her attention.

He looks around and spots me. With the detective at his heels, he strides over.

"Bill," he barks. "Tell this bleedin' woman what happened so I don't have to."

The female detective flashes her warrant card as she approaches. "Detective Sergeant Banner. And you are?"

Despite her diminutive stature, the detective's cold blue eyes, sharp features, and commanding voice ooze authority. I duly give her my name, together with a sixty second synopsis of what happened. Sergeant Banner then turns her attention to Clement who is now leaning against the fence and staring off into the distance.

"Your name, Sir?" she demands.

"Bastin. Cliff Bastin," Clement replies.

The detective scribbles his name down while I'm left puzzled as to why he gave it. Is that his real name?

"And is Mr Huxley's version of events as you remember them?"

"Exactly," he mumbles without looking away from the paddock.

I can feel Sergeant Banner's impatience simmering as she glares at the back of Clement's head.

"Detective," I intervene. "My friend here is probably suffering from shock so I'd suggest interviewing him at a later date."

"And I'm suffering from a possible murder," she snipes. "So I don't really care what you suggest. He needs to start talking."

Her rudeness is both unnecessary and unprofessional. I withdraw my wallet and flash my own identification.

"I said, detective, he'll speak to you later," I growl. "Now, unless you want me to call the Chief Constable, I suggest you back off. He needs medical attention."

Judging by her scowl, Detective Sergeant Banner is not used to having her orders thrown back at her. However, a potential rollicking from her boss proves deterrent enough.

"Fine," she snaps. "Get him seen to and then I will interview him."

The detective storms off without another word.

I join Clement at the fence and stare at the bleak Surrey countryside.

"You okay?" I ask.

"Not really."

"Do you…want to talk about it?"

"It?"

"What happened in there."

"Nothing to talk about. If I hadn't taken her down, she'd still be alive."

"I know, and I'm sorry it ended like that, but she was about to stab Gabrielle. You did the right thing, Clement."

"Maybe, but not everyone will see it like that."

"You mean the police? I really wouldn't worry about them."

"I couldn't give two shits about the police."

"Well, who then?"

He doesn't answer so I have no choice but to draw my own conclusion.

"It's not...the voice you're worried about is it?"

He snorts a hollow laugh before turning to face me. There is no mirth in his eyes. "Nah, Bill. The voice has gone."

"Oh, that's good, right?"

"No it ain't. No voice, no chance of leaving this bleedin' place."

"I'm sure we can get a lift back to the cottage."

"Not what I meant."

"Well, what then? If you didn't talk in riddles, I might be able to help."

He pushes himself off the fence and strides away. He gets a dozen yards away before calling back to me. "You coming?"

"Where?"

"To get Frank's car. I wanna get back to London."

"I'll meet you back in the car park. Give me five minutes."

He continues on his way, swiping away the cordon tape before disappearing beyond the stable block.

Left alone, I take the opportunity to gather my own thoughts.

From the moment Clement slapped that newspaper on my kitchen table, this day has been the epitome of an emotional rollercoaster, culminating in the death of a woman whose real name I didn't even know until a few hours ago. I've met a sister I didn't know existed, who, due to my mistakes, is likely to need therapy for the rest of her life. I've met the man who was on the wrong side of my father's infidelity; a man who must think I'm a complete liability as far as his daughter is concerned. And finally, my errant saviour; a man carrying an entire suitcase of issues.

I might need more than a few weeks in Sandown to get over this.

For now though, I need to find the stroppy detective and ensure she has everything she needs before I leave. No matter how cut and dried Amy's death might have been, I know there will be many questions asked over many months. The wheels of the judicial system turn even slower than those of parliament.

A puff of my cheeks and I trudge away from the fence. Five steps later, someone calls my name. I turn in the direction of the voice and my shoulders slump.

"William," Mr Davies calls again, striding towards me.

Here we go.

"Mr Davies. How is Gabrielle?"

Perhaps an incendiary question, considering my actions put his daughter in harm's way.

"She's...okay," he wheezes, coming to a halt.

I give him a moment to catch his breath. No doubt he'll need it to vent properly.

"I...I wanted to thank you before we head off to the hospital."

"Thank me?"

He draws a couple of sharp breaths. "Yes."

"I'm not sure I deserve any thanks, Mr Davies."

"Don't be modest, William. I heard what you said in there."

"You did?"

I have no idea what I might have said to warrant his praise, let alone forgiveness.

"Yes, and I know you pleaded with that crazed woman to release Gabrielle; even forsaking your own safety."

"Well, yes, but it didn't work."

"Not the point. The fact you put Gabrielle's life ahead of your own tells me precisely what kind of man you are."

"Um…thank you, but how exactly did you hear what I said? I presumed you were waiting in the car park for the police."

"I had to go out onto the road to get a phone signal. On the way back I stumbled into Clement and told him what was going on. Thank God he was around because I don't know what I'd have done without him."

"Really?"

"Yes, it was all his idea. We filled a bucket from the septic tank and waited outside the stable."

"I'll have to have a word with him. He couldn't have cut it much finer."

"We thought the police would arrive in time, but then we realised Gabrielle was in imminent danger, and that's when Clement sent me in with the bucket."

"Quite a masterstroke, that."

"Yes, indeed" he replies. "Incredible what you can achieve with a bucket of horse piss and a man as inventive as Clement."

Despite his good-humoured assessment, it does little to mask concern for his daughter.

"Anyway," he continues. "I better get back to the ambulance before Gabrielle starts fretting."

"Will she be alright?"

"I think so. She's a resilient girl."

"I am truly sorry, Mr Davies. Please let her know that."

He offers me his hand. "If you think an apology is necessary, I think it would be better coming from you."

I take his hand. "Right, of course."

"Maybe in a few days' time you can pop over for lunch and meet your sister properly."

"Are you sure?"

"Absolutely, because you know what Gabrielle would love in her life, almost as much as another horse?"

"No."

"A big brother, and you've more than earned that title. Give me a call in the morning."

No words have ever sounded sweeter. William Huxley — former politician, now someone's big brother; I'd call that a promotion. And such is the gravity of my new position, I have to bite my bottom lip to keep my emotions in check.

"And feel free to bring Clement along," he adds. "I'm sure Gabrielle would like to thank him properly, as would I."

"I'll ask, but he can be a little…unpredictable."

"I don't doubt that, but the invite is there."

With a parting nod, he turns and walks away.

My inner glow stays for the entire duration of my conversation with Sergeant Banner. Not even her brusque interrogation can bring me down.

Unfortunately, Clement is not in such good spirits by the time I return to the car park.

"What took you?" he grumbles.

"I was just dealing with that detective. Sorry."

"What did you tell her?"

"The truth, apart from your name. Do you want to tell me why you gave her a false name?"

"What's to tell?" he shrugs. "I don't want the Old Bill knowing my name. Simple as that."

"Dare I ask why?"

"I don't trust 'em."

"And that's it?"

"Yeah."

He's clearly not in the right frame of mind for further questions on the subject.

"Shall I see if there's a cab firm locally?"

"Nah. I could do with the walk."

"Fair enough."

We set off on the two mile walk back to Brooke Cottage. I'm no slouch but Clement's long strides propel him forward at such a pace I'm panting within minutes and struggling to keep up.

Even if I could manage a conversation, it's clear my hiking companion is not in the mood for a chat.

Clement's pace setting ensures we complete a half hour journey in under twenty minutes. On arriving at Brooke Cottage, I collapse into the passenger seat of Frank's car, sweaty, breathless, and suffering a mild stitch.

Before I can offer to set up the navigation app, Clement is already tearing back down the lane.

"Do you know where you're going?"

"I know where I'm not going."

"Sorry?"

"Nothing," he mumbles.

I decide to leave the navigation to Clement. If he needs directions, he can ask. It'll probably be the only conversation I get from him.

We make it all the way to the A3 before he finally speaks.

"Your sister okay?"

"A little shaken apparently, but otherwise she's fine."

"Good."

"I spoke to Mr Davies. He's invited me to the house for lunch in a few days' time."

"Happy families, eh?"

"Early days, but I hope so. He also asked me to invite you."

"I'm busy."

"Don't be so dismissive, Clement. He spoke very highly of you and simply wants to show his gratitude."

"No need."

"I can't persuade you?"

"Nope."

"But…"

"Forget it, Bill."

That conversation brought to an abrupt end, I give it ten minutes before trying another line of questioning.

"Have you made any decisions about what you're going to do?"

"Sort of."

"Can I ask what?"

"You can ask."

"Okay. What are you going to do next?"

"Wait."

"Wait for what?"

"The next person who needs my help, and the next opportunity to go back."

"Back where?"

"Where I'm supposed to be."

"And that's where exactly?"

"Not sure. But it ain't here and it ain't now."

37.

Former Prime Minister, Harold Wilson, famously once said: "A week is a long time in politics."

It would be fair to say the last week has been a long time for me, both in politics and beyond.

The soft glow of the setting sun beyond my office window proves a fitting end to my career. I check my watch and reflect on the final few minutes behind my desk in the Palace of Westminster. For the first time in a decade I have no one to call, nowhere to be, and no decisions to make. In truth, I have been a member of parliament in name alone since last Wednesday. That was the day I tendered my resignation, and I naively thought I could see out my notice period. Not so.

Despite being proven innocent of any wrong doing, the press interest has been intrusive and relentless. It was therefore decided I should go on immediate gardening leave and I'm only here now to clear my desk and say a few goodbyes. And with both those tasks completed, it's time to bid farewell to Westminster.

I'm glad, really, because for the first time in a decade, I feel I have a purpose.

Last Thursday I travelled down to Surrey to lunch with Gabrielle and Mr Davies, or Ken as he now insists I call him. Much to my surprise, his initial suggestion — that we don't tell Gabrielle who I really am — fell by the wayside. As we sat around the table after dessert, the subject was broached and Gabrielle delicately informed I was her brother.

If Ken had devised a plausible explanation for my absence all these years, I will never know, as my new sibling was too excited to care where I'd been all her life. In fact, her primary concern was the thirty years of birthday presents I apparently owe her. We debated the issue and for once, I was happy to concede defeat and agree an extra special present on her next birthday.

I spent the whole afternoon at Brooke Cottage — I could have spent the whole week. I'm pretty sure Gabrielle was joking about her missing birthday presents, but even thirty years of gifts would pale against the single gift I received that afternoon. Perhaps it sounds ridiculous, in that I barely know Gabrielle, but I felt a connection unlike any I've ever felt. Ken might be her father, but there is no hiding our shared genes.

I also received a crash course on Gabrielle's disability, which began with a stern telling off for calling Down's Syndrome a disability. It is, as Gabrielle rightly corrected, a condition, and not one which defines her. As she so succinctly put it: first and foremost she is an independent woman, who just happens to have Down's Syndrome. As she discussed her life in more detail, I couldn't help but notice the pride in Ken's eyes. After just a few short hours, I realised the tiny, frightened woman held at knife point was not a true reflection of my sister. The fact she put it so quickly behind her is a credit to her resilience and positive attitude.

I now see why Ken is so keen to ensure her wellbeing is maintained when he's not around. It's not about looking after her, but looking out for her. I gave him my word I would do that for as long as I'm on this earth.

My change in career also means a change in living accommodation. I've already had most of my possessions moved from the flat in Blackfriars down to Marshburton, and the estate agents have assured me a tenant will be in place within the next few weeks. Hansworth Hall has been re-let to the same company currently in situ and they'll remain there for the next five years at least.

One thing that's clear is I can't stay at the cottage in Marshburton for a while. The press continue to hound me, and the local residents are already sick of the intrusion into village life. That makes my decision to get away all the more sensible and I'm leaving for the Isle of Wight in a few days' time. Despite my initial reservations, I've decided to stay at the Sandown Bay Hotel; not because I'm a fan of the decor or the gloomy rooms, but because I feel sorry for Emma and her struggle to keep the place afloat. I doubt my patronage for a few weeks will make much difference, but it'll help. And besides, Emma was pleasant company on my last visit and I don't wish to completely cut myself off from civilisation.

One person who is unlikely to be going on holiday anytime soon, is Rosa. I'll give her credit for keeping her word, and handing herself in to the police as promised. I was tempted to tell her Amy planned to keep their ill-gotten gains for herself, but decided against it. It would be cruel, and she has enough problems now.

My solicitor thinks Rosa will probably get a suspended sentence, seeing as Amy was the driving force behind the blackmail plot, and I wouldn't argue with such a punishment. She might escape prison, but with a criminal record she'll have the added punishment of severely limited employment options. I think, at heart, she's not a bad person and I wouldn't derive any satisfaction from seeing her suffer.

As for her mother, I've kept my word and made arrangements for Miss Douglas to be transferred to a private care home next week. However, alongside the substantial financial settlement deal I've agreed with the libellous newspaper, they have also agreed to publish an article I'm in the process of writing.

It's probably just as well I'm leaving today because that article will pull no punches regarding our party's policies and spending on social care. For too long, and we're not the only guilty party, we've wasted billions on weaponry and wars when the real battle was being lost under our noses. I'm fairly sure the residents of Orchard House don't wake up in the morning and, while waiting for the overstretched staff to help them out of bed, thank their lucky stars we have a nuclear deterrent keeping them safe. While good people like Anna work tirelessly to help those in need, we cannot continue to undermine their efforts through a lack of funding.

Hopefully, my article will bring sufficient shame to those holding the purse strings.

On the subject of financial matters, Clement steadfastly refused to accept the payment I promised him. After we returned from Surrey, we had a couple of drinks at Fitzgerald's but there was little in the way of celebration. We dealt with Amy, but not in the way either of us hoped, and I think her death really affected Clement. After barely an hour he sloped off and I haven't seen or heard from him since. Fortunately, tonight is my farewell to Frank and Jeanie, and I've been assured Clement will be at Fitzgerald's later. I get the impression he isn't big on friendships so I don't think he's likely to stay in touch, but at least I'll have the chance to properly thank him.

But, as they say: all things, good and bad, come to an end. I won't miss some of Clement's bad traits, but there's far more good than I ever expected to find, and I will miss him, for sure.

I take a final look around my office and switch off the lights.

It's funny, but the routine of everyday life takes on a new perspective when you know the routine won't be repeated tomorrow, or ever again. As I wander through the chilly London streets, I take my time in order to appreciate the architecture and the people passing by. The faces of the pretty young things are still young and still pretty, but now I see them differently. Look beneath the surface and they'll carry the same insecurities, the same fears, and the same scars as anyone else. I no longer envy their youth or their beauty because, as I've learnt, it's not who they are or what defines their time on earth.

Sixty-five million people live in this great country of ours, and every one of us is capable of bringing beauty to the world.

And, unfortunately, a degree of ugliness. In the last fortnight I've witnessed both.

After a slow walk, I arrive at Fitzgerald's just after five thirty. It's busier than usual as Frank appears to have corralled all the regulars. My arrival is met with a cheer and a few dozen smiling faces. Even barfly Stephen is on his feet for a change.

It's a heart-warming reception and a stark contrast to the handful of emails and half-hearted handshakes I received from my Westminster colleagues.

I make my way to the bar and receive numerous pats on the back as I go. I've chatted with each and every person here at some point over the last decade, but I can't say I know them that well. Perhaps my own fault. Nevertheless, it's good to see them all for one final goodbye. My call for a round of drinks is met with another cheer and I ask Frank to set up a tab. No doubt my credit card will receive a hammering tonight, but I couldn't care less.

With the juke box turned up and the drinks flowing, I scour the room looking for the one person I really hoped would be here.

Unsuccessful in my search, I turn to Frank behind the bar. "Have you seen Clement?"

"Sorry, mate. I was gonna call and tell you, but I've been a bit busy this afternoon. He's decided to move on."

"What? When did he decide that?"

"He came in at lunchtime to say goodbye."

"Where's he gone?"

"He wasn't exactly clear on that. Said something about needing to be somewhere closer to home."

"Closer to home? I thought he was born and bred in London?"

"Yeah, so did I, but you know what he's like — a man of mystery is our Clement."

"Oh, that's…disappointing."

"He did leave something for you, though."

"Really?"

"Yeah. I think he gave it to Jeanie. Give me a sec and I'll go grab it."

On reflection, disappointing doesn't sufficiently cover how I feel about Clement's absence. It was at this very bar I first met him, and more than anything I wanted to close the circle. Perhaps a reflection of my life rather than him, but I can now count Clement as one of the few people in my life I've ever been able to truly count on. And if it wasn't for his pragmatism and dogged determination, I'd probably be drinking in very different circumstances this evening.

But clearly the feeling wasn't mutual and that smarts.

"Here you go," Frank says, handing me a flat package about eight inches square, and wrapped in brown paper.

I take the package and place it on the bar.

"Was there any message, Frank?" I ask.

"Nope."

I turn the package over and peel away the single line of tape. Pulling away the paper flaps reveals the back of what looks like a picture frame. Curious, I turn it over to find a black and white photo, carefully mounted in a wooden frame.

I pick it up and study the photo of six men in suits, stood shoulder to shoulder and holding glasses aloft. It takes a few seconds to determine why Clement went to the trouble of having the photo framed. The man stood in the centre has a striking resemblance to my father, albeit a forty-something version. It's not just seeing my father that stuns, but also the backdrop for the photo.

"Frank," I call across the bar. "Come here a second."

He shuffles over and I show him the photo.

"Never seen that one before," he says.

"But it was definitely taken in here?"

He looks a little closer. "Yeah, you can just make out the juke box in the background."

I point to the man in the centre. "I think that's my father."

"Really?"

"The more I look at it, the surer I am. I'd guess he's somewhere in his mid-forties so this must have been taken in the early seventies."

Frank re-examines the photo. "Sounds about right. Your old man was a politician wasn't he?"

"For forty years. I had no idea he'd ever stepped foot in Fitzgerald's, though."

"It was members-only back then, and I'm told it was popular with politicians who wanted to misbehave out of the public eye. Who'd have thought your old man was a regular though?"

"Incredible. Ten years I've been coming here and I didn't have a clue."

I can't even guess how Clement found the photo, and I'm genuinely humbled he went to so much trouble. But as considerate as his gift is, it only adds to my lament — there will be no opportunity to thank him or offer a proper goodbye.

I ask Frank to keep the photo safe behind the bar.

It won't be until tomorrow I spot the reflection of the man who captured the photo; just about visible in the plate glass window next to the juke box — a big man decked in double denim, sporting a horseshoe moustache.

SIX MONTHS LATER

38.

I don't get on with duvet covers. The fact we have twenty-four beds to make is a version of hell I'd rather avoid.

"I think I'll go and see if they've arrived."

"No, you won't" Emma replies. "They're not due for another fifteen minutes, and besides, we've only got four beds left to do."

I shoot her a frown while attempting to stuff another pillow into its case.

"Don't sulk," she adds. "You've only done three beds, anyway."

"I know, but its painstaking," I whine with mock indignation.

I finish making up my fourth bed and saunter over to the window. The view from the third floor is like a picture postcard that changes on a daily basis, and today we've been blessed with bright blue skies and wall-to-wall sunshine.

"Perfect," I whisper to myself.

An arm curls around my waist as Emma sidles up to me. "In every way," she coos before planting a kiss on my cheek.

I turn and pull her to me.

"Thank you...for this...for everything."

"It's me who should be thanking you," she replies. "I can't believe we've actually done it."

In truth, there is much about the last six months to defy belief.

My original plan to stay in Sandown for two weeks fell by the wayside. Those two weeks became three, then four, and after a series of life changing decisions, seamlessly became indefinite. They say you should never mix business with pleasure, but I think in my case, they've become one and the same thing.

It started with an idea, seeded one dark December evening as we sat in front of a log fire in the lounge and watched *Oliver* together. For some reason my thoughts turned to that young woman I met on the estate in Hounslow. I thought about her son, and the hundreds of thousands of children on similar estates across London. If the parents are forced to rely upon food banks, what hope is there for the children to ever go on holiday? Virtually none I concluded.

That thought coincided with Emma's grim forecast for the hotel's future. With dwindling demand and major refurbishment needed, there was going to come a point where the Sandown Bay Hotel simply couldn't afford to open its doors.

And there was I with a big chunk of cash in the bank, courtesy of one libellous newspaper. For the first time in my life, I believe the Gods were trying to point me in the right direction.

I put the idea to Emma and she jumped at it.

With Emma on board there was no holding me back, and I promptly bought a fifty percent share in the hotel from her mother, Dora. That money allowed Dora to escape the damp in her bedroom, and purchase a warden-assisted retirement flat a few streets away — a win-win situation for us all.

The next step involved setting up a charity and planning an extensive refurbishment program for the old place — not as a hotel for paying guests, but to accommodate disadvantaged children from inner London. After a number of meetings and weeks' of research, it became clear we could help hundreds of children every year — children who, in many cases, had never seen the sea, let alone enjoyed a holiday.

Perhaps selfishly, the thought of making a direct and positive impact on so many young lives was irresistible.

By mid-January everything was in place and the refurbishment contractors were booked to start in February. Emma and I went out for dinner that night to celebrate. It also happened to be the night we shared our first kiss. Three days after our first kiss, we spent our first night in the same bed; a bed we've shared ever since.

It would be fair to say Emma has changed my life beyond recognition, and that fateful trip to the Isle of Wight back in October now feels like the greatest blessing. Who would have thought something so wonderful could come from a situation so bleak.

"What are you thinking about?" Emma asks.

"Oh, nothing really. I just can't quite believe we're only minutes away from greeting our first guests."

"We'd better get a wiggle on then," she chuckles. Apparently there's still time for a lingering kiss, though.

A voice from the doorway interrupts us mid-kiss.

"Ewww!"

Our lips part and we turn to the door.

"Will you two please stop with the PDA," Gabrielle orders.

"What on earth is PDA?" I ask.

"Public display of affection," she replies. "It's gross and should be banned."

"Oh, I see."

I step across the room and pose a question. "Does that mean I can't give my little sister a hug any more then?"

Gabrielle ponders this for a moment before throwing her arms around me. "No, they're allowed," she beams.

With the two most incredible women by my side, I make my way down to the reception area.

While Gabrielle and Emma head off to prepare drinks for our first batch of guests, I take a moment to stand behind the new reception desk and ready myself. My gaze drifts around the lobby before falling to the two framed pictures on the desk: one of six men in suits, and one of Gabrielle and I; taken by Ken a few weeks after that fateful day at the stables.

Both pictures summon mixed emotions.

Ken passed away ten weeks ago after his health took a turn for the worse over the Christmas period. Fortunately, Gabrielle and I had already forged a strong bond by that stage, and I do wonder if Ken was only holding on long enough to ensure his daughter would be cared for. I like to think he met his maker knowing she would be.

Two weeks after Ken's funeral, and with Emma by my side, I asked Gabrielle if she wanted to move to Sandown to live with us. I'm not sure what I'd have done if she'd said no, but the lure of living by the seaside proved too much. Her only condition was that Archie had to come too, and he now lives in new stables a few miles away. In some way, I think Gabrielle was relieved she'd never have to visit the scene of Amy's siege ever again.

And so, here we are — my cobbled-together family. We might have been thrown together by the most adverse of circumstances but that only strengthens our appreciation of what we now have. I wouldn't change it for the world.

"They're here," Gabrielle yells across the lobby.

I look up to see a minibus draw up by the front door.

"Right. Here we go."

We head outside where twenty-four hyper excited children are already exiting the minibus. With them are Debbie and Chloe; two volunteers from a London-based charity who organise that end of our venture. We all shake hands before corralling the children into the lobby.

It takes a few minutes of hushing before I can finally deliver my welcome speech.

"Good morning children. I'm Will."

Twenty-four fidgety children look back at me. With broad smiles and excited faces, they reply in unison. "Good morning, Will."

"I know you're all keen to get down to the beach, so, what we'll do is show you to your rooms and then we can head straight down there. Is that a good idea?"

I'm met with a roar of approval.

"Before we do that, let me introduce you to two very special ladies who'll be looking after you."

I introduce them to an equally excited Emma, and a mildly embarrassed Gabrielle. She's much nearer their age, and I suspect I've probably said something she'd consider lame.

"There's just one thing I need to do before you head up to your rooms," I continue. "As you're our very first guests, I'd like to mark our official opening."

Gabrielle and Emma take my prompt and circulate with trays of orange squash. Once everyone has a plastic cup, I take the final one myself.

"Who knows what a toast is?" I ask.

A girl at the front raises her hand.

"Yes young lady."

"It's cooked bread, innit?" she asks hesitantly.

"Um, yes it is, but it's also something we do when we want to mark a special occasion. So, I'm going to say a few words, and then you're going to raise your cups like this."

I raise my cup to demonstrate.

"And then you're going to give me a huge cheer. Okay?"

I'm met with plenty of nods and a few giggles.

I clear my throat and they fall silent. "Right, boys and girls. It's with great pleasure, and a huge amount of pride, that I officially welcome you to Clement House."

Twenty-four plastic cups are raised and a raucous cheer breaks out.

I glance down at the second picture on the reception desk and quietly offer a more personal toast.

"To you, big man. God speed."

FORTY MILES AWAY...

The train pulled into a station he last visited eighteen months ago. Desperation had brought him back.

Over the last six months Clement had lived in three different bedsits across London, and worked a dozen cash-in-hand jobs. He'd met hundreds of people and yet, the voice remained stubbornly silent. He was tired of waiting and now committed to finding his own answers.

He hauled a rucksack over his shoulder and made his way from the platform to the station exit.

Some of his fellow passengers were greeted by loved ones. There was nobody to greet Clement and he cast an envious eye over a young couple in mid embrace — a cruel reminder of a life he once lived.

He set off towards the town centre; trying hard to ignore the pangs of loneliness chasing after him.

As he walked, he'd catch the occasional stranger staring at him. The young, the old, and every age in-between — they knew he didn't fit in here almost as much as he did. In London, people rarely paid him any attention but here in a suburban commuter town, Clement's size and attire made him an oddity. A returned glare was usually enough to shift their attention elsewhere.

Five minutes later he turned into a quiet backstreet; away from the judgemental eyes of the locals.

His final destination lay fifty yards up the road on the left. His pace quickened until he reached a row of three shops, all closed down. He passed a newsagent, a bridal shop, and finally, he stopped outside the property where he hoped to find answers — Baxter's Books.

Across the street, hidden from view, someone watched with interest as Clement disappeared up the alleyway next to the shop.

That someone smiled, and paused for a moment before following the big man.

THE END

BEFORE YOU GO...

I genuinely hope you enjoyed reading Clement's second adventure. If you did, and have a few minutes spare, I would be eternally grateful if you could leave a review on Amazon. If you're feeling particularly generous, a mention on Facebook or a Tweet would be equally appreciated. I know it's a pain, but it's the only way us indie authors can compete with the big publishing houses.

Stay in Touch...

For more information about me and to receive updates on my new releases, please visit my website...

www.keithapearson.co.uk

If you have any questions or general feedback, you can also reach me, or follow me, on social media...

Facebook: www.facebook.com/pearson.author
Twitter: www.twitter.com/keithapearson